PLAYING IN THE DARK

A Glasgow Lads Novel

AVERY COCKBURN

Books by Avery Cockburn

Glasgow Lads

- Play On: Duncan/Brodie novella
- Playing for Keeps: Fergus/John novel
- Playing to Win: Colin/Lord Andrew novel
- Play It Safe: Fergus/John short story
- Playing with Fire: Liam/Robert novel
- Play Dead: Colin/Lord Andrew novella
- Playing in the Dark: Evan/Ben novel
- Play Hard: Liam/Robert novella
- All Through the House: Duncan/Brodie short story

Glasgow Lads on Ice (spinoff featuring curling)

- Throwing Stones: Luca/Oliver novel
- Must Love Christmas: Garen/Simon novel

Standalone Titles

- A Christmas Harbor: A M/M Romance Novella

Foreword

Playing in the Dark takes place in early 2015, just after same-sex weddings began in Scotland. Finishing it in 2018 was like writing historical fantasy! I've tried to keep it real and avoid anachronisms, while at the same time using the nature of Evan's work to foreshadow future events.

I've also tried to make every term clear in context, but if you get confused, there's a list of agencies and acronyms at the back of this book. Enjoy.

To those who work in the dark,
unnamed and unsung.

Chapter 1

22 June 2014

STALE-IRON TANG OF BLOOD.

Reek of stagnant breath.

Squish of soil between bare toes.

Patter of summer rain on a million leaves.

Shift of patchy dark fabric, teasing glimpses of light.

Even now all five senses were noting and remembering, cataloging details which might prove critical in the unlikely event of survival.

Or perhaps it was just habit, born of training and his own insatiable need to understand everything about everything.

Either way, this mental inventory kept him going, kept him sharp, kept his brain from flatlining with panic while it planned an escape.

He was shoved to his knees, the black hood ripped from his head, the dusty gag jerked from his mouth so hard it nearly dislocated his jaw.

Stench of fear-infused sweat.

Pierce of twigs and rocks into bare knees.

Bass-drum pounding in every pulse.

Green leaves dripping with drizzle in the haze of dusk.

After eighteen hours of darkness, he could see at last. Where there was light, there was hope.

A glance uphill confirmed he and his captor were out of earshot of the driver who'd brought them here.

"Last chance," the voice behind him growled. "Give me names and I'll make it painless."

Lies hadn't worked. These people knew what he was.

Stalling hadn't worked. His people would never find him in time.

Fighting back had almost worked. But now his hands were bound and his strength was gone.

The truth was his last resort.

Click of magazine into pistol.

Ink-black of gun barrel.

"Names, please."

His mouth opened in response, parched lips popping apart. This truth could get him killed, and not with a merciful bullet to the brain courtesy of his own Glock. This truth could get him beaten to death, perhaps with the loss of a few significant body parts before everything went black.

The thing he had to say, it wasn't the truth his captor sought. But maybe it was the truth they both needed to survive.

Chapter 2

1 September 2014

A PERFECT DAY TO be set free, Evan Hollister thought as he neared the pedestrian bridge stretching across the River Clyde. The sun was climbing into a sky far too clear and blue to have ended up in Glasgow by anything but accident.

As always, Evan noticed every person he passed. Partly he was looking for subtle incongruities signifying bad intent: wearing a coat too large for their frame or too heavy for the weather (possibly concealing a bomb), strange bulges in pockets (knives or guns), or shoes costing twice as much as the rest of their clothes put together (probably stolen, not that it was his job to enforce the law).

Mostly he was looking for people who were familiar for the wrong reason—not because they worked in the area, but because they were following him. One couldn't be too careful.

In the not-too-distant past, "careful" meant scanning his vehicle for signs of car bombs. These days it merely meant varying his morning commute to avoid a detectable pattern.

Today he'd taken ScotRail from Argyle Street to Exhibition Centre. It was his favorite route, so he rarely used it. But today he couldn't resist, because of the fine weather and because the morning held the promise of life going back to what passed for normal.

As he stepped onto the bridge to cross the river, Evan thought about how his last day in the field had almost been his last day on earth. The beginning of that operation had shattered his life, and its ending had nearly shattered his mind.

But after spending July on mandatory mental-health leave, then August behind a desk assessing threats based on information fed to him through a screen, Evan couldn't wait to go undercover again. Maybe that meant he was daft.

He didn't feel daft. Most days, anyway.

Stepping off the bridge toward his building's front entrance, Evan spied his colleague Adira Mansour approaching from the south. Adira was one of the top analysts at this MI5 regional office. Because the domestic-intelligence agency posted a mere thirty employees here in Glasgow, Evan knew Adira well, though they'd never worked together on an operation. Evan had so far served only in T Branch, which handled Irish terrorism, while Adira worked in G Branch, which handled terrorism from everywhere else.

"Good morning!" he sang out, holding the door open.

"You're unnaturally cheerful for a Monday," she grumbled, but then her eyes widened. "Is this your day of liberation?"

He grinned at her. "Aye, if the Powers That Be declare it. Is that a new hijab?"

"Perhaps." She fingered the rose-and-copper-colored paisley fabric draped over her head and chest. "Does anything escape your notice, lad?"

"I hope not."

On their way to the lift they passed the ground-floor canteen, bustling with the breakfast crowd. Evan saw a blue oval Yes Scotland sticker pasted to the glass beside a corner table. He smirked at the sheer cheek: Government buildings were forbidden territory for political merchandise, especially merchandise advocating a split from the government that funded the buildings.

When the lift doors opened upon MI5's basement office, Evan and his colleague stopped short. Adira raised her fists as though she'd scored a goal. "At last!"

Evan followed her to queue up at the newly installed, space-age-looking security capsule. "Now we can join the twenty-first century."

"More like the twentieth," said an older man ahead of them in the queue. He gestured to the capsule with his ragged brown-paper lunch sack. "We've had these at Thames House for decades."

Adira acknowledged him, then muttered under her breath. "Feel free to fuck off back to London, then."

Evan suppressed a snicker. The daughter of Jordanian immigrants, Adira was over twice his age and a devout Muslim, but her Glaswegian ferocity rivaled that of any teenage hooligan.

As the sack-lunch man slouched into the capsule, Evan imagined how "Clyde House" would appear to someone from headquarters. Situated in several major UK cities, MI5's regional offices had been opened and furnished in the late 2000s, just as austerity was beginning to be inflicted upon the nation. Most of the computers here were memory-starved, the desk chairs were ergonomically hostile, and Evan's team of officers and analysts shared a single, perpetually jammed stapler.

But things were changing. As this month's independence referendum hotted up, the UK government worried that Scottish nationalists might pose a security threat. Evan thought this an overreaction—there was no evidence that even hardcore "nats" sought to address their grievances through anything but the ballot box. But hey, whatever it took to get his office upgraded.

Evan handed over his jacket for the usual X-ray scan, then tapped his pass code into the terminal in front of the cylindrical security capsule. The capsule's bulletproof laminated-glass door slid open with a *whoosh*.

"Cool," he whispered as he stepped inside. There was a slight pause, during which, Evan had learned at headquarters, the capsule judged his weight and height to be sure it was him and that he was alone—and not, say, held at gunpoint. After a moment, the door behind him closed, then the door in front of him opened. Very cool.

He and Adira greeted their colleagues, grabbed coffees from the ancient machine, then sat at their desks in the open-plan main office. As always, the first task was to read the daily threat assessments before their team meetings. Monday's briefs were massive, as terrorists didn't take weekends off and neither did the information they produced. If there'd been an imminent threat, of course, normal working hours would go out the window, but MI5's mission was to sniff out threats before they *became* imminent.

Evan doubted many folk had a more disquieting start to their mornings. The daily threat assessment painted a picture of a world bent on harming itself. It made it easy to forget that good people were actually a thing.

He was midway through a Europol report on vehicular-based terrorism when Kay Northam appeared out of nowhere, as she was wont to do.

"Good weekend?" his supervisor asked in an unusually bright voice for this time of day.

He jumped a bit, grateful he'd set down his coffee before Kay had popped up. It was best to hide how easily startled he could still be. "Erm, it was all right. Yours?"

"Mmm-hm." She eyed him over her tea, contained in a cappuccino cup that dwarfed her hand, the nails of which looked freshly bitten despite a layer of clear varnish. "Did you win in football?"

"It was just a pre-season friendly, but aye, Warriors won." He noticed a black expanding file tucked under her arm. "Is that a new operation?"

"Okay, fuck the small talk, then." Kay set down her cup with a *clonk*, then pulled over a chair to sit beside Evan. "Thus far, your work in T Branch has focused on the Catholic part of Northern Irish sectarian violence. The time has come to switch sides, so to speak."

Evan wasn't surprised. It was no longer safe for him to go undercover in Glasgow's rougher Irish Catholic pubs, where literal terrorists and murderers from Northern Ireland liked to meet funders and plan attacks. Their Protestant counterparts were equally ruthless, but they didn't know Evan—not yet, at least.

Kay opened the expanding file. "Lately we've seen a troubling crossover between members of local Protestant associations—including relatively mainstream ones like the Orange Order—with extreme-right-wing groups, including this new one."

He opened the report she handed him and snorted when he saw the XRW group's name. "'British Values Party'? Did they miss the bit where the government declared tolerance an official British value?"

"They did not, in fact, miss it." Kay withdrew a pamphlet from the black file and opened it with a flourish. "Recruitment materials, distributed at rallies."

The glossy blue brochure featured primitive clip art of Union flags and white-power fists. In their list of "British Values," the BVP had replaced *Democracy* with *Strength,* and *Tolerance of diversity* with *Pride in heritage.*

"If you're assigned to this operation," Kay said, "you'll work with SCD again. They specifically requested your involvement after the way you handled yourself on the last operation."

Evan felt a glow of excitement. Collaborating with Police Scotland's Specialist Crime Division had been a highlight of his two-plus years in the Service. He'd made several friends in SCD, all of whom had top-secret clearances, which meant he could (mostly) be himself with them.

A few had even helped with his combat-stress issues this summer. Though his police mates hadn't been cleared to know what had happened in Belfast, they understood the challenges following an on-the-job trauma. How some days it took everything not to smash one's head against a wall to quash the memories.

Evan skimmed the police profile of the British Values Party. The BVP were headquartered down in Birmingham, but they had a regional coordinator of sorts in Scotland, a man called Jordan Lithgow. "I assume he's my target?"

"Yes. You're fluent in Norwegian, right?"

"I know the version they speak in Oslo—my gran was from near there, and I took classes growing up in Orkney. There are a lot of different dialects."

"I don't think the subtleties will matter to this lad. Like a lot of XRW types, Lithgow is fascinated with all things Norse."

"The whole superior-Aryan-race thing?"

"That's part of it. Anyway, we thought the thrill of meeting someone from the land of ice and snow would help him lower his guard. Also, it'll make it less suspicious that no one in Glasgow knows you."

Evan examined the surveillance photos. In one, taken at a rally, the young man with a shaved head and swirl of neck tattoos was scowling, his mouth twisted in rage. But in the other, taken in a park with his dog, Jordan wore an almost childlike grin. "So I'm to pose as a Norwegian guy to get close to Lithgow?"

"Yes. As friends." Her earnest blue eyes met his to emphasize the last word. "There's no evidence he'd be interested in more."

Thank God. He paged through the report. "Why are MI5 involved? I thought the Service considered these right-wing nutters a threat to public order, not to national security."

"Yes, normally we let police handle domestic extremists, because their activities haven't crossed the threshold between hate crime and terrorism."

Evan suddenly tasted his morning coffee at the back of his throat. "Until now, you mean."

Kay's forehead creased. She looked down at the file in her lap, gripping it along its open edge with both hands, as if by blocking its contents' escape, she could keep them from becoming reality.

"Evan, I'm not keen to send you undercover again so soon. But as I said, the police requested you. More importantly, I knew you'd want this assignment."

"Why?" He attempted a slight joke to allay his unease. "Because I'm dying to use my gran's Norwegian to take down *en gjeng kjeltringer*? That means 'a bunch of bad guys,' by the way."

Kay didn't laugh. "No, that's not why." She handed Evan the rest of the file. "Because the BVP want to attack same-sex weddings."

---

7 February 2015

The most important skill in wedding planning, Ben Reid's mum had taught him, was to act calm and confident even whilst inside, one was utterly shitting it.

Approaching the front door of the semi-posh Glasgow City Centre hotel, he inhaled deeply, then exhaled, a cloud of steam forming as his breath met the cold February air. Then he put on a smile he hoped was more disarming than deranged, ready to greet his brand-new clients.

They met him at the revolving door, yanking him out of the in-between space as though he was the one in need of rescue.

"Ben! Oh my God, Ben," said the shorter of the two men, a stout ginger who looked closer to forty than fifty. "You are Ben, aye? Our emergency wedding planner?"

"I am." He tried to shake their hands, to no avail, as they were clutching both his arms. "You're Gary and Sean?"

"We are," said the taller, dark-haired man who looked closer to fifty than forty. "That is, I'm Gary, he's Sean. And we're both pure grateful you exist."

"Aw, thanks, loves. I'm pretty glad too." He gestured to the lobby's nearest seating area. "Shall we have a wee chat?"

Sean looked at his watch. "The ceremony's to start in eighty-three minutes. We've not even put on our kilts."

Ben had noticed. They were both clad, incongruously, in jeans and tuxedo jackets, probably intending to save the kilts as a surprise for the wedding ceremony.

"Please. Sit." He took a comfy chair, and they both sank into the love seat across from him. Ironically, he felt calmer now in the face of their edgy nerves.

"I can't believe this is happening." Sean clutched a white two-ring binder to his chest like a teddy bear. "When Corinne phoned to say she'd broken her arm this afternoon—"

"A compound fracture, no less," Gary said. "She was hanging bunting."

"So she told me. Poor thing." Ben pointed to the binder. "Are those her notes?"

"Oh!" Sean practically threw it into Ben's lap. "You know, I pictured you being older."

Ben heard the dubiousness in the groom's voice. "I've been helping my mum plan weddings since I was thirteen." When Sean failed to look assured, Ben added, "That was ten years ago." *Well, almost.* "Sorry I couldn't be here earlier."

"Corinne said you were working another wedding this afternoon," Gary said. "Please let us know what we can do to help you save us."

Ben motioned to the coffee kiosk in the corner of the lobby. "I would kill for a green-tea latte and anything resembling real food."

They leapt to their feet and dashed for the kiosk. Ben took another deep breath and opened the binder. He was in fact in need of protein and caffeine, but he mostly wanted them out of his face while he perused Corinne's notes.

Her binder was hundreds of pages thick, which meant he'd never be able to read every detail before the wedding. But at least she used a similar system to his own. By the time Sean and Gary returned with his latte and sausage croissant roll (or "croll," Ben's new favorite word and food), he had a pretty good idea of the challenge before him.

"Good news," he told them. "The hotel is handling most of the logistics, so my role will be to act as stage manager—see to it that everyone's in the right place at the right time—and handle transitions so everything runs seamlessly." Ben adjusted his glasses and gave them his biggest smile yet. "And so you can enjoy the best night of your lives."

Gary and Sean sagged back into the love seat as if they'd just lost all vertebrae. "Thank God," they said in unison, then took each other's hand without even looking down to find them, a move so automatic and natural it was clear they'd had years, possibly decades of practice. Ben felt a flash of wistfulness as he imagined finding someone he meshed with like that.

Then again, it was hard to truly mesh when one rarely hooked up with the same man twice. He'd need to work on that someday.

Ben led Sean and Gary to the two adjoining ballrooms where the ceremony and reception would take place. Luckily, he'd already done a million weddings at this hotel with his mum. How he would have loved to ask her advice on a night like this.

They quickly reviewed when and where the grooms and wedding party had to be to start the ceremony, then Ben gave them strict instructions not to worry or even think about anything but their own parts in the production.

"Mind," he said, wanting to hug the anxiety from their faces, "you've put a lot of work and thought into this night. I know we just met and you've no reason to trust me with something so precious as your wedding, but for now, just pretend you do."

They finally laughed, much harder than his joke deserved.

Ben put a hand on a shoulder of each groom and gave a squeeze. "Now go and kilt up before that photographer over there has a heart attack."

Sean and Gary hurried off toward the guest elevators, and Ben went to greet the photographer and her assistant. He'd calculated he could afford ten minutes each with them, the florist, and the celebrant; followed by fifteen minutes each with the DJ and the hotel's events manager, Richard—a dear friend of his mum's—and still give himself ten minutes alone for a final review.

Ben knew that in Corinne's absence, no one expected this evening to go off without a hitch. Still, it was a challenge he relished.

Soon the photographer had hustled upstairs to take pics of the grooms dressing, the florist had agreed to set up table arrangements herself for a small fee, the celebrant had been briefed on how the grooms would process from each side of the room and meet in the center, and the DJ had been reminded to loop the processional music at a very low volume during the ceremony because Sean got nervous in quiet rooms.

Bang on schedule, Ben found the events manager in the hallway outside the ballrooms, where the early arriving guests were already enjoying prenuptial cocktails. He walked up behind him and touched his elbow. "Richard, it's good to—"

"Ah!" Richard spun to face him. "Oh, Ben, it's you. Sorry." He took the cinnamon-colored handkerchief from his breast pocket and dabbed at the sheen of perspiration near his receding hairline. "It's been a-a stressful afternoon, what with—what with, you know…"

"Corinne's injury?"

"Yes, that." Richard peered over Ben's head and nodded to someone behind him.

"I was hoping we could review the transition between the ceremony and—"

"Excuse me for a moment." Richard brushed past Ben and walked up to a fortyish man with close-cropped dark hair who stood near the window overlooking the courtyard. The man wore the uniform of regular serving staff, someone who shouldn't have the authority to beckon a manager.

Ben stepped over to the wall behind one of the small bars, away from the growing throng of chattering guests. He opened his binder and pretended to read from it, even as his ears strained to hear the conversation between Richard and this oddly officious server.

Unfortunately, only scattered bits were audible, and they only confused him further.

"…not meant to be here…"

"…blow his cover…"

"…look suspicious?"

"…limit exposure between him and Reid…"

Ben held his breath, positive he'd just heard his surname. Then again, it was a homonym of *read*, so it was an easy mistake to make.

When he couldn't stand it anymore, Ben glanced over at the two men, trying to catch Richard's eye.

They were both watching him. After a blink, he offered the events manager an expectant look. *Just hoping to speak with you. Oh, and by the way, WHAT IS GOING ON?*

Richard had a last hushed word with the "server," then hurried over. "So sorry about that. Let's go over the transition like you asked."

Ben forced his focus back to the job in hand. Their review went quickly, but by the time it was over, Ben had to oversee the guests' entrance to the ceremony space and thus had no time for a final review of Corinne's notes, much less an inspection of the reception room. He cursed his own raging curiosity; his attempted eavesdropping had used up valuable minutes.

But once the ceremony began, he found himself lost in the moment, swept up in Gary and Sean's long-awaited dream come true. The way they looked at each other, the way their families and friends beamed at them, dabbing tears even as they laughed at Sean dropping Gary's ring, then Gary dropping Sean's in solidarity, made all Ben's stress worth it. This was his life's calling, no matter his uni degree or his mum's opinions.

Ben was fighting back his own tears when someone tapped his elbow. He turned to see Corinne's daughter Hannah. Fluttering a hand over his heart in relief, he beckoned her out into the hallway. "How's your mother?" he whispered.

"Still in surgery. My sister's with her. Mum asked me to come and assist you, said it'd help her heal or some pish like that."

"Sounds like something mine would say. Thank you." He hugged her awkwardly, the binder between them. "Could you watch over the ceremony while I check the reception room?"

"Sure." She took the ceremony run sheet from him. "Talking of your mum, was she helping with the wedding you did this afternoon?"

"No, that was all me. Mum doesn't—" He stopped himself. "She doesn't have time, as her services are pure booked up for the next two years. Couldn't fit this massive first crop of same-sex weddings into her schedule."

Hannah frowned. "You know people are talking, right?"

"Which people? About what?"

"In the industry, about your mum. They say she doesn't approve of gay marriage and that's why you've started your own business."

Ben's heart started to pound. If word got out his mother was avoiding same-sex couples as clients, then her business—and therefore her life—could be ruined.

"Mum's a bit old-fashioned," Ben told Hannah, "but I'm working on her. She'll come round soon."

Hannah nodded, but the tilt of her head as she turned toward the ceremony hall showed she wasn't convinced.

Cursing his big mouth—he should have simply denied the rumors—Ben hurried over to the reception ballroom. He'd deal with his mother later. Right now he needed to make sure the table arrangement wasn't a complete shambles.

Entering the room, he spied a server striding away from him toward the door at the opposite end. This puzzled Ben, as only half the tables were laid. What could be so important as to leave the job unfinished?

"Excuse me!" His voice echoed against the empty ballroom's high ceiling.

The man froze, reaching for the door handle. After a pause, he turned around. "Sorry?"

"I was wondering if you'd do me a favor, if you've got a wee minute?"

The man looked at the door, then walked toward him.

Ben moved to meet him halfway. "Usually I do this myself, but I'm a last-minute substitute, so I've got a million things to see to."

The man came closer, enough for Ben to see he was tall, mid-twenties, with a well-trimmed sandy-gold beard that matched his slicked-back hair and the metal rims of his eyeglasses. "Heh?" he asked.

"These place settings." Feeling unusually shy in the presence of hotness, Ben went to the nearest laid table. "I like to be sure all the cutlery are straight and their bottoms are lined up properly." He demonstrated, nudging a knife half an inch farther from the edge of the table to align with the spoon beside it. "I know, it's a bit Carson-from-*Downton-Abbey*, but if you'd just humor my strange compulsion, I'd be pure grateful."

"It's not strange at all," the server said, in an accent Ben couldn't place. He adjusted the cutlery on the table beside him. "There. How's that?"

Ben came closer to examine the results. "Absolutely perfect," he said, though it was only ninety percent perfect at best. He looked up at the man. "Do you think you could—"

Hold on. He knew this guy from somewhere important, though maybe only his fantasies. Or maybe Ben's own eyeglass prescription needed an update.

The server raised a brow. "Do I think I could what?"

Ben blinked. "S-sorry, I've been rude, not introducing myself. I'm Ben, the wedding planner."

"Hi, Ben." The man jutted a thumb at his own chest. "Gunnar."

"Gunnar." Hmm, perhaps they *hadn't* met before. Based on the name and accent, this man was clearly Scandinavian not just in looks but in national origin. Ben didn't know any men from—

All at once it hit him, and he saw what lay under the disguise.

The blond hair had been darkened, the waves smoothed into oblivion by styling product. Facial hair hid the chin dimple that was deep enough to swim in. And that Norwegian accent was a less musical version of the sweet Orcadian lilt that had taken up permanent residence in Ben's memory.

But Gunnar's spectacles couldn't hide those ice-blue eyes and their faint tragic glow.

Here was the man Ben had thought about every day—and especially every night—for nearly six weeks.

Chapter 3

ALL EVENING EVAN had avoided Ben in hopes of maintaining his cover. This last-minute wedding-planner substitution had taken the police by surprise. Evan's lead officer had considered dismissing him in the name of caution, then decided it would have looked suspicious to their operation's target.

Especially if that target ever showed up.

"Anything else?" Evan asked Ben.

"That's all for now. Thank you so much." Ben spun away and made a beeline for the table at the far end of the ballroom.

Evan watched him go, unable to do otherwise, and equally unable to forget the night they'd met—at Evan's ex-boyfriend's wedding, of all places. Ben had approached him during Fergus's reception, taking pity on Evan's awkward isolation. He'd been kinder to him than anyone in months, despite what Evan had done to Fergus.

Or rather, what Evan hadn't done.

Adjusting the cutlery, Evan watched Ben from the corner of his eye. The wedding planner was now patrolling the room, stopping every few feet to consider the table angles. His sweet, full lips pursed as he pondered, and his thick, dark brows pinched together beneath his black-framed glasses. His sleek ebony hair was swept up into a quiff that was a cross between hipster and Buddy Holly. A unique face for a unique man.

On the evening of Fergus's reception, Evan and Ben had found each other again and again, with Ben asking increasingly creative questions, going far beyond small talk and easy assumptions. It seemed he wanted to know Evan as he was, not as everyone said he was. That night, for the first time in years, Evan had felt truly *seen*.

As a spy, that feeling terrified him. As a human, it thrilled him. He wanted more.

A voice spoke in his ear. "Zero Three, do you read? Zero Two," said Detective Sergeant Deirdre Fowles over their radio system. "Visual signal."

DS Fowles was watching him from the hotel's security room. She could see he and Ben were alone in a quiet area, which meant Evan couldn't speak out loud.

He scratched his right ear to signal affirmative.

"Zero Three, did Mr. Reid recognize you?" Fowles asked. "Does he know who you are?"

Evan wasn't sure. For a moment there'd been the light of recognition in Ben's eyes, but then he'd seemed to dismiss it. The police knew that he and Ben were acquainted—which is why they'd warned him, too late, of the lad's approach to the ballroom. But they didn't know Evan had asked MI5 to do a background check on Ben so they could date.

He scratched his left ear to signal negative. *No one knows me*, he thought bitterly, *and no one ever will.*

"Copy that, Zero Three," Fowles said. "DI Hayward says you can stay. We'll need you if Backspace ever shows up. In the meantime, keep your distance from Reid. Acknowledge."

Evan signaled affirmative.

"Zero Two out." Fowles went silent.

A glance at Ben showed him facing the other way, shifting one corner of the wedding-party table a few inches to his left, then his right.

How could Evan keep his distance when there might be an attack? He wanted to hover beside Ben, bodyguard style, to protect him from the monster who wished to eradicate him and his clients in the name of purity.

Evan pulled out the phone he used as Gunnar to see if Jordan Lithgow (code name Backspace) had texted him in the last few minutes. Their conversation remained where they'd left it half an hour ago:

GUNNAR

It's starting. Where are you?

JORDAN

got hammered last night rough all day

You chickening out?

After several minutes…

nah their not worth it

Evan gave a frustrated sigh and shoved his phone back into his pocket. Had that BVP bastard lost his nerve, or had he got spooked by something Evan had done or said? If the latter, did Jordan still plan to attack this wedding and simply not tell him?

Now that Ben was here, the thought made Evan's heart trip over itself.

He went back to aligning the cutlery, the mindless task freeing his brain to work out what, if anything, could have tipped off Jordan.

Evan had met Lithgow in October by volunteering at the same North Ayrshire wildlife rescue center. (For some reason, extreme-right-wing types were often animal-welfare advocates, using their objections to kosher and halal slaughter methods as an excuse for anti-Semitism and Islamophobia.) He and Jordan had bonded over normal lad stuff like football, food, and their love of animals.

For weeks Jordan shared no hint of his political views. But

Evan recognized the coded fascist tattoos on his knuckles, and he saw the way the man looked at the volunteers with darker complexions.

"Truth is the living heartbeat of every believable lie."

Evan had learned this from his acting coach, the one hired to teach intelligence officers how to behave undercover. *"If your emotion is real, your words will feel real,"* she'd told the class. *"You may have never lost a child, but you've lost something—a dog, a job, a best friend who moved away. You may never have been held prisoner, but you've felt trapped by circumstance with no dream of escape. Use that. It may save your life one day."*

She was right. Suspicious by nature, terrorists could detect the slightest discrepancy between words and body language. Feelings had to be real, even if their justifications were phony.

So it was on the thirtieth of December, as he and Jordan drove into the countryside to release a rehabilitated stoat back into the wild, that Gunnar revealed how his girlfriend had left him for a woman.

"Aw, no, man," Jordan had said. *"That's a shiter."*

Evan then tapped into feelings about Fergus, who was marrying another man the following day. *"I feel so helpless. Like, there's nothing I can do, because I can never change what I am."*

And there lay the truth at the heart of Evan's lie: He'd lost the love of his life because he was born this way. He'd tried to be an architect like Fergus, to live in this world as an honest, simple, real person. But spying was in his blood and in his soul.

Jordan had taken the bait, offering up vile views about same-sex marriage as they'd stopped at the designated spot in the woods. Gunnar had agreed, mentioning how he'd come to the UK earlier that year partly to escape Norway's lax attitudes toward "moral impurity."

After the stoat had zoomed into the underbrush without looking back, Jordan closed the animal carrier, then leaned close to Evan. *"I've got a plan to sort things."*

A few weeks later he'd arranged for Gunnar to work a single

shift tonight at this hotel, where Jordan was an assistant catering manager. Something was going to happen.

Unfortunately, Evan still had no clue what that *something* was. The hotel had been searched for explosives, and undercover cops were on site ready to nab Jordan if he brought in a weapon—a knife, a gun, a bottle of acid, whatever. But he'd never shown up. According to the surveillance team, Jordan had been at his flat all day, leaving only to buy cigarettes from the corner newsagent.

In case Jordan was sending an associate to carry out the attack, the police were monitoring every wedding guest, with under-cover officers acting as coat check staff offering to stow their outerwear at no charge. A wise precaution, Evan thought, but he doubted Jordan would delegate a task he so clearly relished. Why had he changed his mind at the last minute?

A new voice came over the radio, that of the op's lead officer, Detective Inspector Raymond Hayward. "Zero Three, do you read? Zero One."

With a glance at Ben, Evan signaled affirmative.

"Here's an idea," said DI Hayward. "What if you texted Back-space and told him the wedding planner was Middle Eastern? That might change his mind about not coming."

Evan couldn't believe his ears. Without hesitating, he signaled negative.

"Zero Three, that's not a request."

His blood boiling, Evan scratched his left ear again, this time using his middle finger.

The radio went silent. Ten seconds later, the ballroom door opened and DI Hayward stepped in, dressed in the same server outfit as Evan.

"Gunnar, I'm afraid you're needed in the kitchen." Hayward turned to Ben. "Apologies, sir. I'll send in another staff member to assist you."

Evan stalked out of the ballroom without looking at Ben. He followed Hayward down the hall and through an unmarked door into the security facility. In front of a bank of monitors, DS Fowles sat with the hotel security chief and a pair of constables. Deirdre gave Evan a sympathetic grimace as he and Hayward swept by.

The detective inspector took Evan into a tiny bare room and shut the door behind them. "Switch off your radio so we can speak freely."

Evan obeyed, then said, "Sir, I can't use a civilian as bait for a terrorist attack."

"You *can* do it, because I ordered you to."

Evan was pretty sure that as an MI5 officer outside police chain of command, he didn't have to follow Hayward's orders, but he preferred not to test that assumption. "It's an interesting idea. We could have used an undercover officer with a similar ethnic background, giving them a false name to protect their identity."

"Too late for that," Hayward said. "It takes time to build a legend that can be backed up in case Lithgow ran a search on them. Reid is our best chance."

"Sir, if I tell Jordan Lithgow there's a gay man of Iranian heritage handling same-sex weddings, then Ben Reid will become a top target of every extremist in Scotland. We can't protect him twenty-four-seven."

"We only need to protect him tonight," Hayward said. "Lithgow won't share this juicy secret. You know how competitive these XRW types are. He'll want Reid for himself."

"And if he doesn't, then we've put a civilian at risk for nothing."

"Civilians are always at risk, they just don't know it." Sighing, Hayward combed his fingers through his dark hair. Every strand stood on end, making him look like he was wearing a perpetually alarmed cat on his head. "If Lithgow fades away, Operation Caps Lock will be downgraded, maybe even suspended."

Evan had worried about that. Counterterrorism resources were finite, and tonight's operation must have cost thousands of pounds. "Could you search his flat?"

"There's not enough evidence for a warrant. He's coy on the phone, and everything he told you in person was too vague."

Evan gritted his teeth at the mention of his own shortfall. "I can get better intelligence, or the surveillance team might—"

"Surveillance is expensive. So are you. So are all those undercover cops out there." Hayward gestured at the door, whacking his hand against it. "Ow." He rubbed his knuckles, his face growing redder. "You're the one who scared him off. Now you're the one who'll lure him back."

For a moment, Evan doubted himself, nearly succumbing to the detective's manipulation. *I failed. I'm the only one who can make it right.*

Then logic stopped that spiral, reminding him that even if Jordan's no-show *was* Evan's fault—a theory with no evidence yet —it didn't mean he should follow this dangerous order.

"I won't do it, sir," he said. "Not like this."

Hayward's eyes narrowed, and he lifted his hand into the tiny space between their bodies. "Give me Gunnar's phone."

Evan took a step back, his heel striking the wall. No way he'd let anyone give Ben up to a potential terrorist.

"That phone is property of Police Scotland," Hayward said. "Now hand it over."

"Fine, I'll text him." Evan pulled out Gunnar's phone and brought it close to his face as he thumbed in the message, using his greater height to keep the screen from Hayward's view.

Stay away. Police here. Drugs bust

Evan hit send, then handed the phone to Hayward and said, "Sorry," though he wasn't.

The detective inspector looked at the screen. "Are you—" His lips kept moving, but no more words came out. His grip on the phone tightened with such ferocity, Evan worried the device would shatter.

It buzzed with an incoming message. Hayward read it, then

shoved the phone into Evan's chest and jerked open the door. "Never trust a spook," he grumbled on his way out.

Jordan's reply had just come in:

!!!?!? ok staying home thx mate your my hero

Evan's stomach curdled at Jordan thinking him a hero and a friend. But maybe by warning him off, Gunnar had gained Jordan's trust, which could pay off later in the operation. Assuming the operation continued.

The most soul-twisting fact of counterterrorism work was that sometimes a *few* dangerous people had to stay free in the short term—leaving innocent lives at risk—in order to thwart a *lot* of dangerous people in the long term. It was a troubling tradeoff, but one Evan accepted.

Just not tonight.

THE RECEPTION WENT off without a hitch—apart from the bagpiper playing a wee bit out of tune and the best man being too drunk to give a coherent speech. By the time the guests had cleared out, Ben felt exhausted but giddy, like he'd just finished a triathlon whilst being chased by a tiger.

Now he stood beside the gift table, overseeing the parade of packages heading for the best man's SUV. Elsewhere in the room, Evan—aka, Gunnar—was clearing the tables. As he stretched forward to lift the floral centerpiece so he could remove the table-cloth, Ben took a moment to admire his…everything.

Why was Evan here in disguise? Wasn't he an architect? Perhaps he needed extra money but was embarrassed to admit it. A second job was nothing to be ashamed of, not in this economy.

Or maybe Evan was an undercover cop. Maybe he was working with the man whose conversation Ben had overheard with Richard, the hotel's events manager. They'd said something about *"blow his cover"* and *"limit exposure between him and Reid."* Ben remembered seeing a headline somewhere that certain hotel chains were running drugs out of their kitchens.

Whatever the reason, Evan clearly didn't want his cover blown. So Ben turned away now, leaving him to his secret mission. Besides, he needed to peruse Corinne's notes one last time.

He cursed when he realized the "Brought In" list contained a third page with one item—or rather, three large items. After a quick poll of the remaining wedding party, it was clear Ben was the only person with both room in his car and the sobriety to operate it.

At least it gave him an excuse to do what he already wanted.

Ben strode over to the table Evan was clearing. "I wonder if you could help me...Gunnar, is it?"

"Heh?" Evan turned to him, crumpling the pesto-stained white tablecloth into a ball. "Oh. Hi. What can I do for you?" His smile was smooth and serene. If Evan was worried Ben recognized him, he was hiding it well.

"The vases at these three tables, see, they've been in the McKay family for generations. I need to load them into my car and return them to Mrs. McKay tomorrow."

Evan looked at the vase in front of him. "With or without the flowers?" he asked, turning the *th*s into *d*s.

"With. Sorry, I know you must be knackered, but as you can see"—Ben lifted the vase and set it down with a thud—"they're a bit heavy for one person."

Evan looked at the tablecloth in his hands, then his eyes flickered with that incoming-transmission look. "Okay. I'll be right back."

Hiding his smile, Ben returned to supervising the gift parade, ensuring none of the packages took a tumble or ended up in the wrong hands.

Evan soon returned, and together they lugged the three massive vases out to Ben's car, parked in the alley behind the hotel. Once he'd secured the last of the clay monstrosities on the floor of his back seat, Ben turned to Evan with a grateful smile. "You're an absolute star."

"My pleasure." Evan brushed his hands together, then frowned at his left palm.

"What's wrong?"

"Nothing, just a little cut from the edge of that vase."

"Let me see." Ben stepped close and took his hand. Evan caught his breath but didn't pull away.

Ben was sure they'd shaken hands when they'd met at Fergus and John's wedding. So if this wasn't their first touch, why was Ben's pulse suddenly thumping in his ears? "Do you—do you want a sticking plaster?" he asked, though the scrape really didn't warrant it. "I've got some in the glove compartment."

Evan's eyes met his, the golden-framed glasses lending them unusual warmth. Then his head jerked to the side. "What's that noise?"

"What noise? Where?" Ben's heart now pounded more from fear than desire. Had some hooligan seen them touching hands and decided to stomp them into the dust? That rarely happened anymore in Glasgow, but Ben didn't want to buck the trend.

Evan motioned to the big green rubbish skip against the hotel wall, about twenty feet away. "Stay here." He crept forward, head swiveling, one hand hovering near his hip as if ready to grab a weapon.

As Ben followed, he heard a loud rustling from the large steel container, but he kept going. Better to face a threat together than separately.

Evan paused beside the rubbish skip, head cocked. From inside came a plaintive "Mrrrrow?" Ben's shoulders sagged with relief.

Evan lifted the skip's right-hand lid, murmuring something that sounded like, *Vor ah doo, katungeh?*

Ben came up beside him. At the sound of another soft, sweet

meow, he lifted the left-side lid, wrinkling his nose at the stench of rotting food.

A ghostly form moved inside the skip. Its face turned upward.

"Aaaaaugh!" they cried out, leaping back. Both lids clanged shut.

"What was that thing?" Ben asked.

"I don't—could it be…" Evan lifted the left lid again, cautiously, and peered inside. "That is the most sad creature I have ever seen."

Ben slid next to him to look. The cat was a pale gray, a color which on a paint can would be called *Despair*. Its long fur was matted into clumps near the tops of both forelegs, making it look as though it was wearing shoulder pads. One pale-blue eye was squeezed shut, while the other blinked up at them through a sheen of rheumy pus.

"Mrroww?" it asked again, propping its forepaws against the side of the skip.

"Ben, hold the lid." When Evan's hands were freed, he reached down, extending the backs of his fingers near the cat's head. After a quick sniff, the cat rubbed its chin against Evan's knuckles.

"That face," Ben whispered. "Looks like someone ironed it."

"It is very flat. He's probably part Persian."

"Ooh, I'm part Persian too, so it must be a sign. Let's rescue him. And since I live in uni housing with no pets allowed, I really mean *you* rescue him."

"How?"

"Take him home. Take him to the vet. Be a hero."

For a moment, Evan's eyes turned almost sad. Then he nodded and pulled a pair of gloves from his pocket. "Hold up the lid, and when I pull him out, close it—softly, not to scare him—then get that empty box behind you."

"Right. Fire in."

Evan leaned over, reaching down with both hands, murmuring that *katungeh*-sounding word again, which Ben assumed was Norwegian for *kitty*. He admired the man's devotion to his cover.

Evan lifted the reeking feline from the rubbish skip. Ben set the cardboard box on the ground and held the flaps open so the cat could be placed inside. He'd never seen such a pathetic beast—and yet it was purring. Then again, he'd purr too, had Evan been holding him with such care and consideration.

"Let me drop you home in my car," he said, though he knew the offer would be refused.

"No need. My flat is near." After giving the cat a last pat on the head, Evan closed the box's flaps so they interlocked, then lifted it as he stood. "I guess this is goodbye."

"Is it?" Ben pulled out a business card and slipped it into Evan's outside jacket pocket.

Evan started. "What are you doing?"

"Giving you my card." As Ben pulled his hand back, it brushed against a solid object in the inside pocket, something that felt bigger and heavier than a phone.

"Are you offering to plan my wedding?" Evan gave a crooked smile that flipped Ben's heart. "Is this how you discover a man is single?"

"Caught out." Ben held up his hands in mock surrender. "Text me a pic of our wee boy after he's been seen to."

"Okay." Evan started to turn away.

"Wait! He needs a name." Ben's mind latched onto the song that had been stuck in his head since the grooms' first dance. "How about Terence, as in Trent D'Arby?" He sang a bar of "Sign Your Name," swaying in a way he hoped was awkwardly charming instead of just awkward.

Evan seemed to consider it. "A street cat like this needs a more tough name. What about 'Trent,' as in D'Arby?" He paused. "And Reznor."

"He does looks like something out of a Nine Inch Nails video."

They shared a last lingering glance, and Ben wanted more than anything to touch Evan's cheek, which was turning rosy in the cold air.

Then the box shuddered. Evan tightened his grip as he turned away. "Shhh," he murmured to the cat. "You're in safe hands."

Wonderful hands. Ben headed back to the ballroom for one last check. *Hands I'll be dreaming about tonight.*

He stopped short just inside the back door, then smacked his forehead. Those hands would remain just a dream forever, because if Evan kept Trent, he couldn't bring Ben home without blowing his "Gunnar" cover.

Ben made his way into the ballroom, feeling guilty for his dismay. They'd saved a life tonight, serving a greater good than any romance. Still, he wished that just once, he wouldn't screw himself over by doing the right thing.

Chapter 4

"I DIDN'T THINK you could get any uglier," Evan said as he gazed down into the box beside his couch.

He'd slept there since arriving home at five a.m. from the emergency veterinarian's, where he'd gone after his contentious joint police/MI5 debriefing had wrapped up at three. The vet had trimmed the mats out of Trent's gray hair and shaved patches of it so she could check for mange and ringworm. Now the sleeping cat resembled a Miniature Schnauzer groomed with hedge trimmers.

He watched the cat's flank rise and fall with deep, even breaths, illuminated by the faint sunlight leaking in through the window. The sight made his eyelids heavy, and as they drifted shut, Evan realized he'd slept more peacefully this morning than he'd done in ages. Perhaps this was down to Trent; it was soothing to have someone besides himself who needed Evan to be strong.

Or perhaps it was the fact that at the post-op debriefing, Kay had defended Evan's refusal to use Ben as terrorist bait. He wasn't sure whether she agreed with him or was just being loyal. Either way, his job was secure.

Or perhaps he'd slept better because of Ben himself. The mere thought of that blithe, self-assured man filled Evan with a strange mix of peace and desire. He curled an arm around his pillow, letting sweet, fantastical thoughts slide his mind back into sleep.

A knock came at the door.

Evan sprang off the couch, heart pounding. He crept toward his flat's entrance, raising his hands into a fighting posture.

"It's me," came a deep voice muffled by the wooden door, "and yes, I'm alone."

Evan peered through the peephole to see his father standing in the corridor, his long gray coat already doffed and draped over his briefcase.

After taking a moment to collect himself, Evan opened the door. "How did you get in the building?"

"Hello to you, too." His father swept inside, hanging his coat on an empty peg without pausing. "An elderly couple let me in just as I approached the front entrance. I gave them a brief but pointed lecture on security lapses."

Evan rubbed his arms to shed the rest of his adrenaline rush. "You couldn't phone first? What if I'd been entertaining a naked man or three?"

"Your bedroom blinds are open. They'd be closed if you had naked men in there."

"Not if they were exhibitionists." Evan followed his father into the living room, veering off into the adjoining kitchen. "Coffee?"

"Please. And we both know you'd never date *one* exhibitionist, much less multiples."

This was true, though Evan had no need to hide his sexuality. As the son of a high-level spook, he'd never had the luxury of personal secrets, which were considered a security risk. He'd come out as gay when he was fifteen, so that no one could blackmail his father into betraying his country in order to keep Evan in the closet. With nothing to hide, Evan's own MI5 vetting process three years ago had been swift and smooth.

If only his ex had been so clean, the job might not have destroyed them.

"What happened to him?"

Evan turned to see his dad standing beside the cardboard box. "That's Trent. I don't know what happened to her, apart from getting pregnant and nearly starving to death."

"Pitiful thing." Unbuttoning his blazer, his father crouched down to peer into the box. "It's a marvel she's kept *herself* alive, much less a litter of kittens."

"That's what the vet said." From the cupboard Evan retrieved the two mugs his father had bought for him at the International Spy Museum in Washington, DC. He inserted the one reading Trust No One beneath the coffee-pod machine's spout and hit brew. "She'll be spayed when she's strong enough for surgery. Obviously the kittens will be aborted."

"That's wise."

Evan came over to the box to see Trent blinking up at them with a bleary blue gaze. "A bit sad, though."

"It'd be sadder if she died carrying the kittens to term," Dad said. "Sometimes sacrifices must be made for the greater good."

On the whole, Evan agreed. Such an outlook seemed cold on the surface, but the world needed people who could make tough decisions. Trent needed Evan to save her life, not let sentiment make him *risk* her life.

"Doesn't mean I can't feel bad," Evan said as he took his father's full mug from the coffee machine and replaced it with an empty one reading Deny Everything.

"Of course you feel bad. It's a bloody tragedy. The key is acknowledging those feelings as legitimate but irrelevant." His dad's voice pitched up as he leaned over to pet Trent. "There's a good kitty. Oh, you're a friendly one, aren't you? That's how you survived." He straightened up to take the coffee mug. "She'll be good for you. You must miss having animals since you moved to Glasgow."

True. After growing up on his stepfather's sheep farm in Orkney, Evan found this city's human-beast ratio higher than he preferred. But he'd never mentioned this to his father, whose bursts of empathy always surprised him.

Then again, it was a spy's job to understand people.

"You need company, full stop," his dad said. "You've been cloistered like a Cistercian monk far too long." He swept a disapproving look over Evan's minimalist living room.

"The Cistercians were fabulous architects. Made good beer, too." He gestured to Trent. "What'll happen to her if I get relocated?"

"You'd stay within the UK, so you could take her with you. A cat won't mind the occasional all-night op."

"But what if I—" Evan cleared the sudden tightness from his throat. "What if something happened to me? Who'd look after Trent?"

His father sighed as he settled onto the couch. "Evan, what happened in Belfast was an aberration. Your job won't usually be so hazardous."

"How do you know? We're not even in the same division." Evan's father, a self-proclaimed Cold Warrior, had spent his career as a spycatcher in MI5's counterespionage D Branch. If a foreign intelligence officer set foot on British soil, Hugh Hollister almost certainly knew about it.

"I know because despite what you experienced last year, a quiet life is the norm for MI5 officers. Seven-thirty to four, five days a week. A loving spouse, some squealing children—"

"How long was that your life?"

His dad gave a conciliatory nod. "Not long enough, but that was *my* failing, not the job's."

"So I should do as you say, not as you've done."

"Precisely."

Turning back to the coffee machine, Evan recalled how his father had discouraged him and his older sister from following in his footsteps. *"I want you to be happy,"* he'd told them a thousand times.

Justine had heeded that advice and was currently smashing it as an up-and-coming astrophysicist at St. Andrews University. Evan, however, had made a weak attempt at architecture before accepting his true calling as a spook—a calling which did in fact make him happy, despite the wrecking ball it had taken to his personal life.

"You know I'm proud of you," his dad said, prompting an unwelcome glow deep in Evan's gut. "I got you that award, after all."

Evan glanced at the refrigerator, the front of which held his Certificate of Awesomeness. His father had commissioned a friend's five-year-old to sign the certificate in crayon and color the stars, making it look like an art project for the adored uncle Evan was not. It functioned as a stand-in for Evan's real-life MI5 Commendation for Bravery, which of course he could never tell anyone about, much less display in his home.

On this certificate, the line reading IN RECOGNITION FOR had been left blank. *"So you can mentally fill it in each time you see it,"* Dad had told him.

"Thank you again for that," Evan said. "It meant a lot."

"I know what it's like." His father crossed his legs, smoothing the creases in his smart gray trousers. "How was the wedding?"

"What wedding?" Nobody outside Operation Caps Lock had a need to know about last night.

"Fergus's, of course."

"Oh." It seemed odd that Evan and his dad hadn't spoken since then, but the senior Hollister had been overseas for most of January. Since MI5 operated only on UK soil, Evan assumed his father had been working at a British embassy. "The wedding was fine." *Inasmuch as it was not attacked by terrorists.* "I met someone." He felt a quiver inside at the mention of Ben, even without naming him.

"I know. That's why I'm here." Without setting down the coffee, his father pulled his briefcase into his lap, thumbed the codes on the latches, then opened the case. "Behnam Nouri Reid.

Twenty-two years old, fourth-year geography student at University of Glasgow."

Evan tightened his grip on his coffee mug. After encountering Ben last night as Gunnar, he was dying to be with him again as his real self. This vetting report would determine whether that could ever happen.

His father pulled out a thin blue file and flipped it open. "No foreign travel apart from family holidays to North America, the Continent, et cetera. Spent his gap year working for his mum's wedding business." His dad turned to the second page. "Giti Kirmani Reid is rather interesting. Her family fled Iran when she was ten years old, just after the Revolution. They're of the Bahá'í Faith, see. The Ayatollahs are keen on persecuting Bahá'ís."

"Good on her parents for getting out, then."

"Yes." His father continued. "They came to the UK, where she eventually attended University of Strathclyde and met a Scotsman, Archibald Reid, whom she later married. He's a colonel in the army's Intelligence Corps, currently stationed in Afghanistan. Colonel Reid's location is classified, by the way, and it isn't mentioned in this file, in case you decide to share this with Behnam one day." He held the file toward Evan. "The lad's clean. You can date him."

Evan took a step back, mostly relieved but also a bit revolted. "I don't want to read that. I feel like a stalker as it is, asking Five to vet him."

"You did the right thing, following protocol. Now you can see him with a clear conscience and a complete lack of paranoia." He set the file on the couch beside him. "If things get serious and he seems trustworthy, you can tell him where you work."

At the thought of being so honest with anyone on the outside, Evan felt a giddiness bubble up within him. He quickly tamped it down. "No one told me you'd be doing the vetting."

"I didn't. I'm merely the messenger delivering the good news. Just keep in mind, the Service vetted Reid only for his threat potential, not his suitability for…" He waved his hand at the walls. "This life."

Life with a professional liar, you mean. Evan looked down into the cardboard box. Trent stretched, her back end wobbling, then meowed up at him. He squatted to pet her, his right hip a bit stiff after yesterday's football match and last night's op. "I did miss being near animals."

"You're changing the subject," his father said.

"From what, your prophecies of romantic doom? You going to tell me again to find a nice man in the Service?"

"Why not? There are loads of LGBT folk at MI5. It's just won a Stonewall Award."

"Aye, it's a gay-friendly place to work," Evan said. "That doesn't mean I want to date a fellow spook. I want someone honest and uncomplicated."

"So you can break *his* heart instead of him breaking yours? Like you did with Fergus?"

Evan's fingers froze on Trent's chin mid-scratch. His cheeks burned as if he'd been literally slapped instead of just figuratively.

"Apologies," his dad said. "That was out of order. I only meant you should find someone who understands the sacrifices this job requires."

"Or what? I'll end up like you, married to the realm instead of a person who loves me?"

His father gave a soft gasp, and then the room fell silent, apart from Trent's raspy purr.

"Yes. That's exactly it." His dad got to his feet. "Thank you for the coffee. I'll show myself out."

"Wait." Evan stood and followed him to the foyer. "I'm sorry. You're the only person I can be my real self with, and my real self is a bit of a shit."

"You're not a shit, you're just astute." His father was already smirking as he pulled on his coat. "And you very nicely proved my point."

"Which is?"

"Don't be like me." His dad opened the front door and flicked a hand toward the living room. "Be careful with your new companion."

"She'll be all right, the vet said, once she—"

"Fuck's sake, lad, I'm not talking about the cat."

As always, Evan's father walked away with the last word.

―――――

Dear Ben (may we call you Ben? Well, too late),

My fiancé—I still can't get used to calling him that!—and I are members of the Rainbow Regiment, the fan club for the Woodstoun Warriors. We attended the AMAZING wedding you did for Fergus and John on Hogmanay and heard how you saved the day when they needed last-minute help.

So...guess what? Our wedding is Saturday 18 April and we need rescued. Michael thought I was sorting certain details and I thought Michael was sorting certain details and it turned out both of us were sorting the same details whilst other details got not sorted at all.

Could you help us turn this colossal mess into the best day of our lives, or at least not one of the worst? Please?

A hopeful future client,

Philip

BEN ROLLED his chair back from his desk, shoving one foot after another against the floor of his one-room student flat. He considered going for a run, but that plan had two flaws: 1) it was pishing down raining and 2) he hated exercise.

He would happily overcome both obstacles to avoid answering this email. He hated to disappoint potential clients, especially friends of John and Fergus.

But after last night's conversation with Hannah, Ben had made some inquiries, and it turned out that people in the wedding industry *were* talking about his mother. Most of what Ben had learned today was hearsay, like *so-and-so said they heard that a lass who worked at one of the florists—can't remember which—had heard from someone at the dressmaker's…*

But the rumors were unanimous: Ben's mum was refusing to handle same-sex weddings, as evidenced by the fact Ben was doing so on his own. His activities were shining a spotlight on her prejudice. If he stopped, maybe that spotlight would dim.

He continued to roll his chair, careful to stay atop his thick Turkish rug so the sound of the wheels wouldn't disturb his neighbor in the flat below.

It was hard for other people to understand Mum's position. Most days it was hard for *him* to understand it, even though she'd raised him in the same faith, a faith he'd committed to of his own volition as an adult. He was breaking the rules by endorsing same-sex marriage, but that was a risk he was willing to take. It wasn't fair to drag his mum into it, not when the community meant so much to her.

Ben was already committed to a wedding at the end of the month, but he could stop taking on new clients, at least until…

Until when? Until the rules changed? Or until he couldn't take it anymore?

Whichever came first.

He rolled back to the desk and began his reply:

Dear Philip,

Congratulations on your upcoming nuptials! I'm so, so happy for you, and flattered you thought of me.

Alas, the timing is less than ideal. I'm in my final year of uni, so in April I'll be sprinting to finish my honors dissertation and prepare for exams. I promised myself not to commit to new weddings until I miraculously obtain my degree.

If in a month you find yourself in dire need, please don't hesitate to approach me again. By then I'll know the fate of my dissertation's progress and whether I can take on a new event

*—perhaps as a wedding-day coordinator—or whether I must
flee the country in mortal shame. :-)*

He finished with a list of referrals to other wedding planners
and reliable suppliers. Before he could reconsider, he whispered,
"So sorry," and hit send.

Needing a distraction from his guilt, he clicked the email
folder which automatically collected news alerts pertaining to his
honors dissertation on the tracking powers of geographical information systems. Most of the alerts looked irrelevant, but far down
the list, a certain *Guardian* headline caught his eye:

Fancy a nice sit down? MI5 needs you.

Ben couldn't resist clicking. As he skimmed the article about
recruiting surveillance officers, his heart raced with excitement.
Perhaps "Gunnar" wasn't a cop at all but a spy for the UK's
domestic security/intelligence service, which meant last night's
undercover work wasn't about busting a drugs ring but rather
hunting terrorists.

The shadowy agency seemed to fit Evan's aura of mystery, but
that wasn't necessarily a good thing. Like most of the world, Ben
knew little about MI5 apart from its fictional representation on the
long-running *Spooks* TV program. Though the show made the job
seem glamorous and exciting, it often portrayed MI5 agents as
ruthless and amoral, paying little heed to citizens' privacy or even
human rights.

Ben clicked the link to the MI5 recruitment advert.

One by one, the ad's details chipped away at his certainty. The
agency wanted people who could blend in—average height, no
distinguishing features—and who lived near London or could
relocate there. Evan was tall and unforgettably handsome, and
Glasgow was definitely not a commutable distance from London.

Ben closed the browser tab with an extra-hard keyboard tap, a
bit frustrated but also rather relieved. As much as he supported
MI5 officers' mission in theory, it would be pure weird to date

one, never knowing where he went or what he did—or how much he secretly knew about Ben.

He stared at his phone, wondering how Trent the cat was faring in his new home. Then he glanced above his desk at the Woodstoun Warriors wall calendar, a gift from his friend Robert, a member of the semi-famous all-LGBTQ football team and "Glasgay" icons. Evan was one of their best players, which made his absence from the calendar all the more conspicuous.

He checked Evan's public-facing Facebook profile, which hadn't changed in the month since Ben had sent him an unanswered friend request.

The last post was from home in Orkney on Christmas Day, a photo of Evan and seven schoolmates after winning the mass street melee known as the Kirkwall Ba. Evan's cheek was bruised, his forehead was cut, and his hair was matted with mud, but he and his old friends beamed with breathless joy.

On impulse, Ben clicked *Like*. On a followup impulse, he quickly shut the browser tab, as though that would erase Evan from his thoughts and memory.

Just as he'd finished scanning the rest of the news alerts, his phone rang with a call from an unfamiliar number.

"Ben Reid," he answered in the professional voice he had yet to master.

"Ben. Hi." There was a slight pause. "Maybe you don't remember me, but we met at Fergus and John's wedding."

Oh my God, it's him. He'd know that divine lilt anywhere. "And you are?"

"Sorry. It's Evan." The caller cleared his throat. "Evan Hollister?"

Ben twirled his chair in a full circle as he tried to rein in his excitement. "I vaguely remember meeting an Evan Hollister," he said in a playful tone. "I remember giving him my number, which went unused for nearly six weeks."

"Aye, there were, erm…I had to sort some things. Anyway, I'd like to see you again. Maybe for dinner? Maybe Saturday?"

Ben grimaced at the calendar. "Friday might be better."

"I've got a match Saturday, so I can't go out on a Friday night. Not without avoiding all the things that make going out worthwhile."

Ben's mind glowed, imagining all those things. "Saturday is Valentine's Day." He spun his chair again. "That's a lot of pressure for a first date."

Evan gave a soft laugh that turned Ben inside out. "I think we can handle it."

Chapter 5

FOOTBALL WAS FULL OF TRIGGERS.

Evan felt it each time a player came at him from behind, even here at practice session, surrounded by trusted teammates. At the approach of pounding footsteps and heavy breath, a klaxon blared in the base of his brain, urging him to fling back an elbow with all the force in his threatened body.

He didn't give in to that urge. If anything, that brief jolt of fear sharpened his play. Every nerve and muscle strived for escape, whether by a deft double scissors feint or a nimble Marseille turn. His manager, Charlotte, had pronounced his dribbling "dazzling," but to him it just felt like survival.

Charlotte wasn't as thrilled with how long he held onto the ball, pressing forward as far as he could instead of passing to his teammates, who all thought him arrogant for it. Evan had fed that belief with barbs about their lack of speed. As long as they considered him a dickhead, they'd never notice he was broken.

Now he was dribbling down the middle of the indoor practice pitch, zigzagging toward the goal, trying to shake his final defender, Warriors center-back Liam Carroll.

Ahead of him, forward Duncan Harris shouted for the ball. Evan did a quick flap-flap move to try to shake Liam but gained only half a step on the speedy defender. It was enough to see clear to Duncan, but something stopped Evan from passing.

Liam stepped forward and poked the ball back between Evan's legs. His body collided with Evan's, sending him sprawling on his arse.

"Oops," Liam said with no regret as he zipped around Evan to steal the ball. The tackle had been perfectly legal—and perfectly humiliating.

As Evan rose from the turf, recovering his breath, he imagined Charlotte's imminent rants.

"You do realize we Scots invented passing 150 years ago for a reason?" she'd said more than once. *"You'll never earn back your teammates' trust until you give them yours,"* she'd also said, more than twice.

But at the end of tonight's practice, Charlotte had no lectures, only urgent news: The draws for the next two rounds of the Scottish Amateur Cup had been released. In the tournament's early rounds, the Warriors had been lucky to play against sides from lower divisions, so they'd had a relatively easy run so far.

Judging by their manager's face, the team's luck had finally ended.

"Round seven will take place the seventh of March," Charlotte said, reading from her phone screen. "It's a home match."

"Yes!" Duncan said beside Evan, pumping his fist.

"Against Moray Rovers."

Duncan dropped his arm. "Shit."

"Who are they?" asked left fullback Katie Heath, who'd just joined this season.

"Last year's finalists," said striker Colin MacDuff, rubbing the wound that lay beneath his football shirt. "Fucking hell."

"It gets worse." Charlotte lowered the phone. "If we beat Moray, we'll face either Stirling Hill or Forthside in the quarterfinal."

Evan echoed his teammates' groans. Forthside United—appropriately abbreviated FU—had held the cup for three straight years.

Charlotte continued. "But you're not to think of the quarterfinals—not this year's, which we may never play, and certainly not last year's. We focus on the match in front of us. Understand?"

Evan's face flamed under his teammates' glares. MI5 had deployed him to Northern Ireland directly before last year's quarterfinal. With no safe or legal way to explain his absence, he'd invented a story about running off to Brussels with a fictitious Belgian lover. He'd broken the hearts of every Warrior—especially Fergus, who had replaced Evan as captain.

Since returning last July, Evan had tried to redeem himself through hard work, dedication, and of course scoring and assisting as many goals as possible. But most of the Warriors—Fergus included—probably wished Evan would disappear again forever.

"There's something else," Evan said. "In April we'll be needing to make up the league matches that got postponed by the weather. We'll be playing a brutal schedule, probably twice a week for over a month."

"True," Fergus said, "but so will every league team. If anything, we're fitter and better prepared, thanks to our training schedule. Most amateur players treat football like a hobby." He cast a proud smile over their teammates. "Warriors treat it like a calling."

"We're at a disadvantage," Evan said. "We missed an extra league match on Saturday because of the Cup."

"Aye, we're the only team in our division still in the tournament." Charlotte looked at Evan. "You're worried we'll not have enough healthy players?"

He nodded. "If any of us get injured between now and April, Warriors might not be able to field a full squad for some matches, not without risking further injury."

"We could do with some new blood." Fergus rubbed the dusting of ginger stubble on his chin. "Maybe another open trial?"

"And who'll be coming to it?" Evan asked Fergus. "All the people we rejected from the trial we held six months ago." After the Warriors' charity match last summer—an event that had made them international LGBTQ icons—every queer footballer in the Central Belt had wanted to sign up. Only two players out of the dozens who'd applied had been good enough to join even as substitutes.

"You've got a better idea?" Liam snapped.

"I can scout for quality players at the gay football league's matches," Evan said. "Like I used to do."

Fergus tilted his head back and sighed at the ceiling. "So we're back to poaching, then."

"I prefer the term 'active recruitment.'"

"Whatever you call it," Fergus said, "it makes the gay teams hate us."

"They already hate us, so I don't see—"

"Lads, lads." Charlotte stepped forward. "Gonnae no chew each other's heads off? I'll have a wee chat to the board about it and let you know Saturday."

As the players gathered their gear, Evan was approached by right fullback Jamie Guthrie. "If you need another pair of scouting eyes, I'll go with you."

Evan straightened up from his kit bag, amazed a teammate actually wanted to hang out with him. "Thanks."

"Nae bother." Jamie toweled off his own face, muffling his voice. "You recruited me from Glasgow Greens, so it'd be, like, full circle and all. Plus it'll be fun."

"Even if we go to a Greens match?"

Jamie lowered the towel to stare at him. "Can I wear a disguise?"

"Aye, we'll both need them. If they recognize me, I'll be the one needing a permanent substitute."

"We'll be like spies!" Jamie's face froze. "Oh God. I didn't— sorry, I cannae believe I said that word."

Evan kept his face straight. "What word?"

Jamie blinked. "Right. So...erm, yeah, just let me know." He hurried off to help Colin and Duncan collect the practice cones, though they were nearly finished.

This had been Jamie's first slip-up since he'd been involved in Evan's original MI5 vetting. The agency had requested four names as references, then each of those people in turn had been asked for four more names. Evan had given MI5 Charlotte's name, and she in turn had offered them Jamie's because, as she'd told Evan later, *"The lad knows how to keep a secret."*

Though Jamie and Charlotte never knew which agency Evan had applied to or whether he'd been hired at all, they must have suspected that his sudden departure last year had been connected to his work. They'd had to remain silent in the face of his team-mates' recriminations, unable to defend him without raising suspicion and risking national security.

The thought of vetting reminded him of Ben. Evan needed more intel, the sort MI5 couldn't provide.

He approached center-back Robert McKenzie, who was seated on the floor, leaning forward with the soles of his feet together in a deep groin stretch. "You know your friend Ben? Fergus's wedding planner?"

"I was wondering when you were gonnae make your move." Robert stretched his arms forward, spreading his fingers over the fibers of the artificial turf.

"We're having dinner Saturday." Evan sat beside him. "I don't want to make an arse of myself, so any insights you could give me..."

Robert looked amused. "Ben's great. He's kind and funny, constantly buzzing about one thing or another. And he's honest—sometimes too honest. Cannae keep a secret to save his life."

Good to know, Evan thought.

"Which is ironic," Robert continued, "considering his Grindr username is IllusiveMan. Erm, you knew that's how we met, right? On Grindr?"

Evan shook his head but smiled to ease Robert's embarrassment over the hookup app. "Illusive as in deceptive?"

"Illusive Man is a character from the *Mass Effect* video game. He's a bad guy, but he's got his reasons."

"Reasons for what?" Liam asked, creeping up behind them. Evan pretended to be as startled as Robert.

"Gonnae stop eavesdropping, ya knob?" Robert beamed up at his partner. "This yin's finally ready to woo Ben Reid."

"Ben's too good for you," Liam told Evan, then turned back to Robert. "Your place the night?"

"Aye. Shower's fixed."

"Good." He tapped Robert's hip with his toe. "Though I do prefer you filthy," he added before walking off without a glance at Evan.

"Sorry about him," Robert said.

"I understand. Fergus may forgive me one day for hurting him, but his mates never will."

"I'm glad you came back. You're the reason this team's not bottom of the league table." Robert rubbed his thighs as he straightened his legs. "Besides, I believe in second chances."

"Thanks."

"But if you hurt Ben, I will personally break every one of your limbs." He patted Evan's shoulder as he stood. "Even if it means Warriors get relegated."

Evan sighed. Sometimes he wondered whether he should move on for good, leave his team in peace. But he needed the Warriors and the exquisite everyday normalcy of football. His therapist and psychiatrist had agreed, else he never would have been allowed to return to Glasgow.

Now he watched as Robert and Liam left the building together. Lifelong best mates, they'd always been close, but ever since Robert had come out as bisexual and fallen for Liam, their synchronicity had taken on a sweetness and heat that anyone could see was true love.

Evan had once known that sort of bond with Fergus, before his job had driven them apart—little by little, then all at once, like a glacier inching toward the edge of a continent before plummeting into the sea.

Maybe his dad was right. Maybe it was time for Evan to find a new land.

Chapter 6

BEN FELT LIKE CINDERELLA.

He wasn't wearing a ball gown or high heels, and he'd spent the day working on his dissertation and bingeing on *Better Call Saul* rather than cleaning ashes from a hearth.

But he *was* pulling up to a castle (of sorts) in a carriage (of sorts) summoned by his own Prince Charming. A prince who was right now striding over from the castle's front entrance.

For a moment, Ben wondered if he'd been mistaken about "Gunnar." Evan moved down the front stairs with an easy grace, his posture holding none of the reticence of the allegedly Norwegian server. His blond waves gleamed in the streetlight, rippling in the breeze without the gel that had steamrolled Gunnar's hair. And his cheeks and chin were so smooth, Ben already longed to reach out and stroke them.

"How much, mate?" Ben asked the taxi driver.

The driver waved his hand. "It's been seen to."

Evan opened the cab's back door. Ben slid out of the car, keeping his eyes on his companion's face. The smile was the same he remembered from Fergus and John's wedding, but it held none of the sadness it had contained that night.

"It's good to see you again," Evan said.

"You too. Thanks for the ride." To stop himself staring at Evan for clues, Ben looked up at the front of the Sherbrooke Castle Hotel. Its turrets were draped in fresh snow, which glowed with the hotel's warm floodlights and the blue haze of dusk. "I've never seen this place so beautiful."

"You've been here before?"

"Just for weddings my mum and I did."

Evan looked chagrined, and the doubt in his eyes mirrored Gunnar's expression when asked to help with the vases.

It was you.

"We could go somewhere else that doesn't remind you of work," Evan said.

"That would eliminate every fine establishment in the West of Scotland. Besides, it's Valentine's Day—we'd never find a table." Ben threw an admiring gaze over Evan's dark-blue suit, which was smarter than the one he'd worn to Fergus and John's wedding. "Not anywhere we wouldn't look out of place."

They entered the lush lobby and crossed the red-and-green-plaid carpet beneath the bright brass chandelier.

"This venue has an in-house wedding coordinator," Ben told Evan as they approached the grand central staircase flanked by enormous white-and-pink-rose displays. "So when Mum and I've done weddings here, it's mostly emotional rather than logistical —" Ben stopped in front of the sign at the foot of the staircase. "Oh my God, the Gallagher-Black wedding. That's one of ours."

"Were you meant to work tonight?"

"No, my mum and I—" Ben shrugged, trying to shake the urge to hide. "Forget it. I'd hate to ruin your appetite by moaning about my family issues."

"I played football in a snowstorm today. Literally nothing could ruin my appetite." Evan took Ben's shoulders and turned him toward the adjacent dining room. "Besides, there's a fireside table with a bottle of Shiraz awaiting us."

Evan smelled amazing, and Ben wanted to step closer and press his nose against his neck. "I'm starving too."

They entered the hotel's restaurant and settled into plush chairs at a table by the roaring fire. As Ben explained the rift with his mother and his decision to stop handling same-sex weddings, Evan sipped his wine and listened sympathetically.

When Ben was finished, Evan asked, "If your mum accepts you for who you are, why is she so opposed to marriage equality?"

Ben's first instinct was to demur, as he didn't usually discuss religion with someone he'd just met. But something about this man made him want to open up.

"Because she's Bahá'í," Ben said. "We both are. Or at least I was. No, I still am. I don't know." He finally took a sip of wine, partly to be polite and partly…to rebel? He wasn't sure.

"Bahá'í—is that a sect of Islam?"

"No more than Christianity is a sect of Judaism. It was started in Persia by people who were originally Muslim. The Bahá'í Faith is less than two hundred years old, so our beliefs are pretty modern."

"For instance…"

"We see men and women as inherently equal. We fight for racial equality and encourage interracial marriage. We see other religions as different expressions of the same faith rather than as threats to eradicate."

"Sounds peaceful," Evan said.

"It is," Ben said with a sigh, wishing it was that simple. "We're all about unity and harmony and respecting differences. But we don't condone sex outside marriage, or same-sex relationships at all. And by 'we,' I mean the Faith as a whole. Obviously I condone those things." *Or at least I engage in them, which makes me a hypocrite.* "Many Bahá'ís I've met are the same way."

"Like Catholics who use birth control?"

"Exactly. There's edicts, and then there's real life." Ben decided to leave it at that so as not to ruin his own dinner or scare Evan away.

"What will you do after you finish uni, if not weddings?" Evan asked. "You're studying geography, right?"

"I am." Ben was impressed Evan had remembered this fact six weeks after learning it. "Contrary to popular belief, geography's not about looking at maps or memorizing capitals. It's the study of humanity's relationship with the earth. Which is fascinating, but in reality, most geography students end up working for oil companies."

"And you don't want to work for an oil company."

"God, no. Not since my third-year lecture course on climate change."

"What about clean energy? There's loads of marine-power research going on in Orkney, for one."

"Yes, but…it's deeper than that." Ben adjusted his glasses on his nose. Evan's reaction to his next words would reveal their chances for a second date. "Knowing climate change is going to turn the world into an absolute hellhole—it's beyond depressing. But helping people get married? *That* lets me believe in the future, just for one day."

Evan's eyes softened. "I get it. Everyone should have work that means something to them." He brushed his fingertips over the back of Ben's hand. "And you deserve to be happy."

Ben's head swam for a moment, as though he'd gulped his entire glass of wine instead of taking a single sip. "You don't think I'm selfish?"

"I don't know you very well yet, but I doubt there's a selfish bone in your body."

"Ha." Ben's face warmed, and not just on the side nearest the fireplace. He reached for his wine glass. "Or maybe I just like working in the world's most kilt-intensive industry."

Their starters arrived then, interrupting their flirtation.

"Sorry our reservation is unfashionably early," Evan said as they tucked in. "We've got tickets for something at half past eight."

"What sort of something?"

"It's a surprise."

Ben waved his tiny fork. "Yas, I love surprises!"

"I sensed you were the adventurous sort."

"I am, I am." He ate a mussel, closing his eyes with bliss at the perfect aioli sauce. "What about you?"

Evan paused as he placed a bit of gravlax onto his ciabatta wedge. "I've had a few *mis*adventures, which tend to make one crave a humdrum life."

Ben paused with his napkin halfway to his mouth. Evan's tone had turned grave, matching his expression but providing an odd counterpoint to his rippling, upbeat Orkney accent.

Then Evan's lips twitched up at one corner. "But not for long."

Their eyes met, and Ben returned Evan's smile. He wanted this lad badly, for more than his delicious physique and heart-stopping face. He wanted to unravel the mystery inside Evan's mind, discern whether he was man or monster or both. To do that, he had to play it cool.

But Ben's own curiosity was a force even he couldn't resist. "Tell me about Fergus."

"*THE HARDEST PART OF THIS JOB,*" Evan's father had once told him, "*is not the secrecy, the sacrifice, or even the risk to life and limb. It's letting people believe you're boring.*"

But Dad was wrong. The hardest part was seeing hatred and mistrust in the eyes of people who mattered. To Evan, telling himself he'd done the right thing by leaving Fergus was like taking aspirin for an amputated arm.

He sat back in his chair. "What do you want to know?" Obviously he couldn't tell Ben everything, but he needed to seem forthcoming. It wasn't honesty which set people at ease, but rather the *appearance* of honesty. It let people tell themselves the story they wanted to believe.

Ben clearly wanted to believe Evan was a good man.

"Why did you leave Fergus?" he asked. "Were you in love with this Belgian fellow?"

Evan mentally replaced *this Belgian fellow* with MI5 so he could be as truthful as possible. "I struggled with the decision for weeks. In the end, deep down, I saw no other option. Following my heart meant betraying the man I—the man I'd loved for years. Which is no excuse, of course, for the pain I caused."

Ben examined him for a moment, then helped himself to another steamed mussel. "Had you outgrown Fergus?"

"We'd grown away from each other. Once I graduated and Fergus continued for his Master's, we had less in common. I wasn't happy in my first architectural job, and it spilled over into our relationship."

"This job you hated, are you still in it?"

Evan kept his expression neutral, wondering whether Ben had recognized him as Gunnar last weekend. They'd stood so close together as they'd rescued Trent. On the other hand, it had been dark in that alleyway.

"No, I found another position in civil service. Working for the government sounds tedious, but I love my job." This was true. "My colleagues are good folk, and the projects are challenging." This was also true. "Fergus, though, he saw it as a step down." *Not that he ever asked me about my job, which made it tragically easy to become a spy.*

"He didn't respect your work."

"Why should he? He's an artistic genius. I'm a toddler stacking blocks."

Ben tilted his head. "Is that a direct quote? Did Fergus call you that?"

Evan looked away, scanning and cataloging details of the restaurant even as he wrestled with how to present his past to Ben. "I won't run Fergus down. I've betrayed him enough as it is."

This was the truest statement of all. Merely joining MI5 had been a disloyalty; Fergus hated the agency for its support role during the Troubles in Northern Ireland. In a cruel twist, MI5 had assigned Evan to T Branch, the section now fully in charge of Northern Irish–terrorism intelligence.

"Enough talk of heartbreaks." Ben cast a sly glance over the restaurant. "Let's guess which of these couples followed the 'Fuck First' rule."

Evan nearly choked on his wine. "Sorry?"

"The relationship guru Dan Savage, he says that on romantically pressurized holidays—Valentine's, anniversaries—couples should have sex before going to dinner. Otherwise they'll be so full of food and drink they won't be up for it later. Then everyone feels a failure, maybe even thinking their lack of rumpy-pumpy on an artificial holiday means they shouldn't be together."

Still coughing, Evan wiped his eyes with his cloth napkin. "Brilliant advice. As for who's taken it, definitely the blue dress and black suit at your nine o'clock."

Ben squinted at the sixty-something couple sitting ten feet away. "Why do you say that?"

"They keep touching each other—hands stroking, feet brushing beneath the table."

"Maybe they're horny."

"Horniness is all about tension. Those two are basking." Evan extracted another mussel from its shell. "Postures relaxed, eyes soft. They look like they could be on holiday. Don't stare at them, by the way."

Ben jerked his head back. "Maybe they're simply drunk."

"They're still on their first glass of wine."

"They could've been drinking at the bar whilst waiting for their table."

"No." Evan kept his voice low. "When they sat down, she still had snow in her hair."

Ben stared at him. "When did you notice all this?"

"Not sure, I just…remember what I see." Evan adjusted the maroon cloth napkin in his lap. *Try and act human*, he told himself. *The Sherlock Holmes routine is making him suspicious, not swoony.*

"Have you heard anything I said tonight?" Ben asked.

"Every word."

"Then what's my mum's name?"

Evan nearly blurted out the answer before remembering he'd learned it from his father. "I don't think you told me."

"Oh." Ben bit his lip. "I can never keep track of the things I say. I open my mouth and words just pop out, whether I want them to or not."

"It's the Glaswegian in you. Where I'm from, people can be maddeningly reserved." From the corner of his eye, he saw their server approaching with the main course. He picked up the bottle of Shiraz to keep her from filling his glass. "More wine?"

"Nah, thanks." Ben covered his own glass, which was still half full.

Giving himself a small, unwanted refill, Evan wondered whether Ben abstained from alcohol, like most Bahá'ís. He'd considered not ordering wine—he'd had enough booze in Belfast to last a lifetime—but thought it might seem odd. Evan needed to play the role of a man who knew nothing about Ben, and play it so well that he believed it himself.

It was exhausting, this pretending not to be a pretender. No wonder he'd not dated or even hooked up with anyone since returning to Glasgow seven months ago. It was easier just to be alone.

As the server laid out their course, Evan reviewed his surroundings, noting who had departed and who had arrived. He hated not having his back to the wall, but at least the dark window beyond his dinner companion would reflect any movement behind him.

Ben made a rapturous noise. "This tortellini is astounding. You must try a bit before you fry your taste buds with the chili glaze on that duck." He speared a tortellini, then made a circle in the air with the end of his fork. "Best close your eyes for full sensory awesomeness."

Evan parted his lips, but his eyes wouldn't shut. The thought of descending into darkness amidst all these people...

"Too late." Ben popped the tortellini into his own mouth, then released another orgasmic sound.

"Tease."

"You wouldn't close your eyes."

"Okay, okay." Evan took a calming breath, then squeezed his eyes shut. Immediately his pulse accelerated. "Hurry, my duck's getting co—" The pasta cut him off with its sweet creaminess. He emitted his own moan of pleasure, keeping his eyes closed to savor the taste.

When he opened them again, Ben was smiling. And just like that, Evan knew he would go on pretending, no matter how it drained him. He would go on layering lies upon truths upon lies, in the desperate wish that someday he could be real with this man.

He only hoped that if that day came, Ben wouldn't hate him for what he was.

Chapter 7

EVAN WAS DEFINITELY A COP. Ben could see it in the way he assessed his surroundings, the way he took control of a room the moment he walked in, the way he noticed and remembered small things like the snow on the hair of the woman who'd already had sex today.

It made Ben feel safe and excited at the same time.

After dinner they took a cab to the date's second surprise. When the taxi pulled over, Ben couldn't suppress a squeal. "Electric Gardens!" He shoved open the door and stepped out into the falling snow.

Glasgow's enormous Botanic Gardens lay lit up before them, the golden Kibble Palace greenhouse looming like an alien spacecraft.

They joined a group of about a dozen people, all booked into the final time slot of the final night. "Did you pull strings to get us in?" Ben asked Evan.

"Not unless buying tickets online counts as pulling strings."

Right. And there just happened to be a fireside table available on Valentine's Day.

As the group began to move off, Evan gave Ben's hand a subtle glance that asked whether he should take it.

By reflex, Ben shifted away. To cover his timidity, he pulled his gloves and slouchy beanie hat from his pockets and put them on.

Evan also slipped on his gloves, a sleek black leather pair that hugged his knuckles. "Mind if I…?" He loosened the knot of his red tie, the vivid blue stripes of which matched his eyes.

"Good idea." Ben tried to undo his own tie, but the thick gloves made his fingers clumsy.

"Let me." Evan stepped close. "All right?"

"Aye." Ben willed his hands to stay at his sides as Evan slipped the knot free with a deft touch. It took all his control not to drag this man off the garden path and behind the nearest sparkly hedgerow.

"There." Evan undid the top button of Ben's shirt, then stepped back. "Now we can breathe a peedie bit."

Speak for yourself, Ben thought, his head spinning. He smiled at Evan's first use of the Orkney word *peedie* to mean *wee.* Maybe it was a sign he felt relaxed enough with Ben to be himself—whatever that meant.

As they wandered with their group through a musical tunnel of light, Ben reviewed what Evan had shared over dinner about his life. He'd seemed to weigh every word as it left his mouth, as though his tongue was a delicately calibrated scale.

Born in London, Evan had been two years old when his parents divorced and his mother took him and his older sister back to her native Orkney Islands in the far north of Scotland. There she married a local farmer and had two more sons. Evan also had a cat, which Ben knew about, having been with "Gunnar" when said cat was found.

But these were surface trivia. Even the story of the breakup with Fergus sounded like a carefully curated biography. If Ben was an open book, then Evan was one of those top-shelf library treasures, accessible only with a rickety ladder and written permission from an archivist. The sort of book which people got murdered over in Dan Brown novels.

As they exited the tunnel of light, Ben heard a new song with a rapid, pounding beat. "The fire dancing!"

They followed the thumping music along the snow-wet path until they came upon a woman in a tight red top, gold mask, and black-and-white-striped leggings. She raised her arms to display two long chains ending in flaming spheres. The scent of kerosene made Ben's nose crinkle.

But he forgot the smell, forgot everything, the moment she began to dance. The burning spheres became an orange blur as she spun them, first close beside her like a pair of lassoes, then diagonally, gyrating her hips, then finally linking the chains in front of her to create a fiery pinwheel.

Ben gasped as the flames nearly grazed her face. "Hope she's not wearing hairspray," he murmured.

Suddenly one of the balls leapt up, seeming to hurtle straight toward him.

"Whoa!" Ben stepped back, using Evan's body as a shield. Then he felt stupid as the dancer caught the ball by the chain's handle and continued her performance.

At least I made Evan feel all manly. Cops probably like that sort of thing.

Sure enough, Evan angled a protective shoulder in front of him. On impulse, Ben took his hand. Through their gloves he could feel the warmth and strength of Evan's fingers. His heart beat faster.

Then the dancer began to switch hands with each swing, passing the chains back and forth in front of her, then behind her, then—*Whaaaaat?*—through her legs, stepping over the spheres as smoothly as if they were puddles of water and not, well, great balls of fire.

Ben looked over to see Evan's reaction, and the sight nearly took the strength from his knees. Before him, at long last, stood the man behind the mask.

Evan's eyes filled with wonder as they followed the fireballs' path, his lips curving into faint smiles, then wider and wider *O*s.

For once he seemed purely in the moment, neither calculating nor analyzing.

He looked more beautiful than ever, and Ben wanted to see that face above him, beneath him, at close, close range, its guard down in the grip of ecstasy.

The acrobat finished with a flourish, then bowed to the crowd. Ben let go of Evan's hand so they could applaud.

"That was amazing," Evan said, eyes still gleaming with delight.

Ben forced himself to look away, unable to stop picturing Evan naked and sweaty on a heap of twisted sheets.

Their group continued on, over pathways that seemed to undulate with shifting patterns of light. As the falling snow reflected and refracted every glow, turning the Botanic Gardens into Glasgow's very own faerie world, Ben wished it would never end.

Alas, closing time soon arrived, whereupon the Gardens' staff not-so-subtly encouraged visitors to toddle off.

"Where to now?" Ben asked Evan as they battled the stiff wind on their way to the main entrance/exit.

"I'm out of surprises. Two per day is my limit."

I doubt that.

"Pub?" Evan asked.

"Mmm, nah." Ben stopped to fix his scarf, which was flapping in the wind. "Technically my religion forbids me to drink alcohol." *And date men,* he added mentally before he could block the thought.

"Oh." Evan rapped his knuckles against his head. "I'm so sorry. I ordered wine at dinner and didn't even ask—"

"How would you know? Anyway, I'm not strict. Wedding planners have to taste food and drink so we can recommend them to clients." He tossed the end of his scarf over his shoulder, but it promptly blew back again. "Sometimes I drink a wee bit socially, so people don't feel like I'm judging them."

"I promise not to feel judged if you never drink with me again.

Here, let me get that." Evan reached out and pulled the end of Ben's scarf around his neck, then tucked it into the front of his coat. "How far is your place?"

Ben shivered at this near-proposition combined with this near-touch. "May I be frank?"

"Of course."

"I like you too much to fuck you." Ben paused long enough to see Evan's surprise and confusion. "Tonight, at least."

"That's a relief." Evan stepped back. "Now I can stop seducing you."

"Oh, had you started?"

"I don't know." Evan released a crooked smile. "You tell me."

Ben's mouth opened, releasing a series of stammered syllables. It felt like Evan was seeing straight inside him, reading every deliciously filthy thought. Standing there in the snow with his black leather jacket and windblown hair, Evan couldn't have looked more enticing if he'd been doing naked bench presses in a tub of whipped cream.

"Hmph." Ben turned away and marched over to the grass, where he started scooping up fresh snow.

Evan came over to stand behind him. "What are you doing?"

"You think you're so hot," Ben muttered as he formed the snow into a loose ball. "This'll cool you down." He spun around, grabbed Evan's open shirt collar, and shoved the snowball inside.

"Aaaugh!" Evan sprang away, releasing a half laugh, half shriek. "I can't believe you—och!" He clawed at his chest, which now bore a wet stain.

"I thought Orcadians were meant to be rugged."

"Orkney's climate is"—Evan yanked his shirttail out of his trousers—"actually quite mild." He cursed as the wet mark spread to his belly. "Gulf Stream and all."

"What about your Viking blood?"

"It doesn't stop frostbite!" Evan shook out the front of his shirt, letting the snow drop to his feet.

"Sorry," Ben said in a not-sorry tone. "Buy you a coffee as penance?"

"This date is my treat. I'll buy the coffees." Evan put a hand to his coat pocket. "Hold on. Where's my phone?" He patted his other pockets, eyes widening with horror. "It must have fallen when I took out my gloves."

"That was near here on our way in, almost an hour ago." Ben looked round with dismay. "Could be covered in snow by now."

"We were next to that green bench when I—wait, is that…" Evan dashed forward and knelt beside the bench.

Ben followed. "Did you find it?"

"Fucking hell. Knew I should've bought a waterproof case." He handed the phone to Ben. "Can you fix it?"

Ben examined the screen, which was completely black. "Maybe the battery's—aaaaeeeeeee!" He leapt to his feet as a chunk of snow slithered down his back. "Oh my God. Get it out. Get it out!"

"Relax. It'll melt." Evan snatched his phone from Ben's hand. "Eventually."

Ben danced around, flailing his arms at his own back. "You treacherous bastard!"

"I see Robert's told you my Warriors nickname."

Ben scooped a handful of snow off the bench and chucked it at Evan without forming a ball. Naturally the wind blew it back in his face. "Oh, get to fuck, snow!"

Through his water-bleary glasses, Ben saw Evan crouching down, no doubt preparing the final death blow. He rushed to stop him, but slipped and toppled forward, landing on Evan in a graceless but effective tackle.

They tumbled together in a cackling heap, and when they rolled to get up, found their legs were tangled. Their struggle stopped.

Evan's face was so close, it would have been easier at that moment to kiss him than not kiss him.

"Get a room, lads!" shouted a lass passing by. Her companions added a wolf whistle and a catcall.

Still giggling, Evan and Ben stood and brushed the snow off each other's coats. As they proceeded toward the gate, Ben said, "I never imagined Evan Hollister could be such fun."

Evan laughed again. "Me neither."

"So TELL me more about your job," Ben said as he snuggled into the corner of a big puffy couch at the back of the coffee shop.

Evan sat down beside him, trying not to spill his brimming caramel mocha all over his shirt, which was still damp from their snowball skirmish. "It's not as fun as wedding planning."

"But it can't be boring if you love it like you say." Ben curled a leg up between them. "Give me a day in the life of Her Majesty's risk-management architect Evan Hollister."

Evan was prepared for this question, having devised plausible civilian parallels for his MI5 duties. "First thing: coffee." He took a sip of his mocha. "While the caffeine kicks in, I read reports, then prioritize the ones needing immediate attention."

"For instance?"

"Let's say there's a building which might be architecturally unsound. Obviously resources are limited, so I need to judge how dire it is. In extreme situations, lives may be at risk. So I confer with my colleagues, then bring urgent cases to the attention of my superiors. Are you still awake?"

"Mm-hm. Do you ever travel to find out for certain?"

"Sometimes. Data is useful, but there's no substitute for seeing it firsthand."

"So you're like a health inspector for buildings?"

"Pretty much," Evan said.

"And which agency do you—"

"Sorry, but I've been wanting to ask all night: Is that a Teletubbies tie?"

Ben brightened. "Yes! My dad gave me this." He lifted one end of his undone necktie. "See, there's three guys dressed as Tinky-Winky—the one that televangelist said was gay—and they've got a sack of Mardi Gras beads."

Evan leaned in to examine the cartoons on the white silk background. "Wow, that's…"

"Random, right? I've no idea where my dad found it, but it's a good conversation piece, if nothing else."

Exactly why I mentioned it when I needed a diversion. "Your dad, does he work with your mum's business?"

Ben laughed. "No, he's in the army, stationed"—he flicked his hand—"somewhere in the world. He's pretty high-ranking, so I guess his location would be a clue as to where the military thinks there might be trouble. Can't have civilians knowing that."

Evan wished his own father hadn't told him Colonel Reid was stationed in Afghanistan. It felt unfair to know more than Ben knew. "Does it bother you? The secrecy?"

Ben looked down at his tie, tracing the Tinky-Winkys. "Obviously I'd prefer to know where my father is, but not if it puts him or his troops in danger. I know what he's doing is important, that he may literally be saving our lives right this moment."

"Do you worry about him?"

Ben picked up his giant cup of hot cocoa. "Would it help?"

"I guess not." Evan was pleasantly surprised by Ben's pragmatism. Or maybe he was just pretending not to worry, the same way Evan had minimized his concern for Ben's welfare to Kay so he could stay on Operation Caps Lock. After spending a few hours with this man, Evan wanted more than ever to return to the operation, to protect Ben from people like Jordan Lithgow.

"I didn't see much of my father growing up," Evan said, "what with living in Orkney and him in London. But he always came for my birthday and my sister's, and we'd go south to him on alternate Christmases."

"Must've been a culture shock."

"Aye, all those fancy shops and restaurants, and in London

they get a whopping eight hours of daylight in December." He felt his smile fade. "Visits were always short, because his job was demanding. Like your dad's, just not overseas."

The café door opened. Evan turned to see a pair of teenage girls, who'd been outside for a good while, judging by their reddened noses and staticky hair. Then he did a quick visual review of the rest of the place, taking note of the fire exit in the back—something he should have done when they'd first arrived.

"Why do you do that?"

Evan looked at Ben. "Hm?"

"Scan your surroundings wherever we go. Is someone following you? Or are you a bandit looking for a place to rob?"

Evan shrugged and kept his face impassive. "I like to be aware. I guess it's a footballing instinct. I play midfield, where mindfulness is key. You've got to anticipate where the ball's going, what all the players are thinking."

"Like ESP?" Ben asked, then licked the chocolate whipped cream atop his cocoa.

"Kinda," Evan said, his gaze glued to the furrow Ben's tongue had carved into the cream.

"Then tell me what I'm thinking."

"I don't need to read your mind to ken what you're thinking." Evan picked up his spoon. "If I wait a few moments, you'll tell me."

"Oi, you!" Ben made as if to kick him.

"Careful." Evan shielded his cup. "First you freeze me and now you're trying to scald me."

"Maybe I just want to see you in a wet top." Ben grinned and waggled his foot atop his knee.

Evan felt himself blush. "Your turn. Tell me about a day in the life of Ben Reid."

Ben groaned. "I'm sooooo behind schedule on my honors dissertation."

"What's the topic?" Evan asked, since he didn't know.

Ben sat up straight and cleared his throat. "'From First Kiss to

Wedded Bliss? The Marriage of Geographical Information Systems and Social Media.' Basically it's a history of how social networks have become more locational. Originally I thought this trend was a good thing, but now I'm not sure. Hence the question mark in the title."

"What's the downside?"

"For people who want to mine that information—companies and investigators and all—there's just too much of it now, and it's not reliable."

Evan agreed. Mass surveillance was popular amongst some politicians, but it was no friend to the average citizen *or* the average counterterrorism officer. Every day at work, sifting through surveillance data felt like searching for a needle in a needle-stack—and that was just the classified stuff. The open-source intelligence Ben referred to was more like the Needle Himalayas.

"Of course, for users," Ben continued, "there's a massive loss of privacy. People give away so much information, either forgetting or not caring that it can be used against them. Like, remember the photo site Imageo?"

"Aye, it used to be huge."

"And now it's dead, because thousands of users had their identities stolen. Imageo got bought by a bigger company who promised to make it safer, but they couldn't figure out how to do that without ruining what was great about it. That's my dissertation's big question: How do we balance openness and security?" Ben gave a long sigh. "It's also the big question of our whole society, which makes it *so* hard to answer in a wee undergraduate research paper." He mimed stabbing himself in the heart with his spoon. "But it's far less boring than other topics I was offered, like 'Spatial organization of households' or 'Biosecurity and the badger cull controversy.'" He stopped and looked at Evan. "Oh my God, talking of boring, look at me blethering on."

Evan could listen to Ben all night. "I wish I could help, but I barely use social media at all." MI5 had let him keep his Facebook profile because it would look more suspicious to delete it, but they also discouraged overly personal posts. Evan's presence in the world was like that of a camouflaged animal, obscured but not invisible.

"I noticed," Ben said with a glare. "At least with Twitter and Facebook, location can be hidden. But some apps are useless without it. Like Grindr: What's the point of finding guys to hook up with unless they're nearby? Talking of Grindr, Robert and I didn't—I mean, not that it's anyone's business, but we didn't do anything. He wanted Liam to be his first." Ben's smile became a grimace. "Och, I probably shouldn't have spilled that detail."

"It's kind of romantic."

"Right?" Ben took a small sip of cocoa, then pulled it away. "Ow, still too hot." He stirred it carefully. "Perhaps I went over the top ordering cocoa with chocolate whipped cream and chocolate flakes."

"It looks amazing."

"Want to try?" Ben held out his mug. "I won't even make you close your eyes."

Evan leaned forward, keeping his gaze locked with Ben's as he slid his tongue up the side of the whipped-cream dollop. Ben's pupils dilated, and he swallowed hard, his Adam's apple rising and falling. With a languid blink, Evan licked a slow, deliberate circle around the tip of the dollop, then descended the other side until he tasted hot cocoa. He lapped a few drops into his waiting mouth, then sat back on the couch and swallowed. "Tasty."

Ben cleared his throat and looked around. "Your tongue should not be allowed in public."

"That'd be a shame. We never know when we might need it."

Ben bit his lip and glanced away. Then his knees clapped together three times as though applauding. It was the cutest thing Evan had ever seen.

"I HAD A BRILLIANT EVENING," Ben said as they shared a taxi down Great Western Road. "Next time I'll plan it, and it can be my shout."

"No, I'll pay. You're still a student."

"Don't worry, I've something dead cheap in mind." He grinned at Evan to cover the twisty feeling inside him. It would be murder saying goodnight to this man.

In a few minutes they were pulling up in front of Ben's student housing block. Evan turned to the driver and said, "Wait here, mate. I'll be right back."

"Ooh, walking me to my door," Ben said as they got out of the cab. "How gallant."

"You never ken what sort of ruffians are about at this hour." Evan put his hands in his coat pockets, looking almost nervous. "I had a brilliant evening too, by the way. In case I've not said it."

"Good." Ben mounted the bottom step in front of his building. "This is where you kiss me goodnight."

"Is it?" Evan moved closer, and thanks to the stairs their heights nearly matched. "You're a bossy one, aren't you?"

Ben's pulse began to pound, providing his head with a delightful buzz. "I can be. But I liked having someone else see to everything tonight. It's good to be looked after."

Evan took Ben's face in his bare hands. "I'd be honored to look after you." Then he kissed him.

For the first moment, all Ben could think about was how Evan's eyes hadn't left his since the word *kiss* had been uttered. Which meant he hadn't checked to see whether any "ruffians" were watching.

In the second moment, when Evan's lips coaxed his apart, Ben stopped thinking. His tongue trembled, along with his knees, and he felt himself tilt forward, succumbing to the pull of a tenfold gravity. For an instant he worried they'd topple over in an embarrassing heap.

But Evan held him up, as strong and solid as the concrete they stood upon. Ben reached inside Evan's open coat to place a palm against his chest, where he felt a racing heart whose speed matched his own.

This was *not* a goodnight kiss. This was a let-me-stay-and-show-you-what-else-this-mouth-can-do kiss.

When Evan let him go at last, Ben almost stumbled back. He pulled his coat tighter around himself. "Right." His eyes felt glazed and his cheeks, flushed. "I'll just..." He fumbled for his keys. "Go."

Evan's disarming smile reappeared. "Phone me when you decide what we're doing Saturday night."

"But I want to surprise you."

"No." Evan caught the door as Ben opened it. "I hate surprises."

Ben started to laugh until he saw Evan's frozen expression, so like the one he'd worn when he'd been told to close his eyes for a bite of pumpkin tortellini.

"All right," Ben hurried to say. "I'll send you the itinerary. But a warning"—he moved in to murmur in Evan's ear, letting his lips and breath caress his skin—"it'll make waiting that much harder."

Chapter 8

EVAN WAS STILL THINKING about The Kiss when he arrived at the office Monday morning, this time via the subway from Buchanan Street to Kinning Park. It was his least favorite route, culminating in a sometimes dodgy thirteen-minute trudge through Southside Glasgow, but nothing could dim his mood today.

He couldn't remember the last time a kiss was just a kiss and not a preamble to something "more," a kiss that wouldn't get lost in the fog of subsequent fumbling and fucking. This kiss had been a single pure act Evan could hang on the wall of his memory like a favorite painting in a gilded frame. For the rest of the week he could pull out the memory of this kiss—admire it, relive it—whenever he needed to feel real.

As he booted up his computer to read the daily threat assessment, Evan hummed a bouncy tune that had been stuck in his head since Saturday night in the coffee shop with Ben.

"Awfully cheery for a yin whose career is hanging by a thread."

Evan looked up to see Detective Sergeant Deirdre Fowles, dressed in plainclothes and bearing a visitors pass on a lanyard round her neck.

He answered her banter with a smile. "I thought our Caps Lock meeting wasn't until eight."

"Our bosses are having a 'pre-meeting' to discuss SCD's internal review of the last wedding."

"Have you read it? Am I still on the operation?"

She looked round, then pulled up a chair close to Evan's. "I've not read all of it, but I wrote one part, about some new intelligence you'll like."

"Yes!" Evan pumped both fists.

"What's got you over the moon this morning? Hot date?"

"Actually..."

Deirdre's jaw dropped. "I was joking, but that's brilliant. Gaun yersel, lad!" She gave his shoulder a hearty punch.

Evan couldn't help beaming as he briefly outlined his date with Ben. It felt odd to tell a story in such a casual way, completely unlike debriefing a superior or confessing to a therapist. It meant Evan had a life again.

As Deirdre recounted her own Valentine's Day escapades, they were interrupted by intelligence analyst Lewis Sawyer, along with Ned Carmichael, king of all things technical.

"Oi, lad and lass." Lewis waved to get their attention. "It's meetin' time."

Ned pointed at Evan. "Kay specifically requested your presence."

"And you know what that means." Lewis gave a toothy grin. "You've been exonerated, ya wild rogue, you."

When Evan entered the meeting room, Detective Inspector Hayward was sitting beside Kay, who as always was positioned at the head of the table. To Evan's surprise, DI Hayward met his eye and gave him a nod of respect, which Evan promptly returned. It was best for the operation if the two of them left their quarrel in the past, pronto.

He hoped that his eight-day hiatus from Operation Caps Lock hadn't jeopardized his link with Jordan. As instructed, Evan had sent a message to him early last week saying Gunnar was going out of town for an undefined length of time.

Kay opened the meeting, then handed things off to Hayward, who asked DS Fowles to present the latest in police intelligence.

Deirdre had them turn to page three of the report she'd distributed. "After the wedding, the key question was why Jordan Lithgow—Code Name: Backspace—failed to show up for his allegedly planned attack. It was suggested that he'd been unwittingly tipped off by the behavior of our undercover MI5 officer."

Evan scanned ahead in the report for evidence it wasn't his fault.

Deirdre continued. "Backspace was clever enough to use a burner phone for his BVP communications. Sadly for him, he wasn't clever enough to destroy that phone before chucking it in a rubbish bin near his flat. Our surveillance officers retrieved it that night."

Evan suppressed a smirk as he read the transcript of a text-message spat between Jordan and a BVP leader, dated a few hours before the wedding.

[Unidentified person, thought to be BVP chairman David Wallace]: Don't even fucking think about this thing you want to do tonight.

[Backspace]: WHY NOT???

[Unidentified]: Not part of our mission. Trying to reach mainstream folk, mind?

[Backspace]: Fuck mainstream. I'm not alone. Met a comrade.

Evan assumed Jordan was referring to him.

[Unidentified]: Don't care. You do this and we disavow you in a heartbeat. Focus on the big picture and the real enemy, mate.

Based on the time stamps, Jordan's reply took several minutes:
ok

"BVP's ultimate goal," Deidre said, "is to attract new members and gain a louder voice within society. The 'real enemies' referred to here are immigrants, especially Muslim ones."

"Evan, your reaction?" Kay asked.

"I'm a bit surprised that Backspace is bowing to this guy's

wishes," Evan said. "With me, he acts like he's one of BVP's leaders, but this clearly shows he's second tier."

"Based on your knowledge of his personality," Hayward asked, "do you think he'll listen, or do you think he'll go rogue, especially if he thinks you've got his back?"

Evan considered it. "He seems to identify with this organization, so I think for now he'll obey orders. But Jordan craves approval and camaraderie. If he gets that from me, he might not care so much what the BVP leader says." He blanched as he followed the trail of logic. "Then he'd be more likely to attack a same-sex wedding."

"Let's consider a change in strategy," Kay said. "Evan, we'll need you to cement Backspace's ties to BVP. They're holding an anti-immigration rally in Glasgow on the twenty-eighth. Cozy up to David Wallace, show Backspace he can't use you to defy his leader." His supervisor tapped the chewed-up cap of her pen against the report. "As a bonus, you can get us a list of other Orange Order members attending—technically they are MI5's whole connection to this operation."

Evan nodded. The investigation had to cover some form of sectarian conflict or risk veering out of MI5's purview. He couldn't understand why the agency still distinguished between right-wing "domestic extremism" and outright terrorism. A neo-Nazi's victim would be just as dead as one killed by the IRA or al-Qaeda.

When the meeting wrapped up, Kay dismissed the rest of the team and asked Evan to stay. Lewis gave him a surreptitious thumbs-up as he sauntered out.

When they were alone—as alone as anyone ever was at MI5—Kay turned to Evan. "I'm pleased the joint review supports my response at the post-op debriefing." She cocked her head. "You remember that debriefing—the one featuring a boxful of stray cat. How's he doing, by the way?"

"She's well, thanks. Getting spayed today. So what's this private meeting about? I thought I wasn't in trouble."

"You're not. But the wedding did raise another issue." She folded her hands atop a three-inch stack of reports. "When you returned to Glasgow after Belfast, we hoped you'd continue your exemplary personal distance from your outside acquaintances."

Exemplary personal distance, i.e., lying to everyone he cared about.

Kay continued. "But this man you're involved with, his profession makes him a potential victim, which makes you incapable of being impartial."

Evan looked away and scratched his neck, his collar suddenly itchy. He wanted to say Ben didn't matter to him. He wanted it to be true. But even if he could convince himself, Kay would never believe it.

Instead he said, "My interest in Mr. Reid didn't affect my decision not to use him as terrorist bait. I would've done the same if he'd been a perfect stranger." He remembered what he'd learned on their date. "If it helps, Ben quit doing weddings. He's got just one more, on the twenty-eighth."

"That does help, actually." Kay made a note on her jotter.

Evan weighed whether to push his luck on Caps Lock. He wanted to surveil Ben's final wedding, but knew if he mentioned it now he risked looking biased. On the other hand, surveillance ops required lots of planning, and with the wedding less than two weeks away...

"Could you also request a police presence at that event? In case—" Evan swallowed. "In case something happens."

"There's been no specific threat like there was on the seventh. Police Scotland can't afford armed officers at every same-sex wedding."

"There aren't many—a few per week at most, now the big rush is over. Most are small ceremonies or simple conversions of civil partnerships to marriages. Not exactly easy or tempting targets for terrorists."

Kay set down her pen in that way she had: deliberately, with both hands, as though its ink was combustible. "Evan, your three years in T Branch are nearly over, and the other branches have no open positions at the Glasgow office."

He hadn't wanted to think about moving, but the looming possibility had haunted him for months. "Is that a change of subject, or…"

"Not really." She sighed. "I do wonder whether you'll be better off at Thames House with a clean slate."

Evan cursed himself. By appearing desperate to protect Ben, he may have just signed his own relocation to London. "I don't need a clean slate."

"You might find work easier in a place with no attachments."

"My dad works at Thames House. He's an attachment."

"I meant attachments outside the Service." Her eyes crinkled. "It can't be easy being the son of an MI5 legend. I can understand why you'd want to carve out your own niche here in Glasgow, but you'll never reach your potential in this remote outpost."

"Compared to Orkney, Glasgow feels like the center of the universe. And I love how having a small staff means we all do a bit of everything." On any given day, Evan could find himself making copies and coffee, then installing surveillance equipment, then meeting undercover with a ruthless killer before returning to Clyde House to answer the anti-terrorism hotline. "In London I'd be forced to specialize in one narrow subject."

"That's how you become an indispensable expert."

"That's how I die of boredom." He slid forward to the edge of his chair. "Back on the farm, everyone in my family has to know how to do every task. Being an indispensable expert means when you're gone, your work doesn't get done. Seems a dodgy way to operate." At her level look, he shifted in his seat. "In my entirely unseasoned opinion, that is."

Kay sighed again. "Your versatility has served you well here. But when the Service wants you in London, that's where you'll go."

"I'll work wherever I can best serve. But if you've any influence that could keep me here a while longer…"

"Not much influence." She gave a grim smile. "But maybe enough for now."

On his way back to his desk a few minutes later, Evan gave his colleagues a confident grin to show them everything had gone well and he was still on Operation Caps Lock.

But all he could think about was being trapped inside the concrete behemoth of Thames House. He probably wouldn't go out into the field again for years, because at headquarters, MI5 would have dozens of more experienced undercover officers.

If Evan wanted to stay in this job, then sooner or later London would be his home. Which meant nearly everyone he cared about, including Ben, would be left far behind.

Chapter 9

IN BEN'S EXPERIENCE, it was hard to look truly absurd at Glasgow's Grand Ole Opry, but Evan was coming close.

Though Ben had brought the pimp-purple ten-gallon Stetson himself, he hadn't expected his companion to wear it for more than a moment. But here they were, nearly an hour into their second date, with Evan still in the hat, which looked rather fetching with his gray-and-black poncho.

"You're a better line dancer than I am," Ben panted as they left the floor, tugging the front of his T-shirt to cool himself. "Did you go on YouTube for lessons?"

"I'm a fast learner." Evan bobbled as a drunken ginger lady careered into him. He steadied her, then touched the brim of his hat. "Ma'am," he said before turning back to Ben. "Or maybe I just missed my calling."

"Don't give up your day job." As they joined the queue for the saloon, Ben seized his own segue to gather clues about Evan's profession. "Talking of jobs, as much as I love weddings, it's rather luxurious not working on a Saturday." He nudged Evan. "What about you? Standard Monday through Friday hours?"

"Pretty much."

"No night shifts? No emergency situations? What if a building

was falling? You might be needed as a consultant by the police."
He watched Evan's reaction to the *p*-word.

But Evan just shrugged. "Maybe." He looked at the Opry's
events chalkboard on the wall. "What's this shootout thing?"

"Quick-draw duels," Ben said, well aware Evan had changed
the subject. "They use cap guns, obviously, not real ones. There's
still time to sign up for tonight's shootout, if you'd like to have
a go."

Evan's eyes flashed with excitement, which he quickly blinked
away. "Nah, I'm all right."

A wistful Faith Hill ballad began then. Ben raised his chin and
smiled at the opening lyrics. "I love this song."

Evan crooked his arm in invitation. "Want to dance?"

Ben looked at the center of the room, where men and women
—and only men and women—were swaying together. "I've never
slow-danced with a man here."

"So let's change that."

He edged closer so he could whisper. "But then they'll know
we're gay."

"I'm wearing a purple cowboy hat," Evan whispered back. "I
think they already know."

Ben wiped his mouth to smother his smile. "Right, but it's one
thing to be gay and another thing to…you know."

"What, *act* gay?"

"To be gay together. As a couple." Saying it said aloud made
Ben realize his own cowardice. "Fuck it, let's do this."

As he took Evan's arm and wove through the crowd to an
empty spot, he felt like his heart was slithering down into his
large intestine. But the thought of hiding who he was out of fear
made him feel even sicker.

Ben rested his hand on Evan's shoulder and tried to obey Faith
Hill's gentle reminder to breathe.

This is fine. Everything about Evan inspired confidence: the
low, calm angle of his brows, the determined set of his square jaw,
and the relaxed posture of his broad shoulders. Between his

physique and self-assurance—born of success on the football pitch and whatever the hell he did for a living—surely no one would mess them about.

"You all right?" Evan asked. "We can stop if you're uncomfortable."

Ben realized he was tensing every muscle. He exhaled, letting his hip relax against Evan's so they could move together.

A few of the other dancers were noticing them. Most had no reaction, and two older couples even sent them warm, slightly patronizing smiles. Ben felt better, but also a bit like a fluffy animal in a zoo.

He focused on Evan again. "Well done on the Clint Eastwood circa 1964."

"Sorry?"

"The poncho. Man with No Name, right?" At Evan's blank look Ben prompted, "Sergio Leone's spaghetti-western trilogy?"

"To be honest," Evan said, "I bought this poncho from the thrift shop so I could wear regular clothes underneath. And because I thought it looked cool."

"It does. Ooh! We could watch the first film tonight if you fancy. I've got it at my mum's house. Her TV's much bigger than the one in my flat. And she'll be out all night at a wedding in Inverness. We could pop some popcorn, curl up on the couch, and…" He gave Evan's poncho a flirtatious tug. "Whatever."

"Och, state of these *Brokeback Mountain* yins," came a man's voice, far too loud and close.

Ben flinched. "Who said that?"

Evan's eyes narrowed as they focused behind him. "Doesn't matter."

"Is he talking about us?"

"Doesn't matter."

"It's bad enough what they get up to in their own bits," the man complained again, louder. "They shouldnae bring it here."

Ben's stomach felt squeezed like a sponge. He peeked over his shoulder to see a middle-aged man in a red pleather vest glaring at them. His wife looked down in embarrassment as she tried to slow-dance-steer him away.

"That's Tombstone Tim," Ben said, "the shootout champion." *This song should be over by now. Is it some sort of extended remix?*

"He won't hurt us." As he focused on Tim, Evan's gaze turned as steel-cold as his voice. "I won't give him the chance."

A shiver rippled over Ben's back. "Is it wrong that the thought of you getting violent kinda turns me on?"

Evan's eyebrows popped so high, they were lost in the shadow of his cowboy hat.

Ben kept talking, raising his voice so he couldn't hear Tombstone Tim's complaints. "I mean, I've always been more of a peace-love-and-understanding guy. It's why I hate football, with all the shoving and shouting and kicking—and that's just the fans —and why I prefer curling, because it—"

"Stay here." Evan let go of Ben and moved past him. Ben peered around Evan's shoulder to see the shootout king headed their way, his wife hanging onto his arm in a futile attempt to prevent the confrontation.

Suddenly Maisie, the Grand Ole Opry manager, stepped between Evan and the gunslinger. "Bad news, Tim!" She lowered her voice to say something Ben couldn't hear.

Tim threw up his hands. "Again?! He's a fucking coward, that Black Hills Boy." Then he stalked off the dance floor, tugging his wife behind him.

Maisie turned to Ben and Evan. "If that arsehole bothers you any more, it'll be my pleasure to hoist him by the oxters and chuck him into the street."

"Thanks, Maisie." Despite the rescue, Ben's face was still burning. "What's he raging about now?"

"His opponent skedaddled. Now he's got naebody to fight. He cannae win tonight's shootout without a willing victim." Maisie checked her watch. "Gotta clear the dance floor after this song." She turned for the stage.

"I'll do it," Evan said.

Maisie stopped. "Do what, mate?"

"Sign me up." Evan turned to Ben, whose face burned hotter under that fierce gaze. "I'll fight Tombstone Tim."

EVAN SHIFTED his borrowed weapon from hand to hand. It was made of plastic, its black muzzle featuring a bright orange tip marking it as a toy. It was nothing like the Glock he'd carried in Belfast—the one he'd last seen pointed at his own face.

He had to lose this shootout, though it would kill his pride. After Ben's probing questions about his job, Evan couldn't risk raising more suspicions by being competent with a weapon.

"It's best of three," said Ben, who stood with him at the edge of the dance floor while the Opry prepared for the shootout. "The objective is obviously to draw first, but you also need to aim for that black box between you and your opponent. It'll detect the flash of light from your revolver."

"And that's the last of the raffle winners," Maisie said from the stage. "You know what that means, cowboys and cowgirls. It's time for the shoooootouuuuuut!" The crowd whooped and hollered. Across the floor from Evan, the bellend in the red pleather vest was already high-fiving his friends.

"Pecos Paul and Sir Scallywag, to the floor, please," Maisie said. Two gunfighters stepped out, including the one who'd lent Evan his spare cap gun. They shook hands, waved to the crowd, then retreated to their respective corners to stand within a half-circle wire "cage," which Evan assumed was to protect them from flying beer bottles.

"Gunfighters, are you ready?" Maisie asked. "Fire!"

Evan jumped at the crack of the cap guns. "She doesn't give them much time."

Ben nodded. "You'll need lightning reflexes."

"Round Two," Maisie said. "Gunfightersareyoureadyfire."

Again the weapons were drawn faster than Evan could see,

proving it wouldn't be a challenge to lose this shootout. He rubbed his chest to calm his pounding heart.

"That's you up next," Ben said.

Maisie spoke into the microphone. "In the near corner, can I have Tombstone Tim?"

The man strutted backward into the open cage, waving his hat and stirring the crowd into a professional-wrestling-level frenzy. Half the spectators seemed to worship Tim, and the other half seemed to hate him.

Maisie covered the mic with one hand and asked Evan, "What's your gunfighter moniker?"

"He's the Man with No Name," Ben called back.

Maisie gave a thumbs-up. "In the far corner, let me have the Man with No Name!"

Evan imagined a spotlight shining upon him as he strolled toward his cage. His boot heels striking the hardwood floor thumped loud in his ears, even as the cacophony of whistles and shouts rose around him. He didn't look at Tim, much less offer a handshake he knew wouldn't be accepted. Evan gave the crowd a cool nod, touching the brim of his hat. *I hope I did that right.*

When he reached the cage, he adjusted his poncho to give himself access to his holster. Then he glanced over to see Ben gazing at him with a mix of fear and hope, the same expression new Warriors fans often wore, afraid to believe people like them could be as good as everyone else.

Maybe Evan would try to win. Just a peedie bit.

"Gunfighters, are you ready?" This time Maisie paused for nearly two seconds. "Fire!"

Evan whipped the gun from his holster, so fast it went flying from his hand before he could touch the trigger. The weapon clattered against the floor, spinning round and round until it finally stopped, pointing back at him.

In his panic, he'd not seen whether the black box had lit up, indicating a kill shot. But based on the way Tombstone Tim was bent over laughing, Evan presumed himself symbolically dead.

Blotting out the crowd's jeers, Evan walked through the acrid cloud of cap-gun smoke to retrieve his borrowed weapon. He picked it up and inspected it for cracks—he would've felt horrible if he'd broken someone else's toy—before stuffing it back into his holster. Then he kept his face stoic as he returned to his cage.

As Maisie announced Round Two, Tim was still laughing. As she said, "Gunfighters, are you ready?" Tim was *still* laughing.

But when she said, "Fire!" and Evan drew his gun and pulled the trigger before his opponent could move, Tombstone Tim stopped laughing.

"Yaaaaassss!" Near the stage, Ben jumped up and down, waving his snow-white Stetson. "Get in!"

Evan maintained his stoic facade, but inside, every nerve sparked with adrenaline. He wanted to win so badly he could taste it, almost as badly as he wanted to taste every inch of Ben's body.

Tombstone Tim was pacing in front of his cage and moaning to Maisie about how she'd said "Fire!" too soon. When she ignored him with a serene smile, he retreated into position, hand twitching at his side, all traces of gloating gone. His eyes gleamed with ferocity as they locked onto Evan's.

"Quiet, please." Maisie cleared her throat, waiting for the crowd to hush. Soon even the clink of bar glasses came to a halt.

"Gunfighters, are you ready?" Maisie asked. Then she paused, letting time stretch out for two…three…four seconds. "Fire."

This time it felt like slow motion—the draw, the pull of the trigger, the snap of the hammer. Tim's revolver flashed, and instinct made Evan touch his left side to check for a wound.

The crowd stayed quiet, accentuating the echo of cap-gun fire in his ears. *What just happened?*

The floor judge stepped forward and examined the black box before raising a hand toward Evan. The Opry exploded.

"That's the Man with No Name," Maisie said over the whoops and whistles. "Congrats to the mysterious stranger, winning on his first try."

Evan couldn't move his feet, he was so shocked. Tombstone Tim was already barreling through the crowd toward the bar.

"You did it!" Ben slammed into him, wrapping his arms around Evan's neck and toppling both their cowboy hats. "I'm phoning a cab this instant."

"Why? What's wrong?"

"Nothing." Ben moved his mouth to Evan's ear. "I just can't wait to get you alone."

Chapter 10

Ben was grateful his old bedroom was on the ground floor, just a few steps from the front entrance to his parents' house. He didn't want to wait the extra ten seconds it would take to climb the stairs.

"You slept in the library?" Evan asked, taking in the shelves and the fireplace as Ben dragged him inside his room.

"What can I say?" Ben pushed aside the hem of Evan's poncho and hooked his fingers through his belt loops. "I love books." He yanked Evan close and kissed him hard, slipping one hand down to stroke him through his jeans.

With a deep groan, Evan lifted him off his feet to pin him against the wall. Ben spread his legs and locked the heels of his cowboy boots around the back of Evan's thighs, taking care not to stab him with the plastic spurs.

Evan had gone on to lose the final shootout to Sir Scallywag—the kindly bloke who'd lent him his spare gun—but the loss hadn't dimmed Ben's exhilaration. Watching Evan outdraw Tombstone Tim had been the highlight of his year thus far. The icy self-assurance, the warp-speed reflexes, and finally the raw, gleeful astonishment had taught Ben more about this man than all their hours of conversation had done. Here was a man who could take control without taking himself too seriously.

Also, it was hot as fuck.

Now, up against his wall, Ben had everything he'd been dying for. Every bit of Evan was crushing him: lips, hands, hips, cock. The mad grinding through their jeans was growing painful, but he wasn't about to make it stop. Letting go of each other long enough to undress seemed ludicrous.

When Ben began to slide down the wall, Evan cupped his arse with both hands to support him. Feeling those fingers grip his cheeks, Ben imagined them fucking just like this, with Evan pounding him from below.

This mental picture, along with the insistent rhythm of Evan's cock against his own, sent Ben spiraling toward orgasm. He gripped Evan's shoulders and moaned.

Evan broke their kiss. "You okay?"

"Yes." Ben strained against him. "I'm gonna come."

Evan glanced at the bed. "Shall we—"

"No! Don't stop. I need to." He gasped for air. "Now."

"Me too."

They pressed harder together, their thrusts turning ragged and desperate.

"Wait, you first." Evan tightened his grip and took a step back from the wall. "Just ride me."

Ben gave it his all, jerking his hips faster and faster, chasing the delicious friction, climbing a jagged peak that seemed to recede the higher he got. Clutching Evan's back, he fixed his gaze on the fireplace against the opposite wall.

This'll be so awkward if it doesn't work. Also, I'm already so sore I want to scream. But he couldn't stop, couldn't stop, not for anything.

"I've got you, Ben." Evan shifted his feet to widen his stance. "Come for me. Come for me now."

"Yes!" Ben tried to say, but it came out as a strangled

"Yeghuhgh!" as his orgasm swamped him, all the more intense for its momentary elusiveness. Stars danced before his eyes, sparking against the dark fireplace. "Now you."

Evan pressed him to the wall again, burying his face in Ben's shirt collar to muffle his groans. Ben noticed with gratitude he'd shifted slightly so he could drive himself against Ben's hip rather than his now-aching cock.

Evan's body buckled as he came. Still clinging to his back, Ben could feel the shudders rippling through Evan's muscles and imagined how they would feel against his own bare skin.

Finally Evan lowered Ben to the floor. "I canna say…" he gasped out "…that was how I pictured…our first time."

"Me neither." Ben sagged against the wall, his shaky legs barely able to support his own weight. "I do so love surprises."

"I don't." Evan stepped close again, and this time his touch was pure gentle as he cupped Ben's face to kiss him. "But maybe you could teach me how."

EVAN WRAPPED A LUXURIOUSLY soft towel round his waist—a much-needed bit of comfort after that ferocious journey to orgasm—then switched on the clothes dryer holding his rinsed-out pair of briefs. He couldn't remember the last time he'd come in his pants like that, so desperate for release he'd practically injured himself.

Looking back, he was glad it had been so frenetic. If he'd not been drunk on lust and adrenaline, he might have had time to think. Time to remember. Time to panic.

He walked barefoot from the utility room, across the hallway's cold tile into the kitchen, where Ben was arranging open containers of ice cream on the salmon-marble worktop. "Interesting choice for winter," Evan said.

"Science says ice cream warms you up, just like eating spicy foods cools you down. At least, I hope that's what science says."

Ben turned to Evan, his Dapper Dan T-shirt now paired with gray-and-black plaid sleep trousers and neon-green socks. "Ooh, check you." He licked chocolate ice cream off his thumb as his gaze roamed Evan's naked legs. "Are you as sore as I am from our mad wallbanger?"

"Aye, I think bruising might have occurred. Worth it, though." He held out the boxer shorts and pajama trousers Ben had offered him. "These didn't fit, but thanks."

"Ooft, sorry." Ben set the clothes on the nearest kitchen chair, then turned back to the ice cream. "On the bright side, our temporary injuries give us time to watch the film before bed." He angled his head to look at Evan from the corner of his eye. "You're staying the night, right?"

"If you like." He'd left out extra food for Trent, just in case. "What about your mum?"

"She won't be home until late tomorrow morning." Ben held out the ice cream scoop. "You can leave before then."

As Evan helped himself to an equal amount of each of the four flavors, he tried not to take it personally that Ben wanted to evict him at daybreak. "Your house is beautiful."

"That means a lot, coming from an architect. All I know is it's very red."

"It's cozy." Given the home's location in Bearsden—one of the UK's wealthiest districts—Evan had expected something more palatial and ostentatious. But the Reids' villa was human-size and understated, employing the warm colors and cool textures of the American Southwest.

As they carried their ice cream into the living room, Evan said, "When I first heard of Bearsden, I thought, 'How convenient they've made it easy to find all the big hairy men.'"

Ben chuckled. "I've heard a hundred variations on that joke. I've *made* at least a dozen myself."

"Sorry." Evan sank onto the plush russet leather couch, his face flaring with embarrassment.

"Don't be. It's good we got it out of the way." Ben knelt before the square wooden coffee table and opened both drawers. From one he withdrew the remote controls, and from the other a Blu-Ray box set. "I'm obviously not a bear, but I am an otter, FYI."

"Erm…okay." He watched Ben scoot over to the TV to insert the disc into the player.

Ben stood and turned to him. "I do shave some hair." He put a hand to the small of his back. "And of course I trim other bits. But I don't wax. I tried it once and nearly passed out from the pain."

"Ah." Evan's Scandinavian heritage meant he'd never needed much manscaping himself.

"I only mention it," Ben continued, "because a lot of guys see my slimness and assume I'm a twink. Then my top comes off and they're disappointed, and sometimes it becomes a"—he lowered his gaze to his shifting feet—"a racial thing. Like they have a closer look and realize my tan doesn't come from a bottle. One of them even said, 'I'm not into—' I won't repeat the word." Ben pushed his glasses up his nose, still not meeting Evan's eyes. "It's funny, cos one look at my Scottish dad shirtless proves I got my hairiness from him."

"I'm sorry." Evan set down his bowl of ice cream, harder than he'd intended.

Ben stepped back like he'd been slapped. "I can phone a taxi, or if you don't want to wait, the Hillfoot train station is—"

"I meant, I'm sorry you had to go through that." He stood and went to him, thinking of people like Jordan Lithgow who'd be happy to see Ben suffer. "Tell me who these racist pricks were, and I'll—"

"What, shoot them with a cap gun?" Ben smiled up at him. "Thanks for the chivalry, but I wasn't looking for sympathy. I just wanted to be forthcoming before we got naked. I wanted to be sure I was your body type."

"I haven't got a body type. I'm attracted to personality." *And a clean background check.* "Specifically, your personality." He kissed Ben softly. "And your mouth, to be perfectly forthcoming myself."

"Ooh." Ben tapped one of Evan's shirt buttons. "You're too good to be true, Mr. Hollister."

Evan swallowed his dismay at these apt words. "I'm not."

"Not good or not true?" Ben stepped back with a smirk. "Relax, I'm kidding. Mostly." He headed for the five-panel bay window. "While I draw the blinds, want to turn off the big light? It'll make a better viewing experience."

Evan moved toward the switch near the living room doorpost. When he reached it, he stopped, heart hammering his chest. "Put on the film first so I won't trip on my way to the couch. My manager would have my head if I got injured in a freak Blu-Ray-watching accident."

Ben gave him a curious look but did as he asked. In a moment the TV glowed with the bright desert sky of the disc's main menu. Evan turned off the light, then returned to the couch as fast as he could without losing the towel round his waist.

Ben sat beside him and covered their legs with a thick black-and-white plaid blanket. Then he pointed the remote at the TV. "Ready?"

Evan took a moment to gaze at Ben's blue-lit face. "Fire."

———

BEN HAD SEEN *A Fistful of Dollars* so many times, he'd grown immune to the mind-snapping tension of its opening sequence. Watching the Clint Eastwood classic with Evan was like reliving that first viewing.

When the Man with No Name (aka, the Stranger) confronted the Baxter gang—*"My mule don't like people laughing"*—then gunned down all four before they could get off a single shot, Evan let out a spontaneous, "Wow."

"Indeed. Now you see why your poncho turned me on."

Evan eyed Ben's bootlace tie, which he wore loosely fastened like a necklace. "This turned me on," he said as he slipped his fingers beneath it, "because all night I wanted to do this."

He tugged on the tie to pull Ben toward him. Their mouths meshed, cold and sweet with ice cream.

A loud buzz came from the back of the house.

Evan jumped, tightening his grip on the tie. "What was that?"

"Ow. It's the clothes dryer." Ben rubbed the back of his neck as Evan let go. "Your underwear's ready."

Evan blinked rapidly. "Right. Sorry." He got up and moved into the hallway, switching on every light on his way to the utility room. Soon he returned, once again in his jeans and socks, his eyes comically wide. "Hot pants."

As they continued watching the film, Ben found himself leaning into Evan, snuggling against his soft blue flannel shirt as though they were a real couple.

Wait, *were* they a real couple? It had felt like it tonight at times, like when Evan had put himself between Ben and Tombstone Tim. But their frantic come-fest against the wall had been like any other anonymous encounter, with a singular (*sinful?*) objective.

A sudden jolt broke through Ben's contemplation. He turned to see Evan's eyes fixed on the screen, where the Rojos gang were beating the crap out of the captive Stranger. Evan flinched at the sound of each blow, despite the cartoonish quality of 1964 sound effects.

When one of the villains offered the Stranger water to drink, then poured it over his head instead, Evan sat up straight. "Pause it. Now. Please."

Ben fumbled for the remote control. "What's wrong?"

Staring at the frozen screen, Evan swiped his tongue, then his teeth, over his top lip. "He gets out, right?"

"Of course." Ben tried not to sound patronizing. "I promise you'll love how he escapes." He held out the remote, hoping Evan would feel better if he could control the experience. "Whenever you're ready."

Evan swallowed, then pressed play, but he kept the remote control. When Ben instinctively put his arm around his shoulders, Evan didn't flinch, but he didn't relax either.

As they watched the Rojos gang interrogate the Man with No Name, Ben stroked the back of Evan's ice-cold hands and pondered his hypervigilance—how he'd hesitated to close his eyes at the restaurant, how he'd balked at turning off the living room light.

"I hate surprises."

If Evan was a cop, he must have encountered the ugliest of human behavior. Ben prayed he'd been but a witness and not a victim himself.

As promised, the Man With No Name soon escaped by ambushing his captors with a giant rolling barrel of gunpowder. Evan's body relaxed, and his hand warmed beneath Ben's. The two of them snuggled closer on the couch, limbs intertwining, hands wandering beneath the blanket with no particular destination.

"This is my favorite part," Ben whispered against Evan's cheek as the Stranger emerged from the dynamite smoke to to rescue his innkeeper friend—as much as anyone could be a friend to the Man With No Name.

"Interesting," Evan said, his fingers drawing maddening circles inside Ben's thigh. "Usually it's the villain who walks out of the fog when everyone thinks he's dead. Here it's the good guy."

"He's not a good guy." Ben pressed his lips to Evan's ear. "But he is a hero."

Evan turned his head, and the look in his eyes made Ben feel like he'd just given a quiz show's million-pound answer.

"I'm so sorry," Evan said.

Ben's heart pounded. Was Evan about to run away? "Sorry for what?"

"For interrupting the film again." He took Ben's face in his hands and kissed him.

Ben succumbed to this deluxe version of last week's goodnight kiss. It wasn't like the suffocating kisses they'd shared against his bedroom wall, but it stole his breath just the same.

When Evan's mouth moved to his neck, Ben glanced at the TV, where the Stranger was about to have his final showdown. "We're missing the best part."

"No." Evan's lips against his ear made Ben shiver. "We're not."

Chapter 11

EVAN HAD PREPARED for this naked-in-bed moment all week, and not just by buying condoms. With the help of his therapist, he'd planned what to do if *that* night crashed his mind in the form of a flashback or an unbidden memory: He would take a deep breath and find something concrete to ground himself in the here-and-now.

So here they were undressing—on opposite sides of the bed, to avoid any painful high-impact collisions. Evan's fingers shook as he tried to undo the buttons of his flannel shirt.

Ben noticed straight away. "It is a wee bit chilly, isn't it? I'll put on the fireplace." He went to a wall switch beside the bookcase. There was a slight hiss, then small flames whooshed to life. "Plus it'll give us light, so I can turn this off." He came back and reached for the bedside lamp.

"Leave it on." Evan cleared his throat. "Just for now."

Ben nodded, looking a bit uneasy. "I can see you better that way, since I'm blind without these." He took off his glasses and laid them next to his bootlace tie beside the alarm clock. After a brief hesitation, he pulled off his T-shirt and dropped it on the floor. Then he rubbed his arms and looked away. "Yes, it's chilly."

Evan's anxiety dimmed at the sight of Ben's self-consciousness. All he could think about was touching him everywhere, removing all doubt from Ben's mind that he was beautiful.

Forgoing the rest of the buttons, Evan lifted off his shirt, along with the white T-shirt underneath.

"Wow." Ben stared at him, the ties of his undone sleep trousers dangling from his hand. "It should be illegal for you to wear a top."

Evan felt his face flush as he unbuckled his belt. "Thought you said you were blind."

"Shortsighted, technically. Besides, your muscles are incandescent. I bet they can be seen from space." Ben tugged down his sleep trousers. "Ooh, talking of space." He straightened up to reveal a pair of bright-green cartoon boxers featuring Marvin the Martian. "These were in my old chest of drawers here. Obviously, I wasn't wearing them on our date, nor was I planning to come back here and explode in my pants."

"They're cute." Evan stepped out of his jeans and gestured to his blue silk briefs. "Mine are boring."

"There is nothing boring about that sight. At least, not that I can tell from here."

They stood and looked at each other for a moment. Ben tucked his thumb under the waistband of his boxers. Evan did the same with his briefs. Neither moved.

Ben's eyes crinkled. "So we're equally bashful about whipping out our cocks for the first time. Now *that's* cute."

Evan laughed. Nothing about this situation—the man, the setting, the mood—resembled the last time he'd had been to bed with someone.

Still, he couldn't help glancing at the door.

"I locked it," Ben said, reading his mind. "But check it if you like."

Evan didn't want to look paranoid. "It's not that I don't trust you."

"Go on, it'll only take a second. I promise not to be insulted."

So Evan went to the bedroom door, which was indeed locked.

The door was locked that night, too.

He took a moment to acknowledge this rogue musing. *Thanks for the reminder. On you go now.* Arguing with thoughts just made them cling to the inside of his brain, and that was how spirals began. Better to simply stand back and let them pass, to offer them respect but not appeasement.

"Sorry," Evan said. "I should've taken your word for it."

"I don't blame you," Ben said as he got into bed. "You're in a strange house."

There was no sign of the Marvin the Martian boxers on the floor, so Evan kept his briefs on as he slid under the soft duvet.

They faced each other at arm's length without touching. Ben's eyes seemed larger than ever without his glasses, which had left a pair of indentations on the bridge of his razor-straight nose. Dark hair spread across his chest and down over his stomach, thick enough to shadow the skin beneath without obscuring it altogether.

Ben swallowed audibly, then slid his hand over Evan's beneath the duvet. Evan turned his hand to lock with Ben's. They remained like that for several seconds—then, as though heeding some signal only they could hear, they tugged each other closer at the same moment.

As they kissed, Evan drifted his palm up Ben's arm, savoring each inch of warm skin on this, the first man he'd touched in eight months. He sighed at the feel of Ben's fingers gliding over his bare waist, then rising to wrap around the back of his shoulder. He relaxed into their embrace and reminded himself there was no rush, no agenda—and most of all, no danger.

Outside, a car door slammed. Evan jerked back and looked toward the floor-to-ceiling window at the other end of the room.

"It's the neighbor," Ben said. "Not Mum."

"Are you sure?"

"I've spent most of my life in this house. I know every sound."

Evan kept his gaze on the long teal curtains and tried to steady his breath. How could he explain that it wasn't the thought of being caught by Ben's mother that had set his heart racing?

Over the last seven months, Evan's MI5 doctors and supervisors had watched him closely, looking for signs of Post-Traumatic Stress Disorder. He'd devoured the latest research and seized on every treatment to stave it off, more or less successfully. The fact he'd kept his sanity after Belfast was, in his opinion, his life's crowning achievement.

Of course, there was no guarantee. *"Every brain is unique,"* his doctor had said. *"We don't know why some people develop PTSD and others don't. Escaping it doesn't mean you're stronger, just luckier."*

A hand touched Evan's chest. He flinched, but only on the inside, a feat in itself.

"Shall we go to my flat instead?" Ben asked. "Or maybe yours? Or would you rather, you know, say goodnight?"

"No, none of those." He laid his head on the pillow again. "I'm fine here." When Ben arched an eyebrow, Evan added, "Relatively."

"Relative to where?"

He gazed into Ben's soft, dark eyes and told the utter truth. "Everywhere."

EVAN DIDN'T SEEM fine at all, but if this bed was the place he felt most comfortable, Ben wasn't about to eject him from it.

As they kissed, hands exploring, Ben had to remind himself it was possible, however incongruous, that a man as big and strong as Evan could be fragile. But what had made him so? Did Ben have the courage—or even the will—to deal with it? He barely knew Evan, and much of what he did know was disturbing or incomplete.

With a soft growl, Evan ran his palm down Ben's chest, then up again, spreading his fingers as they plowed through the thick hair there. Ben arched his back to meet this appreciative touch, reveling in the feeling of being wanted.

Then he reciprocated, sliding his palm over Evan's pecs, which felt as smooth as they looked—like carved marble, only warmer.

He couldn't help smiling. "This is like making out with Michelangelo's *David*."

Evan guffawed, instantly blushing. "I hope not, as that statue has disproportionately small genitalia."

"Does it? Why?"

"It was a Renaissance thing, hearkening back to the Greek fascination with prepubescent beauty."

"Och, that's rather pervy in a modern context."

They laughed together, but then the smiles faded from their eyes, replaced by a new heat.

Evan reached forward and slid his hand up Ben's neck, into his hair, then kissed him. It was a kiss that both begged and possessed, and it sent molten wax flowing through Ben's veins. He moved forward, sliding his thigh over Evan's hip to bring their bodies together.

At this press of warm flesh against his chest, Ben felt his cock stiffen—somewhat painfully, but it was an ache he could ignore, if needs must. He wasn't sure what they were about to do, but he was ready for anything.

The gas fireplace made its simulated-wood-crackling noise. Evan jolted in his arms.

"All right?" Ben asked.

Evan's gaze darted toward the center of the room. "I'm fine, just..." He looked down between their bodies. "Still fair sore, you ken? I don't think I'll be able to—"

"Me neither," Ben said. "Too bad, as I was pure looking forward to riding you proper." Clearly soreness wasn't all that was making Evan uneasy. "Shall we stop, then?"

"I'd rather not." Evan looked at him with more sincerity than Ben had ever seen in those eyes. "I want to keep touching you.

And kissing you. And have us keep doing both things to each other until we fall asleep."

Ben melted inside a little. "I would really fancy that. A lot." He skated his fingertips over the planes of Evan's torso. "Warning, though: I might still spontaneously come just from touching your abs."

Chapter 12

EVAN STARED AT THE CEILING, knowing if he left this bed right now, he could be at the Hillfoot train station in ten minutes. Ben wouldn't try and make him stay, even if he'd still been awake, which he wasn't. He would understand.

But just in case, Evan would write the most honest note allowed by law, explaining how he'd had a lovely time but wasn't ready to be close to someone just now. How Ben deserved better.

He'd leave the note right here on this pillow. Right here.

But the minutes and hours passed, and Evan didn't move. The thought of going out into the cold again…

Finally he looked at Ben sprawled on his back beside him, his profile standing out against a pure blue light. Before falling asleep, Ben had switched off the lamp but turned on a humidifier the size and shape of a cricket ball (*"For my sinuses, so I don't snore your ears off."*). It gave a steady, soothing hiss, and its cobalt glow cast the lampshade's shadow upon the ceiling.

Evan sighed. There'd be no sleep until he made sure every room was as secure as this one. He slid from the warm bed, pulled on his jeans and T-shirt, and crept out into the hallway.

The stairs were thickly carpeted and solidly built, making no creaks as he climbed. The wallpaper in the foyer and stairway was a rich red-and-gold Victorian pattern, the sort his fellow architects would have deemed "trying too hard." He was glad his current profession didn't involve assessing the hipness of his surroundings. Memorizing details was a lot easier if he didn't need to form opinions about them.

The upper floor contained a bathroom and three bedrooms, the smallest of which held the impersonal decor of a guest room: a neutral blue duvet cover, a trio of matching landscape paintings, a set of folded towels at the foot of the bed.

He continued to Mrs. Reid's office. One wall featured three massive calendars, of the current year and its two successors. Evan noticed certain wedding-free dates common to each year, the next being 20-21 March, which was marked NAW-RÚZ, the Persian New Year.

He stepped into the master bedroom just long enough to confirm it was empty, then crept back downstairs to the library, where he locked the door, took off his jeans, and slipped back into bed.

Perhaps the perimeter check had been what he'd needed to sleep, because when Evan opened his eyes, the room was painted with a dusky gray light, and the space beside him was empty.

Somewhere in the room, Ben spoke in an urgent whisper. "… none other God but Him, the Help in Peril, the Self-Subsisting."

After a moment, Evan heard a soft rustle. The trajectory of Ben's voice changed a bit. "Exalted art Thou above my praise and the praise of anyone beside me…"

Evan guessed this was the Bahá'í medium obligatory prayer, to be said between sunrise and noon, then twice again later in the day. Ben's voice held none of the bored drone Evan usually heard people pray with. He sounded as though he was speaking to a real person, trying to convince them—or himself—of something vital.

Ben shifted position again, and when he spoke, his voice was softer, perhaps blocked by the end of the bed as he reached the final, seated portion of the prayer.

Evan marveled at this impulse to speak to a higher power. His mum and stepdad were ostensibly Church of Scotland but had never been particularly observant. Evan shared his father's cynicism toward religion, born of watching people bomb one another —and innocent bystanders—in the name of their versions of God. He'd seen firsthand in Belfast and Glasgow how sectarianism drove people to wall themselves off from "enemies" whose choice of church made them less than human.

His leg twitched in a sudden jerk.

Ben's prayer halted. "You awake?"

"Only just." Evan rolled onto his back. "Sorry, didn't mean to interrupt."

"No bother," Ben said as he stood. "I can finish reciting the name of God later."

"Don't start over on my account."

"I won't. I'm meant to say *Allah-u-Abha* ninety-five times a day. I got to twenty-one before I stopped. I should've gone to another room, but I didn't want you to be disorientated waking alone."

"Thanks." Evan warmed inside at Ben's thoughtfulness. "How do you keep count?"

"I'll show you." Ben crawled onto the bed to lie prone, propping himself on his elbows, then took Evan's hand. "I touch the tip of my thumb to each knuckle and fingertip on the opposite hand." He demonstrated, beginning with Evan's thumb before moving on to his fingers. "There's fourteen knuckles on one hand, plus five fingertips, and five fingers on the other hand. Nineteen times five equals ninety-five."

Evan's entire arm tingled from Ben's soft, deliberate touch. "That's brilliant."

"There's also an app that vibrates after the ninety-fifth time you touch the screen, but I like this better."

"Me, too." Evan cleared the huskiness from his throat. "You can finish now if it'd be easier."

"Nothing could make it easier. Feels so awkward after not praying for months." He glanced at the bedside table clock, its antique bronze face topped by a pair of alarm bells. "Mind, you should leave within the hour, in case Mum's home early."

"What made you want to start praying again this morning?" Evan thought of the Bahá'í precept against premarital sex. "Did last night make you feel, erm, sinful?" He hoped Ben would laugh and deny it.

Instead his eyes drooped at their corners. "I'm not ashamed of being gay. I'd feel just as conflicted if I was straight." Ben rubbed his cheek, which, though unshaven, looked freshly scrubbed. "Bahá'ís don't believe that sex is wrong or impure. I was taught that it's a perfectly natural impulse, one of the most beautiful parts of human experience. But also that marriage was created to make a place for those impulses."

"Why?"

"Because when you're in an equal, loving union, then sex is constructive instead of destructive. And by 'constructive' I don't mean just making babies. It's about nurturing each other, building each other up."

"Okay." So far none of this sounded odd to Evan. "Couldn't two people be in an equal, loving union without marrying?"

"One would think. But there's something, I don't know, *divine* about having that unique bond with one person for the rest of your life." Ben tapped his fingertips on the bed. "I don't judge others for premarital bonking, I swear. Fault-finding is a big no-no for Bahá'ís."

"So you don't judge others, but you judge yourself."

"Sometimes." Ben pulled his pillow beneath his chest and hugged it. "See, being Bahá'í isn't about mindlessly following a set of archaic rules. We're taught that we're rational souls, so we should use our discretion when it comes to applying the laws of our faith."

"So you can decide for yourself whether to follow them?"

"Not in a capricious way, like, 'Eh, I don't fancy being chaste, so I've decided that law's rubbish.' We should reflect on whether our actions nurture our souls. Whether they serve God or only serve ourselves."

Evan felt a bit lost. "Like what?"

"This'll sound weird," Ben muttered as he combed his fingers through the flop of dark hair on his forehead. "When I'm with a Grindr hookup, it's all about them. I *make* it all about them, and they either don't notice or they don't care because they just want to get off. And I, for want of a better word, *specialize* in lads who are coming to terms with their sexuality. I make them feel good, and not just physically. I bring them peace." Ben slowly shook his head. "And I'm not ashamed of that, not on any level."

Evan wanted to kiss him then, to absorb a few iotas of the radical kindness dwelling within this lad. But he didn't want to derail their conversation just when he was on the brink of understanding. "So it's your own pleasure which feels wrong. When someone makes you feel good, it doesn't nurture your soul?"

"Basically, I guess." Ben looked at him again, pressing his cheek into the pillow. "When we were rutting against the wall, I wasn't thinking of you as a person, only a body. I wasn't thinking anything but, 'Yaaaaaaaasss!'" He waved his bare feet in the air.

Evan risked a gentle joke. "If it helps, I was thinking the same thing."

"It doesn't help, but thanks." Ben picked at the seam of his pillowcase, looking as though he might weep. "It feels like I moved away from God by putting my own needs above yours."

"It didn't seem that way to me. Besides, you deserve to get what you want."

"Mm. Maybe." Ben switched on a winsome smile. "Maybe it's all about being a Leap Baby."

Evan blinked at this sudden shift in tone. "A what?"

"I was born the twenty-ninth of February. I've had but five proper birthdays in my life. I'm not complaining—on the regular years my parents still celebrate it on the twenty-eighth, or on the first of March."

"Great," Evan said, "but what's that got to do with sex?"

"Birthdays make people feel special. I've had seventy-five percent fewer than other people."

"You realize that being a Leap baby makes you *more* special, right?"

"Not special, just unusual. Och, you must think me a loon. I can't even enjoy an orgasm without throwing a morning-after moody."

"With all the selfish pricks out there? Your attitude's kinda refreshing."

"Don't patronize me."

"I'm not. Listen…" Evan reached out to take Ben's hand. Then he paused, wanting to get the words right. "Please understand how much it would mean to me to make you feel good. How happy it would make me. How much peace it would bring me."

Ben's face softened. "Really?"

"Really. Giving and taking don't have to be opposites." He pulled Ben's hand to his lips and kissed it. "They can be a team."

Ben's eyes grew suddenly damp. He turned his head to press his face into his pillow.

"Ben." Evan moved forward and kissed his upper arm, just below the sleeve of his T-shirt. "Let me make you feel good."

"You mean now?"

"Aye, now." Evan hesitated, peering over the cliff of uncertainty. Then he leapt. "And later."

Ben's smile erased the sadness from his beautiful brown eyes. Then he rolled onto his back. "I suppose…if you must."

I must, Evan thought as he slowly undressed him, his lips lingering on each new inch of skin. *I really must.*

Because there was no choice. Or rather, Evan had made his choice, between the security of solitude and the riskiness of romance. Before meeting Ben, Evan's fear had always made this a simple, even automatic decision. But now there was something bigger and stronger than his fear.

In a way, that was the most terrifying part of all.

Ben couldn't remember the last time he'd just lain back and let a man make him feel good. In fact, he'd only gone along with this idea to make Evan happy.

But now that it was more than an idea, now that Evan was settling between his legs, nudging his own bare knees beneath Ben's thighs, all doubt was dissipating like fog beneath a hot sun.

Evan ran his hands up Ben's legs, then slid his palms under Ben's arse and clutched him hard.

Ben groaned and tilted up his hips. As he closed his eyes, the last thing he saw was Evan's head descending.

Soft lips enveloped the head of his cock. Ben drew in a half gasp, half hiss. There was still a ghost of soreness from last night, but it faded with each gentle stroke of Evan's tongue.

"Is this okay?" Evan whispered.

"Oh yeah." A low laugh rumbled in Ben's chest. "It's okay."

He felt the curve of Evan's smile. "Show me what you want."

Ben opened his eyes. "Hmm?"

Evan gazed up at him and licked his lips. "Put your cock in my mouth."

It stiffened in response to the command. Ben grasped his shaft and shifted his foreskin down to expose the head. He guided it against Evan's glistening lips, which parted in an instant. Instead of thrusting inside, Ben slid his cock head around the rim of Evan's open mouth.

Evan moaned, his tongue slipping out for a taste. Ben echoed the sound, fully hard now. With his other hand, he tilted Evan's head, just enough to let himself slip inside, halfway this time.

"God." Ben dug his heels into the mattress as the sensations flared out through his body. "More." Evan took him deeper, squeezing Ben's arse with both hands. When his cock was secure within Evan's mouth, Ben reached lower to cup his own balls. "Ow." Those were even more sore.

Evan halted, casting up a questioning look.

"That was my fault," Ben said. "But talking of pain, won't your neck get stiff like that?"

Evan released him carefully. "Maybe." He slid off the end of bed, then went to the side near the fireplace and knelt on the floor. "Come here."

Ben shifted over, mesmerized by the sight of this magnificent man on his knees before him. "Shall I sit up, then?"

"No need." Evan took Ben's legs and looped them over his shoulders. His long arms reached around Ben's thighs so he could take his cock with all ten fingers. "How's this?"

Ben wanted to say "Perfect," but couldn't find the breath as Evan began anew. The strokes of his hands and mouth remained light, yet his face was fervent, like he'd never felt such hunger or tasted anything so delicious. Ben pulled a pair of pillows beneath his head, the better to watch. He wished for his glasses so he could properly see past Evan's bare, muscular back, down to his presumably perfect arse encased in those tight blue briefs.

For a moment Ben thought about how, when he'd get a blowjob or a hand job from a Grindr hookup, his pleasure was mostly for the other lad's sake, for demonstration purposes. His sighs and moans had been mere feedback, encouragement. Lessons.

But this...Ben just wanted it. Needed it. Hoped it would never end.

He squirmed with each wave of sensation, but Evan held him fast, forcing his awareness to shrink to the length of his cock and the skill of what enveloped it. It felt like he was mapping every contour of Evan's mouth, even the deeper parts he couldn't explore when they'd kissed last night.

Evan turned his head at a new angle, making Ben groan. He looked up at the sound, and when their eyes met, Ben felt something click into place between them, something sweet and sincere yet full of fire.

Evan let go of him and rose up, sliding between Ben's legs as he spread his body over his and brought their faces together.

"Are your knees getting sore?" Ben asked.

"No." Evan's gaze focused on his mouth. "I just saw your lips and had to taste them again."

"Oh," Ben managed to whisper. "Go on, then."

Evan's eyes crinkled. "But I canna decide which one first." He took Ben's bottom lip between his teeth, then gently sucked it between his own.

Moaning, Ben slid his palms down Evan's back, barely stopping his fingers from plunging beneath the waistband of his briefs. He wanted to beg Evan to fuck him right here, right now, but more than that he wanted to savor this almost reverential kiss.

Evan switched to Ben's top lip, giving it the same devoted treatment as the other. Ben's cock jerked against Evan's warm, taut belly, as though begging for attention.

Evan glanced down, then met his eyes again. "Ben…do you want to come in my mouth?"

OH GOD YES PLEASE NOW NOW NOW, he thought, but could manage only a shaky nod.

After a last, lingering kiss, Evan moved down again. "I'll be going a peedie bit stronger, so tell me if it's too much."

"'Kay." Ben prepared to flinch at Evan's firmer grasp, but there was only a hint of pain, which gave way to a whole new level of pleasure as Evan's mouth joined in, sliding up and down faster and faster, his tongue pressing harder with each stroke. Ben watched Evan consume him—head bobbing, jaws bulging, face flushing—and again wished for his glasses so he could see every masterful detail.

But then his vision blurred anyway as his orgasm swept over him.

"Yes! Oh…" Ben's legs jerked up, thighs spasming, toes spreading wide. A flood of hot come surged forth, coating his cock within the exquisite chamber of Evan's mouth, a place he never wanted to leave.

When he could finally speak again, Ben blurted out the first thought that came to mind: "That was far better than I expected."

Hearing his own words, he opened his eyes to see Evan standing beside the bed staring at him. "Wait," Ben said. "That came out wrong."

"What did you mean?"

Ben decided to be honest, since backpedaling might imply an even greater insult. "Most guys who are even half as gorgeous as you are, they don't bother developing skills." His voice slurred a bit in the post-orgasmic haze. "Maybe they think a man can come just by looking at them."

"Okay," Evan said, drawing out both syllables.

"But not you," Ben said quickly, then covered his face. "Sorry, this must be the worst compliment you ever got."

"Not the worst." Evan sat on the bed. "Definitely top five, though."

Ben peeked at his face to make sure he was joking.

Evan gave him a wry grin. "I'm happy you enjoyed it." He leaned over to kiss Ben's cheek.

Ben grabbed his face and kissed him full and deep. His own taste on Evan's tongue made him want to return the favor, pronto. But that would defeat the purpose of the whole taking-without-giving thing, so he simply whispered, "Thank you."

Then he closed his eyes, rolled over, and let himself relive the last twelve hours as he drifted off into the sleep of the satisfied.

———

EVAN DRESSED QUIETLY, as Ben had already dozed off, a lopsided smile on his charming face. Buckling his belt—careful not to let it clink—he realized he'd not so much as glanced at the door while he was on his knees just now. He'd been so focused on Ben that he hadn't the headspace to relive the past. That seemed a good sign.

He left the bedroom, shutting the door softly behind him, and headed for the foyer. Passing the living room, he stopped when he spied the pairs of bowls, spoons, and mugs on the coffee table.

The fact there were two of everything would be a dead giveaway that Ben had had a guest, which seemed to be forbidden.

No sooner had Evan washed, dried, and put away one set of dishes than a car door slammed out front—this time definitely not that of a neighbor. He began to wash the second bowl to cover up his attempted coverup, then took a deep breath, awaiting his reckoning.

The front door rattled with a key, then creaked as it opened. Evan kept the tap running so Ben's mum would hear him before she saw him. No point in startling her any more than necessary.

"Erm...hello?"

Evan turned to see a face familiar from her wedding planning website and the photos in the house. Giti Reid was taller than he'd expected, but her black hair and olive skin were as elegantly made up in real life as in the pictures.

"Hello." He dried his hands on the closest tea towel. "I'm Evan. I hope I didn't startle you."

"Not really, I..." Mrs. Reid half-turned toward the hallway. "I saw what I assume is your jacket on the peg." Rather than looking as uncomfortable as he felt, she just looked angry. "I pretty much joined the dots."

Evan could only imagine what she was imagining. "Ben's sleeping. I'm away in a moment, once I've finished the washing-up."

"Stay for a coffee." She gestured to the kitchen chair nearest him. "Please," she added, though this was clearly an order, not a request. Was she being hospitable, or was she hoping to interrogate him? Either way, she was no doubt reeling at the live evidence of her son's immorality standing in her own kitchen.

Evan maintained his serene smile. "Thank you, that would be lovely. Shall I wake—"

"No. Sit." Mrs. Reid tugged off her black leather gloves, one finger at a time. "Let's get to know each other first."

A LIFELONG EAVESDROPPER, Ben had been twelve years old when he'd bought a stethoscope to replace the traditional empty glass against the wall. At this moment, he'd never been more grateful for the upgrade.

Standing upon the head of his bed, he pressed the stethoscope's bell against the wall's thinnest spot, marked by a tiny penciled dot.

"...hard enough leaving Orkney for Glasgow," Evan was saying. "I canna imagine the culture shock coming here from Iran."

"At the time Iran was very Westernized," Ben's mother said. "But that was changing. My parents could see the writing on the wall." There came the familiar hiss of butter meeting a hot frying pan. "The day my older sister was expelled from university simply for being Bahá'í was the day my father told us to pack our bags. She was told she had no human rights because Bahá'ís weren't human. Every Bahá'í who could afford to leave, left."

"What happened to those who couldn't?"

Ben knew he should run to the kitchen and derail this conversation. Evan was broaching a topic Mum never discussed. Ben himself had heard the stories only from his father.

"The Iranian government," Mum said, "claims the Bahá'í Faith is not a religion but a political movement. They accuse us of being enemy spies in league with the so-called Zionists."

Evan remained silent, letting her continue. Ben heard the muted suction thumps of the refrigerator opening and closing, the jam jars rattling in their rack on the door.

"They claimed we were a security risk," Mum said, "so their treatment of us was not religious persecution but rather a defensive measure to protect the state."

Ben's fingers tightened on the stethoscope. Now that she'd given Evan the political background, would she change the subject and let him draw his own conclusions?

"There was a man I called 'Uncle,' though he was no blood relation. He was a leader in the Bahá'í assembly. When he was arrested for spying, they promised to release him if he recanted his faith and converted to Islam. Of course he refused." There was another long pause. "In the end, they used a firing squad."

Ben's eyes heated with sympathy. Evan's voice was barely audible through the wall. "In the end?"

"After he was tortured," Mum said, her voice curdling with bitterness. "Over two hundred Bahá'ís have been killed in Iran since the revolution, and thousands more have been imprisoned or sacked from their jobs or expelled from university." She raised her voice over the sound of a wire whisk against a stainless-steel mixing bowl. "Now those people come here wanting to steal our freedoms with their *sharia* laws." The mixing bowl banged against the marble worktop. "And the police do nothing. They don't want to offend the Muslims by arresting the ones who break the law."

Ben sighed. She was clearly still watching those fearmongering TV documentaries.

Evan took a few moments to respond. "I think the vast majority of UK Muslims support our values. It's the handful of violent extremists I'm afraid of, especially as a gay man. I understand they object to my orientation, but my safety deserves more protection than their prejudices."

"I agree," Mum said.

Ben rolled his eyes. So she believed gays shouldn't be assaulted in the streets. How liberal of her.

Evan spoke again. "I worry things'll get worse now we've got marriage equality. Bigots like that see it as an affront to their values and they want to fight back."

Ben winced at Evan's misstep. Had he just called Mum a bigot, however obliquely?

His mother's voice came closer, approaching the breakfast table. "One can adhere to one's values without being a bigot."

Rationalization powers, activate! Ben pitied Evan for the pasting he was about to receive.

"I'm sure Ben's told you of my opposition to gay marriage," Mum said. "I don't favor discrimination, but—"

"Of course you dinna." Evan's tone was as warm as ever. "You clearly love Ben, and he adores you, as I'm sure you ken."

"Oh. Well." She cleared her throat. "Yes, we're very close."

"And you want him to be happy."

"Right, but—"

"Just like your parents wanted you to be happy. It's why you came to the UK in the first place."

Ben smirked. This guy was good. Really good. Or maybe it was that mesmerizing Orcadian accent—which, Ben noticed, Evan was leaning into at the moment, no doubt to make himself seem sweeter and less threatening.

After a moment there came a sizzling sound: onions and peppers, Ben assumed, and not Evan's fingers, based on the lack of screaming. "My son is a natural with the wedding couples," Mum said, "but he should focus his talents on his field of study. He could have a great future someday and make a difference in this world."

Now that they were discussing him, Ben stopped listening out of shame. He replaced the framed painting above the headboard to cover the pencil mark. Then he hid the stethoscope back inside the hollowed-out interior of his 1939 *Collier's World Atlas and Gazetteer*—one of his largest vintage volumes—which he then replaced on the bookshelf by the fireplace.

As he finished dressing, Ben thought of all the things he'd told Evan. Had he given up those secrets willingly, or had they been extracted? Evan hadn't used any interrogation tricks Ben recognized from TV or books. He'd simply listened. He'd made it feel safe to be honest, even as he was lying about his own profession and skulking about other people's houses in the middle of the night.

After a futile attempt to de-sex his unruly hair, Ben crept down the hall toward the kitchen.

His mother had her back to the door as she poured eggs onto the pan, her free hand holding the loose sleeve of her black cardigan safely away from the gas flame. The air was heavy with the sweet-clay smell of French roast coffee.

It was the usual Sunday-breakfast tableau, but for one tall blond addition.

"Good morning." Evan offered a tranquil smile from where he stood at the table grating a wedge of cheddar cheese.

"I was about to wake you." Still facing the cooker, Mum spoke in that forcibly carefree voice which meant she was furious. "Breakfast is nearly ready."

"Smells delicious." Ben rubbed his eyes as if he'd just woken. "Sorry for being a terrible host and not doing the introductions."

"We've managed without you." Evan shared a secretive smile with Ben's mother.

Wondering what he'd missed, Ben headed for the coffee pot. "You're home early, Mum."

"I sent you a text when I left Inverness at eight this morning."

He must have left his phone—and all common sense—on the couch last night after he and Evan had started groping each other.

Ben poured his coffee, trying not to slosh it onto the worktop. His face felt flaming hot, while the rest of him was near-shivering with unease.

His mother turned to Evan. "What sort of toast would you like?"

"I'm afraid I canna stay. Need to feed my cat before going oot again." Evan carried his mug to the sink. "Thank you for the coffee, Mrs. Reid."

"Please, call me Giti," she said with a warm smile that confused Ben all over again.

He walked Evan to the front door. "Did she freak out when she saw you?" he whispered.

"Not on the outside." Evan took his jacket and poncho from the coat peg, then leaned in to murmur, "There are worse places she could've found me than at the kitchen sink."

Ben's cheeks flared even hotter at the thought of Mum barging into his bedroom while Evan was kneeling between his flailing legs.

"She seems lovely," Evan said. "Which isn't surprising, considering…well, considering you."

A million questions wanted to burst out of Ben's throat:

How did you get her to open up?

Why did you sneak upstairs last night?

Why do you sleep like someone's chasing you?

Instead he asked, "You're going out today? Anything fun?"

"Jamie and I are scouting the gay football league for players to recruit. We'll be wearing disguises so the teams don't recognize us for the poachers we are." Evan shrugged on his jacket. "I need to hurry if I'm to meet Jamie at Queen Street Station by half past twelve."

"I could drive you to the match," Ben said.

"I thought you hated football."

"Yes, but I love subterfuge."

Evan laughed. "All right, then."

"Great, let's go." Ben reached for his own jacket, but Evan stopped him, his smile vanishing.

"What, to my place?"

"I want to meet your cat. You said you need to feed him."

"Her."

"Right. Her." *You are* very *good, Mr. Hollister.*

"Tell you what." Evan pulled on his gray knit cap, which mercilessly brought out the blue in his eyes. "It'll be faster if I go home and meet you at Jamie's. Besides, if you leave now, your mum'll think you're avoiding her."

She'd be right. Ben managed to hide his annoyance. "True. Also, I need a shower." He reached out and straightened Evan's jacket collar, though it didn't need it. "Maybe next week we can shower together at yours," he added, expecting resistance.

Evan merely smiled and gave Ben a soft but firm kiss. "Sounds perfect."

More bewildered than ever, Ben watched from the doorway as Evan hurried down the street toward the Hillfoot train station.

"He seems nice," Mum said behind him, her tone holding none of the kindness of her words.

Ben winced, then turned to face her. "I'm sorry for inviting Evan to stay, after you asked me not to bring home any, erm…" *sex mates* "…anyone. I never meant to disrespect you. It's just that we wanted to watch a film and—"

"Was this the first time you brought a man into this house?"

"Yes." He met her eyes so she'd know he was telling the truth. "The very first."

"I see." Mum looked down at the tea towel in her hands as she folded it in half, then in half again, then again. "So he must be important to you."

"He is, actually." Ben heard the marvel in his own voice.

"I wish I could…" She cleared her throat, sounding on the verge of tears. "You know I love you more than anything, and I accept you for who you are."

"I know." He could feel it, and besides, their faith forbade any sort of prejudice.

"I want you to find love," she said hoarsely, "and I want to be happy for you when it happens."

Ben held his breath, afraid to hear what would come after the *but*.

She met his gaze with overflowing eyes. "But if you enter a relationship with this man—or any man—it would be the end for you as a Bahá'í."

"Mum, nothing's changed." He looked away. "I've not exactly been celibate at uni, and yet I'm still a Bahá'í."

"I know that. By being discreet and staying single, you've let our community look the other way and pretend you were chaste. That way they don't have to—" She stopped short.

Ben suddenly felt like he'd swallowed a boulder. "Don't have to what?"

"To take action."

He could barely get the words out. "But that's…that's discrimination."

"Discrimination is forcing our rules onto non-Bahá'ís. Expecting our own people to follow those rules is not." Her voice softened. "I would fight for you, *nouré cheshm-am*. I would fight until my dying breath, if that's what you want."

She could cushion it with terms of endearment—even "light of my eye"—yet Ben heard her unspoken words as if she'd shouted them: *But please don't ask me to.*

He nodded, his neck creaking with tension. "Okay." He desperately wanted to end this conversation so he could go home and think about it—or better yet, *not* think about it, a strategy that had always served him well.

"Ben, we know this isn't your fault, and that you're suffering from a spiritual affliction. We want to help—"

"Mum, please…" He shuddered at the term *spiritual affliction*, then rubbed his arms to cover his reaction. "I'm tired and hungry." Half of this was a lie, as eating felt impossible. "Can we just have our breakfast and talk about this another time?"

"Of course." She came to him and took his hands. "I know you'll do what's right for you. And whatever you decide, I'll support you. No matter the cost."

Ben wanted to pull away, then felt guilty for the impulse. How could such soft words feel so harsh? Because they were laced with warning?

"Thanks, Mum," he said, since it was what she wanted. "That means a lot."

As he followed her back to the kitchen, he thought about what she'd just said, that he would do what was right for him. But how could he, when he had no idea what that was?

Chapter 13

As he hurried down the street toward Jamie's flat, Evan pondered Ben's eagerness to play spy. His boyhood bookshelves were loaded with novels, comics, and biographies about espionage. Judging by their overall condition and the creases in their spines, the books were several years old and thoroughly read.

Perhaps Ben's enthusiasm for the spy world meant he would accept the truth about Evan. It could also mean he wouldn't be fooled much longer.

MI5 had given Evan the green light to tell Ben about his profession, but common sense said to wait until they'd grown closer. One of Evan's colleagues had had her cover blown by a resentful ex, a breach which had jeopardized her career *and* her safety. Evan was serious about Ben—and he sensed the feeling was mutual—but he didn't yet know if he could trust his new lover with his life.

Jamie was waiting for Evan outside his flat. For this week's undercover mission, the fullback was wearing a blue Captain Sulu T-shirt that read It's OK to be Takei, his long, sandy hair flopping over his shoulders instead of in its usual ponytail. Like Evan, he wore a cap pulled down over his bloodshot blue eyes. He had just as much a need for disguise as Evan, if not more—his musical performance in a viral Warriors video the previous summer had made him internet-famous.

"All right, mate?" The brawny Glaswegian gave Evan a bro-type hand grasp. "You should know, I'm pure hungover."

"I didn't sleep much myself."

"Aye, but you've got a better reason." He lowered his voice. "Does Ben know, by the way? About your job?"

"My job as an architect?" Evan said reflexively. "Of course he knows."

Jamie's blank stare lasted longer than it should have. Then he blinked. "Right."

Evan hated having to lie to his teammate, especially one who'd so generously taken part in his MI5 vetting process. But just because Jamie and Charlotte had signed a copy of the Official Secrets Act didn't mean they could be trusted with the full truth.

Ben's car turned the corner at the next junction. "That'll be him," Evan said, relieved the conversation was over. He tugged down his cap and fidgeted with the padding he'd worn under his flannel shirt to disguise his build. Evan would have deployed his glasses and beard if Ben hadn't already seen them on "Gunnar."

Jamie shoved his hands in his pockets and watched the red hatchback crawl down the narrow side street. "I hope it was worth it."

"Sorry?"

"Whatever you had to do last year, when you left us. When you broke Fergus's heart." Jamie gave him a nervous sideways glance. "I hope you saved a lot of lives, or banged up a bunch of baddies, or whatever it is you do."

Evan couldn't answer—could never answer as long as he lived. And right then he realized that being known a peedie bit was worse than not being known at all. Because no one could ever know him completely. The wall around him could never truly disappear. At best—perhaps with Ben—it could become translucent, distorting, like a wall of ice.

The car gave a cheery beep as it pulled up beside them. Ben

shut off the engine, then hopped out and struck a pose. In an instant, Evan's mood turned right side up, like an inverted turtle flipped onto its feet by a kind passerby.

"What are you laughing at?" Ben regarded his cackling companions beneath the brim of his black fedora. "Too obvious?" He tightened the belt on his black trench coat, then swept off his sunglasses to reveal his regular pair underneath.

"Promise me you're wearing something under that trench coat," Evan said.

"Of course not." Ben sidled up to the curb, eyes darting left and right. "You might need me to create a diversion whilst you recruit your new assets."

Evan went up to Ben and tugged his lapels aside to see a bright red basketball jersey beneath. "Nice."

"It's the only sporty clothing my wardrobe contained." Ben smoothed the front of the jersey, which featured a flaming ball falling through a hoop above a white 1. "It's got sentimental value, possibly talismanic magic." He gave a brief wistful smile, then asked, "Why do we need the disguises again? Not that I'm complaining."

"Cos they hate us," Jamie said. "When Evan was captain, Warriors pinched the best players from the gay-league teams, especially Glasgow Greens. That's where I came fae." He slipped on a pair of pitch-black sunglasses. "Words were said."

Ben arched an eyebrow in Evan's direction, and it felt as though he could see into his sordid soul. But he simply took off his trench coat and fedora, tossed them into the back seat, and said, "Let's rock."

On the drive to Edinburgh, Jamie and Evan outlined their "legend," as Ben insisted on calling it: They were Stuart and Bruce, a couple of lads from Cumbernauld who'd recently discovered the joys of football.

"Gives us an excuse to ask other fans about the players," Jamie said from the back seat. "We play dumb, see, which I'm naturally good at."

"Are Stuart and Bruce boyfriends?" Ben asked.

"Just mates," Evan said. "If we pretended to be boyfriends, we'd have to remember more fake details about each other."

"But that's what makes it fun." Ben gasped. "We should all be boyfriends! We can say we're in a triad. It'll make us more interesting."

"It'll make us more memorable." Evan looked out the car window at a passing sheep farm that reminded him of home but for the presence of trees. "We want them to forget us."

"I understand." Ben heaved a dramatic sigh. "As I'm sure you'll understand if I drop you in Falkirk so you can take the train the rest of the way."

Evan stared at him, then glanced back at Jamie to see if he'd heard right. "Ben, are you threatening us?"

"Just stating my transport fee."

Evan checked the dashboard clock. There was no guarantee they'd get to Edinburgh on time if they caught a train now. "Fine. You're our boyfriend."

"Yaaas!" Ben slapped his palm against the steering wheel. "So. My name's Wullie McTweedy, and the three of us met in the steam sauna at Club 212."

As Ben spun his lust-to-love tale in a broad Glaswegian brogue, Evan's sleep-deprived mind fought to store the details. It didn't help that Ben kept editing his story on the fly.

"Wait," Jamie said as they entered the roundabout for Edinburgh's bypass. "Are we still doing the furry thing or not?"

"No," Ben said. "Mind how Bruce got carried away that one time at the zoo gift shop?"

Evan glared at him. "A minute ago you said it was you who did that. We either keep our stories straight or we don't keep them at all."

"Sorry," Ben said with no regret. "Just having a bit of fun."

"This is serious," Evan said. "If we don't find new players soon, then this spring we'll all be on the pitch longer than we should be, which means we'll make mistakes that lose matches. Warriors could end up relegated."

"I don't know what that means," Ben said.

"And many of us could end up injured," Evan said. "Do you know what *that* means?"

Ben was silent for a moment. "I'm sorry," he said, and this time it sounded sincere. "I don't want you to get hurt."

Evan felt a tweak in his chest and cursed his own gruffness. "It's all right. I appreciate your enthusiasm."

His phone buzzed in his pocket. As he reached for it, he realized it was the one in his *left* pocket: Gunnar's phone, which had been silent for two weeks.

He pulled it out to see a text from the only person who had this number.

JORDAN

ARM?

He was also the only person Evan knew who abbreviated the standard Scottish man-greeting *All right, mate?*

Evan slipped the phone back into his pocket without answering. The last conversation Jordan had started with *ARM?* had led to him offering Gunnar a temporary job at that hotel, not to mention the investment of thousands of pounds of law-enforcement money to try and catch him in a terrorist act. Evan needed to carefully consider his reply.

"Maybe we *are* taking this too seriously," Jamie said. "We're amateur footballers, for fuck's sake. If we cannae have fun with it, what's the point? Life's got enough dire problems." He rolled down his window. "Also, this is the first Sunday in months when the weather's not turning our baws into wee marbles."

Evan drew in a lungful of air that held the earliest hint of spring. Jordan's text was the clearest reminder possible that there were more important things in life than sport. "You're right. Let's just enjoy the day."

It's only football, Evan thought. *What's the worst that could happen?*

"So if the goalkeeper can use his hands," Ben asked the fan to his right, "why can't he just carry the ball down the field and chuck it into the opponent's goal?"

From his left, he felt the nudge of Evan's knee, probably a hint he was overdoing it. He gave Evan's thigh a reassuring squeeze.

"He cannae touch it with his hands outside the penalty area." The green-hatted supporter beside Ben pointed to one of several regions bordered by white lines, then gave him the once-over. "You new to the sport?"

"Oh aye, brand new, and I've hunners of questions." He jutted his thumb at Evan and Jamie. "When I ask my boyfriends, see, they just laugh, but I think secretly they don't know the answers theirsels."

"Like what questions?" A hipster-looking fan on Green Hat's other side leaned over. "My name's Thom, by the way. Thom with an *h*." He flashed what he must have thought a disarming smile. "This is Allan."

"Hiya, Thom with an *h*." Ben fluttered his lashes, hoping he looked more impressed than he felt. "Okay, so, why's there nae orange card? Why do the refs go straight fae yellow to red? It seems pure unfair."

"Ah." Thom stroked his dark goatee with a thumb and middle finger, looking like he was trying not to laugh. "The red and yellow cards are based on traffic lights. It's a universal thing, so players who speak different languages know what's going on."

"Ohhhh, that makes sense." Ben turned to Evan and Jamie. "Youse could've just telt me that instead of rolling your eyes, ya bastards."

"Cheers, mate," Evan said to Thom. He put his arm round Ben's shoulders and pulled him close to whisper, "Careful."

Ben giggled and slapped Evan's chest. "Not here, Bruce, we're in public! Christ, you're insatiable." He turned back to his new acquaintances. "Anyway, this is my first real live match. I've seen a few on the telly, but—" One of the nearby players on the pitch put a hand to the side of his nose. "Oh God, please don't," he exclaimed, then realized he'd slipped into his own West End prep-school accent. He tried to make up for it after the player shot a wad of snot from the other nostril. "Och, that's pure mingin'."

"Guy's gotta breathe somehow," Allan said.

Evan asked him and Thom a question about one of the players —some sort of midfielder—which began a conversation Ben didn't care to follow. This dull-as-dirt match hadn't changed his belief that football was a lot of running about with fuck all to show for it. He half-wished he was home watching his recording of last night's curling final.

The game was giving Ben far too much time to recall what his mum had said this morning, how being with Evan could get him cast out of the Bahá'í Faith. His chest hurt just thinking about it.

As usual, he'd come up with the perfect response an hour later in the shower: *If I'm suffering,* he'd imagined himself saying, *it's not because I'm gay, and it's not because I've got a 'spiritual affliction.' It's because humans who claim to believe in a big-hearted God somehow invented a small-minded rule which goes against all the rest of our beliefs. They're too stubborn to admit they're wrong, and too impressed with their own progressive values to admit they're prejudiced.*

Yes, that would've been brilliant. But in the moment, standing before his mother, he'd felt as small and helpless as a baby bunny glimpsing its first hawk.

It shouldn't matter, anyway. He and Evan didn't have a relationship. And after what had happened to Fergus, Ben couldn't count on anything. He would just enjoy it while it lasted, live in the moment...like this moment here, with Evan's thigh and shoulder against his, the warmth and subtle pressure slowly unraveling Ben from the inside out.

He cleared his throat and scanned his surroundings for a

diversion. Near the stand, a footballer was warming up beside the pitch. The wind rippled the bright-yellow pinny he wore over his top, obscuring the logo of the club and its sponsors.

"Do all gay teams have alliterative names?" Ben asked, breaking into the others' conversation. "Here we've got Glasgow Greens and Leith Legends. And of course there's the famous Woodstoun Warriors."

Thom's posture stiffened. "Do *not* mention Warriors here."

Oops. "I've never been to one of their matches," Ben said, "but I hear their opponents' supporters can be pure dicks." He took in the park around them with a smile. "Not a relaxed atmosphere like this," he added, hoping to smooth things over.

"I don't get it," said Allan. "Why do Warriors subject themselves to so much abuse? If they joined our league they'd have more fun—and they'd probably win the title every year."

"They're too good for us, Allan," Thom said with a sneer. "They think they're superior cos they play against straight teams. As if sharing a pitch with breeders has got anything to do with quality."

Ben gave a nervous titter. "Now, now. Some of my best mates are breeders."

Thom ignored him. "Warriors think they're helping the cause, but all they've done is turn themselves into a circus act. You seen their calendar?" he asked Ben.

"Aye, it's…nice."

"It's not 'nice,' it's porn," Thom said. "They're tarting themselves up for money."

He felt Evan's thigh tense beside his. "I heard the profits all went to charity," Ben said.

"Doesn't matter. It's the message it sends: 'Ooh, we're gay —objectify us, demean us, but also put us on a fucking pedestal.'" Thom turned sideways in his seat, clearly relishing the soapbox. "Warriors are an insult to the gay football leagues. By assimilating into straight culture, they make us look bad. People ask the Greens, 'Why can't *you* play against heterosexuals?' Like we're cowards hiding in our gay ghetto."

"Pack it in, Thom." Allan turned to Ben. "I think their publicity is brilliant. Gives queer kids someone to look up to, lets them know they're just as good." He pulled a fresh bag of crisps from the plastic bag at his feet. "I've no problem with Warriors now they've left us alone."

Ben glanced at Evan, who wore a slight frown as he thumbed something into his phone. The bright sun made his screen unreadable from an angle, but whether he was texting someone or taking notes, the task seemed to consume his attention.

Ben turned back to Allan. "What do you mean, now they've left you alone?"

"Their captain." Allan paused as he munched his crisps. "The old one. I cannae remember his name. Anyway, that bawbag used to scout the gay teams and steal all the best players."

"Like Colin MacDuff," Thom said.

"Aye, massive loss to us. Massive. And then there was Jamie what's-his-name, though we don't miss him as much. He was a bit slow." Allan nudged Ben with his elbow. "Not just with his feet, if you know what I mean."

"Oh…" Ben couldn't bear to look at Jamie's reaction. In the Bahá'í Faith, vicious gossip was one of the worst sins. He had to change the subject for everyone's sake. "Is that a new flavor?" he asked, pointing to the crisps.

Allan lifted the bag to reveal a salt-and-vinegar label. "Only if you lived under a rock the last century."

Ben felt his face grow hotter. *You are making an absolute arse of this mission.*

Thom snapped his fingers. "Evan Hollister!"

Ben jolted at the name. "Who?" he said with a squeak.

"Evan Fucking Hollister," Thom repeated, "aka, the Poacher. He'd sashay up to our best players after a match and ask them to join his team. Right under our manager's nose, the cheeky bastard. But then my boyfriend—Dean, our deep midfielder—

actually *tried* for Warriors and got rejected for alleged lack of quality."

Ben looked over to see Evan tug his cap farther down over his eyes. Jamie was chewing his gum harder than ever, knee bouncing as his heel tapped a staccato rhythm against the wooden stand.

"They are pretty selective," Allan said. "That's why they do so well." He shoved another crisp into his mouth. "Just seems wrong. Being gay is about being inclusive, know what I mean?"

"Hmm." Ben knew the discussion would probably dissipate if he let it. Yet he couldn't resist an argument. "But why should Warriors lower their standards? If their purpose is to win, they should take only the best." He continued, though Allan looked ready to interrupt. "One of my mates is in a world-class gay men's choir. They've been to European championships. They reject ninety-eight percent of the lads who audition."

"That's different," Allan said. "Football's not our realm. It's an incredibly homophobic culture. But this gay league gives us a safe space for us to enjoy the game we love."

"What's that got to do with Warriors?" Ben gestured to the pitch. "If this is just about having a laugh on a Sunday afternoon, who cares if this Edward guy takes all the good players?"

"*Evan*," Thom snapped. "And just cos we want football to be fun doesn't mean we don't care about winning. Doesn't mean we don't miss Colin and Jamie. They weren't just players, they were our mates. And now they never even come round to see us play, cos Evan Hollister told them they were too good for us." Thom sniffed. "Fucking snob."

"Don't call him that!"

Ben froze as he realized he'd said those words aloud. But the horse was out of the stable, so he might as well hop on and ride it.

"Look, I don't know the man," Ben said, "but clearly he's trying to do what's best for his team. And look how it's turned out. Warriors are international legends after that charity match last summer. Now imagine some queer footballer kid out there in the world, thinking they're alone, when one day they discover the

Rainbow Regiment fandom. They make friends, they follow the team, they start believing in something that makes them believe in themselves. But you'd take that away because of your petty jealousy."

"Wullie..." Evan murmured, but Ben ignored him.

"If you had your way," Ben said to Thom, "Warriors would sink down into this tedious mediocrity"—he flapped his hand at the pitch—"just to make you and your precious Dean feel better. But mediocrity never changed the world."

"Wullie..." Evan said again, slightly louder.

"And you." Ben turned to Allan. "You moan about Warriors being exclusive, but they've got women and trans folk in their team, and a female manager. What have you got here? A fucking sausage fest."

"Wullie." Evan took his hand, which Ben now realized had been gesturing toward him and Jamie.

Allan had clearly noticed. "Why are you pointing at them when you talk?"

Ben shoved his hands between his knees. "I was pointing toward Glasgow. Which we are all from." Oh God, he'd dropped the accent, too. "Which we-we're all fae."

"Cumbernauld, actually," Jamie corrected. "It's miles better."

Thom was staring hard at Evan's face. "It's him."

"Who?" Allan asked.

"Evan Fucking Hollister. Poacher prick extraordinaire."

With a sigh, Evan took off his hat. "Look, I can explain."

"This better be good." Thom leaned over and lowered his voice to a growl. "Cos if I tell the rest of these Greens supporters who you are, you'll be drawn and quartered faster than you can say, 'I'm a whore to mainstream values.'"

Ben tried to remember whether they'd agreed on a cover story in the event of exposure. Evan's hesitation told him they had not.

"He's not here to poach," Ben said. "He's here to make you an offer."

Chapter 14

"WHATEVER IT IS, the answer's no."

"Just hear me out." Evan stood on the pitch in front of his old nemesis Martin Gibson, hoping today's victory had put the Glasgow Greens manager in a receptive mood. Thom and Allan—currently lurking in the stand ten feet away, glaring down like ravenous seagulls—had scoffed at Ben's brilliant idea, but it had kept them from outing Evan and Jamie to the rest of the fans.

"You've got ten seconds," Gibson said.

Evan put on his warmest tone. "I'd like to invite you to play a friendly match with the Warriors."

The manager gaped at him. "Why?"

"For charity," Evan said. "And for a chance to spotlight the gay football league. A lot of people think Warriors are the only LGBTQ team in the country, and we'd like to correct that misconception."

Gibson started to nod, then looked away, scratching at his red-blond stubble. "Why isn't your manager asking me herself?"

Because Charlotte didn't know about it until I phoned her ten minutes ago with Ben's idea, and then she was too furious to speak at all. "She wanted to," Evan said, "but I asked her to let me come." He took off his cap in a gesture of humility. "It should be me offering the olive branch, since I harmed you in past seasons."

The manager squinted at Evan's face, then at the hat he was symbolically clutching. "Why the disguises?"

"I wanted to be sure your lads were good enough to play us," Evan said, figuring a bit of infamous Hollister arrogance would lend some authenticity. "They definitely are."

"Thanks," Gibson said with heavy sarcasm. "We're pure honored."

"We should've reached out sooner, but our team has been in disarray after Colin MacDuff was nearly killed."

The manager's face softened. "Poor lad. He was our best player by a million miles."

"Ours, too." Evan took a step away, wanting to leave the discussion on a note of connection. "I'll let you think it over, talk to your team."

"Tell Charlotte I'll phone her when we decide." Gibson made a shooing motion toward the park exit. "Now gonnae get out of my sight."

Evan made his way back to Jamie and Ben. "A solid maybe," he told them.

"I'm so, so sorry for blowing your cover," Ben said as they made a hasty exit from the park. "I ruined everything."

"'Ruined'?" Jamie said with a laugh. "Seeing their faces when Thom and Allen recognized us was the best part of the day. That's how boring that match was."

Ben goggled at him. "But they said mean things about you."

"Nothing that wasnae true." Jamie shrugged. "Footballers get slagged off all the time. It's worth it for the extra sex—I mean, for the love of the fans."

On the drive back to Glasgow, Evan did his best to keep up with Ben and Jamie's road-trip banter, even getting in a few pelters himself at his own expense. But most of his mind was working over what had just happened in Edinburgh.

His primary concern wasn't Ben's big mouth. Robert had

already warned him about that. If anything, Evan was in awe of Ben's ability to think on his feet. Though his bright idea would complicate the Warriors' lives, a charity friendly match with the Greens was long overdue.

What bothered Evan most were the things Thom and Allan had said about him and the Warriors. Were they beacons of hope or exploiters of their own sexualities? Had their high standards become a form of snobbery? Evan had always thought he was supporting equality by making the Warriors successful, but maybe he'd sacrificed other values on the altar of excellence.

Perhaps his attitude from work had carried over into football. If things went wrong in his job, people died. Compared to that, relegation to a lower league hardly seemed worth worrying about.

He pulled out his phone to review the text conversation with Jordan he'd held during the match:

GUNNAR

Back in Glasgow now. Any work for me?

JORDAN

sorry M8 not now

looked at other places but their not so easy

Evan interpreted that to mean it would be harder to carry out an attack against a same-sex wedding at a venue where Jordan didn't work. Hopefully that difficulty would put him off the whole business for good.

Moving on to other projects?

lol yeah check this

Attached to that message was a BVP flyer for an anti-immigration rally in Glasgow next Saturday, the same one Kay had asked Evan to attend as Gunnar.

> Cool. Might have work that day but will try to come

thx going back to our roots gotta mind the real enemy

At the end of the message he'd included a string of emojis: a mosque, a red circle with a line through it, then several downward-pointing arrows.

Evan frowned, wondering whether he was ready for this hate rally. Until now, his undercover work had mostly been one-on-one with a single target. Fitting in with a crowd of suspicious-minded folk required a whole other level of craftiness than being one gullible person's fake friend.

Glancing up from his phone, Evan noticed they were entering Glasgow and the car had fallen silent. He checked the backseat to see Jamie with his head drooped forward, mouth slack, strands of sandy hair dangling over his cheeks.

"When did he fall asleep?" Evan whispered.

"About a minute after you checked out of the conversation." Ben's voice was as tight as his grip on the steering wheel. "I can't believe you're not raging. I convinced you to trust me, and I wasn't worthy of that trust. I'll never forgive myself, and I totally understand if you never want to see me again."

Evan snorted. "Is this your way of never seeing *me* again?"

"What? No! Why would I want that?"

"After what those lads said at the park, about me being a snob and a poacher—"

"They were full of pish. Look, I meant what I said to those judgmental knobs. What you're doing is important *because* it's different, *because* it's harder. Your job isn't to make bad players good, it's to make good players great. Never apologize for that." Ben tilted his head. "Unless you were an arse about it, in which case I don't approve."

Evan didn't laugh. "I tried not to be. When I rejected players, I told them face to face. I gave feedback on how they could improve and encouraged them to try again. Like Colin—he didn't pass his first Warriors trial, but he worked hard with the Greens, then came back to us and got in the team."

"See? You're a good guy. In fact, in this scenario you're a good guy pretending to be a bad guy for a great cause."

The thought made Evan's head reel. It bothered him that Ben was so determined to see the best in him. Then it bothered him that it bothered him. What was he afraid of?

Being found out, of course. Evan may not be the villain most people thought him to be, but he was certainly no hero either.

"WHAT IF, at each place setting, we use a different color ribbon to tie the menu to the napkin?"

"It would reinforce the rainbow theme." Ben switched on his kitchen kettle, glad that Candice couldn't see the look on his face. He was used to clients coming up with new ideas mere days before the wedding, but his schedule between now and Saturday was tighter than the jeans he'd worn to the Grand Ole Opry.

"Ooh, we could use those fancy curly ribbons!" Candice's tone verged on manic, and Ben worried she was suffering prenuptial insomnia.

Ribbons don't come in "curly," he thought with a frown. *They have to be made that way by hand. By* my *hands.* "I'll phone the venue and see if I can get napkins and menus after Friday night's rehearsal."

"Brilliant! It won't be a bother?"

"Of course not." Folding 126 napkins, tying them to 126 menus, then curling 126 ribbons should keep him up only until… och, one or two a.m. He really needed an assistant, but as this was his last wedding, what was the point?

After contacting the venue, Ben sat before his computer with a fresh cup of tea, almost relieved to focus on uni work instead of work-work. Each was a means of procrastination for the other.

For his dissertation he'd downloaded a new program called WhoWhatWhere. The software supposedly used basic identifiers like name and number to produce a report delineating the last few months of someone's life. Ben thought it would be illustrative to compare the profile of a social-media butterfly like himself to that of a hermit like Evan.

He entered his name and number, then clicked retrieve. "Wow."

On the screen before him was a dispassionate display of Ben's gallivanting about Glasgow: posting pics of himself here, rendezvousing with a hottie there, checking in here *and* there, and basically advertising his whereabouts nearly every moment of every day. In other words, having a life.

The first tab showed a map, which shaded the most common destinations. There was nothing unexpected there, so he clicked on the INTERESTS tab:

- *Education*
  - *Formal events*
  - *Curling*
  - *Gay nightlife*
  - *Country and Western music*

"Where you go is who you are," his advisor had once said. This theory was basically the foundation of Ben's entire field.

He'd known his phone was a massive repository of open-source intelligence, and that his number linked to his email and social-media usernames. This program had simply gathered the data Ben had put into the world, turning it into an elegant report that any intelligence agency or marketing firm would kill for. Though not a surprise, it still felt a bit creepy.

What bothered him most wasn't what was included, but rather what was missing: his faith. The report contained no record of him attending a Bahá'í devotional meeting or even a study circle to discuss the words of the prophet Bahá'u'lláh. The Glasgow Bahá'í community numbered only in the dozens, so he'd been close to several members. Like Mum, they didn't condemn his sexuality per se, but they were definitely not chuffed about his wedding activities.

What would they think of this...thing he had with Evan? Would they be sad like his mum? Would they cite their leaders in the Universal House of Justice, who claimed that support for same-sex relationships was a symptom of society's degradation?

Ben switched programs and brought up his copy of the letter the UHJ had released last year on the matter. It had so outraged him he'd read it only once—skimmed it, really, to keep his eyes from burning—and never opened it again. Looking back, he realized it was this edict that had led him to stop going to prayer group and eventually to stop praying at all.

He read it again now, feeling the urge to look through his fingers like a kid watching a scary movie.

Of course it emphasized how wrong it was to persecute or discriminate against people of a "homosexual orientation" and said that gay Bahá'ís shouldn't withdraw from the community but rather should be supported by it. But it also reminded Bahá'ís that premarital sex and same-sex acts were strictly forbidden.

And then there was this, in case Ben might hope for some wriggle room:

To accept Bahá'u'lláh is to accept His Teachings, including those that pertain to personal morality, even if one must struggle to live up to His standard. It would be a profound contradiction for someone to profess to be a Bahá'í, yet reject, disregard, or contend with aspects of belief or practice He ordained.

Ben read those lines five times, then reread the entire letter twice before closing the document and leaping up from his chair, as though he could somehow escape the truth by walking away from the computer.

According to his mum, he'd been allowed to stay in the Faith despite all of his Grindr hookups, because those encounters had been "discreet." Yet now that he might have found something real and powerful, *that* could get him chucked out of their community? It made no sense.

As he heated more water for tea, a new and horrible thought occurred to him: Perhaps he'd lied to Evan. Perhaps Ben's anonymous hookups had felt okay not because he was helping those lads find peace, but because they were *secret*. They hadn't forced him to choose between his faith and his sexuality.

Evan was anything but secret. They'd slow-danced together in public, an act that had terrified and thrilled Ben to his core.

Could Evan be the one to take him into the light? Was Evan worth it? After two dates, Ben had no way to know.

The kettle dinged, and just like that, it came to him: He *did* have a way to know more about Evan, a way to take a wee peek at the mysterious book of that man's life.

Ben went back to his computer and reopened the WhoWhat-Where software. Then he reconsidered. This data was all open-source and therefore publicly available, but he felt like a stalker checking up on Evan's activities.

He reviewed their private communications—what there was of them. Though Evan had accepted Ben's Facebook friend request, he never seemed available to chat there, and he'd still not added a new post since Christmas.

Their text conversations were a bit more fruitful, like this one from the previous week:

BEN

Fave band?

EVAN

Franz Ferdinand

!?! I expected something less bouncy. Something darker

FF have their dark moments. Some lyrics are
pure Glaswegian despair

But they're darkness you can dance to

Darkness you MUST dance to

Evan had gone on to explain how when he was a teenager,
growing up different to everyone around him, Franz Ferdinand
had made him feel less alone, less weird, less afraid to come out
and be himself.

Their music was sorta gay when I was accepting
being totally gay.

So Evan wasn't paranoid about opening up. Perhaps his
barely-there social-media presence was down to his demanding
schedule.

Ben decided on a compromise, setting the report to its most
basic output: simple location tracking. He wouldn't delve into
Evan's interests or other personal information.

*I just want to see where he goes every day. I deserve to know what
the man I'm dating does for a living, right?*

Ben entered Evan's name and number and hit search. The
hourglass on the screen flipped over once, then twice, then a third
time. Then a fourth time.

Finally the results page came up. The map was much emptier
than his own. There were gaps in coverage every weekday
between seven a.m., when Evan left his flat near George Square,
and four-thirty p.m., when he reappeared either there or at a gym
in the Merchant City area.

His workday—the very thing Ben wanted to explore—was
completely blacked out.

Where do you go? Ben wondered. *And what do you do when you
get there?*

Chapter 15

EVAN HAD SPENT the last two hours getting into character. He'd listened to Gunnar Einarsson's favorite Scandinavian death-metal bands—on earphones, so as not to scare Trent—while applying his neatly trimmed beard, inch by inch, using an advanced silicon-based adhesive that wouldn't dissolve even in this morning's drizzle.

Yet despite Gunnar's sympathy for the British Values Party, when Evan arrived at their "Value our Britishness" anti-immigration rally, he was relieved to see they were far outnumbered by pro-immigrant counter-protesters.

He stopped for a moment on the street corner, pretending to answer his phone.

"All stations from Zero Two," he said into the microphone on his jacket cuff. "Eyes on Backspace and Alt-Tab. Visual signals only, going forward."

Detective Sergeant Fowles's radio crackled. "Copy that, Zero Two," she said. "Good luck. Zero One out."

Evan tugged down his knit cap to be sure the earpiece was covered, then pushed through a group of protesters, hoping that none of them knew him in real life. At least Ben was halfway across the city preparing for a wedding.

At the march's gathering point, Jordan stood near the unfurling BVP banner. He brightened when he spied Evan.

Jordan clomped over in his combat boots, beaming like a kid whose best friend had just showed up at his birthday party. "Thanks for coming!" he said, as always speaking loudly and slowly, as though Gunnar wasn't fluent in English like most Norwegians.

"Thanks for inviting me." Evan waved a dismissive hand at the counter-protesters. "Who are all these people who hate free speech?"

"Och, they always show up—and more of 'em each time. These leftists reproduce like rats, just like the people they think they're helping. Here, sign." He handed Evan the clipboard. "Fill in my name where it asks how you heard of us."

Do you get a free autographed Mussolini poster for every ten referrals? Evan flipped up the plastic sheet protector and wrote Gunnar's information. "Who did you mean, 'the people they *think* they're helping'?"

"Immigrants," Jordan said. "They're better off going back where they come fae. Some of those countries are pure shite, but at least they fit in there. Everyone's got a place in the world, and Britain can't be that place for everyone, know what I mean?" His eyes widened. "Nah, I don't mean you, mate. I'm not against, like, all immigration. Just for the yins who cannae…you know."

"Assimilate?"

"Aye. It's about values." He pointed to the word on the BVP banner. "How do you say, 'value' in Norwegian?"

"*Moral*." Evan emphasized the second syllable. "Spelled like in English."

"That's brilliant, man." He took back the clipboard and flapped it like a wing. "I pure love how many words are the same in both languages. It proves our ancestors were badass Vikings."

Instead of delving into linguistic history, Evan pointed to the tall, blandly good-looking blond standing behind Jordan speaking into a radio. "Who's that?" he asked, though he already knew.

"That's the yin started all this. Oi, David, here's the Norwegian lad I telt you about."

"Base out," the man said into the radio, then tucked it under his arm and extended a hand to Evan. "David Wallace. Gunnar Einarsson, right?" As they shook, he tugged Evan closer and spoke in a low voice. "I confess I looked you up to be sure you are who you say. Impressive history."

"Mmm." Evan gave the standard Norwegian modesty shrug. He knew the BVP had already checked up on him, according to the agents who'd been put in place to reinforce his cover. Gunnar's "impressive history" included a loose association with a right-wing fringe group, as well as an egregious lapse in child-maintenance payments for his three-year-old son—whose mother was the girlfriend who'd left him for another woman.

David turned to Jordan. "Be a good lad and pass around the signs, would you?"

Jordan's smile faded, but he did as he was asked, scooping up a pile of the placards and making his way toward the marchers.

"I've been dying to meet you," David said to Evan. "Making international connections is crucial to our long-term vision." Despite the Scottish surname, Wallace hailed from Birmingham in the English Midlands, though he had but a moderate "Brummie" accent, with just a hint of the singsongy quality.

"How so?" Evan asked.

"It's all about bringing our ideas into the mainstream. We'll be more accepted if regular folk can see we're part of a global movement. Gotta trade boots for suits, know what I mean?"

Evan knew what he meant but wanted to hear and record more, so he put a hand to his ear. "Heh? Sometimes I hear English wrong in loud places."

"Sorry, mate." Wallace spoke more slowly. "We need fewer guys who look like that." He tilted his head toward a cluster of Jordan's leather-clad skinhead friends, their thick, bare arms adorned with fascist-coded tattoos. "And more guys who look like you and me."

Evan mirrored his smirk, hiding his own dismay. Wallace was more dangerous than he'd thought. While Jordan fitted the neo-Nazi stereotype, Wallace looked like he'd just stepped off a Marks & Spencer business-casualwear display. No doubt this media-friendly "everyman" would soon be on TV making seemingly civilized arguments for mass deportations.

"Look at these protesters, Gunnar," David said. "What do you see?"

Evan scanned the crowd, which seemed composed mostly of university students. "I see a lot of naive young fools."

"And I see potential." David's clear green eyes took on a faraway look. "Any one of them could join us tomorrow."

Right, because they're white.

David pointed to the ground they stood on. "Mark my words, mate. This is where it starts."

"Gunnar!" Jordan was waving at him. "Come and meet my pals from the lodge."

Evan wanted to know what Wallace meant by *"This is where it starts,"* but one of his assigned priorities was to collect names of Orange Order members involved with the BVP. Mingling with Jordan's Orange associates—who were much more vanilla-looking than his skinhead mates—Evan tried to gain as much information and take as many photos with his lapel camera as he could without looking suspicious.

Finally the march began, moving up Buchanan Street. The throng of counter-protesters grew in size and passion, over-flowing the pavement despite police efforts to corral them.

A few marchers bailed in the face of opposition, worried their pictures might be posted online and lose them jobs, customers, or friends. Jordan railed at each deserter, calling them cowards, while Evan envied their escape. The humid air was making his fake facial hair itch even more than usual. He longed to yank it off and go home—or better yet, join the protesters.

They neared the rally point at the top of Buchanan Street, where a podium had been set up for the BVP speakers. Here the crowd of counter-protesters was at its thickest and fiercest, forced to stay on one side of the street so the BVPers could take the other side.

Tucking his chin to hide his face as much as possible, Evan scanned the participants. At this end of the road, the protesters were a more diverse group of all ages and ethnicities. They were modern-day Scotland—or at least modern-day Glasgow.

His gaze froze on one face, towering above the others. *You've got to be kidding me.*

Standing across the street, holding a sign reading IMMIGRANTS MAKE US GREAT, was none other than Evan's ex-boyfriend Fergus. Beside him stood his husband, John, waving a sign and chanting at the top of his voice.

Evan pulled out his phone and frowned at it. "It's my boss," he told Jordan.

The lad's eyes flashed with annoyance. "You're not going to work, are you? We're outnumbered here."

"No, it's about a job tonight. I'll be right back."

Evan ducked into an alleyway and put the phone to his ear. "Zero One, do you read? Zero Two," he said, identifying himself into the police radio transmitter.

"Go ahead," said DS Fowles.

"Just spotted a close associate. Highly likely I'll be recognized. Require strategic extraction."

"Roger that," DS Fowles replied. "Zero Two, can you make an excuse and leave?"

"Negative," Evan replied, thinking of Jordan's fury at the others who'd abandoned the rally. "Can you arrest me? Forcibly, if possible?" He recited his exact position.

"Zero Two, I'd be delighted. Heading your way now with a two-man tactical team who know the score. Once I'm in position, come at me and pretend you're going for a weapon. Then I'll…"

Evan waited for her to finish the sentence. "Zero One, I did not copy that. You'll what?"

"I'll stop you," she said. "Forcibly."

"Take me down fast, before anyone can get a photo of me. And don't use a baton."

"I wouldnae hit you for real," Deirdre said, sounding insulted.

"I know." Still, the BVP guys would lose respect for him if he got battered by a woman, even one as formidably built as DS Fowles. More importantly, Evan wasn't sure he could stop himself fighting back. "No baton."

Deirdre sighed. "Copy that. Apologies in advance, and I promise you'll be feeling better in no time. Zero One out."

Evan scowled at his phone as he returned to Jordan and David. "My boss, she's such a...how do you say, bawfaced cow?"

They laughed, then Jordan asked, "How do *you* say 'bawfaced cow,' like in Norwegian?"

Evan thought a moment. "Literal translation would be something like *pungtryne ku*, but a closer equivalent would be *jævla hore*, which means 'fucking whore.'"

They dutifully repeated the slur to themselves. Gunnar basked in their admiration while Evan silently apologized to women everywhere.

Deirdre arrived, flanked by a pair of uniformed officers. As she stopped in the middle of the street, the cops positioned themselves on either side, taking wide stances to look more intimidating.

"Right, then." DS Fowles and one officer turned to face the BVP folk while the other faced the counter-protesters. "I need you all to please take ten steps back."

Evan stepped forward and gestured to the opposition. "Why do we have to move and they don't? There's more of them."

Jordan stepped up beside him, to Evan's dismay. "Aye, and we're the ones with the permit."

"Sirs, would you please move back?" Deirdre's voice was low and calming, honed through her years on the street.

Meeting Deirdre's gaze, Evan took another long step forward, hoping Fergus was too far away to see through his disguise.

"Last warning, sir." Deirdre held out her left palm as her right hand moved to her belt.

Evan gauged the distance between them. One more step and he'd be inside her reaction gap, where she'd have to defend herself.

"C'mon, mate," Jordan said behind him. "She's not worth—"

"This is *your* last warning," Evan told Deirdre as he moved forward, reaching inside his jacket.

Her right hand came up.

"Mate!" Jordan shouted.

Evan didn't see the spear-thin blast of chemical spray before it hit his face. But the sudden, blinding fire stopped him in his tracks.

"Fuuuuuuuuuu*aaaaaaaeeeenn*!" Somehow he managed to switch languages mid-scream. *"Faen! Faaaaaaen!"*

His knees went suddenly weak. He dropped onto the stone pavement, wishing he could claw his own face off. Despite his spectacles, his eyes gushed tears so hot and thick they felt like blood.

"Din jævla hore!" he shrieked. *"Brenn i helvete, din jævla hore!"*

"Sir, you're suffering the temporary effects of PAVA spray," Deirdre said as she handcuffed him. "Keep your eyes closed and try to breathe normally. We're gonnae put you in the police van, and you'll be feeling better in about twenty minutes."

Behind him, the BVP guys were now chanting, *"Jævla hore! Jævla hore!"* at the top of their voices.

As the cops helped Evan to his feet, Deirdre recited the reason for his arrest and the fact his words could be used in evidence. "Do you understand?" she concluded.

Evan nodded, wondering whether she secretly enjoyed bringing an MI5 officer to his knees. Surely DI Hayward would have a laugh when he found out.

When they were alone in the back of the police van with the door shut, Deirdre uncuffed him and pushed a box of tissues into his hands. "Sorry, mate, but you did say no baton. Mind, don't wipe your face."

"Thanks for the rescue." Keeping his eyes shut, he blew his nose, careful not to rub his skin. "Also, I hate you forever."

"That's fair." There was the sound of paper rustling, then the click of a pen. "Now tell me the names of everyone you met and anything else you can remember about them."

Good idea. Evan had planned to write the information in a report once he got back to the office today, but recounting it now would take his mind off the pain.

When they finished the list, Deirdre asked, "By the way, what did you call me? In Norwegian, after I sprayed you?"

He couldn't bring himself to translate *jævla hore*—his gran would have definitely disapproved. "*Brenn i helvete* means, 'Burn in hell.'"

"Before that, I mean," Deirdre said, now in banter mode. "Cos it kinda sounded like you called me a whore."

"Technically, Gunnar called you a whore." His voice was still clogged with tears. "And those fascists loved it, so, mission accomplished."

"Huzzah." Deirdre was silent for a moment. "It's great they were outnumbered by counter-protesters, but that can't make us complacent. For every dunderhead who showed up at this rally, there's dozens more at home spreading lies online."

"More like thousands." Evan coughed hard, his throat spasming at the spray's residual fumes. "This is only the beginning."

CLYDE HOUSE WAS NEARLY empty when Evan stepped out of the security capsule into the MI5 office. During his hour-long stay at the police station, his eyes had stopped burning, as Deirdre had promised, but his cheeks still felt raw from the spray-induced tears and the subsequent removal of his fake beard.

Ned got up from his desk to greet him. "Och, the state of your face." He tugged the sleeve of the baggy flannel shirt the police had given Evan after removing his PAVA-contaminated jacket and top. "The lumberjack look's not bad, though."

"Thanks, I think." He drew a hand through his damp hair, where he felt a few remnants of Gunnar's gel. "I'll need another shower when I get home. First, though…" Evan looked toward his own desk.

"Write a report." Ned patted his arm. "I just made coffee. You want some?"

"More than anything in the world." Evan started toward his desk, then caught sight of the three monitors at Ned's work station. One of the screens was showing the news. He wandered over to see if his altercation at the rally had been documented by a journalist. He hoped not.

Instead the BBC featured the same disturbing report Evan had first seen this morning. He'd been too focused on becoming Gunnar for it to sink in at the time.

Ned approached with their coffees. "Sad about Boris Nemtsov."

"Not to mention suspicious." Evan took his cup and gestured to the shot of Moscow's Moskvoretsky Bridge, where a prominent opponent of the Russian president had been assassinated the previous night. "Directly in front of the Kremlin, just to show they can get away with it."

"And the CCTV cameras there just happened to be offline for servicing." Ned sank into his creaking chair and folded his arms over his tea-stained tan cardigan. "Remember the good old days when we all thought Nemtsov would become President?"

"Sort of. I was ten at the time."

"Thanks, now I feel old."

"I remember because in December 1999 it was my mum's turn to have me and my sister for Christmas, but we begged to spend the holidays with our dad so we could be in London for the big Y2K celebration."

Ned laughed. "And Boris Yeltsin ruined it by stepping down on New Year's Eve."

"Exactly. My father lost his mind, like, 'Why is this absolute nobody, Putin, suddenly president of Russia?' Justine and I were left watching fireworks on TV while Dad ran off to Thames House for an emergency meeting."

No doubt that's exactly where Hugh Hollister was right now, trying to work out what Nemtsov's murder could mean for Russian activities on British soil. Putin had dozens of friends and enemies in the UK, and several of the latter had already died of mysterious causes.

Evan went to his desk, where he switched on his computer and both monitors. Ned's mention of CCTV cameras had given him an idea. Within a minute he was watching a live shot of the street outside St. Andrew's in the Square, the eighteenth-century classical-style former church where Ben's wedding would soon take place.

Fortunately, Glasgow's CCTV network had been upgraded before last summer's Commonwealth Games. *Un*fortunately, coverage of the city was still spotty, with the lion's share of cameras mounted in the central shopping districts or on streets packed with nightclubs and pubs. Near St. Andrew's Square, there was but one CCTV lookout, and its pair of cameras pointed only up and down the pavement, not at the building itself.

He left the two viewpoints up on his second monitor, then began writing his report of the day's events.

Gunnar's phone buzzed in his pocket.

JORDAN

u ok?

Evan looked at the clock. Enough time had passed that he could have realistically been released by the police.

GUNNAR

Fine now. No charges just a caution since I didn't have a weapon. How was the rally?

> David gave a brilliant speech could barely hear him over the rockets screaming

Evan calculated whether Gunnar would recognize the slang.

> rockets???

> Sorry rocket means idiot. Talking about the protesters. None of them got arrested obvs

> obvs means obviously

> I know. Anyway the rally was great. Can I have David's number to thank him for making me feel welcome?

After a minute's pause:

> you can talk to him thru me

Evan smirked. The lad was jealous, probably worried about being cut out of the loop. Classwise, Gunnar had more common with the BVP chairman than Jordan did.

> I'll say good things about you

Jordan immediately texted back with David's number, which Evan in turn entered into a warrant-request form for phone surveillance.

Boom. A good day's work.

By the time he'd finished requesting the warrant, the CCTVs on his second monitor showed wedding guests arriving at St. Andrew's. Evan turned his full attention to the images.

Directly in front of the former church was a bus lane, part of which served as the venue's loading bay, in which vehicles could stop but not park. Soon two white luxury cars appeared there, a Rolls Royce and a sleek Jaguar. A bride stepped out of each car, their views of each other blocked by huge black umbrellas. Evan smiled, imagining the umbrellas were Ben's clever idea to keep the brides from seeing each other before the ceremony.

Shortly after the nuptials began at two o'clock, the street outside St. Andrew's was empty apart from regular traffic and stray pedestrians. Evan took note of each car, confirming it continued on its way and didn't return for a second pass.

At a quarter past two, a small white SUV pulled into the loading bay where the brides' cars had been. An entire minute passed, and no one got out. Evan strained to see how many people were inside, but the tinted windscreen obscured his view.

"Ned, have you got a second?"

"Barely." Ned looked at his watch as he strolled over. "My daughter's match is at three, and it's a half hour from here. She's starting in goal for the first time today."

"Well done, her." Evan took a screen grab and zoomed in on the SUV's yellow registration plate. "I need to identify this, but the image is too fuzzy at this distance." He knew that unlike on TV, a photo's resolution couldn't be "enhanced," as no fancy program could add pixels that weren't there to begin with. But he also knew that Ned had software which could interpret letters and numerals from much vaguer patterns than the human eye could discern. "Can we get a reasonable guess?"

Ned bent over, putting on his glasses to peer at the image. "Ooft, that's a rough one, but I might be able to give you a list of permutations—a long list—which you can then try to match to that vehicle." He straightened up. "Does Kay know you're doing live surveillance on your own?"

"Well, I'm not really on my own, am I?" When Ned harrumphed, Evan said, "C'mon, mate. Just this once, for my peace of mind." After a pause he added, "I'll give wee Lindsay an hour of goalkeeper drills."

Ned sighed. "Make it two hours and I'll run the reg plate myself." He headed for his desk. "Send me the image."

While Ned worked his magic—with his much faster computer

—Evan watched the SUV do absolutely nothing. With every motionless minute, his pulse sped up another notch, as he wondered what sort of weapon the vehicle might contain and whether Ben might soon be on the receiving end of it.

To make matters worse, the sky was clearing. According to Evan's research, the wedding party and guests had to leave the main room after the ceremony so the St. Andrew's staff could set it up for the reception. During rain or cold, everyone gathered in the downstairs cafe; but when the weather was fine, people ventured out front for photos upon the picturesque portico featuring the city's crest and motto, LET GLASGOW FLOURISH, upon the tympanum at its peak.

The portico barely twenty feet from that SUV.

Chapter 16

BEN STOOD to the side of St. Andrew's, watching with pride as Lauren and Candice held hands and gazed into each other's eyes. Thanks to him, they were able to think only about the love they shared and not about whether the wee pageboy would eat their wedding rings.

Just as they exchanged said rings, the clouds parted outside. Sunlight streamed through the stained-glass windows, provoking a collective gasp of awe. Ben exchanged a jubilant glance with the photographer, who was no doubt chuffed they'd be able to take pictures outdoors on the portico.

The moment's excitement paled next to Ben's anticipation of tonight. He and Evan had a late dinner planned, followed by a birthday breakfast tomorrow at Ben's favorite West End "bruncheria," after which Evan allegedly had something "very important" to tell him. Maybe he'd read Ben's mind and knew that all he wanted for his pseudo-birthday was the not-so-pseudo-truth.

The ceremony was nearing the end, so Ben moved toward the entrance, where he was met by the photographer's assistant. Together they swept open the doors at the exact instant the recessional music began, letting the fickle afternoon sunshine flood the path of the happy brides.

Lauren and Candice seemed to be floating on air as they came outside clutching each other's hands.

"We did it!" Lauren said with a whoop, throwing her arms around Ben's neck.

"Congratulations!" He gave her an air-kiss, careful not to muss her makeup, before being tugged into an embrace with a beaming Candice.

Ben felt a lump form in his throat as he carried out his post-ceremony duties. This could be the last time he'd arrange a receiving line, the last time he'd distribute bottles of blowing bubbles to guests, the last time he'd dissuade a flower girl from picking her nose during the photo shoot. Where else but in a wedding would he find such blithe hope for the future?

He stopped on the edge of the portico stairs, just now noticing the white SUV that had sat in the loading bay since...well, at least since the end of the ceremony. He'd thought it was picking up guests leaving before the reception, but no one had entered or left the vehicle since its arrival. Through the tinted windows he could barely make out two figures, one in each of the front seats.

"Deborah, we discussed this when we bought gowns," Lauren was telling her maid of honor. "If you wanted to stand closest to us in the photo, you had to choose the red bridesmaid dress instead of the green."

"And I telt you, gingers cannae wear red," Deborah shot back. "If I'd put that thing on me, the fire brigade would be hosing my wee arse down by now."

Ben's phone vibrated in his pocket. He pulled it out to see an unfamiliar number. He answered it anyway.

"This is Kevin with Merchant City Cake Masters," growled the voice on the line. "I've been circling the streets near St. Andrew's for twenty minutes and some fandan in a white SUV's stopped in the loading bay. Gonnae chase it away for me?"

"Absolutely. See you in a minute."

Ben had taken one step toward the nuisance vehicle when he heard Deborah's rising rage behind him.

"I'm your best mate!" she shouted, verging on tears. "Why should I be stuck halfway down the line like some meaningless cousin?"

"Cos that's how rainbows work!" Lauren said.

Ben glared at the SUV, then turned to deal with this emotional crisis. The baker could make another pass in his van if he had to. Right now Ben had to solve this impasse before the whole day was ruined.

EVAN STARED AT THE SCREEN, rocking his feet against the floor, waiting for help to arrive. After receiving the vehicle report from Ned—the SUV was registered to a car-hire company—Evan had done what any concerned citizen would do: He'd called the cops.

"The rental company will be much happier giving information to you than to MI5," he'd told Detective Inspector Hayward. *"We make people nervous."*

After some argument, Hayward had agreed to phone the company and send a patrol car to investigate the SUV—which, after all, was parked in a loading bay, considered by many Glaswegians to be a hanging offense.

"They should be there by now," he told Ned, who'd elected to stay until the end of their impromptu operation.

"From the way DI Hayward talked," Ned said, "we should be grateful they're sending anyone at all."

Evan gave a grunt of agreement. In his experience, police were understandably skeptical of MI5 instincts. Cops lived in a world of black and white, while spooks dwelled in ambiguity and uncertainty, relying on intuition to guide them. Gut instincts didn't hold up in front of a judge.

"Ever wish you could just arrest them yourself?" Ned asked.

Evan shook his head. "We know far too much to be trusted with that power. The day MI5 officers can bang up our own citizens is the day this country becomes a police state."

"Still. Must be maddening for a lad of your age and energy level to sit here in a windowless room while someone else swoops in and nicks the bad guys."

"As long as I know—"

Evan cut himself off as the SUV drove away.

"Check the other cameras in the area," he told Ned. "See if we can track it from here."

He picked up the phone to dial DI Hayward, then stopped and looked closer at the image. There was a slim man in a suit standing on the pavement, facing the departing SUV.

Ben.

Evan's gut flipped at this reminder of the stakes. "Get out of there," he whispered, though there was no rational reason to worry. It was just Evan's intuition again, warning that something was very, very wrong.

Ben spoke into his phone, then turned and walked out of the shot, back toward the venue.

Evan dialed Hayward's number. When the detective inspector answered, he said, "They're headed south on Turnbull Street. Can your officers intercept?"

"On what grounds?" Hayward asked. "That wee voice in the back of your head?"

Ned tapped Evan's shoulder. "Put him on speaker." When Evan did as he asked, Ned said, "If whoever's in that vehicle is a subject of interest but *not* an imminent threat, we shouldn't overtly pursue him. That would alert him and his associates we're aware of them. Investigation scuttled."

"I agree," Hayward said.

Evan was outnumbered. "What about *co*vert pursuit? Something more subtle."

"Sorry," Hayward said. "If you want tactical surveillance officers ready to jump into their cars at a moment's notice, you'll have to go to London."

Or back to Belfast. "So what can we do?" Evan asked.

"Gie's a second." Hayward's keyboard tapped in the background. "I'm having the dispatcher radio the uniformed officers who are already on their way. We'll have them patrol the St. Andrew's Square area for a while, see if anything else suspicious happens."

"Thanks." Evan let out a long exhalation. "What about the car-hire company?"

"Closed until Monday morning."

Evan's jaw clenched. For all its big-city bustle, sometimes Glasgow still felt like a backwater town.

His desk phone rang then, as did everyone else's. The call was coming in on the regional terrorism tips hotline. If no one here picked up after three rings, it would be forwarded to the twenty-four-hour UK-wide hotline at Thames House. Considering the callers were usually conspiracy-theory-addled crackpots, Evan never answered it when it wasn't his turn.

He answered it now.

"West of Scotland Anti-terrorism Hotline." Hunched over the phone at Lewis's desk, Evan listened to the caller take a deep breath, then another.

Finally a distorted voice gasped out three words that stopped his heart.

"Let. Glasgay. Perish."

BEN WAS STARTING to wish he'd hired an assistant, or better yet cloned himself. No sooner had he sorted the furious baker—who was finally able to park in the loading bay after the white Outlander had taken off at Ben's approach—than he was roped back into the rainbow crisis.

Together with the photographer, Ben settled the issue by suggesting two sets of wedding-party pictures: one with the colors in the scientifically correct order, and one with the maids of honor directly beside their brides. Everyone was happy with the compromise, until they'd all lined up and realized the yellow bridesmaid had gone missing.

As Ben charged back into the venue to hunt her down, cursing the way his new shoes were pinching his toes, he mentally recited the words his mother would say to clients after an unforeseen setback: *The important thing is, you got married and no one died.* The latter part was still up in the air, considering Ben had just rugby-tackled the pageboy to keep him from running into traffic.

When he got inside St. Andrew's, he stopped short. Half the chairs were still lined up in ceremony formation. By now they should have all been arranged round the tables with place settings being laid by stressed-out servers. Yet the only staff present were the venue manager and his assistant, up near the altar. The manager had his phone to his ear. As Ben approached, he caught the end of the conversation.

"—staff in pairs to search for suspicious items, like you asked. Yes, of course I told them not to touch anything. Now when will your officers be arriving?"

Ben looked at the assistant manager in alarm. She gave a tight shrug, fidgeting madly with the buttons of her white blazer.

Outside, a siren blared in the distance.

"That better be them now," the manager said into the phone. "Yes, I'm *trying* to remain calm. Let me go and do my job." He hung up.

"What's going on?" Ben asked.

The manager pocketed his phone. "There's been a bomb threat."

For a moment, Ben's mind blanked with fear. Then he said, "What can I do to help?"

"Go with Sydney here to search for any guests still in the building. Get them outside with the others, but don't frighten them. When the police arrive, they'll set up a cordon outside, and I'll need your help corralling people behind it without starting a panic."

"So we're not telling them the truth?" Ben asked.

"The police say that the more information gets out to the wider public, the harder it'll be to investigate. And if it's a hoax—which it probably is—the attention just rewards the hoaxer. People only need to know enough to be safe." He gestured to the door to the hallway. "If you don't mind."

Ben went with the assistant manager down the empty hall, which echoed with the clop of Sydney's shoes. "The catering staff's already evacuated," she said.

He glanced into the kitchen, noting food sitting out on the work surfaces. The aroma of roasted lamb and potatoes was a poignant mockery of the dire situation.

As they passed the cleaning-supplies cupboard, Ben heard a noise inside.

"What was that?" He stopped and put his ear to the door, barely able to hear the rustling within over the pounding of his pulse.

Sydney tried the knob, but it was locked. With trembling hands, she found the key on her fob and opened the door.

"Oh!" She stepped back to reveal the yellow bridesmaid adjusting the straps of her dress while her partner fumbled to refasten his belt.

"There you are," Ben said to the bridesmaid. "Hurry outside now. They're taking wedding-party photos."

"Sorry." The yellow lass grabbed her sparkly bag from the floor and dashed past him.

Ben turned to the man, who was married to one of Lauren's cousins. "You should go out the back exit so no one suspects." He pointed down the hall. "Quickly now."

After the man stumbled out, mumbling an apology, Ben and Sydney continued their search for stragglers.

"Do they know where the bomb is?" he asked her.

"That's the problem, see." Sydney's voice shook. "The police said it could be inside, or the threat could have been a ploy to get people *outside* so they could be attacked there."

"Oh my God."

"But most of the guests were already out front when the threat was phoned in. So the police reckon they would've already been attacked if that was the plan."

This was all so unreal. Ben thought of the white Outlander parked in the loading bay. He wished he'd had time to see the faces of the two people inside, or to memorize the registration number on the SUV's plate. "What did the threat say? Why are they after us?"

She shook her head. "Not a clue."

They finished their search, finding no more guests. When he at last stepped outside to join the wedding party, Ben discovered a quartet of uniformed police officers setting up a cordon far from the building. While two of them unrolled the boundary tape, the other two patiently herded people toward the southern side of the square.

Ben had an idea. He approached the photographer and said, "Mate, why don't we take the wedding party down to Glasgow Green for some fun pics in the park? It'll be a good distraction. Maybe some of the guests will follow, rather than glaring at the officers doing their jobs."

The photographer and Ben posed the idea to the brides, who decided to turn the five-minute walk into a procession of sorts. The wedding party got into it, cheering and tossing invisible rice at the couple as they made their way down the pavement. Ben silently thanked God for giving him such level-headed clients.

More police cars passed, followed by a Strathclyde Fire and Rescue truck. Under the noise of sirens, Ben heard his phone ring.

He answered Evan's call. "You won't believe what just happened."

"Are you safe?" Evan asked.

"Well, currently we're—wait, are we on TV?"

"No. Are you safe?"

"Then how did you know about—"

"Answer me!"

"Yes, I'm safe." Ben swallowed, his throat suddenly dry.

"Everyone's out, and I assume the bomb squad or whatever is going in now. But how did you know?"

Evan let out a hard breath. "Can you come over tonight? Not sure what time yet. I might need to work even later than you."

"Come over?" Ben felt a strange warmth mixed with fear. "You'll actually tell me where you live?"

"Aye." After a long pause, Evan said, "I'll tell you everything."

Chapter 17

EVAN PACED his living room floor, fidgeting with the buttons of his shirt, a soft blue Henley he'd chosen for this occasion. He wanted to look respectable but non-threatening when he told Ben the truth.

Assuming Ben ever showed up. He'd sent no reply to Evan's *all clear please come* text message containing his home address. After today's weirdness, Evan wouldn't blame him for staying far, far away.

No bomb had been found at St. Andrew's, so the wedding reception had finally been allowed to proceed, once the police had questioned all those present—including Ben—about what they'd seen and heard.

MI5 and Police Scotland weren't yet certain it had all been a hoax. Threats were often phoned in not by the perpetrators but rather an innocent associate or even a conspirator having second thoughts. Or perhaps the men in the white Outlander had planned to shoot or stab the evacuees but had chickened out without telling the person who'd phoned in the tip.

The call itself had been made from an untraceable burner phone, but its signal had pinged off a mobile tower near St. Andrew's, so theoretically the people in the SUV could have made the call themselves. But why? Certainly a bomb threat would instill fear, but not as much as an actual attack.

Now his task was to explain all this to Ben. During this evening's debriefing, Kay had reviewed exactly what Evan could reveal about what had happened today, about his job in general, and about his past ops. He hoped he could resist sharing more than he should, but Ben's eyes had a way of tearing down Evan's well-honed defenses.

By now, Trent had stopped following him back and forth and was sitting on the arm of the couch watching him pace, occasionally batting him as he passed by.

His mobile rang with the number for his building's security system. He answered, nearly dropping his phone before it could reach his ear.

"It's me," said a terse voice. "It's Ben."

Evan entered the code to unlock the building's entrance, then hurried to put Trent into the bedroom. "Sorry, lass, it's just for a few minutes," he told her as he shut her inside.

He went back to watch through the peephole. When Ben's form appeared to the left through the fish-eye lens, Evan opened the door as slowly and calmly as he could manage.

Ben stopped several feet away. "Hi," he said, barely above a whisper. He'd changed clothes since this afternoon, but his hair was mussed from the wind and his eyes drooped at the corners with what looked like exhaustion.

"I'm glad you came," Evan said.

Ben examined the open doorway like it was the entrance to Dante's Inferno, but then stepped across the threshold and into the narrow foyer. "Where's Trent?"

A loud mew answered from behind the bedroom door.

So Ben had recognized him as Gunnar from the start. Either he'd hidden his awareness well or Evan hadn't looked for clues, wanting to believe his cover was intact so he could go on protecting Ben.

"Trent's right here." He opened the bedroom door. The cat

dashed out and wound round Ben's legs in a figure-of-eight. "She's happy to see you."

Ben crouched down to pet her. "Trent's a girl?"

"I wasn't lying when I said I had a female cat."

Ben gave him a look that said, *But you lied about everything else.*

Evan briefed him on Trent's veterinary adventures, then asked, "Can I take your coat?"

Ben seemed to think about it, then shrugged it off and hung it on a wall peg. "You're about to tell me a very good story, aren't you?"

"A true story."

"Hmph." On his way to the living room, Ben peered into the bedroom and bathroom as though checking for an ambush. Then he sat on the couch, but on the edge of the seat, placing his hands carefully, almost symmetrically on each knee. His head remained still while his eyes darted to take in the room. "I thought your place would be...I don't know, prettier."

"The flat came furnished." Evan shifted his feet, debating whether to sit beside him.

"Still, I thought with you being an architect and all..." Ben scoffed. "But you're not really an architect, are you?"

"Actually, I do have a degree in—"

"Just tell me what happened today," Ben said sharply. "Who was the target?"

"Not a 'who,' as far as we know." Evan sat across from him in the armchair. "A bomb threat was phoned in, a threat which seemed related to St. Andrew's in the Square. The caller didn't mention any people or motive for the threat."

"Surely you must have theories?"

"We do." Evan forced himself to hold Ben's gaze. "They're classified."

"Why? Don't the public have a right to know about dangers?"

"Mmmrap!" Trent flumped in the middle of the floor between them and rolled onto her back.

"The public also have a right to security," Evan said.

"Announcing exactly what happened today could inspire copycat attacks, or it could teach today's perpetrators—if they exist—how we deal with this sort of threat, which makes it easier for them to strike next time." He softened his tone. "Just know that you're safe."

"I don't feel safe. In general, that is." Ben crossed his forearms, placing his hands on opposite knees. "Here with you, I feel safe. Ish. Safe-ish." He gave a tiny, mirthless laugh. "I mean, if a cop can't protect me, who can?"

"Meeerw!" Trent extended her paw toward Ben, gazing at him upside down.

Evan hesitated. He could let Ben believe he was a police officer. He could say he worked in Specialist Crime Division. It would edge closer to the truth without actually revealing it.

But he wanted to be real with Ben, as real as he could ever legally be.

"I'm not a cop."

"But you were working undercover as Gunnar the waiter." He gestured to Trent as she leapt onto her heated cat perch by the window. "She's proof, and you knew I'd recognize her when I came over, so don't pretend—"

"I'm not a cop," Evan repeated.

"Then what are you?" Ben sat back, crossed his arms, and waggled his foot, looking like a hipster headmaster. "I'm waiting."

"Right." Evan drew in a long, deep breath, then let it out. "Sorry, I've never said what I'm about to say, not to anyone on the outside. Just give me a minute."

Ben grumbled, then looked away to watch Trent shove her face beneath the lowered blinds. "Why is her shelf plugged in? Is it a kitty massage table?"

"It's for heat. I'm an intelligence officer with Her Majesty's Security Service." *God, that sounds even more pretentious out loud.*

Ben jerked his head to stare at him. "You're…"

"I work at MI5. We gather information and assess threats—"

"I know what MI5 does." Ben planted his palms beside himself as though the couch was a boat threatening to capsize. "Fuck."

Evan wanted to go to him, but knew it might scare him off. If anything, he should give Ben some space. "Sorry, I never offered you a drink." He stood more quickly than he'd intended, thanks to his nerves.

Ben shrank back at the sudden movement, then gave a spastic nod.

Evan went into the kitchen. "I could make coffee or tea, since we'll probably be up for a while. There's also—" His heart sank when he saw Ben approaching but looking toward the foyer.

"Please don't go," Evan said. "Not yet."

Ben took a step forward, then sagged against the kitchen door-post. "What sort of booze have you got?"

"I KNEW you weren't what you seemed," Ben said after Evan had given him a minute to let it all sink in—and to consume a bit of whisky, which had served only to remind Ben why he didn't drink. "But MI5 was not one of my guesses."

Evan poured his own dram, then sat across the table from him. "What else did you think I could be, apart from police?"

"Loads of things crossed my mind." Ben counted off on his fingers and thumb. "Assassin. Vigilante. Gangster. Mercenary. Ninja." He paused. "Also superhero, but that was in a dream I had." In a way, the last one seemed closest—this felt like the movie moment when a superhero's friends realized he was more dangerous than they'd ever dreamed.

"You thought I could be a ninja," Evan said, "but it never occurred to you I was a spook?"

"Of course it occurred to me. But last month I saw an advert for jobs at MI5. They wanted ordinary-looking folk who could work in London."

Evan's look of confusion suddenly cleared. "Ah, you're

thinking of surveillance officers, the people who track our targets on foot or in cars. That's not what I do—I mean, I've done it on occasion when needs must, but mostly I work in an office like any normal person."

"What do you do in that office?"

"Assess threats," Evan said.

"Terrorist threats."

"Aye, that's our main purpose these days. Keeping the public safe from those who want to harm us."

Ben drew his thumbs over his brows, his eyes aching from glaring. It was like a stranger had walked in mid-blink and taken the place of the man he was falling for. "Is any of this real?" He gestured between them. "Is Evan Hollister even your true name?"

"God, yes. We're real. I'm real. At least I'm trying to be." He reached across the table to touch Ben's arm. "And I am Evan Hollister as much as you're Ben Reid. The only thing I've lied to you about is my job."

Ben pulled away. "But your job is who you are. It's not like being a bank clerk or a bricklayer. Surely being a spy affects the way you think, the way you act with 'normal people.'"

"You're right." Evan's head drooped as he looked down into his whisky. "I'll understand if it's too much and you never want to see me again. But I'd be…" He pressed his lips together, then rubbed them hard. "I'd be devastated, because I really like you. A lot." He raised his eyes to meet Ben's again.

The feeling of foreignness began to fade. Ben stood up. "I just need to check something." He planted his palms on the table, leaned over, and kissed Evan.

After a soft grunt of surprise, Evan kissed him back. He smelled, tasted, *felt* the same as ever. This was still the man Ben craved, and now what lay between them was no longer a packet of lies, but the truth.

Part of it, at least.

AFTER THAT SOUL-PLUNDERING KISS, Evan was more relieved than ever that Ben hadn't tried to bolt—mostly because it would have crushed Evan's heart, but also because it would have made this next bit even more unpleasant.

Evan set Ben's tea and his own coffee on the table, then sat across from him again. "Now that you know what I do for a living, this needs signed." He opened the slip file sitting upon the corner of the table and pulled out a copy of the Official Secrets Act declaration.

Ben scanned the sheet, then flipped it over to read the provisions on the back. "I don't understand. Specifically what 'government information' do I have access to? Is this about today's operation or whatever?"

"Yes, but that's not all." Evan wrapped his hands round his coffee mug to keep from fidgeting. The Service had trained him how to lie about his job, but there was no manual on how to tell the truth. "When you enter this life, you discover that the world is much more complicated than you ever imagined. And by telling you what I do, I've brought you into that life. I did it because I wanted to be truthful with you, and because I believed you could handle it."

Ben looked flattered but skeptical. "Whatever gave you that idea?"

"The way you talk about your father and the sacrifices he's made—that your family has made—for his military service. I thought you'd understand."

Ben's eyes softened. "Yes, unfortunately." He went back to reading the provisions. "This is intense. I need to sign this to keep dating you?"

"You're legally bound by it even if you don't sign." He set a pen beside the sheet. "So you may as well agree to its terms."

Ben's face pinched, but he picked up the pen. "What are the 'serious consequences' this thing speaks of?"

Evan shifted his feet under the table. He hated to scare Ben, but that fear could keep them both safe. "You could be fined or sent to prison."

"Ooft."

"Or I could die."

Ben jolted in his seat. "What? Why?"

"Security-service officers are prime hostage targets for terrorists. By now you know what some of them do to their—to their captives." He swallowed hard, his mouth dry after uttering that last word. "Sometimes on video."

Ben went pale. "God…" He signed the form with white-knuckled fingers, then pushed it across the table. "I'll never tell a soul."

"That's an easy promise to make, but a hard one to keep. Remember how you felt when we went to the Glasgow Greens match and those fans were running me down? You wanted to defend me, and I appreciate that, but if that happened in any other circumstance, you'd need to play along. Let people think I'm awful."

Ben's face fell. "You must have wanted to leave me after that match. You must have thought I can't keep a secret to save my life."

"Robert warned me about that, so I wasn't shocked."

"I accidentally grassed him up once to Liam. But it was for the best in the end. Honesty usually is."

"Not when it gets people killed."

"Right. Sorry." He took a long sip of tea. "Who else knows you're MI5?"

"My parents and sister. Also, several other people involved in my vetting know that I applied for a secret government job, but they don't know which agency or whether I was accepted." He met Ben's eyes, wanting to burn the command into his brain. "Never talk to anyone about what I do, even if they act like they already know."

"Okay." Suddenly Ben sat back in his chair. "Fergus never knew, did he?"

Evan lowered his chin as fresh guilt washed over him. "No, he never did."

"And you were never in Belgium." Ben spoke faster now, unraveling the biggest secret of all. "MI5 only work inside the UK, right? So you couldn't have just run off to another country for three months and kept your job." He slapped the table. "Which means you didn't leave him for another man. You left on an assignment."

Evan nodded, his chest full of lead.

"I knew it!" Ben leapt up from the table and punched the air. "You were never a lying, cheating heartbreaker. I knew it, I knew it, I knew it."

"But I *did* lie to Fergus. I *did* betray him—not for another man, but for the Service. I did break his heart." Evan's voice cracked. "And he will never, ever know that I broke my own heart, too."

Ben's triumph suddenly deflated. "You let everyone think you were cruel. You had to play the villain when you were actually defending the realm." He pulled his chair closer and sat again. "Do you ever regret it?"

Evan remembered going online that sunny day in July and seeing photos of children at the parade that never got bombed. "I don't regret making that choice, but I do regret the hurt I caused."

Ben put his hand over Evan's. "Can you tell me where you went, what you did?"

Evan shook his head. "I can say only that it was a successful operation, in that we stopped a planned attack."

Ben's eyes went round and wide. "Wow."

"But even if the operation had failed, it would still have been worth it. I would still have no regrets—or rather, my regrets would be outweighed by the certainty I'd done the right thing. See, this assignment couldn't be done by just anyone."

"Why not?"

Evan looked away. It was more than prudence keeping him silent about his unique profile. It was shame. "I can't say."

"But you foiled a terrorist plot. You saved lives."

"Not singlehandedly. My team was—"

"You're a hero, do you know that?"

Tell that to Fergus, whose life I shattered. Tell that to Patrick, whose life I— "It's complicated," Evan said, his throat thickening. "And classified."

"I won't ask about it anymore. I don't want to make you uncomfortable." He squeezed Evan's hand. "But you can tell me how you feel. Tell me anything, anytime. I won't judge."

The thickness in Evan's throat rose to his sinuses. He sniffled hard, blinking back rebellious tears. "Thanks," he whispered. "That means a lot to me."

"Are you kidding?" Ben kissed Evan's knuckles. "It means a lot to *me* that you're sharing all this. That you trust me enough to—" He broke off, glancing at the Official Secrets Act form. "Wait. If you couldn't tell Fergus where you work, then why can you tell me? How do you know I'm trustworthy?"

In a way, this was the part Evan had dreaded the most. He reached into the file and pulled out the sealed envelope containing Ben's vetting report. "This is how I know."

As BEN FINISHED READING the brief account of his life as prepared by Her Majesty's Government, he'd never felt so small. "This is awful."

"Is the report inaccurate?" Evan asked. "I've not read it myself. I didn't want to violate your privacy."

"It's not inaccurate, it's pathetic! Look at this." With the pages on his palm, Ben bobbed his hand up and down as though weighing them. "My entire life summed up on three sheets of A4 paper—single-sided, even! And two of those pages are about my parents. I'm so boring."

"Believe me, that's—"

"My most radical actions have been a tonsillectomy and three parking violations, all of which I paid, like a well-behaved boring citizen."

"Is it the contents of your dossier that bother you, or is it the fact this file exists at all, thanks to me?"

"There's that, too." Ben checked the date on the vetting report. "This was done before you phoned to ask me out."

"Yes, I needed clearance to do that."

Ben's jaw dropped so hard he felt it click. "You…so, what, you met me at your ex's wedding, then asked MI5 to paw through my personal information so we could have dinner together?"

"It's protocol."

"But surely they don't surveil their employees all the time to make sure they're behaving?"

"No, but if they found out I'd broken the rule, I could be suspended or even sacked. There's a double standard, of course— straight men often get more leniency than women and gay men." Evan fidgeted with the cuffs of his shirt sleeves. "Sorry, I know it's invasive. For what it's worth, you're the first person I've fancied enough to have vetted."

Ben scoffed. "Ah, thanks for the honor."

"That night we met, I thought we connected. I thought you were worth it."

"We did, and I am." Ben folded his dossier and shoved it back into the envelope. Then he thought of something else that didn't compute. "You said I was the first person you'd had vetted, but what about Fergus? You were in love with him. Robert told me you two were planning to move in—" Ben stopped when he saw Evan's stricken look. "What's wrong?"

Evan ran his finger over the grain of the wood table. "When I first joined MI5, they vetted Fergus. He was clean. I could have told him then what I was doing, but I knew he wouldn't approve. He hated the agency for political and moral reasons."

"Didn't he notice when you stopped being an architect?"

"He knew I'd left my firm, but I told him I was working as an architect for a government agency. Mind on, we weren't living together, so most days he didn't know where I was, especially as he was busy working on his Master's."

"So he had his head too far up his arse to suspect his boyfriend had become a secret agent." Ben shifted his unwanted whisky on the table. "So it all went to shit when you left Glasgow for this heroic operation?"

"A few months before that. Last February when they passed the marriage-equality law, Fergus and I decided to move in together." Evan gestured to Ben's report. "To simply date someone, it's enough to know that they are who they say they are and have no connections to criminals or hostile foreign nations. But when cohabitation or even marriage is on the cards, the Service likes to dig deeper." He paused. "A lot deeper."

Ben felt a chill encircle his stomach. "And they found something."

"Not about Fergus." Evan waved his hands as if erasing an invisible white board between them. "I can't say more."

Ben was sorry he asked. "This thing in the deep background check...was it the reason you could never tell him who you worked for?"

Evan nodded, eyes closed.

"Just one more question," Ben said, and to his relief Evan showed not an ounce of exasperation. "What if one day we—I'm not saying *marry*, but if we stay together long enough..."

"You're worried something will turn up in a deeper vetting?"

"Of course I worry. My mum's an immigrant."

"She's a UK citizen."

"So? She's Middle Eastern, and the way things are headed in this country, that alone could be a crime one day."

"Not to MI5." Evan's eyes were pure serious. "Regardless of the political winds, we care only whether someone is an actual threat. Our limited resources can't track every person in an unpopular ethnic group." His brows lowered in determination. "We literally have no time for racism."

Ben felt somewhat reassured by Evan's matter-of-fact explanation—and by the way his face had switched to "professional setting" just now.

"How much contact do you have with your family," Evan asked, "apart from your mother?"

Ben wondered whether Evan already knew the answer. "Not much. None of them even live in Iran anymore. Mum's parents are dead, and the only cousins I've met live in Canada. We're all pretty unremarkable, which now I realize is a good thing."

"It is." Evan spoke softly. "Look, Ben, if our relationship does...deepen one day, I don't think there'll be a problem like what I had with Fergus."

It broke Ben's heart to think of Evan's life ripped apart by forces beyond his control. Even now his face was painted with regret and still held a tinge of fear. He probably hadn't even wanted to reveal this secret tonight, but the St. Andrew's evacuation had forced his hand. Evan had no doubt been nearly as unprepared and overwhelmed as Ben.

Ben stood slowly. "Are we still having brunch at noon tomorrow, then?"

Evan looked up with trepidation. "If you want."

"I do. And I'm glad the reservation's not too early." He reached out a hand to Evan. "Seeing as we're about to have a very late night."

Chapter 18

As Evan stood in his living room kissing Ben, he wondered what he'd done to deserve such a man. He'd revealed everything—well, everything that wouldn't get himself sacked or imprisoned—and somehow Ben still wanted him. Why would anyone sign up for this life?

He pulled back for a moment. "Sorry, I just need to confirm: After all I've told you, you're sure you still want to be with me?"

"I'm sure I want you more than ever," Ben purred, standing on tiptoe to steal another kiss.

"Because you think spies are cool?"

"Oh, fuck off, I'm not so shallow." Ben made as if to slap Evan's chest, but instead smoothed his shirt, his eyes following his hand as he spoke. "It's because now there's no more pretending. I can stop wondering who you are and start getting to know the real you."

Whoever that might be. "I can never share everything. There'll be times when I have to lie to you."

"I don't care." Ben's hand stilled on Evan's chest. "No, of course I care. But it's not a deal-breaker. If you need to hide things from me, I'll try not to take it personally, or freak out thinking you're cheating or losing interest. When you get that faraway look in your eyes I'll try not to wonder what you're thinking about. I'll know that it's...unknowable." Ben finally tilted his head up to gaze into Evan's eyes. "Whatever we could have together, now it can truly begin."

A wave of near-dizziness swept over Evan. He pressed his forehead to Ben's.

"Did I make you swoon?" Ben asked.

"A bit."

Ben examined Evan's face with serious eyes. Then he wrapped his arms around him. "It must feel strange telling the truth after all this time."

Evan simply nodded, his cheek brushing Ben's hair.

"If you want," Ben said, "we could just sleep tonight."

Evan's insides shimmied with anticipation and trepidation. "I'm not sure what I want, to be honest." He pulled back and looked toward the bedroom. "We could just...see what happens."

"I like that idea." Ben headed for the bathroom. "I just need a minute to piss. And by 'piss' I mean fix my hair. But also piss."

Evan carried the two abandoned half-drams of whisky into the bedroom, shutting the door to keep Trent from following.

The moment he neared his bed, he knew: In this room with this man, he felt safe.

Evan stripped off his clothes, then slid beneath the soft blue duvet. Soon a knock came at the door. A moment later Ben entered, his hair slightly tamed and his glasses missing.

He stopped and squinted at Evan's bare chest. "Something more than sleep, then?"

"Aye." Evan wiggled his feet beneath the covers. "A lot more, I think."

Ben tore off his own clothes, tossing them in a pile near Evan's. Then he went to the end of the bed, where he lifted the duvet and burrowed beneath.

Evan felt a sudden spike of panic. "What are you doing?" he asked as Ben crawled up between his legs. "You'll suffocate."

"I can breathe fine," came his lover's muffled voice. "Besides, it's cold."

"Then let me keep you warm." He pushed back the duvet and pulled Ben up to lie atop his chest. As their mouths met in a long, deep kiss, Evan felt his pulse first slow with calm, then speed up again with excitement. Soon it seemed daft to worry about losing sight of Ben's face.

"Definitely warm now." Ben gazed at him. "God, you're impossibly gorgeous."

Evan tried to keep his expression mild as a snippet of memory intruded:

"Such a pretty face. He'll make a beautiful corpse."

Ben must have noticed his dismay, because he asked, "Are you embarrassed when I compliment your looks?"

Evan hesitated. Better to appear bashful than broken. "A bit. Just my silly Orcadian modesty."

"Sorry." Ben turned his head to look at the bedside table. "Hey, is that a mini-humidifier like the one I've got?"

"Aye." He kissed the edge of Ben's jaw, bringing his own focus fully back to the present. "I bought it a few days ago, hoping you'd soon stay the night."

Ben's mouth slowly opened. "So you *were* planning to have me come over. Which means you were planning to tell me about your job. There'd be no hiding it once I saw Trent."

Clearly Ben thought Evan had been forced into sharing his secret sooner than he'd wanted. "After breakfast tomorrow I planned to bring you here to explain everything." He wrapped his arms around Ben's waist. "For your birthday, I wanted to give you the truth."

Ben's face softened. "Wow."

"And also another gift. Don't worry, I'm not that cheap."

"I don't need another gift. Just having all of you, that's what I need."

Evan quirked an eyebrow and glanced at the nonexistent space between them. "So what are you waiting for?"

Ben smiled and kissed him again, even more deeply than before. When they parted for breath, he said, "I was thinking...I know you're bigger than I am and sometimes I come off as a bit of a femme. But there's no need to adhere to stereotypes."

Evan wasn't sure what he meant. "Sorry?"

"I'm saying don't feel obliged to top if you'd rather..." He swept a hungry gaze downward. "...not."

"Oh, I see." Evan felt turned on—and a bit relieved—at the proposition. *Anything to make this time less like the last time.* "Are you saying you want to fuck me?"

Ben looked away, and even in the dim light it was obvious he was blushing. "I dunno. Maybe?"

Evan remembered what Ben had told him last Sunday, how he had trouble owning his desires. He drew his leg up to brush the outside of Ben's hip. "You can fuck me, *if* you tell me you want to. And if you tell me *how much* you want to."

Ben swallowed, looking uneasy. "Erm..."

"Repeat after me. I want..."

Ben met his eyes. "I-I want."

"Inside you."

Ben's lashes flickered, and down below, his cock twitched against Evan's belly. "Inside you."

"As soon as humanly possible."

Ben relaxed a fraction. "As soon as humanly possible."

"Good. Now tell me in your own words."

"Oh." Ben propped himself up, hands on either side of Evan. "Erm, I-I don't—"

"Tell me what you want." Evan reached down and began to stroke himself. "Tell me so I'm dying for you. Tell me so I canna wait to—"

"I want to fuck you." It came out as a shaky whisper, but only the first time. "I want to fuck you, Evan." Ben's eyes turned sharp and stern. "I want to bury myself in your beautiful arse until you scream my name." His eyes widened gleefully, as if he was scandalized by his own words.

"Yes." Evan pushed at one of Ben's hands. "Feel how hard you made me by saying that."

Ben seized him, then let out a growl as his palm wrapped around Evan's cock. "I want you. I want all of you." He moved down and put his hands behind Evan's knees. "Take these. Spread for me."

Evan did as he was told, pulling his thighs up and apart. He watched as Ben ran his tongue down his cock, then his balls, swirling over their undersides. Then he felt Ben's hands on his arse, parting his cheeks. With a single glance at Evan's face, Ben descended.

Wait. I don't— Before Evan could protest, he felt Ben's warm, sweet tongue sweep across his hole. He cried out, as much in surprise as in pleasure. Rimming wasn't something he'd ever fancied—giving or receiving. It had made him feel far too *known.* Even now, despite the molten sensations flooding through him, it seemed a threat, like he'd unlocked one too many doors.

But Ben now knew his biggest secret. If Evan could open up his mind, then surely he could allow this.

Especially when *this* was unraveling him to the core. With hazy vision, Evan looked down to see Ben's long dark lashes fluttering, and to watch the corners of his jaws moving as his tongue worked its way up, down, over...and finally, just a bit, inside.

"Ah!" Evan let his head drop back for a moment, savoring this liquid exploration that set his cock pulsing with need. Then he raised his head again to see Ben watching him. When their eyes met, Ben smiled, his stubble brushing the skin between Evan's cheeks.

Evan's gaze tripped past Ben to the bedroom door. *There's no one there, no one coming. You're safe. For real this time.*

Ben's fingertip joined his tongue, slipping easily into Evan's wet hole.

"Ohh..." Every cell in Evan's body began to spark as he felt Ben's breath against his balls. Ben's mouth opened to surround one, then stayed open as he teased with tiny licks. "Please...."

Ben drew Evan's ball into the warm, wet embrace of his mouth. Evan shuddered and writhed, his bedroom door the most distant of concerns.

When Ben finally paused to raise his head, Evan let go of his legs, just now noticing all four limbs were tingling. "I feel like it's *my* birthday instead of yours," he panted.

Ben grinned as he pushed up on his hands. Then he glanced at the bedside table. "I'm not keen on rifling through a spy's things, so if you could fetch me what I need…"

"Of course." Evan opened the drawer and pulled out a small wooden box.

"Ooh, *très* flash." Ben took the box and sat on the edge of the bed to examine it. "Is there a secret to opening this?"

"As you turn the latch, you must say the magic phrase."

"Which is what?"

Evan gave an exaggerated shrug. "Try it and find out."

With a smile, Ben closed his eyes and whispered something Evan couldn't hear. The latch turned in his hand. "It worked!" he said with a melodramatic gasp. "I feel like King Arthur pulling Excalibur from the stone."

"What did you say?"

"You should know. It's your box." Ben flipped through the assortment of condoms.

Evan nudged his knee against Ben's back. "I ken *my* magic phrase, but what's yours?"

"I said, 'Heaven I stroll.'" Ben set one of the condoms and the small bottle of lube on the bedside table, then returned the box to the drawer. "It's an anagram of your name."

"You can do anagrams in your head?"

"No, but there's this thing called the internet." He tore open the foil packet.

"What were some of the other anagrams?"

"I only remember a few." He paused as he rolled on the condom. "'Latrine shovel' was the worst, but 'Halest lover in' wasn't bad. If I'd known your middle name I could've found out where you were the halest lover." He downed the rest of his whisky, then coughed. "Oh God, that's awful."

"You didn't need to finish it."

"I did, because I want to kiss you." He reached for the lube. "I thought you might not want to taste where my tongue has just been."

Evan went cold inside. "Did I—was it bad?"

"God, no." Ben reached down between Evan's legs. "You taste amazing. Everywhere. I was just being courteous."

It wasn't long before Evan was ready—literally gasping for it, his mind too swamped with lust to spare a thought for fear.

When Ben attempted to enter his body, Evan felt it offer one final moment of resistance, as if asking permission from his mind. *Are we really doing this again after all these months? After what happened the last time?*

"Yes," he answered, and that was all it took.

HEAVEN I STROLL. Never had an anagram felt so apt. As Ben slowly moved deeper within Evan, he did feel as though he was visiting some otherworldly realm. Their movements, their breaths, even their blinks seemed synchronized.

"Ow." Evan's eyes popped wide, dispelling Ben's illusion.

He stopped. "Sorry. You okay?"

"Aye, I just—it's been a long time since I've had a real live cock in me."

Ben laughed at this uncharacteristic frankness. "I don't do this often either—top or bottom—so I'm out of practice. I'll try to be more careful."

"You're perfect. This is fine." He glanced behind Ben toward the door.

Ben turned his head, expecting to see Trent approaching the bed, but the door was still shut. "Are you sure? I could pull out and we could switch."

"Don't you dare." Evan took Ben's arse with both hands and drew him deeper inside. Then he winced a little. "Just give me a minute."

He slid his arms beneath Evan's shoulders and let his own hips go loose. "Here, you take over. Take what you need."

Evan smiled, then grasped Ben's arse tighter. With their chests pressed together, Ben held still, letting Evan guide him back and forth, in and out. He noticed with relief that relaxing his body let him rein in his excitement. "This is better. If I'd kept fucking you of my own power, I'd probably be on the brink of coming."

Evan's eyes sparked with amusement. "Why, do I feel good?" He punctuated his question with a quick flex of his inner walls.

"Ooft." Ben struggled to keep it together. "Are you fishing for a compliment? Is my rigid, quivering stauner not enough to stroke your ego?"

"It's enough to stroke everything. Well, almost everything." His gaze went to the ceiling as he took a deep breath. Then, as he let it out, he pulled Ben deeper than ever. "Oh!" His eyes rolled up. "Now there's everything."

Yes. Ben had been dying to see that beautiful face close up, painted with pleasure. Now all he could do was stare as Evan's dimpled chin tilted up, as his tongue and teeth turned his bottom lip wet and red, as his golden hair glowed against the dark-blue pillowcase.

Evan clutched at him, fingers and thumbs digging into his glutes. He began to thrust upward, consuming his cock again and again. Ben had never felt a body react to his with such raw hunger.

Then he moved his hands to Ben's hair. "Now you. Just like this." His eyes held a determined light. "Soon I'll need it hard and fast, but not yet. I just want to look at you. I want to kiss you while you fill me up."

Ben grasped the underside of Evan's pillow for stability, then eased forward, this time feeling no resistance.

Their mouths meshed, muffling their groans. Ben swore he

was growing harder with every silky slide in and out of Evan's body. Soon those strong thighs were wrapping round Ben's waist, holding him steady so he could find his rhythm.

And when he found it…it was the closest thing to magic he'd ever felt. He watched, mesmerized, as Evan's expression cycled between aching need and pure delight. Their moans seemed to harmonize, rising in pitch and volume with each minute.

Before long, Ben needed more—or maybe less. Either way, he couldn't go on like this. "Evan…" he said between gasps. "Can I…"

"Pound me till we come? Yes. Please."

Ben planted his hands on the smooth planes of Evan's pecs. "I warn you, I won't last long."

"Good. Me neither." After another fleeting glance toward the door, Evan grasped his own legs and pulled them higher than ever.

Bracing himself, Ben drew back, then slammed forward.

"Yes!" Evan's neck turned to cords of muscles. "More."

Ben did it again, harder, and again, and again. He pinned Evan's shoulders to the bed, savoring his own illusive strength.

Evan pulled his legs back farther, his feet nearly to his head now, letting Ben rise higher on his knees to drive into him with more force. As Ben quickened his rhythm, Evan begged for more and more and more, his pleas turning to sobs.

Then Evan's voice pitched high and tight. "Oh God yes! Please…just like that. Make me come, Ben. Make me come."

"Do you need my hand?"

"Just your cock." Evan let out another moan. "Just keep…" His grip tightened on his ankles, knuckles turning white. "Ohhhh."

The sound of Evan's pleasure, combined with the sight of that gorgeous body rocking beneath him, brought a familiar thickness to the base of Ben's shaft. Instinct told him to slow down to stave off his own orgasm, but Evan's voice kept urging him on.

God, I know this is a terrible thing to pray for, but please let him come soon.

Just then Evan screamed, face contorted, his entire body quivering and spasming. Ben barely recognized the man beneath him, so utterly out of control.

He felt the surge from within at the same moment he saw Evan's cock release its shower upon his chest and abs. He gave one last, deep thrust, holding himself inside to feel the rhythmic clutch of Evan's arse, doubling, then trebling the intensity of his orgasm. Ben's sweat-slick hands slipped from Evan's shoulders, and he collapsed atop him in a reckless heap.

Evan pulled him close as they spent themselves together. He grasped Ben's arse once again and rose against him. "So good..." he said in a shaky whisper. "So good."

Ben wanted to echo that sentiment—wanted to use a word a thousand times bigger than *good*—but couldn't make his tongue form syllables. He carefully withdrew from Evan's body even as those arms and legs still held him close. His eyelids grew heavy, and he longed to fall asleep here on Evan's chest, feeling that heartbeat slow with his own.

Finally Evan murmured, "It's Fredrik, by the way."

"Hmm?"

"My middle name. One *e*, no *c*."

"Ah." Ben buried his nose in Evan's neck and sighed. "Thank you for sharing."

Evan broke into a giddy laugh that quaked them both. Then he let his arms fall to the mattress with dramatic thuds. "My God, that was..."

"Yeah." Ben reluctantly shifted off him, then managed to dispense with the condom despite his fingers' exhilarated trembling.

Evan groaned as he got out of bed, but by the time he reached the door his movements were once again graceful as a panther's. "Back in a minute and tidy you up. Don't move."

I couldn't if I wanted to. Ben stretched his languid limbs, toes pushing into the fluffy duvet at the foot of the bed. It was well after midnight. For the first time, the arrival of a non-leap year March 1st didn't seem anticlimactic, as though his birthday had passed in a blink. If anything, he felt like he'd lived a year in one day.

It had all culminated with Evan sharing his most solemn secret, placing his utmost trust in him. Ben's throat thickened as the truth hit home: This relationship was serious.

What they'd done in this bed had been a true connection of body and soul. So Ben couldn't feel ashamed, not when he believed with all his heart that he'd been created this way—not as a test but as part and parcel of the gift of life.

When Evan appeared at his bedroom door with a washcloth and towel, Ben held out his palm and said, "Wait. Do the walk."

Evan stopped. "Sorry?"

"The one from the opening credits of the *Spooks* TV show. The slow-motion, don't-fuck-with-me-I've-the-most-important-job-in-the-country walk."

"Sorry, that walk is strictly for senior officers," Evan said as he approached the bed at normal speed. "I could be sacked for going slo-mo without proper training."

"I'd never tell your bosses." Ben put on his best pouty face. "Pleeeeease?"

"Fine, fine." Evan went back to the door, where he paused. "Don't look directly at me. The walk's magnificence has been known to scorch the most resilient retinas." He disappeared into the hallway.

Ben sat up to get a better view.

In a few moments, Evan reentered the room, still naked, still holding the washcloth and towel. This time he moved in a slow, protracted swagger, swinging his arms and scanning his surroundings with an all-seeing sneer.

It was kind of hot, but mostly hilarious. By the time Evan reached the bed, Ben was curled into a ball laughing.

"Mocking my life's calling, aye?" Evan wrestled Ben onto his back, soaking him with the washcloth as he squeezed it. "You need a lesson in respect."

Ben laughed harder. "What are you going to do, waterboard me?"

They both froze. Ben's face heated even as his spine laced with cold. "I'm so sorry." He put a hand over his mouth, wishing he could stuff the words back inside. "What a horrible thing to say."

Evan set the cloth on Ben's chest and climbed off of him, looking shaken. "It would've been worse if I'd said it."

"Because you're a white government agent and I'm Middle Eastern. But you didn't say it. I did."

"Still." Evan sat on the edge of the bed, shoulders hunched. "We are what we are."

"Is that a problem?" Ben felt the breath tremble in his throat.

"Not to me, and not to the Service." Evan hung his head. "But if you see me as some sort of secret-police torturer—"

"I don't."

"A lot of people do. They think we're like the characters on that show you just made me act out."

"I *don't*," Ben repeated, wiping his own chest with the warm, damp cloth. "It was just a poor joke. Sometimes words fly out of my mouth like—" He stopped, unable to think of a non-weapon metaphor. "What if I was Muslim?"

"You're not."

"But what if I was?"

"Then you'd be a different person." Evan turned to look at Ben, twisting the towel in his hands. "Right? If you were Muslim or Christian or atheist or anything else? Isn't being Bahá'í who you are? Isn't it partly down to your religion that you're so…"

"So *what*?" Ben asked. "So *weird*?"

"So wonderful." Evan moved to sit next to him, then drew the soft, dry towel over Ben's chest and throat. "You are the loveliest person I've ever met," he said, his gaze following his own hand. "Maybe it's your faith or maybe you were just born that way, but whatever the reason, that's what you are. Anyone would be daft not to want you in their life."

Ben opened his mouth but could emit only a barely audible "Oh."

"'Oh' what?" Evan asked.

"Oh…kay." Ben nodded. "Okay."

Chapter 19

WHEN EVAN WOKE to the morning sun, the first thing he noticed was the taste in his mouth, the faint tang of whisky mixed with the salt of another man's sweat. The second thing he noticed was the shift of his mattress under a weight not his own.

Instinct made him flip over, his heart pounding. He saw what he'd expected: a sleeping Ben. He hadn't forgotten falling asleep nestled against this body, so why had he felt such alarm just now?

Why wouldn't *you?* He knew that no matter how thoroughly his mind had processed the memories of his last night in Belfast, his body would never forget. He'd had a similar reaction the first time Trent had jumped on his bed in the middle of the night.

As if beckoned by Evan's thoughts—but more likely by the sound of him waking—the cat leapt up beside him with a *Prrrow!* before mashing her head against his chin.

He glanced at the bedside table clock to see it was nearly half past nine. "Thanks for letting us have a lie-in," he whispered to Trent.

Beside him Ben stretched, then opened his eyes. "Well, hello there, beautiful. And Evan."

"Happy birthday."

"Thank you." Ben reached out to pet the cat. "Why didn't you change Trent's name when you found out she was a girl?"

"Because she seemed like a Trent."

"She is rather gender-nonconforming." Ben stroked her throat, eliciting a baritone purr.

"Also, it seemed wrong to rename her without you." Evan lifted Trent and placed her between them so he could roll onto his side. "Talking of names, how do you pronounce your given name? The full version of it, I mean."

"It's said like it's spelled. Behnam." He emphasized the second syllable.

Evan attempted it.

Ben shook his head. "You left out the *h*. Behnam," he repeated.

Evan tried and failed again.

"Not so harsh," Ben said, laughing. "It's not like *loch*. It's just Behnam."

Evan tried a third time, letting the *h* caress his throat without getting stuck there.

"Yes!" Ben fixed his gaze on Evan's lips. "Not only accurate, but hot as hellfire."

Evan brought his mouth to Ben's cheek and said it again. The word was so beautiful, it could only be whispered. "Do you like your name?"

"Sure. It's different, but not too different."

"Then why Anglicize the nickname?"

"Because B-E-H-N would look pretentious, like that Thom-with-an-*h* guy at the Greens match." He grimaced as Trent trod upon his head to reach her usual napping spot at the top of his pillow. "Also, people would overthink it and say *bean* or *bechin*, and I've not got the patience for that."

Outside, a police siren wailed. The sound was a few streets away but drawing closer. Evan turned onto his back to look at the window.

"What is it?" Ben asked.

"You don't hear the siren?"

"Oh, that. I thought maybe you heard something unusual for Glasgow. Like sheep or silence."

"Sheep and silence are what I grew up with—or rather, sheep and wind. In Orkney when there's a siren, everyone stops what they're doing. Here, no one even pauses." *Except me, apparently.*

"Nah, we're used to living in a police state."

Evan snorted. "Believe me, we do not live in a police state. If we did, my job would be a lot easier. Then again, it wouldn't be a job I'd want."

"Good to know you're a values-based spook." Ben's smile faded. "I have my own sneaky confession." He stroked Trent's back as he spoke. "Before last night, I was confused and suspicious as to why you rarely did social media. Also I wanted to know where you worked. So last week I used this GIS software called WhoWhatWhere. It takes someone's name and number to create a map of their comings and goings."

Evan tensed. "And you used it on me?"

"It was also for my dissertation, did I mention that? I wanted to contrast your online profile with my own."

"So this was all open-source intelligence?"

"Of course."

Evan let himself breathe. Ben would have discovered no information that hadn't been willingly and strategically released into the world. "What did you find?"

"Nothing, because you turn off your phone when you leave for work."

"It's required. The public don't know where our regional offices are. They don't even know for certain we have one in Scotland." Evan moved his head so he could see Ben around Trent's meandering form. "Can I try your software?"

"Sure, it's at my flat. Anyone can download the beta version, but it's a bit buggy and uses a fuckton of RAM, so it's not yet fit for public consumption." Ben's eyebrow gave a skeptical tilt. "Why do you want it? Haven't you guys got much better surveillance?"

"We do, but I'm curious about something, and I don't want to wait until tomorrow for the answer."

Ben's expression darkened. "Is this to do with yesterday's incident?"

"No, I swear." This was true, as far as Evan knew, but Ben's software could tell him if it *wasn't* true. If one of the BVP guys had switched on his phone's GPS and traveled anywhere near St. Andrew's…

Ben gasped and sat up quickly, provoking Trent to vault off the bed and run from the room. "Talking of surveillance, is your flat bugged?"

"Highly unlikely. It was swept before I moved in."

"But you don't have it rechecked."

"Not every day. That'd be awful expensive."

"So you can't say for sure no one's listening." Ben's eyes widened. "Or watching!"

"No, but the same goes for anyone. There are spy planes that can read the writing on…" He picked up the empty condom wrapper from the bedside table. "This, for instance."

"Stop the bus!" Ben's voice pitched up. "Spy planes can see through walls?"

"Not that I know of, but technology's always improving."

That got him the side-eye. "You're having me on."

"Completely."

Ben laughed, but then crossed his arms and glanced side to side. "What about our calls and messages? Does MI5 track those?"

"Definitely not." Evan's lips twitched. "That's GCHQ's job."

"Och, away, you!" Ben thwacked him in the face with a pillow, then climbed atop him.

As they kissed, Evan could feel Ben's morning stauner stiffen into something more determined. He ran his hands down over Ben's bare waist, then cupped his arse. "Last weekend you mentioned wanting to ride me properly?"

Ben's eyes lit up. "I did! And today's my birthday, sort of."

"Not 'sort of.'" To stop himself grinning about his plans for later, Evan kissed him again. "Not to me."

BETWEEN EVAN'S tongue working miracles on his mouth and Evan's fingers exploring inside, Ben was soon dying for him. His hands shook with need and nerves as he prepared Evan with condom and lube. It had been months since he'd done this at all—he didn't trust the finesse of most of his Grindr partners—and *years* since he'd done it with someone he truly cared for.

The look in Evan's eyes when Ben took him inside reminded him what sex could be like with a man who mattered.

"Oh..." Evan's neck arched nearly as much as when Ben had entered him last night. "God..."

"All right?"

"Yeah, I just—again, it's been a long time." He lifted his head to look down at where they'd just joined, then stole a quick glance at the door again.

What was that all about? Ben wondered. Maybe it was just typical spy vigilance. But if that was the case, wouldn't he do it all the time, not just while they were in bed?

Evan took a long, slow breath, then released a crooked smile that made Ben melt. "Glad I already came last night, or this would be over in about ten seconds."

"That'd be a tragedy." He slowly rolled his hips, taking Evan deeper with each spiral. Evan wrapped one hand around Ben's waist to steady him, and ran the other hand over every inch of his chest. Soon his thumb and fingers arrived at Ben's left nipple, taking first a teasing swipe, then circling closer until they joined in a light pinch.

Ben groaned, and Evan tweaked harder, sending bolts of pleasure in every direction and opening him up fully inside.

"Ohh..." The delirium was making his head spin, so he bent over and kissed Evan. He was about to ask his lover if he wanted to go harder, if he wanted to flip him over and pin him down, if he wanted…anything. But then he remembered that Evan seemed to like when Ben voiced his own desires.

Also, it *was* his birthday.

"Fuck me," Ben said in a hoarse whisper. "Please."

Evan smiled again, this time not crookedly at all. He seized Ben's hips with both hands and began to thrust upward, fast and smooth.

"Yes!" Ben clutched Evan's shoulder with one hand and his pillow with the other. Wordless noises rose from his throat as Evan's cock glided over his prostate again and again, pumping him full of what felt like a growing ball of liquid sunlight.

Ben's thighs tightened around Evan's waist as he felt the first hints of orgasm appear on the horizon. He didn't want to come soon but couldn't bring himself to halt this glorious ride.

A sudden twisting pain made him cry out.

Evan stopped immediately. "What's wrong? Did I go too deep?"

"No, that's not what hurts. Let go." He eased himself off Evan. "My thigh's cramped." He lay down on his back and tried to stretch his leg. The muscle seized again. "Ow! Ow ow ow ow."

Evan sat up and touched Ben's outer thigh. "Right here?" When Ben nodded, he began to massage it gently. "Does this help?"

"Not really." Ben covered his face. "This is so embarrassing."

"It happens."

Not to you, I bet, or the other footballers you've been with. He hissed as the pain grew fiercer. "I need to walk it off." He got out of bed and paced in front of the curtained window, lifting his knee with each step. "Sorry about this."

"It's all right. We can change position if you want."

"Okay." The cramp eased as the blood flowed back into his leg. "I could get on my stomach and you could do me from behind. That way my legs could stay straight."

Evan seemed to consider. "Or you could lie on your back."

"Then I've still got to spread my legs, which is what's getting old at the moment." When Evan said nothing, Ben turned to see him thinking, his brow furrowed. "Know what I mean?"

Evan looked away. "Why don't we take a break and come back to this later? Maybe after breakfast?"

Something wasn't right. What had made Evan go from hot to cold in the blink of an eye?

"Listen." Ben sat on the bed in front of him. "You asked me to tell you what I wanted. Now I'm telling you I want you to pound me like a dog, but you won't oblige. What's going on?"

"I JUST..." Evan pressed his fingertips to his eyes until red spots appeared. How to explain this without sounding a complete nutter?

Sometimes he'd had been able to push past his fears—to close his eyes and taste that tortellini, for example. Other times, like right now, his fears had pushed past him.

Evan lowered his hands. "I need to see your face. It's not just a preference, it's a...I need it."

Ben's gentle expression told Evan that this request came as no surprise. Perhaps he'd noticed other "quirks" like leaving a light on or watching the door.

"Here's an idea." Ben leapt up and opened Evan's wardrobe.

"What are you doing?"

"Don't worry, I'm not judging your clothes—unless you want me to. I was hoping there'd be one of these." He stepped back with a flourish, revealing the full-length mirror on the inside of the wardrobe door. Then he swept the duvet off the bed and belly-flopped upon the end of mattress. "How's that, then?"

Evan crawled up behind Ben, whose sparkling eyes met his in the wardrobe mirror. As a bonus, the doorway was even more visible now. "Perfect."

He put on a fresh condom while Ben waited on his stomach,

toes tapping the bed in anticipation. Evan slicked himself down with one hand and used the other to massage Ben's sore thigh.

Then he got himself into position, straddling Ben's legs, the tip of his cock against Ben's still-pliant hole.

"Give it to me," Ben said. "All at once this time."

Evan obeyed, thrusting so hard the bed's feet groaned against the wooden floor.

"Yes!" Ben clutched the edge of the mattress. "More. Give me more."

Evan held him down flat and did it again, provoking another howl of delight. He kept going, pulling back slowly, nearly departing Ben's body before slamming back inside. Each time Ben cried out louder, begged harder.

Undulating his hips, Evan increased his pace, in search of a rhythm and angle he could sustain but would still drive Ben mad. Ben's thighs pressed tight together, his cheeks squeezing Evan's shaft.

Best of all was the sight of Ben's face in the mirror, radiant with delight, his dark eyes lifted to meet Evan's.

"God, you're so hot," Evan said.

Ben shifted his gaze to himself, then pressed his face into the mattress.

"Yes, you are. I'll show you." Evan wrapped his arms around him, then sat up, taking care to keep their bodies together and avoid an awkward angle. He pulled him back against his chest to sit in his lap, his own thighs flanking Ben's. "Is this okay?"

"Mm-hmm, as long as I can see you."

Evan rested his chin on Ben's shoulder and splayed his hands across his chest and abdomen. "Then see this," he whispered.

Reluctantly Ben drew his eyes to his own image in the mirror. Evan caressed him slowly, hoping his fingers and palms could express his awe as they drifted over Ben's body, worshiping every inch.

Ben gave a timid smile, which widened as Evan began to fuck him again, rocking their bodies together slow and sweet. Then he reached up to turn Evan's face to meet his own. They kissed, devouring each other's soft cries.

Holding him tighter, Evan picked up the pace. Ben broke the kiss and looked in the mirror again. "Okay, you win. That does look amazing. Even the bit with me in it."

"Told you." He tugged Ben's ear with his teeth. "Will you touch yourself for me? I want to watch you come."

Ben's smile lit up the room. "I was thinking the same thing."

"Are you close?"

"I can be." He planted a hand on Evan's leg and took his cock in the other. "Just keep doing that."

Evan lifted Ben's hips a few inches, spread his own knees farther apart for leverage, then began to thrust upward, as fast as he could.

Ben's fingers dug into Evan's thigh as he stroked himself. He leaned back against Evan's shoulder, displaying his slender, naked body in all its glory. The sight of Ben pumping his cock, the head flashing in and out of his long, tan foreskin, threatened to send Evan over the edge himself.

"Yes! You...I..." Ben's throat seemed to close on his next words as his neck turned taut. His eyes squeezed shut and his lips curled back in a near-snarl. Then all at once he stopped, his face going slack and his eyes opening wide. "Oh..."

Their eyes met in the mirror as Ben's hole spasmed around his cock. A moment later, his come spilled out to drench his fist. Pulling out of Evan's embrace, Ben leaned forward to brace himself on the mattress with his other hand, his whole body jerking.

Suddenly Evan heard it all again—the crash of a door slamming open, the shouts of rage drowning out cries of ecstasy. He looked out the bedroom at his empty hallway, to remember where he was and *when* he was. Then he turned back to the image of Ben, to remember who he was with.

Resting on his forearms now, Ben seemed too dazed to notice Evan's momentary lapse of reality—or his rapidly fading erection.

At least the timing of his softening was fortunate, since Ben might be too sensitive now to continue. Evan withdrew and took off the condom.

Ben revived then. "Your turn." He sat up, reached back, and wrapped his fingers around Evan's shaft. Then his brow furrowed as he no doubt compared what was in his hand to what had just been inside him.

"Wait." Evan shifted on the bed so that he was fully facing the door. "Okay. Now try."

With a languorous smile, Ben turned to face him. This time when he took hold of Evan's cock, it jerked and stiffened in response. "There we are." He turned his head to watch them in the mirror. "We do look good together."

"Aye." Evan watched too as Ben stroked him back to full hardness. He vowed never again to get lost in that dark past, not while he was in the presence of this man who deserved every last speck of his attention.

And when he finally came, Evan felt nothing but Ben's hand, saw nothing but Ben's face, then tasted nothing but Ben's neck as he pulled him close and held on tight, his breath verging on sobs at the feeling of being finally, utterly known.

Chapter 20

DESPITE THE FACT he was stuffed with brunch, Ben was looking forward to bringing Evan back to his own flat so they could get naked together again. Tragically, Evan first had to stop at Robert's to fetch a pair of shin guards he'd lent him.

"It's just that he won't be home later and I really need them back," Evan said, again apologizing for their detour as they entered the lobby of their mutual friend's block of flats.

"It seems suspicious, being my birthday and all."

Evan stopped at the lift, dropping his shoulders in defeat. "Fine, it's not shin guards I'm fetching. It's your gift."

"Aha!" Ben did a victory dance. "But why's Robert got it?"

"You'll understand when you open it. But try not to notice when he secretively slips it to me?"

Ben crossed a finger over his heart. "I promise I'll not see a thing."

As they entered the lift, Evan pulled out his phone. "I'll give Robert a quick text in case he and Liam are still undressed."

Ben made a pouty face. "But the sight of that would make such a good present."

When they knocked on Robert's door, he called out, "Just a second!" Liam's laughter followed, low and wicked.

The door swung in, and Evan gave Ben a gentle push to propel him into the flat…

…which was full of people, only one of them Liam.

"Surprise!" Ben's friends surged to surround him.

He heard a squeak come from his own throat. "Oh my God."

His mum stepped out of the crowd to hug him hard. "Did you think I forgot?"

"No. Maybe." He laughed in relief. "It's not really my birthday."

"Of course it is. See?" She pointed at the far wall, where a colorful banner read HAPPY 5.75TH BIRTHDAY BEN! "And you'll never guess who's joined us."

He gasped. "Taylor Swift?"

Everyone laughed. Robert steered him toward his desk, where a massive computer monitor showed a face Ben hadn't seen for six weeks.

"Dad!" Ben gripped the back of Robert's desk chair. "It's really you?"

"Of course." His father sat before the screen in his combat fatigues and green beret. "How's my lad?" he asked with a wide grin.

As they all sang "Happy Birthday," Ben did a blissful scan of Robert's one-room student flat, laid out much like his own. Along with Robert and Liam and Ben's uni friends, Andrew and Colin were there, as well as—to his surprise—Fergus and John. In addition to balloons and streamers, the place was decorated with stuffed animals, including foxes, kangaroos, and what looked like a flying squirrel.

When the song ended, Robert handed Ben a lemonade and a pair of earphones. "Your da's got fifteen minutes before he's back on duty." He pulled out his chair. "Have a wee chat and we'll see you when you're done."

Trying to cram as many words as possible into a quarter hour, Ben updated his father on the progress of his honors dissertation and carefully deflected when asked about his wedding business.

As usual, his dad couldn't discuss his work or even where he was located. Ben told himself it didn't matter, as long as he was safe(ish) and doing what he loved.

With a few minutes to go, Ben waved over his mum to chat in his place. After saying goodbye to his father, he got up and reached for his lemonade to wash down the lump forming in his throat.

Evan appeared at his side. "Good chat?"

"Lovely." He took another sip. "I miss Dad."

"I know."

Of course he knew. Evan's own father had been scarce most of his life. At least Ben's parents were still happily married.

He noticed the party decorations again. "So what's with all the animals?"

"Every guest had to bring something relating to a creature who leaps. But not frogs. Your mum said you were sick to death of the frog cliché."

"Wait—you planned this together, the two of you?"

"Three of us, including your dad."

Ben was speechless. Evan must have arranged all this before last night, before he'd had to reveal his job. So he'd not been forced by circumstances into a more serious relationship than he was ready for. Evan had wanted to be part of Ben's life.

"I also got you this." Evan took a flat square white box from his pocket.

"Ooh!" Ben lifted the box's lid. On a bed of cotton was a bracelet of round black stones. The clasp was held by two bronze bird heads.

"A mate from my school does handmade jewelry in Orkney," Evan said. "The birds are meant to be Odin's ravens, Huginn and—"

"Muninn, right: Thought and Memory. Odin sent the ravens out every morning, and they were to report back to him on the news of the world." Ben grinned. "I've done enough online role-playing games to know my Norse mythology." He hugged Evan hard. "I love it! Now you must tell me your birthday so I can start planning your party, pronto."

"It's the ninth of November."

"And what did you do for your last birthday, the big two-five?"

"Nothing," Evan said flatly.

"It's impossible to do nothing." Ben laid the bracelet over his wrist, already musing which of his shirts it would best match.

"We'd had a tough game the day before, so I stayed home and recovered from that."

"Did you win?" Ben fumbled with the bracelet's clasp.

"We lost. Here, let me." Evan set down his cup, then wrapped the bracelet around Ben's wrist and lowered his voice. "After the match, Fergus announced his and John's engagement."

Ben looked up at him in horror.

"It wasn't fun." Evan snapped the clasp shut, then straightened Ben's bracelet. "But now it feels like ages ago."

"Because of me?" he asked with a playful lilt, expecting Evan to say, *maybe* or *mostly* or something equally coy and sarcastic.

Instead he looked Ben in the eye and said, "Aye. Because of you."

AFTER TAKING part in a close-quarters dance-off and busting a bunny-head-shaped piñata, Ben finally found a few minutes to eat cake with his mum.

"Last chance to eat and drink during daylight," he told her, as if she needed reminding about the annual Bahá'í fasting period.

"Be sure to set your alarm early tomorrow and have a big breakfast."

"Already got the sunrise and sunset schedule posted on my fridge. And in my app, of course."

"Good idea." She paused before asking, "So how was yesterday's wedding?"

Ben took a moment to swallow his bite of cake before replying. She'd never asked about his work, and she must have known full well how yesterday's wedding had gone. News of the "suspected gas leak" had been all over the telly and the internet. "Everything that was under my control went as well as could be expected."

"Were you frightened when the police evacuated everyone?"

"I knew it was only a precaution. These things happen, you know. And the couple handled it beautifully." Ben gave a quick cough, uncomfortable at having mentioned Lauren and Candice, but then resenting his own discomfort. He was proud of what he did, except when he was with his mother. "Anyway, the food was still good—apart from the lamb being a bit dry—and the venue agreed to extend the reception an extra two hours."

"That's lovely of them." Mum stabbed at her cake without eating it. "How many more of these weddings are you planning?"

"Erm…" Ben had dreaded this conversation. "None. I'm finished with weddings."

"Because of exams?"

"Yes." The lie came too easily. He looked over at Evan, who seemed to be sharing a pleasant conversation with Fergus and John. Then Ben turned back to his mum. "Actually, I'm just telling people it's because of exams. The real reason is you."

"Oh?" She looked half pleased, half anxious.

"It's not because you disapprove," he said. "It's because people in the industry have been talking. Apparently, my handling of same-sex weddings has highlighted the fact that you are not."

Her expression clouded. "Oh."

Ben swallowed hard, feeling stray cake crumbs scratch his throat. "Mum, I never meant to shame you. I never wanted anyone to think you were prejudiced. I just wanted to help people."

"I know," she said softly, staring at the floor. "You're a good man."

Guilt stabbed at him. He *had* wanted to give same-sex couples a day they'd never forget, but he'd also wanted to spite his mother, show her he was his own person. The fact his rebellion was a righteous one didn't erase the fact he'd wanted to hurt her.

So it was down to him to bridge this gap between them. "Evan said you planned this party together."

"Mm-hm," she said with a faint smile.

"You must have started the day you two met—the same day the thought of me dating a man practically had you in tears."

"Evan's a hard one to say no to. Just like you."

Ben was confused. "So that whole love-the-sinner-hate-the-sin routine last Sunday morning—was it all an act to make this party a bigger surprise?"

She looked aghast. "Of course not." His mother lowered her voice. "The way I feel about you and Evan is complicated, because the situation itself is complicated."

"I know it is." He fought to keep the annoyance out of his voice. "I'm dealing with it."

"Ben, there's no loophole. The teachings are clear, which means the Bahá'í Faith's position is clear."

"The position could change. We can grow and evolve in our understanding. We can use our rational souls to, erm—to penetrate the mysteries of existence, like Abdu'l Bahá said." Ben wished he'd done more Bahá'í reading lately so he could dredge up more quotes from memory. "Look at Christianity and Judaism —some of their sects embrace same-sex unions. If they can break with thousands of years of tradition, why can't a rational, revolutionary religion like ours break with less than two hundred years' worth?" He held up a palm in *stop* position. "And please explain without blaming it on our Islamic roots."

"There's no explaining, Ben. There's only accepting, even when it's hard—*especially* when it's hard." She sighed and gave him a heartbroken look. "That's why it's called 'faith.'"

Chapter 21

FOR ONCE, Evan couldn't wait to spend the day at his desk. He arrived a half hour early at the office Monday morning, this time taking the bus from West George Street to Festival Park. It was the commute with the least amount of walking, a relief after his strenuous bedtime adventures with Ben.

Today he and his team would figure out who was behind Saturday's shenanigans at St. Andrew's Square. Or at least start the process of figuring it out. Or at least follow a few leads and hope they led somewhere. Intelligence work often required the patience of a sedated saint, to use a Ben catchphrase.

Without even fetching a coffee, Evan dived straight into the investigation. First he wanted to determine whether someone from the BVP rally could have been lurking outside St. Andrew's in the white SUV.

Using the city's CCTV database, he brought up the footage at the top of Buchanan Street. If the rally had still been in progress during the wedding, it would eliminate his primary suspect: Jordan Lithgow.

But the footage showed the street in its normal Saturday afternoon shopping bustle. The rally was over, its participants gone.

No surprise there. Detective Sergeant Fowles had told Evan the

BVP folk and their counter-protesters had been ordered to disperse at one o'clock. They could have been anywhere by the time the wedding started at two.

Kay approached his desk. "I've sent your warrant request for David Wallace up to the Home Office for final approval."

"Thanks." Last night Evan had plugged the phone numbers of David and Jordan into Ben's open-source intelligence software WhoWhatWhere. It had produced no results, as both men were canny enough to turn off the location setting on the mobile phones they used for British Values Party business.

MI5 surveillance, on the other hand, didn't need GPS to track a phone—with a warrant, they could do it using mobile-tower signals alone.

"How long do you think approval will take?" Evan asked Kay.

"Anywhere from a day to never."

"*Never*?" The Home Office rarely rejected surveillance warrants—mostly because MI5 officers rarely requested them without substantial cause. No one wanted the extra work involved in surveillance unless it was crucial to an operation.

Kay sighed. "Due to the Service's notorious history of surveilling politicians, Her Majesty's Government is now reluctant to sign off on a warrant for members of political parties."

Lewis looked up from his desk. "Sorry to eavesdrop, but BVP's not a real party. They've no candidates."

Kay turned to him. "They claim they plan to stand someone in the next council elections."

"They can claim whatever they like," Evan said, "but that doesn't make it true."

"Seriously, Kay," Lewis added. "All anyone's got to do now to avoid surveillance is stick the word 'party' in their name?"

"Of course not," Kay said. "There's simply a higher threshold of suspicion for politically active persons."

"We're five months post-independence referendum," Evan said. "Everyone in Scotland is politically active."

"Everyone but *us*. That's the point." Kay patted his shoulder before walking away.

"My feeling?" Lewis said to Evan in a low voice. "The public already think we stalk everyone, so we might as well do it. Either way no one trusts us, but if we spy, at least we get something out of it."

Evan gave a noncommittal grunt, unsure how to respond. Lewis was barely thirty. Would Evan be that jaded in five short years? Would it even take that long?

Turning back to the job in hand, he logged into MI5's image search software, which would retrieve every photo and video posted to social-media platforms within provided parameters. He included the more obscure social networks, figuring a terrorist might prefer to upload an image to a site with little active traffic so it could be shared with associates but kept out of the public eye.

In one of these images, Evan hoped to find evidence of pre-wedding reconnaissance, or maybe even a clearer picture of the occupants of the white Outlander—which the rental-car company claimed had been stolen after their office closed Saturday at noon.

He drew a one-kilometer radius around a satellite image of St. Andrew's in the Square, then entered a date range of the previous Friday through the present. The program digested the request, its creeping status bar telling Evan he had time to finally get a coffee.

When he returned to his desk, the search was still going. He eased his tension by cleaning protein-bar crumbs out of his keyboard and refereeing an office debate on whether Sam Allardyce should see out the season managing West Ham United.

Finally a list of images appeared. Evan groaned at its size: 1,056 photos, 213 videos.

He viewed a short, shaky video of the evacuation itself, taken by one of the bridesmaids. Ben appeared briefly, assisting one of the older guests across a junction near Glasgow Green. Evan saved the video in case it contained details he didn't yet know were useful.

Then he sifted through dozens more photos and videos taken throughout the weekend, mostly by tourists with a chronic lack of imagination. After two hours without a break, his eyelids began to itch, and his neck felt like a steel spike. With cramping fingers, he scrolled one more time.

"Well, hello." A video's display frame showed the wedding guests filing out of St. Andrew's. The angle was high, perhaps from an upper floor of one of the three-story blocks of flats on the square. The ten-minute video had been posted Saturday night to Imageo, the site Ben had reminded Evan about on their first date. It was titled *12520_7121197125_165189198.mp4*—probably a file name generated automatically by the device.

In defiance of his stiff neck, Evan clicked.

The video began with a slow scan of the square and the side of St. Andrew's. The image was slightly blurred by the window a few inches in front of what seemed a simple phone camera.

The pavement outside St. Andrew's was empty but for a few passing pedestrians, as was the loading bay. Evan's heart raced faster with every second that nothing happened.

"What are you waiting for?" he whispered. Had the filmmaker phoned in the anonymous tip? Or were they working with a potential attacker and wanted to record what they thought would be the ensuing carnage?

The white Outlander appeared at last, pulling slowly into the loading bay and giving Evan a sense of déjà vu. Soon Ben appeared from the front of St. Andrew's. As the wedding party and guests filed out, the camera grew shakier. Evan turned up the volume on his earphones to hear what sounded like rapid, nervous breathing.

After dealing with a wedding-party kerfuffle and stopping a tiny tuxedo-kilted pageboy from running into the street, Ben trudged toward the Outlander with determination. Though Evan knew what was going to happen, he struggled not to chew his nails in suspense.

The SUV drove off, the squeal of tires audible even through the pane of glass.

Hang on. Evan rewound the video, restarting it before the Outlander left the loading bay.

There it was—just as Ben neared the vehicle, the man filming let out what sounded like a soft curse. Evan couldn't make out the word and wasn't sure it was in English. He let the video play on.

Minutes passed. Ben helped arrange the wedding party, then disappeared inside St. Andrew's.

Suddenly the phone camera tilted, then swooped downward. There came a clattering, and the video went dark for a few seconds.

When the camera swept back up to face the window, the man had shifted to the left. Evan could now see a reflection in the glass near one edge of the video's frame.

His pulse quickened. The reflection was of a laptop, sitting open behind the man. On the screen was a—

The video ended.

"Fuck." Evan replayed the last ten seconds frame by frame, trying to get a better look at the reflected laptop, but the image was too blurry, showing nothing but a white glow on a dark background. "Fuck!"

"Need help?" came a voice beside him.

Evan looked up at Ned. "Did I summon you with my thoughts?"

"You summoned me with your cursing. I know computer-generated frustration when I hear it."

"If a photo is uploaded to a platform before it's cropped, you can find the full version, right?"

"Aye, it's easy. You just—"

"Can the same be done with videos?" Nothing in the video suggested it had been cropped, but it was too suspicious not to examine every possibility.

"Sometimes." Ned peered at Evan's screen. "People still use Imageo?"

"Not if they want the world to see their posts."

"Hm, I can't keep up with what's popular. My daughter says she's leaving Facebook cos it's got too many old people. When did you want to give her that goalkeeper training session, by the way?"

"Next week, after our cup tie," Evan said. "Will you reconstruct this video for me?"

"I'll give it a go."

Evan sent his colleague the link, then followed him to his desk. Ned opened the page and said, "That's an odd title."

"Probably just the file name generated by the device."

"Nah, those names are usually date, underscore, time. That's not the structure here."

"You're right." Evan felt stupid for missing the pattern. "Maybe the number is a code. The XRW types like to use A for 1, B for 2, et cetera, for their tattoos and all." He thought of Jordan's knuckles inked in a calligraphic *88*, which equaled *HH* or *Heil Hitler*. "But this can't be that simple."

"Go and try it." Ned flicked his hand toward Evan's desk. "It'll keep you out of my nonexistent hair while I work."

Evan hurried back to his desk and copied the file name onto his jotter:

12520_7121197125_165189198

The first group of numerals gave him *ABEB0*. There were no relevant results for the word or acronym *ABEB*, which meant the code had a higher-level key than the $A = 1$, $B = 2$ code used by the extreme-right-wingers. Cryptology wasn't his strong suit, but their office's GCHQ liaison had a copy of the world's best decryption software.

He tore the sheet from his jotter and started toward her desk. Then he stopped and looked down at the paper, for the first time seeing the 2 and the 0 as a unit.

It's a 20, you fool.

Relieved he'd not embarrassed himself, Evan went back to his desk and changed *B0* to *T*, the twentieth letter of the alphabet.

ABET. A real word—one associated with crime, no less.

The conversion of the second set of numerals, *GABAAIBE,* gave him no joy. He went back to the first grouping. *1* and *2* could be *12,* which would make the first word...*LET.* And the second word definitely began with *G.*

Oh.

Oh no.

Oh fuck no.

It took but a minute to confirm that the file name spelled out the same three words that had rasped over the anti-terrorism hotline Saturday afternoon:

LET GLASGAY PERISH

"Got it!" Ned raised both fists high. "There's an extra forty-three seconds at the end of the video."

Evan took the sheet of paper with the code and went over to Ned, who started the video at the original ending.

Through the window, a few dozen guests roamed beside St. Andrew's while the wedding party took pictures on the portico. A woman in a yellow bridesmaid dress came out of the front door and was greeted with what looked like relief.

Evan's gaze flicked between this main scene and the reflection in the glass. Assuming the phone's camera was using autofocus, a tiny adjustment in position might bring the laptop into momentary clarity.

The man filming the video let out a frustrated noise, then shifted his weight.

"There!" Evan said. "Go back."

Ned stopped the video, then reversed frame by frame until the reflection came into sharp relief. The laptop was sitting on what was probably a bed, based on the height relative to the windowsill. On the mostly white screen was a black rectangle featuring white Arabic letters above a white disc with black letters.

Evan drew in a breath. "Is that..."

"I hope not," Ned whispered. Then he raised his voice. "Adira, can we trouble you for a second?"

She held up a finger, then after a final word with one of the junior analysts, came over to Ned's desk. "What do you—" Adira stopped when she saw the screen, then looked up at Evan. "Tell me that's not part of Operation Caps Lock."

"It is. Tell me that's not the flag of ISIL."

"I'm afraid so." Adira sighed. "Whoever this is, they're either part of or inspired by the group calling itself the Islamic State."

Chapter 22

BEN CONSIDERED himself on the far E end of the extrovert-introvert spectrum. Yet his stomach was aflutter as he entered the grounds of Firhill Complex to watch Evan play. Football still felt a foreign land to him, and the Glasgow Greens "spy" match hadn't whetted his appetite for the sport and its fans.

Unable to spot Evan amidst the two clusters of players, Ben headed for the home stand, which was crammed out with fans waving rainbow paraphernalia. Though it was nearly a half hour before kickoff, the supporters were already chanting at full volume.

"Ben Reid, get yourself over here!"

He looked up, relieved to see John Burns waving at him from one of the stand's top rows.

Ben climbed through the crowd to reach his former client, who was sitting with their friend Lord Andrew Sunderland as well as Duncan's partner, Brodie, whom Ben had met at Fergus and John's wedding.

Andrew stood to let Ben sit between him and John—and probably also so he could keep his seat on the aisle. "You've gone all in, I see."

"Of course." Ben tipped his tie-dyed rainbow cap at Andrew,

who smiled back from behind rainbow-rimmed dark sunglasses, a cheeky contrast with his otherwise tasteful outfit.

As he sat down, Ben tilted his rainbow flag so as not to poke the woman in front of him. "Evan says this is a really important match. They need to tie or something?"

John laughed. "When a match is in an elimination tournament, it's called a 'tie.' Like a 'cup tie,' for instance. It's got nothing to do with the final scoreline."

"Why?"

"Another mystery of football," said Brodie. "Dinna fash, we can be confused together."

"Deal." He reached back to fist-bump Brodie, glad to have found a kindred spirit, then turned to look at the players on the pitch.

Oh. Oh wow.

He'd glimpsed Evan's violet-and-white-striped football shirt hanging in his wardrobe. But now it hugged the contours of Evan's chest and shoulders as he warmed up, trotting about and swinging his arms in large circles. Ben remembered how those muscles had felt against his palms last weekend when Evan lay naked beneath, above, or beside him.

He suddenly no longer needed his jacket.

As he stood to remove it, he saw Evan look toward the crowd, shading his eyes against the low sunlight slicing across the field. When he saw Ben, he broke into a wide smile, then blew him a kiss with an expansive sweep of his arm.

Ben waved back at Evan so hard he thought he might dislocate an elbow. "Score lots of goooooooooals! And assists!" he added, so as not to look greedy.

Evan laughed, then fell back in line with his teammates' warmup, now jogging with high knees.

Ben watched him for a moment before realizing the rest of the Rainbow Regiment had fallen silent. They were all looking in his direction with wide eyes—and wide mouths, in a few cases.

He glanced up, hoping there was a hot-air balloon or a very

quiet helicopter hovering behind him. Nothing but high patchy cirrocumulus clouds met his eyes.

He sat down, cheeks flaming. "Why are they staring at me? Is this how they treat all newcomers?"

Andrew chuckled. "Only newcomers who get to bed Evan Hollister, the most elusive and therefore most coveted Warrior."

"Elusive?"

"Many of the Warriors who are single find regular companionship amongst the Rainbow Regiment."

Ben squinted at Andrew. "Are you saying—"

"They fuck the fans," John said.

"Ah." That made sense. As fit as these lads and lasses were, they could probably have their pick of adoring supporters.

"But not Evan," John continued. "The Regiment calls him 'Brother Hollister' cos he acts like a monk." He nudged Ben with an elbow. "Until you came along, going where no fan has gone before. They're probably wondering what your secret is."

"So am I, to be fair."

"Nonsense." Andrew patted Ben's hand. "Let me know if you need tips on ignoring the envy of lesser beings."

Ben smiled, but the scrutiny of the Warriors fans was giving him a severe case of the I'm-not-worthys.

They think I'm punching above my weight, and they're right.

The match began, and within a few minutes Ben was vowing to maintain an open mind regarding football. Moray Rovers took an early lead on something called a "corner kick." Warriors soon answered by scoring on a "counterattack," in which Jamie sent a long, sky-high pass to the speedy Duncan, who brought the ball down with one seemingly magical touch before leaving two hefty defenders in the dust. Ten minutes later, Rovers took the lead again on a penalty call which stoked the Rainbow Regiment's fury to full blaze.

Soon another foul was called near the goal at the other end of the pitch. The players lined up, but this time they were *between* the goal and the kicking person—which appeared to be Evan—rather than behind him.

"How come he doesn't get to kick it from right in front of the goal?" Ben asked John, who had assured him there were no daft questions.

"Because the foul was committed outside the eighteen-yard box," John replied. "If it was inside, it'd be a penalty kick, but this is just a free kick." He nudged Ben. "And your man is one of the best."

Ben stood with the rest of the Regiment as Fergus and Evan conferred near the ball. The whistle blew, and both men stepped back. Fergus ran toward the ball as though to kick it, but at the last second he veered away. Evan stepped forward, planted his foot, and sailed the ball up, up, and over the wall of players. It curled into the corner of the net, past the outstretched arms of the goalkeeper.

"Yaaaaaaaaassss!!!" Ben's unexpected scream ripped his throat. "Fuckin' yaaaaas, ya beauty!" He hugged John, bouncing up and down on the rickety stand as the Regiment cheers rose around him. This feeling was beyond anything he'd ever experienced while fully dressed.

Today, Ben didn't wish he was home watching the curling.

"What happens if they win?" he asked his friends as halftime drew near, his whole body still buzzing from Evan's stupendous goal.

"*When* they win," Brodie said, "Warriors will go to the quarterfinals."

"Gonnae no jinx it!" John said. "The football gods don't like when fans assume victory. Mind, this Moray team went to the finals last year."

"Since when are you such a pessimist?" Andrew asked.

John beckoned him to lean in so the three of them could hear his hushed voice. "Since Fergus was complaining of a tight hamstring all week."

"Oh God." Andrew sat back.

"Is that very bad?" Ben asked.

"Muscle injuries can be brutal," John said, "and hams are the worst. I told him he should rest today, but he wasnae having it. Said the Warriors needed him, which they do."

Ben looked out at the pitch. Without knowing a thing about positions or tactics, he could tell Fergus was important by the sheer number of times he touched the ball. He and Evan were in constant motion, only slowing down when play stopped entirely.

"Just got to hope for the best," John continued. "And of course, stress-eat our faces off." He opened his rucksack to display an array of individual crisps packets. "Who wants some, apart from Andrew, who scorns all processed foods?"

"Me!" Brodie reached between them to grab one. "I'm fair starving."

John offered a packet to Ben. "I've got fizzy drinks, too."

"Nah, I'm fine," Ben told John, but his stomach gave a loud growl of protest.

John glanced down at the noise. "Your belly disagrees."

"It doesn't get a vote," Ben said. "I'm fasting sunrise to sunset."

"Oh! Sorry." John put the crisps back in his rucksack without taking any. "Is it Ramadan already? I thought that was in June this year."

"It is, but I'm Bahá'í, not Muslim. We always fast for the nineteen days before our new year, which starts at sunset on the twentieth of March." He pointed to John's bag. "Don't stop yourself eating on my behalf."

"Och, I don't need that rubbish." He patted his gut. "I'm still burning calories from our wedding reception, thanks to the unlawfully delicious food you got catered for us."

Ben felt a flare of pride at the memory, then an even bigger flare of awkwardness, considering the man he was now dating.

"Does Fergus still hate Evan?"

John looked surprised at Ben's question. After a pause, he said, "I don't know, honestly. *I* don't hate Evan, mostly because if it weren't for his cruelty and stupidity, I wouldn't have Fergus. Obviously Evan's not a heartless eejit now," he hurried to add, "seeing as he's with you."

"Does Fergus ever talk about what it was like before things went bad?"

"Not really." John turned back to the pitch, but his focus seemed to wander over the bare-branched trees beyond. "Maybe it still hurts, or maybe it's just the way Fergus is. By that I mean he's like most men, who only talk about feelings after several drinks or a particularly cataclysmic orgasm."

Ben chuckled, feeling John's warm nature melt away some of his trepidation. "Evan hardly ever drinks, so that's an opportunity missed."

John darted a glance at him. "Since when does he hardly ever drink?"

"Since I've known him. Sometimes he'll have a glass of wine with dinner or a dram of whisky with—" *Confessions of being a spy.* "Why?"

"That's one thing Fergus did tell me about their last few months together. He said Evan could down half a dozen pints and still walk a straight line. It worried Fergus." John chewed his bottom lip for a moment. "I remember this bit cos it was so odd: He said that last year, Evan didn't even seem to *enjoy* drinking. He drank like it was a chore, like it was on his to-do list."

On the pitch, the official blew the whistle long and loud. Evan walked toward the bench with his team, wiping sweat from his forehead with his sleeve. He looked up and gave a smile that warmed Ben's blood in an instant, a smile that was easy to return, but faded the moment Evan turned back to his teammates.

Had Evan's job driven him to drink last year? Ben wondered. In that case, wouldn't Fergus have noticed other symptoms of stress? What would inspire Evan to booze it up with such diligence?

There were so many layers to this man, no doubt many that Ben had yet to discover. On the pitch he was flamboyant, even a bit grandstanding, in contrast to his reserved manner everywhere else. His work at MI5 allowed him no glory, keeping him virtually invisible.

Ben's smile returned as he realized only he saw Evan as the icy spy, the fiery lover, *and* the warm, compassionate man who doted on his stray cat. Ben was the only one who saw all of Evan's sides.

For now, that would be enough.

EVAN COULD ALWAYS TELL when a Warrior's partner was attending a match—not by hearing the player's name screamed with lust and affection from the stand, but by the sudden spike in their playing intensity.

He'd seen it with Colin, when Andrew had come to the fifth-round cup tie two months ago. The fierce striker had played so hard he'd collapsed after scoring the winning goal. And Duncan, Evan had heard, got himself a red card the first time Brodie had shown up at a Warriors match last year. Then of course there was the center-back duo Robert and Liam, whose defensive focus had fluctuated with their friends-to-lovers-to-enemies-to-lovers-to-friends-to-boyfriends relationship. *That* now seemed well and truly settled, much to the benefit of the Warriors' overall goal difference.

Evan and Fergus, on the other hand, had maintained a consistent working partnership throughout their romantic ups and downs, leaving their emotional baggage behind when they stepped onto the pitch. So it used to annoy Evan when a player's performance varied with the state of their love life.

Today, he understood. In the first half of this match he'd sprinted faster, hit harder, passed more sharply than usual, all due to Ben's presence. Evan was a hypocrite, but he was a happy hypocrite.

An effective one, too. Due to the offensive strength of Moray Rovers, Evan was playing central midfield—half offense, half defense—rather than in his usual attacking role, which was currently held by Colin, normally a striker. Taking cues from Fergus in the deep defensive midfield position, Evan shut down Moray's attacks and fed the ball back up to Colin, Shona, and Duncan in the Warriors offense.

Best of all, he'd stopped hanging onto the ball and had started passing it. Maybe being forced to trust Ben had taught Evan how to trust his teammates as well, how to take chances when he couldn't control every microsecond.

Most important for his sanity, this match gave Evan ninety minutes to forget about ISIS—or ISIL, as the government was calling the group now. It was impossible to contemplate terrorist plots when one had a sixteen-stone defender literally breathing down one's neck.

"How are you feeling, stamina-wise?" Charlotte asked Evan when he reached the bench with his teammates at halftime, the score still even at 2-2.

"Great." He toweled the sweat from his face and accepted a Lucozade bottle and orange quarter from a substitute. "Thanks, mate."

"Are you great or outstanding?" Charlotte examined him head to toe. "Be honest. What's your week been like? Working any overtime? Getting enough sleep?"

"No overtime. Good sleep." He'd not seen Ben since Monday morning, due to the lad's interim dissertation deadline yesterday.

"Outstanding, then." She stepped up onto the bench, garnering the players' attention for her halftime talk. "Not bad out there," she told the team. "The conservative approach has kept us in the game to this point. Now we need to go for it."

"Their defense is excruciatingly disciplined," Fergus said.

"And compact," Duncan added from the bench beside Evan, scraping mud from between the studs of his bright red football boots. "It's pure tricky threading passes through the middle."

"Which is why we're gonnae go wide to stretch them out, get their center-backs out of their comfort zone." Charlotte held up their tactical board and pointed to the top. "I want Evan to play on the right for now, cos that's where their weaker fullback is. Beat him down and get those crosses in, okay?"

Evan nodded eagerly. He was dying to go into predator mode again. Next to scoring a goal himself, he loved nothing more than sailing in a perfect cross and watching a teammate head it home.

Charlotte subbed out one of the other midfielders for a more defensive choice to make up for Evan moving forward, then raised her voice to get the whole team's attention:

"Mind, lads and lasses, if anyone thinks to play for a draw, the replay match would be in the middle of the week at Moray. That's nearly a four-hour drive from Glasgow. How many Warriors'll be able to sack off their afternoon's work or uni to get there on time?" She scanned the sea of doubtful faces. "We'd be lucky to field even eleven players, much less subs."

Evan silently agreed. The last thing Warriors needed was an extra game, especially given the accidental friendly match with Glasgow Greens, scheduled for their one free weekend—the weekend they were meant to rest and train before the season's final push.

"Today is win or lose," Charlotte concluded as they stood to return to the pitch. "So let's play like there's no tomorrow."

"How are you handling Evan's job?"

Ben looked at Lord Andrew. They were alone now that John and Brodie had thoughtfully left the stand to eat their halftime snacks without making Ben hungrier. "His job?"

"It must be difficult," Andrew said, "with all the secrets."

Ben remembered what Evan had told him last Saturday night: *"Never talk to anyone about what I do, even if they act like they already know."* He also recalled how a security breach could cost Evan his metaphorical and literal head.

"You mean architectural secrets?" Ben asked, hoping his widened eyes looked innocent instead of scared.

Andrew took off his sunglasses and examined him with a penetrating silver-blue gaze. "Right." He drummed his fingertips against his knees, his eyes darting over the dozens of football fans milling in front of them. Ben knew that ever since his attempted kidnapping, Andrew sometimes had difficulty with crowds. Yet he braved them to cheer on his partner, Colin, at every match.

The silence grew until Ben couldn't stand it. "Why do you ask?"

Andrew ran his thumbs along the seams of his trousers. "Evan's helped me a lot with my…issues."

Ben nodded. Andrew had recently shared his PTSD struggles with his legions of online fans, but before that, he'd confided only in Evan.

"I don't know what happened to him," Andrew continued, "or whether it's anything to do with his job, but he seems to understand what it's like."

"Ah." Ben thought about Evan's fear of the dark and his need to see Ben's face during sex. "I don't know what happened to him either, but I'm glad he was there for you."

"The thing is, I just can't reconcile the Evan I know with the villain some of the Warriors make him out to be."

Ben sensed he'd heard but a fraction of the terrible rumors. "Don't tell me what they say. Bahá'ís are meant to avoid gossip."

Andrew arched one lordly eyebrow at him. "I've heard they're also meant to avoid being gay."

"It's okay to *be* gay, as long as we don't…you know, do gay things."

"Like waving a rainbow flag at a Warriors match?"

"Like having sex with other men," Ben said.

"Ah, so you can be gay as long as you're celibate. What could possibly go wrong? Let's ask a few priests."

Ben bristled at the sarcasm, but he had no defense.

"So what happens if you break the rules?" Andrew asked. "Do they excommunicate you?"

"In a sense. I could lose my voting rights, and I'd no longer be Bahá'í in the eyes of the community."

Andrew frowned. "What about in your own eyes?"

The question made Ben's chest ache. "I'll always be Bahá'í."

"Good. Don't ever let anyone tell you who you are." Andrew touched the seat behind Ben. "Brodie here, his family were small-minded monsters, so he had to make a clean break from them and be nothing but his new, fabulously gay self." He examined Ben. "But I think your situation's more like my own."

"How so?"

"The aristocracy is built upon heredity—namely, having children with other worthy folk of the opposite sex. I'll never fit in with that scheme, but I'll be damned if I'll dissolve my connections with that world and the traditions I love, simply to maintain the illusion of a pure identity." He lifted his chin in his signature haughtiness. "Being a toff is part of who I am, just like being Bahá'í is part of who you are."

"But not all of it."

"Exactly. One day our worlds will catch up to us. Until then…" Andrew swept his palms up and out as though making a proclamation. "We must simply 'live in the tension,' as my therapist says, between our two identities."

Strangely, Andrew's words made Ben feel better, even though they provided no easy answers. It helped to know he wasn't alone in feeling like he was always betraying part of himself.

"Hiya! Are you Ben Reid?"

Startled out of this heavy conversation, Ben turned to see a pair of guys in their early thirties moving into the empty row in front of him, taking the place of the fans who'd stepped away for the halftime break.

"Erm, yeah." He introduced Andrew, whom they already knew from the Regiment and because he was famous.

"I'm Michael," said the taller one, "and this is Philip. We

emailed you last month about our wedding on the eighteenth of April?"

"Ah, right. Sorry I had to say no." Ben tried not to squirm. He hated disappointing people, and doing it to their faces was pure torture.

"Nae bother," Philip said. "You told us to ask again in a month to see if your uni schedule had got a wee bit less mad. If we still needed help, that is."

"Which we do." Michael took a seat in front of Ben so he was looking up at him, like a subject beseeching a monarch. "We're desperate."

"Not to pressure you." Philip fidgeted with the hem of his Warriors COME OUT AND PLAY T-shirt. "I'm sure you're busy."

"He is," Andrew said. "Dissertation and all."

The thought of that looming project, plus exams, made Ben's head spin. Yet he found himself pulling out his phone to check his scheduling app. "The eighteenth is during spring vacation at uni."

Their faces brightened with hope.

"Tell you what," Ben said. "I might be able to do a simple wedding-day coordination package. That means I wouldn't be arranging suppliers—"

"We've got them sorted," Michael said. "We just need someone to keep it all organized and-and-and—"

"And keep us sane," Philip finished.

"That's exactly a wedding-day coordinator's job." Ben wanted to agree right then and there, but he needed to consider both his schedule and how this could affect his mother. "Just upload everything—contracts, invoices, any documentation—to your favorite cloud storage place and email me the link tonight. I'll let you know tomorrow whether it seems manageable."

"Cheers, mate." Michael shook Ben's hand, clasping it between his own. "You're an angel."

"Nah, I'm mostly human," Ben said, though he couldn't help grinning at their gratitude.

"By the way," Philip said, "we've changed the venue. We're

marrying here, after the Warriors' friendly match with Glasgow Greens. Will that be a problem?"

Ben looked over his shoulder at the looming fitness complex. "You're to be married in there?"

"Nah, on the pitch," Michael said. "We got permission to put up a tent for the food and drink next to the building over there."

"Oh." Ben's mind reeled with this project's potential pitfalls. Here there'd be no events manager like at a hotel, so he'd be overseeing every detail. "It's quite a bit more work at a venue like this. I'd need to hire at least one assistant."

"Do it," Michael said. "We'll pay anything."

Philip glared at his fiancé, but then sighed and said, "Aye. Anything."

Ben was torn. With no permanent job in place after graduation, he could use the money. "We'll discuss it tomorrow."

The two men thanked him again, then returned to their seats in the front row.

He turned to Andrew. "An outdoor wedding at a park where the only shelter and public toilets are in a gym?" Ben rubbed his temples, trying to stave off the looming dehydration-hunger-stress headache. "What a nightmare."

"Simply frighten them away by charging an astronomical fee," Andrew said. "By the way, Colin told me about the genesis of this friendly match—that day you and Evan and Jamie went to scout Greens players?"

"Yes, it was my idea, and yes, I see the poetic justice in it now being my problem."

"Still, I heard it was first-class improvising on your part."

"Sadly, I've loads of experience cleaning up after my big mouth."

He couldn't help worrying that someday he'd accidentally reveal Evan's biggest secret. After only a week of knowing he was dating a spy, Ben was mentally knackered. Maybe it would get easier with time, but right now it felt like being in another sort of closet.

As halftime ended, Ben watched Evan and Fergus return to the pitch together, nodding as they spoke and gesturing to various parts of the field.

What did everyone else see when they looked at those two men? Did their fists clench at the thought of what Evan had done to Fergus? Did they wish him an eternity roasting on the spits of hell? If only they knew the truth.

Ben's stomach clenched—this time not from hunger but from dread at the knowledge that the Warriors and their fans would never know what really happened last year. They'd never know Evan for the hero he was.

And Ben could never tell them.

"TODAY IS WIN OR LOSE," Charlotte had said, and the Warriors had taken her words to heart. Evan and his teammates played harder than ever, opening up the Moray defense with wider, faster attacks, risking a devastating counterattack in the quest for that one elusive scoring chance.

Now, Moray had just won a throw-in, but their fullback looked uncertain as he lifted the ball above his head. Evan guessed which Rover he was about to throw it to, and dashed to intercept.

He'd guessed right, timing it perfectly to steal the ball. He did a quick stutter step to avoid a midfielder, sent a lofted pass to Fergus, and shot forward along the touchline, calling for the ball back. The pitch ahead of him was wide open.

But a gust of wind came up, slowing the ball on its flight to Fergus, so that by the time the Warriors captain received the pass, a Moray midfielder was bearing down on him from behind.

"Man on!" Evan shouted.

With no time to take the ball with his foot, Fergus leapt to head it out in front of himself. He raced forward with lengthening strides to pick up the ball, then sent a hard, low pass back toward Evan.

Before he'd even received the pass, Evan saw Fergus pull up, clutching the back of his right thigh.

Oh no. Evan kicked the ball out over the touchline to stop play. The whistle blew.

The two official match physios hurried with their medical bags across the pitch toward the Warriors captain. Fergus was already down, leaning back with his legs outstretched, palms flat on the turf behind him, chin lowered in defeat.

The crowd had fallen silent. Evan looked back at the stand, where John was on his feet, palms pressed to his face. In front of the bench, Charlotte was beckoning Evan. He hurried toward her, accompanied by Jamie, while the rest of the squad gathered around Fergus to offer support and also partake of the water bottles the physios had carried on their packs.

"Looks like a hamstring," Evan told Charlotte. "If he comes off, how do you want to play this?"

"Depends." She handed him and Jamie their own squeeze bottles. "How much you two got left in the tank?"

"I'm all right," Jamie said.

"Me too." Evan took a short sip of water. "You know I'll run myself into the ground if that's what it takes."

"Please don't." Charlotte pinched the bridge of her nose, something she did when trying not to panic. "Okay, I'll make a like-for-like change. Both of you keep doing what you're doing. We're gonnae break through on that right side, I know it." She turned to the substitutes. "Craig, you'll take Fergus's place."

Fergus arrived them, limping off the pitch with the help of the physios. He ripped off his captain's armband and tossed it to Evan.

"Shall I give this to Liam?" Evan asked. Usually the vice-captain got the armband when the captain went off.

"No, it should be you." Before Evan could process the honor his ex had given him, Fergus added, "Liam's on a yellow card, and if he got sent off it'd be embarrassing to pass on the armband again."

Evan examined Fergus's band. It was vivid blue, unlike the black one Evan had used as captain last season, the one he'd sent to Fergus on the day of that fateful quarterfinal—the day he'd left for Belfast.

He'd had to make the cruelest possible break so Fergus wouldn't try to find him or ask questions that could get them both jailed or killed. What could be crueler than an express-delivery envelope containing a discarded armband and a sorry-I'm-in-love-with-a-Belgian note?

In the end, he and Fergus had both survived. But neither had escaped unscathed.

"It's quicker if I do this for you." Jamie took the armband and wrapped it around Evan's biceps, securing it with the Velcro pads. "We have to win now, for Fergus." The fullback tugged the end of Evan's shirt sleeve out from under the band. "Right?"

"Right," Evan replied, still in a haze of memory.

Jamie seized him by both shoulders and shook him. "RIGHT?!"

For a moment, Evan's vision went red, and his ingrained self-defense sequence—step back, reach up, grab head, slam knee—flashed through his mind.

Jamie froze, clearly seeing the look in Evan's eyes. As he started to let go, Evan grabbed his shoulders in return, bunching his jersey in his fists.

"RIGHT!" Evan gave him a shake. "For Fergus!"

They let go with simultaneous shoves, then shared a high-five. As Evan turned to the pitch to get back into position, he felt a new surge of adrenaline that felt limitless.

He'd survived tougher enemies than this. Nothing could beat him—not last year's Cup finalists, not the awesome responsibility of captaining, not even the soul-crushing regret of last year's departure from the team.

Despite the Warriors' defiance, the next ten minutes were shaky while Fergus's substitute, Craig, got fully warmed up. Then the tide began to turn in the Warriors' favor. With fresh legs, Craig was able to block the attacks of the rapidly tiring Rovers center-forward.

When the Moray manager sent in a substitute striker whom Evan remembered from the scouting reports, he gathered the Warriors for a brief talk.

"This guy's pure fast," he told them, focusing on Craig and the four Warriors defenders. "But he's also nervy. If you put pressure on him the instant before he gets the ball, he'll take his eye off it, and bang, it's yours."

"So we intimidate the everliving crap out of him," Liam said, "which is basically what I live for." He gave Evan a grim smile, probably the kindest expression he'd bestowed upon him in nearly a year.

Soon it was clear the Warriors defense had the new striker well in hand, so Evan turned his focus to offense. The Rovers back line had started to fray under the onslaught of Woodstoun's flank attacks.

As the clock neared ninety minutes, the Moray fullback on Evan's side of the pitch was obviously tiring. The exhausted defender's likely substitute was warming up on the touchline, ready to provide relief.

Oh no you don't, Evan thought. *I won't let you off that lightly.*

He dribbled past the Rovers winger, then saw a gap that let him keep driving toward the corner. The left fullback yelped in alarm and headed for him, followed by the center back.

With one last surge of energy, Evan got past both defenders. In the corner of his eye, he saw a teammate's arm go up and heard Colin's hoarse shout.

Planting his foot, Evan swept the ball up and over.

At the far post, Colin rose like a dolphin to head the ball. It whipped into the goal past the helpless keeper.

"YAAAAASSSS!" Colin raced toward Evan, arms spread, their fair skin a stark backdrop to his fierce black tattoos. Evan met him in a victorious embrace, and they were soon joined by Duncan and Shona, whose impact toppled them over. From the bottom of the burgeoning pile, Evan could hear the shrieks of the crowd and knew Ben's was among them.

Once the Warriors had picked themselves up, Evan got their attention and put on his serious voice. "Keep the heads, everybody. We've not won yet. Focus on what you need to do each moment, and we've got this."

They did have it, a few minutes later. When the final whistle blew, Evan sat down on the pitch and put his head in his hands, utterly spent.

"Nope. Not having it." Duncan reached down under Evan's shoulders, then hoisted him up by the oxters. "You'll celebrate with the rest of us, not sit about moping like we lost."

"I'm not moping, I'm processing."

"'Processing.' And here I thought I was the psychobabbler." Duncan pointed at the stand as they walked. "Look, there's Ben and Brodie. Aren't they cute when they're happy? Also when they're not happy, but you know…"

Evan shaded his eyes to see Ben waving his rainbow cap and singing with the rest of the Rainbow Regiment.

Alas, the Warriors' bliss was dampened when they found Fergus sitting on the bench with an ice pack strapped to his thigh.

"I'll need tests to see the extent of the damage," he told them, "but based on my symptoms, the physios say I'll be out at least a month."

"Will you stay on as captain until he's back?" Charlotte asked Evan.

"Of course," he said, "and not a day longer."

Liam snorted. "Aye, right." Then he rubbed his mouth as he realized everyone had heard him.

Fergus gave the defender a glare that said, *And this is why you're not captain.*

After Charlotte's post-match debriefing, Fergus motioned Evan over to sit beside him.

"What is it?" Evan asked, unwrapping a protein bar and offering half of it to Fergus, who shook his head.

"I just need to be miserable for a minute without worrying the team, and I figured your presence would explain it." He began to unwind the strap holding the ice pack against his leg. "This could be the beginning of the end for me. They say once you've had one hamstring injury…"

"Aye, they tend to recur." It was a leading cause of athletes' early retirement. "But there are things you can do to prevent the next one. Have you tried the Nordic method? You kneel down and have a partner hold your—"

"Not everything from Norway is better, okay?"

Evan suppressed a smile at the resurrection of their old bickering topic. "Lutefisk is a well-known antidote to muscle strain."

Fergus rolled his eyes. "*Faen ta deg.*"

Evan laughed. "I can't believe you still remember the Norwegian for 'Fuck you.'"

"I wish I could forget." Fergus bent over and took a clear plastic bag from his kit bag. "For the armband."

Evan unwrapped the band from his biceps—carefully, knowing how protective Fergus was of his possessions—and slipped it into the bag. "Or I could buy a new one if you prefer."

Fergus stared at the armband for a long moment. "Yes," he said softly as he took it back. "In case anything should happen to you."

Evan's words stuck in his throat. He wanted to promise that nothing would ever happen to him, that he'd never let the Warriors down again.

But that promise would be as frail and fragile as a baby bird's bones.

Chapter 23

BEN WAS STILL BUZZING from the match when they entered Evan's flat early Saturday evening. "I wish someone had been filming. I'd give your free kick thing a million views by myself. And now of course I'm totally obsessed with the massive power of your legs."

Evan held him off at arm's length. "Mind on, I'm absolutely reeking of sweat at the moment, legs and all." Stepping away from Ben, he removed his jacket. "You hungry?"

"Famished. I could almost eat Trent." He picked up the purring cat and made chomping noises against her neck. "Just kidding, my beauty."

"While I shower, can you put the macaroni cheese in the oven? Instructions are on the dish in the fridge. It should be ready just after sunset in time to break your fast."

"You cooked for me?"

Evan shrugged. "Usually after a match I make linguine primavera, but I knew you'd be starving and wouldn't want to wait while I chopped the veg."

Ben threw his arms around Evan's neck and kissed him. "You are magic—oh, and yes, rather smelly." He let go.

Evan moved past him to the table to pick up a phone Ben had never seen before. "Need to check for work messages."

"Do you ever get a proper day off?"

Evan didn't answer. His whole face seemed to narrow as he read the phone screen. Even the dimple in his chin furrowed deeper.

"Do you need to handle that?" Ben asked.

"Aye." Evan switched off the phone and set it back on the table. "But I need the shower time to figure out how. The remote control's on top of the telly if you want to watch something."

"No, I need to—" Ben cleared his throat. "I need to pray." It still felt weird acknowledging it out loud. "Ideally a short and a medium one before sunset."

"Word of warning: If you get on the floor, Trent will want to be involved. Speaking as her unwilling yoga partner."

As Ben put the macaroni cheese in the oven, then washed his hands and face at the kitchen sink, he tried not to think about Evan's work phone sitting a few feet away. It killed him not to know what had been so concerning, but it would be illegal—and wrong—to snoop. Besides, the device was surely protected by a password or fingerprint or retina scan (or all three).

He could do this. He could be with a spy. After all, he'd resisted Andrew's attempts to discover Evan's job. He could do this.

His phone bleeped with the notification tone of his Bahá'í Prayers app, reminding him it was nearly sunset.

Right. Priorities.

He used the app's compass to point him toward the Qiblih, the location of the Shrine of Bahá'u'lláh in northern Israel, then took a few deep breaths to put himself into the proper state of mind.

After he'd finished both prayers, the urge to pick up Evan's work phone had passed. He couldn't move, anyway, because Trent had crawled into his lap the moment he'd sat cross-legged on the floor for the prayer's final section.

Twenty minutes later, Ben was already tearing into his second serving of macaroni cheese.

"Is it very difficult, fasting?" Evan asked as he scooped another spoonful onto his own plate.

"Sometimes, but that's sort of the point." Realizing he sounded pious, Ben gave a quick shrug. "At least it's the same number of hours every year. Muslims have it much harder when Ramadan is in the summer." He took another sip of water, trying not to gulp. "Overall, the Bahá'í Faith is pretty undemanding. No weekly services, no dietary restrictions apart from alcohol and tobacco, and best of all, no Crusades or Inquisitions. Just nineteen days of fasting plus the obligatory prayers—which, despite the name, aren't meant to be a burden. We do them when we can, and when we can't, that's okay too." He opened up a bit more, feeling safe with Evan. "I'm happier when I pray every day. It makes me feel, I don't know…" *Closer to God.* "Centered."

Evan brightened. "Oh, like meditation?"

"Sort of." Ben considered leaving it at that, to build a bridge between their experiences. But the two of them *were* different, and they should deal with that sooner rather than later. "Most Western meditation is human-oriented, not divine."

"True. I couldn't meditate if I had to focus on a god I don't believe in." Evan gave him a look of regret. "Sorry."

"No bother." Ben waved his fork. "I don't care if you share my beliefs as long you respect them."

"I do."

"I know." He gave Evan a soft smile, feeling drunk on carbs. "Don't worry, I won't try to convert you. Bahá'ís don't proselytize, like, ever. If someone's clearly seeking, we offer guidance, but how they respond is up to them."

"Still, you clearly love your faith, so why wouldn't you want to share it with others?"

Ben smirked. "Because historically, when other religions have 'shared their faith,' it's usually been at sword point."

"Fair enough. Hey, did you know there's a Bahá'í center in Orkney?"

"Really?" Ben was amazed, as there were only a few hundred

Bahá'ís in all Scotland. "I always picture Orcadians as rather traditional."

"Most are, but there's a constant influx of free-spirited ferry loopers. We welcome all sorts from 'doon Sooth' and beyond." Evan cleared his throat and shifted in his seat. "Talking of Orkney, my sister's wedding is in two weeks, the day after the solar eclipse. Would you like to come with me?"

Ben nearly dropped his fork. "Seriously? Yes! Yes, of course."

"It's the twenty-first. That's a holiday for you, right?"

"Och, right, it's Naw-Rúz. It'd be my first time away from my mum for the new year." He sighed. "The eclipse will be even better up north, right?"

"Ninety-eight percent totality."

"And to see an Orcadian wedding in person..." Ben gasped again. "Will you be in a kilt?"

"They're not really part of our culture."

"Oh."

Evan waited a beat. "But my sister's marrying a Scotsman, so..." He gave a mischievous grin. "Kilts ahoy."

"Yas!" Ben punched the air in triumph. "You're sure it's not too late to add me as a guest?"

"My sister said she'd happily find room for my new partner."

Ben stared at him, his mouth suddenly dry despite all the water he'd drunk. "I'm your partner?"

Evan's smile faltered. "Is that a problem?"

"No, I—" Ben felt his face flush. "It's been six years since anyone called me partner or boyfriend."

"We could call each other *kjæreste*," Evan said, pronouncing it *SHA-rest-uh*. "It's Norwegian for 'dearest one,' and it's non-gender."

"Call me whatever you like. I just hope I can..." *Keep you*. Ben cleared his throat. "I hope I can find some proper clothes. Your family'll have one look at my urban wardrobe and chuck me in the harbor with the other ferry troopers."

"Ferry loopers. If this is moving too fast for you—"

"It's not." Ben took a deep breath. "It is fast, but I like it that way. Not normally, I mean, not with anyone else. Just you."

"Good." Evan linked his hand with Ben's, then leaned·over and kissed him, slow and sweet, as though searching for doubt.

But there was none to be found. As Ben sank into the kiss, the last shred of uncertainty faded away.

Interesting

GUNNAR'S ONE-WORD response to Jordan's text kept echoing in Evan's head as he and Ben did the washing-up after dinner. On one level, *interesting* was a lie; on another level, it was an understatement.

"Does she ever *not* want attention?" Ben asked, tossing Trent's jingly plastic football for the eleventh time.

"Sometimes when she's asleep. It's like having a dog, except she's clean and quiet." Trent yawped with indignation as the tiny football went out of her reach beneath the couch. "She's clean, at least," Evan added.

Such domestic harmony couldn't keep him from ruminating on the link Jordan had sent Gunnar: an essay about how "Western values" like feminism and LGBTQ rights were a threat to all "great civilizations"—the greatest, of course, being the British Empire, as if that was still a thing. Evan marveled that Jordan couldn't see the parallels between such reactionary thinkers and the Islamic extremists they targeted.

Evan's body was here washing the dishes, but his mind was dying to delve into this essayist, see what else he'd written and how influential he was. This urge disturbed him—couldn't he leave his work at the office and enjoy a few peaceful hours with Ben? It was easy to fall into the trap of thinking, *If I stop working, people might die.* Especially since that was true.

He could do this. He could be a good spook *and* a good partner. He could live two lives, without one oozing over into the other. He could do this.

"Oh, big news!" Ben said, tossing another cat toy with a flourish. "Michael and Philip from the Rainbow Regiment asked me to handle their wedding."

Evan froze, recalling the ISIS flag on that laptop screen. "Did you say yes?"

"I've not decided yet. But the poor lads are desperate."

"Hm." Evan turned away and opened the freezer to hide the worry on his face. "Aren't you too busy with uni?"

"Absolutely."

"And what about your mum? Won't she be upset?"

"Yes. It's a dilemma. Ooh, you got ice cream, too? I am pure smitten with you just now." As Evan set the ice cream on the worktop, Ben slipped into his arms. "Do I seem cheap, my affection so easily bought with fatty foods?"

"You're the opposite of cheap." Evan pulled him close and buried his face in Ben's hair. The thought of this man in danger again…

Ben kissed Evan's neck and pulled away. "Now go and rest your tired superhero legs while I make us tea."

Evan headed for the couch, relieved to have a few minutes to cope with his rising dread.

He and his team had spent the week assessing what appeared to be an ISIS-inspired threat to same-sex weddings. Evan, Lewis, and Adira had pored over chat-room discussions and social-media posts about the St. Andrew's evacuation, with Adira handling the Arabic, Persian, Pashtun, and Urdu conversations. Despite the lack of attack, the online activity was eerily similar to that following an actual ISIS-inspired incident. Yet Adira noted that many of the posts, even by supposed Muslims, showed a limited understanding of Islam. The religion's portrayal, she said, was almost a caricature, *as though the true audience wasn't Muslim at all.*

The mysterious white Outlander, meanwhile, had been found

abandoned in a ditch south of Glasgow, far from any CCTV coverage. The police were forensically examining the vehicle, but unless its occupants were already in the DNA and finger-print databases due to a previous arrest, no match would come up.

After procuring a warrant to covertly surveil the video-maker's flat, Evan and Ned had paid a visit to the block of short-term rentals in St. Andrew's Square. While Evan distracted the kindly Ukrainian octogenarian landlady by inquiring after a temporary home for his visiting mum, Ned installed a listening device in the filmmaker's flat—a flat which had remained silent and empty ever since.

The video itself made the least sense of all. With most terrorists "going dark" in the face of government surveillance, who would be foolish enough to post that video where any intelligence officer worth their salt could discover it?

Still, the videographer had used the semi-defunct Imageo site, so perhaps they'd tried to hide it and failed. But maybe that was the point: to leave a trail of bread crumbs, not a trail of neon blinking arrows.

By the end of the week, Evan and his team had begun to wonder whether it was all a stitch-up. The British Values Party had motive to frame Muslims for a potential attack, but Evan doubted those fascist fuckwits could run a pub quiz, much less a complex disinformation campaign. The almost childish numerical code for the video title—A = 1, B = 2—was too simple and common to be a sure signature. Just because neo-Nazis liked to use it for their tattoos didn't mean they'd used it here.

Evan needed to know more, which is why he planned to attend his first BVP meeting next week. He'd be alone in the lion's den—unlike at the rally, he'd have no police backup.

Backups fail anyway, came a rogue thought. *In the end, I'm all I've got.*

Ben appeared with a tray of ice cream and tea. Instead of setting it on the coffee table, he stood before Evan with a determined look on his face. "I've decided to do Michael and Philip's wedding."

Evan fought to hide his dismay. "Are you sure?" On the slim chance the threat *was* real, Ben could be in danger.

"It's just a wedding-day coordination job, so yes, I can find the time. Somehow."

Evan wanted to dissuade him but knew if he pushed too hard, Ben might get suspicious, maybe even guessing why Evan was worried. And if Evan *told* him why and got caught, he and Ben could both go to prison.

Then there was the risk to national security. Ben might warn Michael and Philip, who might cancel their wedding and alert others in the community. Soon the terrorists would know the authorities were onto them. They'd go silent and cautious, remaining on the loose until they carried out a successful attack elsewhere.

"The bigger worry is Mum. She'll throw a strop for sure." Ben set down the tray, then straightened up, crossing his arms. "But I can't live in fear, you know?"

I know. You have no idea how much I know. "Tell me how I can help."

Ben dropped his arms, shoulders slumping in relief. "Thank you. That means a lot." He settled onto the couch beside Evan and gave him a sweet, lingering kiss. Then he picked up the remote control. "Now, if we're to be boyfriends, we must find 'our' show, one we both love equally. It's a requirement, I hear."

They watched the first episode of three new Netflix programs, which Evan barely registered, his mind whirling with a hundred different outcomes, none of them good.

Halfway through the second program, he remembered with a start the reason Kay had let him stay on Operation Caps Lock— had let him stay in Glasgow, full stop: Ben was no longer handling same-sex weddings. Now that his partner was a potential victim again, Evan could no longer be impartial.

He looked down at Ben lying on his chest, fitted perfectly

between his legs with a blanket draped over them both. Trent was curled up on Ben's stomach, somehow sleeping through the lap-quakes of his laughter.

Evan would do anything to protect this happiness from all enemies, real and imagined, and especially to protect the man who had bestowed it. Taking himself out of the operation could make everyone, including Ben, less safe. Evan would stay on Caps Lock and hope that Kay never found out about this new wedding.

And if Ben was determined not to live in fear, Evan would teach him how.

Chapter 24

"THAT WAS ONLY THE WARMUP?!" Ben shouted with what felt like his last breath. "Are you trying to kill me?"

"Hopefully the opposite," Evan said.

Ben staggered after him to the opposite side of the Merchant City gym, past fit and sweaty men he was already too exhausted to admire. As he walked, he tried to subtly adjust his athletic cup, a foreign-feeling device he'd not worn in years.

His first mistake had been asking Evan whether MI5 had trained him to kill grown men with just his pinky fingers. In response, Evan had sung the praises of Krav Maga, developed for the Israeli Defense Forces, who needed a fighting technique that could be quickly mastered by people of all sizes, genders, and fitness levels.

Ben's second mistake was saying that *that* claim sounded like rubbish.

Now here he was, making what was likely his final mistake: letting his boyfriend give him a lesson in "aggressive survival."

Evan found a clear space on a blue mat near the wall. "We'll start with the basic fighting stance." He demonstrated, one foot in front of the other at shoulder width, hands nearly level with his face—the left one out to protect and the right one held back ready to strike. "Don't be flat-footed. Stay on the balls of your feet."

"Stay on the balls. Got it." Ben imitated his stance. "Like this?"

"That's great."

"I did it right the first time?"

"It's not ballroom dancing. There's no points for precision. Next we'll do palm strikes."

Ben followed his movements, smacking the air with the heel of his hand, then pulling back to do it again.

"Keep your balance," Evan said. "Don't overextend." He stepped close and raised Ben's left hand back into position. "And never, ever drop your guard."

After Ben gave a few more practice strikes, Evan picked up a blue vinyl pad from a pile beside the wall. He tossed it to Ben. "Hold that by the side handles, up against your chest, nice and straight."

The pad looked like a punch bag the size and shape of an orthopedic pillow. "Do we hit each other with these?"

Evan laughed. "No, we just hit them."

Ben took a step back. "You're going to hit me?"

"Not you, the bag."

"But I'm holding the bag."

"Not quite." He stepped forward and placed Ben's bag flush against his chest. "Put your feet in fighting stance to help you absorb the impact. Tuck your chin so you don't get whiplash."

Whiplash?! Ben lowered the bag. "Are you sure I can—"

"I won't hit hard. But I will do it right, so you can feel what it's like." He stepped closer. "One of the most important things you learn in Krav Maga is that getting hit is not the end of the world."

"Not for someone like you." Ben thought of all the times Evan had ended up on his arse during last Saturday's match.

"Not for anyone." Evan touched his arm. "It's in all of us to be strong and fierce. One of the best fighters in my class is a sixty-year-old woman with arthritis. If she can do it…"

"Fine, fine." Ben raised the bag the way he'd been shown, then set his feet and tucked his chin. "Okay, I'm—"

Evan struck the bag with a "Hunh!"

"Whoa." Ben tottered back, blinking hard. Then his adrenaline spiked, and he reset his stance. "Do it again."

"Hunh!" Evan's blow came harder this time, but Ben held firm. He could feel the momentum, like Evan was trying to hit *through* him.

After a few more strikes, Evan said, "Got the idea?"

"Oh yeah." He shoved the bag into Evan's arms. "Let's do this." With his aversion to violence, Ben had been dreading landing an actual hit, but after being on the receiving end, it was all he wanted.

"Whenever you're ready."

Ben lashed out, smacking the bag with all the force of a toddler patting a brick wall. "That was shite."

"It was fine. But move a peedie bit closer to me so I get the full force. And put your hip into it. The strike should come from your whole body, not just your arm. And though it may feel silly at first, it helps to yell."

Ben tried again, shouting "Hah!" as his hand flashed out. It made a satisfying *thwack* against the bag. "Wow!" He dropped his arms. "That felt—"

Evan bashed the bag against his chest. Ben toppled backward, sprawling onto the mat.

He stared up at Evan. "I can't believe you just—"

"A real-life attacker won't stand there while you celebrate landing a blow. And he'll do a lot more than put you on your arse." He reached out a hand to help him up.

Ben rolled away and got to his feet on his own. "If I take a class, will they teach me how to do that to you?"

"If not, then ask for a refund."

They continued with palm strikes, Evan urging Ben on as he landed blow after blow. Then he taught him four combinations, calling them out by number for Ben to strike.

While they took a hydration break, Ben leaned against the wall, willing his heart to keep beating. "Will I be able to move tomorrow?"

"Sure." Evan wiped the back of his neck with a towel. "But probably not the day after."

"It's worth it, though?"

Evan nodded. "The best thing about Krav Maga is what it does for your confidence. You don't become fearless, because that's stupid, but you learn you're a lot stronger than you think."

"That's not saying much, as I think I'm pretty weak."

"Most of that confidence has nothing to do with actual fighting," Evan continued, ignoring Ben's self-insult. "When I'm out on the pitch and a opponent's fan calls me names, I take comfort knowing I could put them on their knees in about five seconds, bleeding from at least two orifices."

"Oh." Ben was almost ashamed at the thrill that coursed through him. Almost.

Evan tossed the towel aside. "Ready for punches?"

Ben made a fist. "Promise I'll still be able to give hand jobs after?"

"Not if you do that." He unfolded Ben's hand, then refolded it with his thumb on the outside instead of the inside. "There, now you won't break your thumb."

Ben examined his newly configured fist. It felt awkward and small and incapable of damage. "We don't use gloves?"

"Some people use them to keep their knuckles from getting bruised or cut. I'll wrap my hands for a long session with the bag, but mostly I like to train the way I'd fight in real life, blocking out the pain as I go."

Ben rolled his eyes. "Great."

They began again. Now the bag felt like it contained bricks instead of padding. Ben kept going, trying not to wince, vowing to invest in the thickest pair of gloves he could find.

After that, Evan taught him how to break free of a choke hold from the front, an exercise they did in slow motion so no one's balls got kicked.

"Almost finished," Evan said. "That means it's time for an adversity drill."

Ben clapped his hands. "Sounds fun!" he said, meaning the opposite.

"You'll do continuous straight punches on the bag." Evan held it up to his chest. "When I say, 'down,' you drop to the floor and do press-ups."

"More press-ups?" They'd started with those at the beginning of the session, and Ben had barely managed three.

"Then when I say, 'up,' you jump up and start punching again. We'll do this a few times until I say 'stop.'"

"That sounds like torture."

"It'll feel like it, too. But the point isn't to make you miserable." Evan lowered the bag. "You need to learn to fight exhausted. A real-life attacker won't stop just because you're tired."

"But if I'm attacked in real life, won't I be too jacked up on adrenaline to get tired? Like those mothers lifting cars to save their babies?"

"You canna depend on that," Evan said. "Instinct will tell you to stop when it gets hard. It'll tell you to stay down when you're hit, to curl into a ball and beg them to stop."

Ben's gut twisted at the image.

"Training helps you override instinct," Evan said. "It rewires your brain through repetition. You do this here in the gym where it's safe, and something inside you changes."

Curious, Ben raised his fists and set his feet. "Let's do this."

Evan raised the bag. "Go!"

Ben struck, again and again, knuckles aching. Evan urged him on as he flailed, each punch getting slower and weaker.

"You're doing it, Ben. You're fucking brilliant. Now down!"

"Ugh…" Ben sank to the mat. With Evan's encouragement, he

did two more press-ups before being told to get up and start punching again.

Strangely, his blows landed harder this time, though he could barely feel his arms. Streams of sweat stung his eyes.

"Keep your guard up, Ben. And let's hear your voice."

"Hah! Huh! Fuh!" Ben could feel spittle mixing with sweat on his chin, but he didn't care.

"Down!"

He dropped again without wasting a single breath on whingeing. When Evan ordered him up the second time, Ben staggered a bit.

"All right?" Evan asked. "If you're dizzy, we'll stop."

"Not...dizzy." Ben hit the bag again, harder than ever. "Just..." He couldn't even find the word. He wanted to stop, needed to stop, every cell in his body was begging him to stop...

And then it happened. Something inside him shifted into survival mode.

I don't stop. I can't stop. If I stop, I die.

Panting hard, he pressed forward, driving Evan back toward the wall. His cries became a stew of syllables raining down on the bag with his fists.

Can't stop until he's down. Can't stop until it's over, even if it takes a hundred years.

"Time!"

Evan's command reached Ben's brain a millisecond too late. This time, his fist connected with something that was definitely not a bag.

"Och!" Evan turned away, holding his face.

Ben leapt back, fists raised, pulse pounding in his ears. "Did you say 'time'?"

"Aye." Evan's voice was muffled by his hands.

"Did I just punch you?" He moved forward—cautiously, in case it was a trick.

"A bit." Evan turned to him, wiping his nose. Blood streaked the back of his hand.

"Oh my God, I broke your face!" He would never forgive himself for ruining such a thing of beauty.

Evan laughed a little. "It's not broken. I started to dodge when I realized you weren't stopping. Thank God for reflexes." He pinched his nose and tilted his head back. "How'd that feel?"

"You were right." Ben handed him one of the towels, then used the other to wipe what seemed like an inch-deep layer of sweat from his own face. "It was terrible. It was wonderful. It was…like nothing I've ever felt before."

"You'll take a class, then?"

Ben considered the idea. It was one thing to be awkward and incompetent in front of someone he trusted, and another thing to embarrass himself amidst an entire class of strangers. But he wanted more of this feeling, more of doing something really fucking hard and coming out the other side in one piece.

"Sign me up."

EVAN LAY in the semi-darkness of his bedroom, listening to Ben's breath as it slowly transformed from panting to sighing. Finally it culminated in a laugh so rich and warm, Evan wanted to crawl inside it and wrap it around himself.

"That was…" Ben laughed again. "Never mind. Words fail."

"Luckily we don't need words."

"But they're so fun." Ben skated a finger down the center of Evan's breastbone. "Tell me a secret."

Evan smiled at the request. This was a classic spy technique, getting people to say things they shouldn't while drowsing in the hazy aftermath of sex, during those moments when life felt safe.

"I don't tell secrets, I keep them," he murmured. "It's not just my job, it's my nature."

Ben gave another soft laugh against Evan's shoulder, his breath caressing bare skin. "You already told me the biggest secret, about what you do for a living."

Evan twined his leg with Ben's, wishing the mere fact of his job really was his biggest secret. "And yet here you are, wanting more."

"I am." Ben's hand began to wander beneath the duvet. "Always."

"You want to ken something shameful or just embarrassing?"

"Hmmm…neither. Tell me something wonderful."

Evan thought for a moment. "This secret's about you."

"Ooh, so it's wonderful by default."

"The night we met at Fergus and John's wedding, mind on how it snowed and we all had to stay over at Andrew's castle?"

"Yes! That was such a fun surprise. Although probably not for you. Sorry, go on."

"Well, I woke at half past six when the grooms left. I heard them in the hallway, and they sounded so…" *Perfect.* "Couldn't sleep after that, so I dressed and left my room." He remembered Dunleven's eerie stillness, how the castle's thick carpet had swallowed his footsteps, how the enormous stained-glass window over the grand staircase had turned black, its patterns obscured by the darkness outside. "I went to your room."

Ben gasped. "Really?"

"I didn't break in and watch you sleep or anything creepy like that. I just stood outside your door, working up the courage to knock."

"No courage needed. I would've let you in, in a heartbeat. In half a heartbeat." He snuggled closer. "Imagine us fucking in a castle—and on those million-count linen sheets, my God."

Evan had imagined it many times. Ben would have opened the door, his hair sleep-mussed, still wearing his dress shirt. In some versions of this fantasy the shirt was buttoned halfway and in others completely undone, but in every version it was off before they reached the bed.

"Why did you decide not to knock?" Ben asked.

"Lots of reasons. One, I wasn't sure you'd let me in. I reckoned by that time someone—probably Liam—would have told you what I'd done to Fergus. Reason number two: I liked you enough to want to know you better before we started winching."

"Aw, that's pure sweet."

"But in the end, it came down to protocol. I couldn't risk being intimate with someone I'd just met." He turned his head to look at Ben's face in the mini-humidifier's soft blue light. "The rules are there to protect us both. People like me canna afford to be…" He searched for a word that wouldn't sound paranoid.

"Spontaneous?"

"Foolish."

The corners of Ben's mouth twitched down for a moment, then up again. "But us being together now's not foolish, right?"

"No, it's very wise." Evan kissed Ben's forehead, inhaling the scent of his hair.

"Do you think things happen for a reason?"

Evan pulled back to look at him. "You mean like a master plan by God or the universe?"

Ben gave a one-shouldered shrug. "Sure."

"No. I think people tell themselves that to feel better when something bad happens." He turned onto his back. "I remember when I was a bairn, the day of the Dunblane school shooting, there was this woman on the news. Her son was a pupil there and would've been in the gymnasium when…" Evan closed his eyes. "But he'd stayed home ill that day. She was crying, saying God must have spared him for a reason. I was only six at the time, but I thought she was full of it because it meant God killed those other kids for a reason. Now I look back and wonder how her words must have sounded to the grieving parents."

Ben was silent for a moment. "That was a bleaker answer than I was looking for, but okay."

"I'm sorry. It's how my mind works."

"I get it." Ben slid a hand over Evan's chest, his touch soothing now instead of possessive. "Must be depressing to spend all day focused on aspiring terrorists."

"It does put a dark veil between me and the world. I try to lift that veil when I'm away from the job, but sometimes…"

"It's too heavy?"

"Aye. It's hard to walk out of that office and magically forget everything I know about all the people who want to kill us. But I don't feel depressed. I just feel determined to stop it."

Especially since last week's BVP meeting. Evan had been floored by the number of attendees and their reaction to Gunnar, who'd become a right-wing folk hero after his "martyrdom by Mace" at the Value Our Britishness rally.

The more he learned about their leader, David Wallace, the more Evan thought him capable of the attempted framing of Muslims for the planned wedding attacks. David told Evan that Jordan's "cockamamie wedding scheme" had given him an idea for something "more visionary."

"Big people are watching us, Gunnar," David had said. *"And they like what they see."*

Here in Evan's bed, Ben's gentle squeeze brought him back to the moment. "You can't stop all the bad things happening."

"I know." Evan heard his own defensive tone. "I know," he repeated, more softly. "It's part of our training to accept that fact."

"Wasn't it some IRA guy who said, 'The authorities have to be lucky every time. We only have to be lucky once'?"

"And when we prevent an attack, the public never find out. But they always notice when we've screwed up."

"How does that not drive you round the bend?"

"We just do our best and hope our best is enough. And remember that we canna *stop* terrible things unless we *see* them. So it's the price we pay. One of the prices."

Ben shifted his head on Evan's shoulder. "At the risk of fawning, I feel safer knowing there are people like you looking out for me." He pressed his lips to Evan's collarbone. "You're a good man."

Something flipped over inside him. "I'm not a good man." He

touched his fingertips to Ben's cheek. "But you make me feel like something close."

Ben just smiled for a moment, then said, "When I asked if you thought things happened for a reason, I was referring to us meeting. It wasn't likely, was it?"

"You mean because what sort of saddo attends his ex's wedding?"

"I mean it was unlikely *I'd* be there. I wasn't advertising my services at the time. I only knew Fergus and John because I was mates with Robert McKenzie, and I only knew *him* cos we met on Grindr."

"Was that really unlikely, though? Your flats are a few streets apart."

"I was likely to *find* him," Ben said, "but not to choose him." He turned onto his back. "See, he'd used a pecs pic for his profile. I never chat those guys because the chest is rarely theirs. In his case the pic was highly authentic—you've seen him, right?"

"Yes, he's fair fit."

"My point is, I only chat lads whose profiles show their faces. But for some reason I chatted him, and the rest is history. You and I are together because I broke my cardinal rule for the sake of Robert's pecs."

"Wow." Evan pondered how much less happy he'd be if Ben had swiped left. "While I don't think everything happens for some divine-destiny reason, I do believe you can *make* a reason."

"Like give it your own meaning?"

"Aye, and not just in your head. When something bad happens, you've got a choice. You can let it destroy you, or you can survive and maybe one day lead someone else out of the darkness." He thought of Lord Andrew. "And then maybe your survival made their survival possible too."

"Oh, like in *It's a Wonderful Life*. If George Bailey had never been born, his brother would've died in the ice and never grown up to save those sailors."

"What? Who?"

"That American Christmas film. A guy's about to top himself when a scruffy-looking angel appears and shows him how terrible the world would've been if he'd never been born. Although one could argue that if George hadn't trash-talked his wee brother into sledding down that hill, the poor wean wouldn't have fallen through the ice in the first place. Also, I think it would've made more sense for the angel to show George the world *after* his hypothetical suicide. If he'd gone into the future instead of the past, you know?"

"I've no idea what you're talking about."

Ben tittered. "Never mind. I prefer your version of 'everything happens for a reason.' It makes me feel less like a chess piece." He reached over and touched Evan's forearm. "Also? I'm glad you survived."

Evan started. "Survived what?"

"You tell me." Ben's eyes were gentle and his tone undemanding. "If you can."

"I can't." Evan pushed away the memory. Now wasn't the time to get lost in the past, not with such a perfect present right here.

He turned on his side and pressed his body against Ben's, chest to toes. "I can tell you a different secret."

Ben snuggled closer. "Go on..."

"Here it is." He slid his hand down Ben's back, tracing the now-familiar arc of his spine. "Walking away from your door that night was one of the hardest things I've ever done."

"Was it?" Ben's voice curled with coyness. "Why?"

"Because I wanted you." Evan kissed him, imagining it was the first time, that Ben had just opened the door of his castle suite and drawn him close without so much as a hello. "I wanted to drown myself in you. You were new and sweet and I knew you'd make me forget."

Ben gave a little moan and kissed him back, drawing his thigh over Evan's hip. "But this is better than drowning, yeah? Better than forgetting?"

"Miles better."

It was true. Whatever had guided each step in their journeys before the wedding at Dunleven—be it God or the universe or simple blind luck—Evan was grateful to it.

But since that night, he and Ben had made it happen themselves. They'd extinguished the lights above their lives' diverging paths until they could see only this one, and could walk it only by each other's side.

Chapter 25

THE FOG LAY SO thick upon the harborside streets of Stromness, Ben had to use his electronic key fob to locate his car outside their inn. The alarm chirped ten feet away, startling him and no doubt waking half of Orkney from its pre-dawn slumber.

"Let me drive," Evan whispered.

Ben didn't argue. He was still sleepy after waking at quarter past four to say his long obligatory prayer, in case there was no time later today.

Remembering he needed to eat before his fast began—for the last time this year, yay!—he pulled a protein bar from his coat pocket.

"You won't need those," Evan said. "Mum'll have breakfast ready long before sunrise."

"Not on my account, I hope. I don't want to be a burden."

"I guarantee my mother wants to impress you even more than you want to impress her."

Slowly and silently, they drove into what Ben assumed was the countryside, given the sudden lack of street lamps. Mist meandered in through the car's windows, which Evan had lowered so he could hear oncoming traffic, since their headlights illuminated only a few feet ahead of them. As they climbed the long hill away from Stromness, the fog thinned enough for Ben to see a roadside fence, and beyond it, scattered dark shapes that might have been cows.

"Almost there," Evan said as he swung the car onto a dirt path.

Before Ben could wonder what *almost* meant in these parts, a golden light appeared through the mist. Evan pulled up next to a long, squat building, then laughed at the white-and-blue painted sign in front of them:

PRODIGAL SON PARKING ONLY

Ben and Evan entered through a side door into a mudroom scattered with foot-wiping rugs atop scuffed gray linoleum. They were instantly greeted by a pair of short-haired collie dogs—one of which was missing a back leg yet seemed as agile as its partner —along with the scent of breakfast. Ben's stomach growled in yearning.

"Evan!" a woman whisper-shouted as she hurried in from the kitchen, wiping her hands on her denim apron. She gave her son a hug and kiss, then turned to Ben. "And you'll be Ben, will you no'?"

"I will be. I mean, I am." He shook her warm, callused hand. "Happy to meet you."

"Come but, come but." She beckoned them to follow her past a long wooden table back into the kitchen. "Magnus is oot gaen the sheep their silage, and the boys are still in their beds. Helga kept them up past one o'clock making like she was about to calf. Never did, though. False alarm."

"She's probably waiting for the wedding." Evan made a beeline for the coffee maker. "Ben, will you have some?"

"Yes, please, with loads of milk." He eyed the closest frying pan, which held what looked like a cross between a pancake and a —well, a cake. "What is that? It smells incredible."

She pointed her spatula at her son. "You've not been making Fatty Cutties for him? What sort of boyfriend do you call theesael?"

"The sort who doesn't want to commit murder-by-carbs." He handed Ben a full mug, took a long sip of his own, then gave a sigh of ecstasy. "Mum, I've missed your coffee."

"Did the Dramamine work this time?" she asked him, shifting three enormous sausages onto a serving plate.

"I managed to make it to dry land before spewing, so...I guess?"

"It was a rough ride, Mrs. Hol—erm, Mrs. Muir." Ben mentally kicked himself for nearly using her ex-husband's surname.

"Call me Linda or I'll be calling you Mr. Reid." She broke a pair of eggs over the frying pan that had held the sausages. "Evan, your sister said her flight to Kirkwall yesterday was a nightmare, so whoever got your plane ticket had a tarf time of it too."

"You had a plane ticket?" Ben turned to Evan. "If you get seasick, then why didn't we fly?" The infamous Pentland Firth separating Orkney from the Scottish mainland had been even more treacherous than Ben had expected.

"He bought it months ago," Linda said, "but by the time he decided to bring you, the flight was booked up, thanks to the eclipse."

"You should've flown," Ben told Evan. "I could've taken the ferry and met you here."

"Would you have done that in my place?"

"Of course not," Ben said, "but I've got higher standards for my own chivalry."

"Ooh-hoo-hoo!" Linda grinned. "I see why you fancy him, son."

Over breakfast, she regaled them with the latest wedding challenges. Ben made what he hoped were helpful suggestions in between murmuring, "Yum" and "OhmyGodthisisamazing" after every third bite of food.

Ben could see a lot of Linda in Evan. She was stunning in a way that inspired confidence rather than intimidated. They had the same afternoon-sky-blue eyes that crinkled to slits when they smiled. Her close-cropped hair was even lighter than her son's, though Ben wasn't sure if she was born with that shade or if it was gracefully aging to flaxen white.

Soon Evan's teenage brothers, Thorfinn and Sigur, shuffled into the kitchen, heavy-lidded and yawning. If the names alone hadn't made Ben feel in a different country, the accents would have done, as the two lads muttered and mumbled their way to coffee.

"They'll be a peedie bit friendlier after their caffeine," Linda told Ben. Then she glanced at her watch. "Time to finish the eclipse cake. Folk'll be here at eight."

"Can I help with anything?" Ben offered.

"Thanks, but no, you sit and swadge, then Evan'll show you aboot." She took their plates and headed for the sink.

Ben leaned over to whisper, "How do I swadge?"

"Just chill and digest," Evan whispered back.

"Ah." He sipped his coffee and examined the room around him. The house lay low to the ground, no doubt to cut a minimal profile against the Orkney winds. The ceiling looked about seven feet high, with thick wooden beams that reduced the effective height another several inches.

"Aye-aye, lads." The eighteen-year-old Thorfinn sat down across from them, clanging his plate against the table. "Let's talk blackening."

"The blackest ever." Sigur, who was fifteen but looked almost a twin to his brother, joined them with his own overflowing plate. "We're doing pure treacle. Ordered it in bulk online and watered it down yesterday. Got buckets of it."

"Been saving chicken feathers for six months," Thorfinn added with a grin. "That Sooth boy won't know what hit him."

Ben had never witnessed a blackening in person, but he'd seen pics and videos by a few of his mum's clients. The traditional ritual humiliation of the wedding couple was still common throughout northern Scotland. "You're only blackening the groom?"

"That's usually how it's done in Orkney," Evan said.

"I thought the whole idea was to put the couple through hell together, to kinda cement the bond between them." Ben shrugged. "I mean, if you need a reason other than the joy of torturing your big sister."

"Well…" Evan turned to his brothers. "We could do."

Thorfinn's eyes lit up. "We should do."

"We will!" Sigur pounded the table and hooted. "There's more than enough treacle for two."

Evan gasped and pointed to a faint square glowing on the wall. "Sunrise." He jumped up from the table. "Ben, come and see before it's away."

They hurried out the door they'd entered, leaving their jackets and Evan's family behind.

The moment he stepped outside, Ben forgot about the damp, chilly air, for before him lay a vision the likes of which he'd seen only in Hollywood films.

"Oh," he whispered, and even that tiny noise seemed a blaring klaxon in the face of such serenity.

The green, sheep-spotted fields sloped down toward the mist-shrouded bay, which seemed made of clouds instead of water. As the sun rose over the not-so-distant island of Hoy, its rays were condensed into a golden spotlight by the thick purple cloud above it.

"Don't blink," Evan said. "It'll be gone in a moment."

Ben held his breath, and before his lungs could even think of aching, the sun disappeared into the cloud bank. Still, it was now light enough to provide his first real glimpse of Orkney. "How could you stand living somewhere so beautiful? How'd you ever get anything done?"

"You get used to it, sort of. Also, moments like that are rare, especially this time of year." Evan smiled wistfully. "May is incredible, and in June and July it never gets completely dark. The night sky turns periwinkle, and people stay up late, sit outside, and just…" His eyes went distant, then he swallowed and looked at Ben. "I'd love to bring you back so you can see for yourself."

Now Ben's lungs were aching. "I'd love it too." He moved in for a kiss.

A low groan emanated from the barn to his left.

Evan chuckled. "The kye'll be wanting oot now the sun's up. Let me ask Mum where they're to go." He brushed his lips over Ben's before heading back to the house.

Ben watched him walk away with a newly relaxed posture. For once Evan wasn't scanning his surroundings, cataloging every detail and preparing for attack. It must have felt unnatural to let his guard down, to not see everyone around him as a potential terrorist, to have no calculation more complex than which field to put a cow into.

Evan returned in a moment—carrying their coats, to Ben's relief. They went into the small barn, which was warm with animal heat and smelled of straw and dung, an oddly pleasant combination.

Ben stood back as Evan clipped a tether onto the halter of the closest cow. "I thought this was a sheep farm."

"It is. Sheep are away in the hills." Evan unlatched the stall door and led out the placid black-and-white beast. "These are house kye, just for the family's milk."

Ben followed Evan and the cow out to the nearest pasture, keeping his distance so as not to get trampled. They repeated the process with two more cows. Ben even got to lead one on his own, which made him feel as accomplished as surviving his first week of Krav Maga classes.

"Helga's to stay inside," Evan said as they approached the last stall. "She could be calving any time noo."

They leaned on the stall door to observe the pregnant heifer, who half-heartedly stamped her feet and gave them a sleepy regard.

"They have beautiful eyes," Ben said, then felt stupid at sounding like a shallow city boy.

But Evan just nodded and said, "It's the long lashes." Then he pulled out his phone. "My sister'll be leaving Kirkwall soon. I'd best warn her about the blackening."

"That's kind of you."

"I believe in informed consent. Also loyalty." He thumbed in a text message. "Justine and I may have grown up here, but being born in London and having a surname like Hollister means we've never been considered true Orcadians." He winked at Ben. "Us Sooth folk stick together."

After a moment, Evan's phone dinged. He looked at the screen, then laughed and showed it to Ben:

EVAN

OK if we blacken you along with Darren?

JUSTINE

Fuck yeah equality!!!

It seemed to Evan that by eight o'clock, the entire Orkney Mainland had gathered on the Muir farm. All the big families—the Fletts, Linklaters, Cloustons, Rendells, Firths—and the small ones, too, were keen to take part in the two-for-one celebration of the sun's eclipse and his sister's impending nuptials.

When Evan's neighbors inquired about his job, he would relate a brief and boring architectural anecdote, then change the subject to local controversies he knew they wanted to pleep about. He caught up on the stoat epidemic decimating Orkney wildlife, as well as the growing number of passengers belched onto the island by giant cruiseliners. And, of course, there the age-old analysis of auction mart prices.

"A hundred fifty pence per kilo for a prime Texel?" Evan asked his neighbor Cameron, who raised the pedigree sheep along with Limousin beef cattle. "I can remember when they'd sell for twice that."

"Prices have been falling three straight year," Cameron said.

"And there's a straw shortage doon Sooth, so bedding's got more expensive as well."

Evan's stepfather, Magnus, pointed to the nearby byre. "A long winter comes, and there'll be nothing for the kye to sleep on. We'll be weaving them blankets oot of their own hair."

Evan chuckled with them, but it was clear that while farming had never been an easy lifestyle, it was only getting tougher to make a living. Money was especially tight now, thanks to last year's small crop of lambs after an historically crap winter. This past winter, while warmer, had been just as wet and dim, which meant the Muir farm needed a higher than usual survival rate just to break even.

When Cameron went to congratulate Justine and Darren, Evan finally had a moment alone with his stepfather.

"How are things here?" he asked Magnus. "Financially, I mean."

"Well enough." Magnus scratched at his gray-and-black beard with weathered fingers. "Prices, they go up and doon, you ken? We've got all this farm-planning software, which helps us save a few pence here and there, but in the end it's all aboot minding on that the good times never last, and neither do bad times."

If Ben were here, he'd tell Evan, "Now I know where you get your stoicism." But his partner had long since been rescued from farm talk by the Milfords, a Bahá'í couple from Kent who were pure chuffed to meet "a real Persian." Currently he and the Milfords were helping Justine distribute eclipse glasses, warning each guest, "Wear these or go blind."

"You've got a night lamber hired for next month?" Evan asked Magnus.

His stepfather's eyes rounded. "Aye, and he's charging fifteen pound an hour this year. Worth it, though, to keep more lambs alive—not to mention keep your mum and your brothers and I from killing each other."

Evan did the arithmetic in his head. With a twelve-hour shift for two straight weeks… "Ooft. I wish I could help."

"You help plenty with the gathering."

"That's for a long weekend twice a year. But if I was your night lamber I could save you over two thousand pounds."

"I'm sure your job and your football team would be thrilled for you to disappear for two weeks only to come back brain-dead fae sleep deprivation."

"Dad, our farm is more important than football."

"But not more important than your job." Magnus gave him a knowing look. "See, you'll not be arguing with me there."

Evan wasn't sure. After just a few hours in Orkney, the burdens of work seemed swept away on the relentless wind, each concern like a damp leaf stuck to his skin, now drying up and peeling off, one by one:

David Wallace proclaiming Scotland a "white firewall" against the "plague of immigrants" at last week's BVP meeting...gone.

The Ukrainian landlady at St. Andrew's in the Square giving a fake name for her tenant...forgotten.

The complete lack of matches for the fingerprints and hair fibers found in the white Outlander...reduced to background noise.

It was always like this, morphing back into his old self with these people, debating silage methods and the surest ways to prevent foot scald in lambs. It reminded Evan he'd once been a man who took words at face value instead of analyzing them for six different meanings. A man who didn't look for threats round every corner.

Was this forthright Orcadian his real self, or was it just another persona? Did he even have a real self anymore?

"Of course if you ever change your mind, son," Magnus said, "we'd love to have you back. Your old room's ready for you."

"Thorfinn took it."

"Well, then Justine's old room is ready for you."

"Nah, that's your and Mum's office."

"You ken what I mean."

Evan did know what he meant—that no matter what, there'd

always be a place for him here. It would never be too late to come home.

Sometimes he wondered whether that certainty was what had kept the madness at bay after Belfast. If he'd been "lucky" not to develop a debilitating case of PTSD, perhaps the luck lay right here in the damp Orkney soil, in the bleats and lows of the sheep and kye, in the foundation his family had given him.

And now that "right here" included Ben Reid.

"Hiya!" Ben handed Evan and Magnus the last two pairs of eclipse glasses. "This is beyond exciting, even if the sun'll be only ninety-eight-percent covered. And this place is so amazing, I'm going to get sick of the word 'amazing.'"

Magnus gave a laugh that made Evan glow inside. His stepfather had never been good at faking warmth toward folk he didn't like.

They chatted for a few minutes before Magnus went off to discuss last-minute wedding details with Justine.

Ben edged closer to Evan. "Everyone here's so nice, especially your family. I worried they'd be, you know…"

"Prejudiced?"

"Yes." Ben slid a pair of eclipse glasses over his spectacles and waved a hand in front of his own face. "But I was the one prejudging them. I imagined all Orcadians to be big blond frosty Vikings."

"Like me?"

"Sometimes you're not so frosty," Ben said with a smirk. "You might be the tallest man on the island, though."

"Depends whether my father's plane has landed yet. Also, most Orcadians aren't as Norwegian as my mum's family. My gran came here from Fredrikstad in 1956 for a music festival, fell in love with the island and my granddad, and basically never left."

"That's so romantic." Ben took off his eclipse glasses. "May I kiss you here in front of everyone?"

Evan hesitated, remembering how he'd brought Fergus home

a dozen times and they'd never so much as held hands. He knew of a few openly gay couples in Kirkwall, but they also refrained from public displays of affection. This was still Orkney, after all. "Yes, please."

Ben kissed him quickly, then pulled back and put the dark glasses on again, smiling at the distant harbor. Evan resisted the urge to look behind him to see if anyone was watching.

Justine let out a whoop over by her solar telescope. "It's staaaaarted!"

A queue quickly formed for a closeup view of the eclipse. First in line was Cameron's wife, Ingrid.

She leaned over to squint into the eyepiece, a hand on her lower back. "Have you not got a cloud filter for this peedie thing?"

Justine looked exasperated, as immune as ever to the bone-dry Orkney sarcasm.

Evan put on his eclipse glasses and peered at the sun, which hung low enough over the sea he didn't need to crane his neck. Through the thinning clouds he could just make out the curve of the moon eating away at one edge of the glowing orb.

The sight gave him the sudden, spinning sensation of being on a tiny ball of rock in outer space. The precise astronomical alignment that allowed their tiny outpost to witness this event felt both highly unlikely and strangely inevitable.

Around twenty past nine, the clouds thinned further, draping the sun with a gauzy veil and chilling the air so Evan had to zip his jacket and put on his gloves. At half nine, ten minutes before mid-eclipse, the party's conversation faded, leaving an eerie silence.

"The birds have stopped singing," Ben whispered. "They think it's twilight."

Evan couldn't blame the skylarks for not twittering, or the kye for ambling back to the fence near the byre. Everything felt *wrong*.

Because this was nothing like twilight. The light had dimmed, but the shadows were sharper and shorter than they would have been near dusk. Even the light's color—shades of blue and gray rather than red and orange—seemed off.

Evan looked to the southwest, where the horizon held the bruise-purple hue of an approaching storm. But this was no storm, just the shadow of a hungry moon.

He rubbed his arms to smooth down the standing hairs. His pulse quickened with each minute, and he felt the urge to…what, run? Hide? Pray? He now understood why solar eclipses had terrified ancient people.

Yet even as his primordial lizard brain was cowering, the rest of his mind marveled at the beauty of it all—yes, even the beauty of his instinctive fear. Never before had terror come from such a harmless source. He was in the safest place in the world, with the people he loved most.

When Ben took his hand without a word, Evan's view of the sun wavered, swimming in unshed tears. He looked down to see Ben's cheeks already wet. So Evan blinked, releasing the tears so he could once again witness this imperfect, ineffable miracle.

BEN HAD NEVER HAD such a day. After the mind-blowing eclipse, the party had come back to earth in the filthiest fashion, courtesy of the blackening. Justine and her fiancé, Darren, were doused in buckets of watered-down treacle, then covered in oats, flour, and chicken feathers. Because of the wind and the need to chase down their victims, Justine's three brothers got splashed as well.

Then the wedding party clambered into the back of the Muirs' old pickup truck so Evan could drive them to Kirkwall, aka "Toon," so the couple could be cling-wrapped to a signpost and forced to drink more beer, per tradition.

Ben rode along in the cab, and while the drunken revelers chanted and whooped and used overturned buckets as bongos, he was busy swooning over the landscape. They drove between the Lochs of Stenness and Harray, stunning silver mirrors of the clouds above, then passed two neolithic stone circles as well as an ancient chambered cairn, all of which Evan promised they'd visit Sunday when there'd be fewer tourists. It blew Ben's mind that Evan had grown up a few miles from 5,000-year-old archaeological marvels.

Orkney held a starkness unlike that of Scotland's other remote areas. Whereas the landscapes of the Highlands and the Western Isles rose in rugged defiance, here the terrain seemed to hunker down, as though bracing for Mother Nature's next round of punishment.

When Ben noticed his gaze tripping erratically over the low hills, he realized what he was seeking.

"Where are all the trees?" he asked Evan as they drove. "Do they not grow in Orkney because of the wind?"

"No, it's because every five years on Saint Rognvald's Eve we cut down all the saplings and set them alight at Skara Brae."

"Why?"

"Well, we need something to burn all the brunettes upon."

Ben smiled. "We are stubbornly flame-resistant."

"Aye, that's why your bones make such good accordions."

Ben liked this even-smarter-arsed incarnation of Evan. He liked him a lot.

But Evan grew tense again at the wedding rehearsal, thanks to a row between his father and stepfather. They were meant to walk the bride down the aisle together, one on either side. When they each tried to crowd the other out by veering toward the middle, Justine declared that her mother would escort her, and the two men could "bloody stuff it."

"You didn't tell me your dad was English," Ben whispered now to Evan as they walked down the stone slab street from the church to the restaurant beneath their inn. Hugh was chatting to Justine and Darren several paces ahead of them.

"You knew I was born in London," Evan said.

"I figured that was because your dad worked there. He did, right?"

"He did. He does."

Ben noticed Evan's pace was slowing the closer they got to the restaurant. "You don't talk about him much."

"What do you want to know?"

"Where he's from," Ben said. "What he does for a living. Why he and your mum broke up."

Evan shoved his hands into his jacket pockets. "He was born in Bradford, in Yorkshire. He's got a very demanding government job, which also answers your third question."

Now Ben was the one slowing down. Was Hugh Hollister a spook? If Ben was allowed to know, surely Evan would have told him.

They reached the restaurant and were seated at a table in the crowded dining room, where visitors were still buzzing over the eclipse. The two fathers sat at either end of the table, rival heads of a fractured family.

Once they'd ordered their meals, Darren placed two identical russet-colored gift bags upon the table. "I read online about an old Orkney wedding tradition called 'speiring night.'"

Justine grinned at her fiancé. "I told him I'd never heard of it, but he insisted."

"Anyway," Darren said, "supposedly back in the day, when a man wanted to marry a woman, he'd bring a bottle of fine whisky to her da and ask for her hand. If her father said yes, they'd have a few drams whilst making arrangements."

Evan snorted. "A peedie bit patriarchal, no?"

"That's what I said!" Justine gave her brother a cross-table fist bump, then glared at her dad and stepdad. "Don't either of you tell him no, by the way. I already paid for this wedding, and it's too late to get deposits back."

Ben laughed, but his mirth faded when he saw the two men's faces as Darren handed them their bags.

"I come from Dufftown," Darren continued, "which is where they make The Balvenie whisky. Hugh, I got you the 30 because it was bottled the same year Justine was born."

Justine grimaced. "Don't remind me."

"And for you, Magnus, I chose the Single Barrel 25, since that was closest to the number of years you've known her."

"Aww." Linda smiled at her future son-in-law across the table. "That's pure sweet of you, laddie."

"Aye, cheers." Magnus examined the bottle's label. "Of course, if you'd gaen us whiskies based on hoo many year we spent raising her, I'd have won by a mile." He laughed at his joke, but he was the only one.

Ben rubbed the back of his neck to stop the prickling sensation. Maybe he was lucky that his parents lived several time zones apart.

"True," Hugh said, "but fortunately it's not only age that determines a whisky's quality, but also the environment."

Magnus shot him a dark look. "Whit thee sayen?"

"I'm saying it's a very thoughtful gift." Hugh turned to Justine's fiancé. "Thank you, Darren. This is one of my favorites."

"How wonderful!" Justine's voice pitched high and tight. "I'm sure both bottles are wonderful. *Equally* wonderful."

"Yes," Evan said emphatically. "Wonderful and…different. But also wonderful." His face mirrored his sister's wince.

Ben squeezed his partner's hand under the table and thought of a change in topic. "Evan delivered a calf today."

"Oh yes!" Linda beamed past Ben at her son. "Hugh, you would've been awful proud of the way he took charge of the situation."

Evan blushed a bit. "Technically Helga delivered the calf. I only helped."

"He's being modest," Ben said. "He was up past his elbow in that cow, turning her baby's leg the right way round so the shoulder didn't catch on the way out."

"Oh." Darren looked slightly ill. "Wish I'd ordered the salmon instead of the beef."

Magnus raised his nearly empty wine glass toward Evan. "I

taught him everything he knows," he said, looking straight at Mr. Hollister.

Hugh's steel-gray gaze remained unwavering and unimpressed. "I'm sure he frequently deploys his knowledge of livestock within his chosen field, so to speak."

"I raised him to make an honest living," Magnus said.

Everyone at the table tensed—except for Darren, who just looked bewildered. Ben guessed he didn't know about Evan's job.

"So, Ben," Linda said quickly, laying a hand on his arm, "it'll surely feel strange to be a mere spectator at a wedding, aye?"

"Yes." He nodded vigorously, as if his waggling head could singlehandedly dispel the table's friction. "I'm happy to help if needed. Like a doctor does when someone on an aeroplane has a medical emergency."

Their meals came then, delivered by a waitress who Ben guessed was a schoolyard nemesis of Justine's, based on their catty exchanges.

Evan nudged Ben and whispered, "I thought you weren't allowed to work on holy days like Naw-Rúz."

"Mum and I discussed it. Helping those in need is always the highest calling."

"Good. I'll be needing your help just to survive the next twenty-four hours." He pulled a small envelope from his inside coat pocket and slipped it into Ben's hand. "Sorry if this is cheesy. I didn't know how else to commemorate the occasion."

Ben opened the envelope and pulled out a greeting card. "Oh my God, it's in Persian."

"Supposedly it says, 'Naw-Rúz Mubarak—Happy New Year.' And some other stuff."

"I love it." He wanted to blurt out, *And I love you*, but not in front of everyone. "Thank you."

Of course Evan's mum wanted to see the card, which was then passed around the table for everyone to admire, since apparently there was no such thing as privacy on this island.

The card was but a brief respite from the barbs flying from

either end of the table. Evan and Justine chided their fathers with pleas to *"keep things civil"* and *"save the blood feud for the reception when everyone can take part, heh."* As the family's outsiders, Ben and Darren tried to lighten the conversation with talk of who might be the next *Top Gear* host now that Jeremy Clarkson had been sacked.

"So I was reading this week's *Orcadian*," Hugh said, folding his napkin at the end of the main course. "There's apparently been a spate of vandalism on the West Mainland. And by 'spate,' I mean two cases. Tell me, Magnus, however do you sleep at night amidst such a crime wave?"

Justine sighed. "Dad…"

"You're just jealous," Magnus said, emphasizing the last word, "because we've not been touched by the ills of civilization."

Justine clutched her steak knife. "Dad!" she said to Magnus between gritted teeth.

"If you mean ills like major hospitals and decent broadband connection," Hugh said, "then I suppose you're right."

Magnus snorted. "It takes a sick mind to look doon on a community for being peaceful."

Hugh raised an eyebrow. "A mind stays healthy with daily stimulation by new and interesting things. How long before dementia sets in when a brain's fiercest challenge is whether to store silage in bales or piles?"

"Stop it!" Justine lurched to her feet, knocking against the table. Her wine glass tipped over, spilling its ruby contents over her half-eaten sirloin. "I don't want either of you at my wedding. You can both go and-and-and jump in the harbor instead. I hope you sink like stones!" She stalked off, pressing her cloth napkin to her face.

"Sit, lads. I've got this," Linda told Evan and Darren, who were getting up to follow Justine. "She'll be in the ladies', anyway."

Evan's two fathers glowered at each other for a long, silent moment. Ben's mind went blank, his once-endless well of small talk now dry.

Hugh slid back his chair. "I need a smoke. I'll be in the beer garden if anyone needs me."

"We won't," Magnus muttered.

Ben saw Evan staring after his dad. "Go to him," he whispered.

"You'll be all right?" Evan asked.

"It's literally my job to calm people down before weddings."

Evan managed a tiny smile. "Thanks," he said, then hurried after his father.

"So." Ben turned back to a simmering Magnus and a shell-shocked Darren. "Tell me, Magnus, how did you and Linda first meet? Did you know each other before she moved south?"

"Och aye." A lopsided grin spread across Magnus's face. Despite the fighting, it warmed Ben's heart that this tough old farmer was still besotted with his bride. "We met in primary school. We weren't friends, really—you ken how boys and girls are at that age. But by the time we were teenagers..." He blushed and rubbed his jaw. "Things changed."

Ben sent a curious glance at Darren, who looked less comfortable than ever. Evan had made it sound as though Linda and Magnus had started a brand-new relationship after the breakup with Hugh—which had allegedly occurred because of the latter's demanding job. Had Ben accidentally unearthed a family secret?

"Sounds like a lovely story." Ben lifted the wine bottle and emptied it into Magnus's glass. "Tell me more."

Chapter 26

EVAN FOUND his father lounging on the stone wall surrounding the empty beer garden, puffing on a cigar. He looked like a blazer advert in an upmarket men's magazine with the slogan *Be who you are, wherever you are.* Upon seeing Evan, he reached inside his suit jacket and withdrew another cigar.

They smoked in silence. Half of Evan's mind wondered what to say, while the other half wondered whether Ben would fancy the taste of tobacco on his tongue.

"Seductive, isn't it?" His father gestured to the bar window, through which they could see people laughing and drinking. "The outside world, I mean. It's fun to pretend—for a short while, at least—that you're part of something simple and ordinary, yes? That you live in the same world as everyone else?"

All at once Evan knew why a small part of his heart had ached today. Orkney felt so solid, so substantial. He'd barely noticed this fact when he'd come home at Christmas, smothered by dread of Fergus's wedding and worry over Jordan's plots. But today, Ben had made Orkney feel real again.

His father's rhetorical question had reminded Evan how work could distract from personal angst. So he uttered the phrase he knew every parent longed to hear:

"I need your advice."

"Oh?" His dad's eyebrows popped up, and his posture changed from hunched and bitter to open and magnanimous. "What's the problem?"

"It's an operation. Something's not quite right."

His father hesitated, perhaps preparing to point out that no one—not even other MI5 officers—should know the specifics of an op unless absolutely necessary.

Instead he said, "Go on."

Evan sat beside him on the wall and offered a detail-free overview of Operation Caps Lock. "It feels like we've followed a trail of neatly laid bread crumbs to nowhere," he said in conclusion. "Like we're being baited into suspecting ISIS, but not as a group of flesh-and-blood individual terrorists. More like ISIS the cartoon."

"It wouldn't be the first time someone tried to frame Muslims for a terrorist attack." His father took a pensive puff, then examined the lit end of his cigar as if the answer lay there. "Follow your instincts, Evan, but be careful. Be very careful."

A chill skittered over Evan's shoulders. His dad had never told him to be careful in his job, not even when Evan had been shipped off to Northern Ireland. "What do you mean?"

"There may be forces at work much bigger than any terrorist network." His father tapped the ashes from his cigar into a puddle at their feet. "Can you show me exactly what you found?"

Evan wavered. Though he'd not mentioned same-sex weddings or the British Values Party, he'd probably already said too much. Orkney had a way of making secrets seem pointless. Everyone here knew everything eventually, so why hide anything? Who needed national security in this safe, serene harbor from the world?

"You can trust me," his dad said, "and not because I'm your father." He straightened up, shifting his weight on the stone slab. "I may have resources that can shed light on the mystery."

Evan was tempted. He could follow protocol and suggest his

dad request the information within the agency. But the approval process could take weeks, and the answer might be no. Plus, his dad's inquiries might alert Evan's supervisors that he'd been illicitly sharing information. So by following procedure, Evan could get royally screwed, and the operation could suffer.

Still, protocols were in place for a reason. Perhaps this was a test of Evan's ability to follow them. He wouldn't put it past his father.

The door to the restaurant creaked open, releasing the hum of the pub crowd. "Hiya, sorry to interrupt."

"No bother," Evan told Ben, relieved at being freed from his dilemma. "How is it in there?"

"Darren's parents have arrived for after-dinner drinks." Ben stepped out of the shadows into the pale light of the beer garden's lamppost. "Justine stopped crying and said, quote, 'I'll rescind the wedding restraining order if both my dads promise to play nice.'"

"An offer I can't refuse." His father doused his cigar in the puddle. "Evan, I'll be in touch next week about what we discussed. For now, let's focus on your sister."

Evan averted his eyes as his dad went back inside the bar.

"I think we're released from further socializing." Ben hopped up to sit beside Evan on the wall. "You okay?"

"Aye, fine." Evan examined his face, which was tight with tension. "You?"

"Erm…" Ben scratched the back of his neck. "Tell me again why your parents divorced?"

Evan cocked his head, confused by the question. "Like I said, his job was demanding. Mum realized it would always come first. Dad said as much himself."

"Did that make you angry at him?"

"Sure. When a parent's got bigger priorities, it kinda ruins that whole childhood illusion of the universe revolving around you. But whatever. I don't blame him." Evan took a long puff of cigar so he could turn his face away from Ben, who wouldn't be fooled by such transparent bravado.

"Why don't you blame him?"

"Because his job was—*is* vital. Some things are more urgent than bruised feelings. Would it be wrong for a brain surgeon to miss their kid's football match to save a patient's life?"

"Is your dad a brain surgeon?"

"No, it's just a metaphor, or an analogy, or something." Evan waved the smoke into the gathering wind. The nicotine was accentuating his buzz from the wine he'd drunk at dinner.

"Okay." Ben fell silent, apart from the bounce of his heels off the stone wall.

"So what's wrong?"

"I was talking to Magnus," Ben said immediately, as though he'd been waiting for a prompt. "Trying to cheer him up after the big row at dinner. Asked him how he and your mum met and fell in love. Typical wedding small talk, the sort I've had a million times with clients' families. In my line of work, you think you've heard it all, but then—"

"What did he say?"

"Just that they knew each other at school."

"So? Everyone here kens everybody, even more so back in the day."

"But they were…I guess sort of teenage sweethearts? Magnus wanted her to marry him when they finished school, but she wanted to go to uni down south, be a 'woman of the world,' he said. But Magnus was patient, and when the time was right, he got her back."

Evan had barely heard a word after *"Magnus wanted her to marry him."* His mind was busy replaying every story he'd been told growing up, how Mum had let Dad take the blame for their disintegration.

"It didn't match your version of events," Ben continued, "so I had him clarify. Magnus claims he 'wooed' your mum back to Orkney. I think they were in contact while she and your dad were still—"

"Why are you telling me this?"

Ben jerked back as if Evan had taken a swing at him. "Because it's the truth."

"It's Magnus's wishful thinking." Evan stood and began to pace. "My dad said the divorce was his own fault. Why would he fall on his sword, let his kids grow up resenting him, if she was the one responsible?"

"Maybe he was too proud to admit his wife left him for another man. Or maybe it was for your sake—maybe he didn't want you to hate the guy whose house you had to grow up in. If you'd known the truth then, would it have made life easier or harder?"

"Harder, obviously. But it's not exactly easy hearing it tonight." Evan clenched his fist, wishing he could go back two minutes in time and stop Ben from telling him. "What do I do now? Pretend I don't know? How do I look my mum in the eye tomorrow at the wedding? And Magnus...he was the only father I'd see for months at a time. He saw to that, didn't he? Bringing us up here to the end of the world, a place my real father couldn't just nip off to every other weekend." Evan stopped short. "He changed our lives forever. Magnus didn't just steal my mum. He stole me and my sister, too."

"He didn't steal your mother. It was her choice. And maybe Magnus wasn't the only thing drawing her back here. Maybe she just wanted to come home. Also, if she'd stayed with your dad when they weren't right for each other, she would've been miserable, which means you and Justine would've been miserable too."

"You don't know that. You don't know—" Evan started coughing, his throat dry from the cigar. *You don't know anything. Your parents are together.*

As he struggled for breath, Evan thought about how he'd always sorted his feelings when it came to family. Loving one father didn't mean he loved the other any less. Despite their rivalry, he'd never seen them as opposing forces.

But if what Ben said was true, and one of them had willfully harmed the other, then this had been a war all along. Which meant Evan had to choose a side.

"You can handle this," Ben said. "You're one of the strongest men I've ever met, not to mention one of the kindest."

Evan scoffed. "I'm not kind."

"You are, and so is your dad. You both confessed to being heartbreakers to hide the fact it was *your* hearts broken."

"I *did* hurt Fergus," Evan rasped. "It killed me to do it, but my feelings don't matter."

"They matter to me."

"Ugh." Evan turned away. He couldn't stand to see the sympathy in Ben's eyes. "Why do you always think you know what's best for people? Why do you need to fix everyone?"

"I'm not trying to fix you. I just want you to be happy. I thought you'd want to know the truth."

"The truth fucking hurts, Ben! Just once in your life remember that before you inflict it on people."

Ben drew in a soft gasp, a noise that sliced through Evan's chest. "I'm sorry," he choked out. Then he turned and walked back into the hotel, faster than Evan had ever seen him move.

"Wait," Evan tried to say, but his voice was gone and so was Ben.

He dropped his cigar and pulverized it with his heel long after it had stopped burning, until it was nothing but a brown smear on the wet bricks.

At least he'd proved his own point: He wasn't kind at all.

THANKS to the howling wind and Ben's fear he'd ruined everything, he was still awake when Evan staggered into their room at half past one, whispering a harsh curse as he banged a bony body part against the chair. Then came a groan of discomfort as the bathroom door shut.

Assuming Evan was drunk, Ben braced himself for the sound

of vomit. But the only noises from the bathroom were soft moans of misery, and the intermittent running of the tap. Finally, there was silence.

He was about to check whether Evan was still conscious when the door opened.

"All right?" Ben asked.

"Oh. Sorry, I tried not to wake you."

"I wasn't sleeping yet. I'd only just turned off the light. Phoned my mum to wish her a happy Naw-Rúz, then did some, erm, reading." He didn't want to admit he'd been praying, mostly for forgiveness for his reckless gossiping.

Evan sat on the bed to remove his shoes. "Is she missing you?"

"She's happy for me that I'm here. She wanted to know all about my day. It took almost an hour to tell her everything. Well, not everything."

"It was eventful." Evan stripped off his dress shirt and trousers, then draped his clothes over the back of the chair.

As he turned to face the bed, they said, "I'm sorry" simultaneously, then "For what?" also simultaneously.

"I'll start," Ben said. "I shouldn't have run to you telling tales about your parents. I didn't think how it would make you feel."

"I should never have blamed the messenger." Evan pulled back the covers and slumped into bed facing Ben. "It's unforgivable the way I spoke to you."

"It's not. I forgive you." Still, he was afraid to reach out and touch Evan.

"Justine says Magnus told you the truth. I was only two when our parents split up, but she was seven, so she remembers the fights." He rubbed his face. "Not really fights. Mostly Dad begging Mum to stay."

Ben's heart twisted. His own boyfriend/best mate at school had left Scotland to attend university in America. How much worse would it feel to lose an entire family? "I'm sorry."

"My sister said we moved in with Magnus as soon as we came to Orkney. I said, 'But I remember living with Gran,' and she said,

'No, Gran just looked after us sometimes on a weekend so Mum and Magnus could be proper newlyweds.' Then she bought me a few sympathy Skull Splitters. Justine did, not Gran. Gran's dead. We miss her."

"A few Skull Splitters?" Ben had seen the local ale's Viking-adorned label and knew it to be 8.5% alcohol by volume. "Are you very hammered?"

Evan gave a loose laugh. "Apparently drinking's not like riding a bike. If you more or less stop for nine months, your liver turns back into an amateur." He wiped his face again, half rolling onto his back. "I boaked into the harbor. Justine stopped me falling in."

"I guess that's what big sisters are for."

"Did you know Skull Splitter was the nickname of Thorfinn Einarsson, the seventh Earl of Orkney? That's who my brother's called after. My brother Thorfinn."

"Fascinating. How do you feel now?"

"Worst has passed. That tile in our bathroom is fair cold." He turned to face Ben again. "So I was lying there with my head on the floor, staring at the wall behind the toilet—which is surprisingly clean, by the way—and I had a massive epiphany."

"Oh?" Ben wasn't sure he wanted to hear this.

"All my life, see, I thought it was my dad's job that ruined everything. I thought a spook could never have a real relationship."

So Hugh Hollister *was* a spy. Ben felt uneasy—he probably wasn't meant to know for sure.

Evan sniffed. "I thought I would always hurt the people I cared about. I thought the job did something that made us…unlovable."

"You're not unlov—"

"And I made it true. I hurt Fergus. I hurt him. Told myself it was worth it cos I was trying to save lives, but it's still eating away at me. And then…" He covered his face with both hands. "Then someone else got hurt even worse, and at work they told me, 'Sorry, it's unfortunate, but he's collateral damage, he shouldn't have been palling about with terrorists.' As if he had a choice."

Wait, what?

"I mean, you canna choose your family, right?" Evan continued. "But you can choose not to fall into bed with an undercover MI5 officer."

Ben's stomach went cold. Had Evan been some sort of honey trap infiltrating a terrorist cell? And the man he'd tricked...*collateral damage.*

Whatever Evan had done, it had to be highly classified. And here he was with his loose lips and amateur liver, spilling details of an operation.

"Not that he could've known," Evan said. "Too innocent and too desperate for—"

"Hang on." Ben reached out to touch him at last. "You were saying something about an epiphany?"

Evan paused. "Right. So I'm lying there beside the toilet just noo when I realize that what you telt me about Mum and Magnus, it fucking obliterates everything I always thought about this life I chose." He grasped Ben's hand. "We can be happy. I know it's not easy and it never will be, but we're not fucking doomed."

"You thought we were doomed?" Ben's mouth went dry with alarm. "Yet you were still with me?"

"I couldn't not be." Evan's voice grew hoarse. "I brought you into my life even though I thought myself a time bomb. And I'm not sorry. Ben, you're the best thing that's ever happened to me by a million miles, and I'm so lucky, I'm so..." He pressed his forehead to Ben's. "Fuck, I'm so drunk. I think I need that tile floor again."

Still dazed by Evan's confession, Ben helped him into the bathroom and soaked a cloth in cold water for his face. "Want one of your motion-sickness ginger sweets?"

"God, yes," Evan murmured beneath the cloth as he settled onto the floor. "You're my hero."

Ben fetched the sweet for him. "Shall I stay?"

"No, you go and sleep in peace." He gave Ben's ankle a quick squeeze. "Thank you."

Ben left the bathroom, shutting the door behind him, then returned to bed. But sleep was further away than ever, and peace seemed lost for good.

Chapter 27

"I LOOK RIDICULOUS."

"Pish. You look gorgeous and you know it."

"But I *feel* ridiculous." Evan examined himself in the wardrobe mirror, wondering how his green-and-blue kilt would stand up to Orkney's gale-force winds. "I should wear something underneath."

"We've discussed this," Ben said as he threaded the sporran strap through the kilt's belt loops. "No true Scotsman—"

"What did I tell you about calling Orcadians Scottish?"

"If you wear something under your kilt then I won't be able to do this." Ben snaked a hand beneath the hem and reached up to grasp Evan's arse.

Evan jolted. Ben had been a bit standoffish this morning, so this sudden groping was a surprise. "Your hands are cold."

"We can solve that." Abandoning the sporran, Ben straightened up behind Evan, pressing close as he placed one hand on each bare cheek.

Evan watched them in the mirror, feeling a stir from the inconvenient semi-erection he'd sported since Ben had started dressing him. "You look gorgeous too. That's the suit you wore on our first date."

"Mm-hm." Stooping slightly, Ben reached between Evan's thighs to caress his balls. "How much time have we got?"

"What, before the wedding?"

"Yes. You need fucked in your kilt, and we can't assume you'll be sober after the reception."

Evan felt his face burn—from excitement at Ben's declaration and from shame at his own behavior. He couldn't remember what he'd nattered on about here in their bed last night, apart from an apology for being a dick and a clumsy statement about the bright side of the truth about his parents' divorce.

But Ben wasn't quite meeting his eyes today, so Evan must have said something disturbing. He hoped it wasn't *I love you*, because even though those words were true, he wanted to be sober the first time he uttered them.

Ben led him to the end of the bed. "If it's the mess you're worried about, we could both wear condoms. Or you could tell me when you're near orgasm and I'll suck you off."

This was matter-of-fact sex talk, even for Ben. The lack of ceremony unnerved Evan, but after last night, he was desperate to reestablish their bond. "We've got half an hour."

"Perfect." Ben undid his trousers. "Now bend over so I can lick you."

Evan's knees went weak, making it easy to obey. He draped himself over the foot of the bed, turning his head to see their bodies perfectly framed in the wardrobe door mirror. He watched Ben kneel behind him, stroking himself with one hand and using the other to lift Evan's kilt.

Then both hands were on him, parting his cheeks. And there it was, that long, exquisite, determined tongue, reaching for him, then disappearing from sight at the same moment Evan felt its touch.

"God..." Evan shoved his wrist to his mouth to keep all of Stromness from hearing his cries. A cufflink clinked against his teeth as he bit down on his shirt.

Ben made an appreciative noise, then began a series of long, luxurious strokes interspersed with rapid, tickling touches with the tip of his tongue. Evan writhed beneath Ben's firm grip, his aching cock pressed against the kilt's silky lining. Through blurring vision he saw Ben's face buried between his cheeks, then felt that tongue press within him.

Finally Ben let go, leaving Evan quivering all over. After fetching the lube and a condom, he stood behind Evan and let his trousers drop to the floor. He was otherwise fully clothed; he'd not even removed his glasses, which frankly was a really hot look.

Evan watched Ben slide one slicked-up finger inside his wet hole. Eager for more, he put his knees on the bed and raised his hips.

"That's right," Ben said. "Lift up for me."

Evan obeyed, keeping his head and arms pressed to the mattress. With his arse in the air and his kilt draped forward over his tuxedo jacket, he looked pure slutty in the best way.

When he felt ready, he said, "Now, Ben. Fuck me now," expecting him to quickly oblige.

Instead Ben froze for a long moment, staring down at him.

"What's wrong?" Evan asked.

Ben gave a jerky head shake, then took off his suit jacket and laid it carefully over the chair. "Everything's fine." But as he put on the condom and lubed it up, his forehead was still lined with tension.

"Undo your bottom shirt buttons," Evan said. "I want to see your cock."

Ben did so without replying, then parted his shirt as he shifted forward to bring them together. Evan didn't watch the place where they joined. Instead he studied Ben's face, which at first showed no reaction. He moved a bit deeper, murmuring, "All right?"

"Yes." Evan meant it only in a physical sense. Something about Ben was definitely not all right. His movements were clinically efficient, and he was talking a lot less than normal. But maybe his efficiency was due to the time constraint, and his silence due to the periodic passing of people through the corridor outside their room.

Then Ben moved deeper still, and Evan stopped wondering. He stopped caring that his boyfriend had traded affectionate caresses for a commanding grip. If Ben held some secret resentment, it was manifesting itself in a rock-hard self-assurance.

"Mmmph." Evan had to press his mouth to the bed to muffle his cries. Holding him in position, Ben drove harder, lighting the first great sparks within him.

Then he quickened his pace, sliding relentlessly over Evan's prostate. With the duvet between his teeth, Evan checked the mirror to see Ben's body bucking and releasing, his jaw tight and determined.

Then Ben looked into the mirror. As their eyes met, his rhythm broke, and on his next thrust he slipped out entirely. "Sorry." He refocused on his cock, carefully putting it back where it belonged.

The next thrust was the deepest yet. Evan gave a shuddering moan he couldn't suppress.

"Are you close?" Ben asked.

"Not yet. Are you?"

"Oh yeah."

Evan watched the mirror as Ben's back arched and his head tilted back. And there it was: that look of pure delight he'd come to crave.

"God…" As Ben went at him faster and faster, his glasses started to slip down his nose from the sweat and rapid motion.

In the end, his orgasm was near silent, his cry stifled by a bitten lip as he ground against Evan, giving him every thick, throbbing inch.

Finally he withdrew carefully and dispensed with the condom. "Turn over and slide down," he said breathlessly, holding Evan's kilt out of the way.

Evan obeyed. "It won't take me long to—och!"

His head slammed back as Ben swallowed him whole. In the mirror, he saw his kilt tossed above his waist, his stockinged legs now angled high. Ben drew back a few inches, rolling Evan's cock around his mouth, the head bulging visibly against the inside of his cheek. Then he shifted Evan's arse and plunged his fingers inside, curling them at just the right spot.

"Yes!" Evan hissed, reaching back to grasp a pillow just in time. He shoved it against his face as he came, nearly screaming, in the grasp of Ben's masterful mouth.

For a few minutes he just lay there on the bed in a daze, listening to Ben washing up and brushing his teeth in the bathroom.

When Ben came back into the room, he examined Evan with a detached gaze, then came over and reached for the kilt buckle. "Let's take this off so you can clean yourself proper. They say there's no such thing as too much lube, but I may have proved that wrong. Sorry."

"Better too much than too little." Evan stood, relieved to feel not even a pinch of pain. "So I'll not be walking funny before the entire congregation."

"Hah. Right?" Ben's broad grin returned in an instant, making its previous absence even more painfully obvious.

Evan leaned over and kissed him, wishing he knew what Ben had been thinking as they'd fucked. Wishing he knew what to say, now and later, to make it all right.

THROUGHOUT THE WEDDING, Ben tried to focus on the happy couple. He pitched in when asked for help or advice but for the most part hung back—*God forbid I should try to "fix" anyone*, he thought bitterly.

The ceremony went smoothly, apart from a mixup with the unity-sand ritual. Due to a miscommunication and a shared favorite color, Justine and Darren had accidentally ordered the same sand, which meant their souvenir bottle, rather than displaying a distinct pattern of two alternating colors which symbolically blended at the top, ended up a container of…blue sand.

Despite the raucous reception, Ben couldn't drag his mind away from the events of the last twelve hours. Normally his physical connection to Evan felt almost divine; not so this morning. He'd felt far away from Evan, his trust at an all-time low, but he'd fucked him anyway. It definitely didn't meet the does-this-act-serve-others-or-myself? standard, a standard Ben treated pretty liberally to begin with.

The whole time Evan was splayed out before him, kilt above his waist, all Ben could think about was what he'd done with that terrorist lad in…wherever he'd disappeared to last year. Had he writhed and moaned in such a way beneath that man, maybe exaggerating his pleasure to manipulate through flattery? Worse, was he doing it even now, in Glasgow, as "Gunnar" the hot Norwegian?

How much of what he and Ben had was even real?

With all these doubts swirling through his mind, sex was the last thing that should have happened this morning. They should have talked instead.

Hopefully it wasn't too late for another dose of truth.

As the reception wound down, he found Evan chatting to some of his mates from school. "Shall we go for a walk?" Ben asked. "I could do with some fresh air."

Fear flashed through Evan's eyes at Ben's solemn tone, but he said, "I know where there's a great view. It's just a peedie stroll."

After a round of farewells, they found their coats and slipped out the inn's side door. They walked past the harbor down the seaside road, which twisted back to wind through Stromness, the tarmac changing to rectangular stone slabs laid between cute shops. Like some of the country roads, the street here seemed meant for two-way traffic though it was barely the width of one vehicle.

The claustrophobic lane turned back into a proper road

leading out of the town, where sporadic houses sat a mere dozen yards from the water.

"Are we okay?" Evan asked.

Ben stopped. He'd wanted to talk but now found the prospect terrifying. "Of course we're okay." He glanced back at the glittering lights of Stromness, where he'd learned a fraction of a very dark truth. "I want to put my feet in the water."

"It's freezing."

"I don't care."

"Then let's go where it's less rocky."

They continued in silence for a few minutes before Evan stopped at a rusty gate. Ben followed him down a set of concrete steps. At the bottom they sat to remove their shoes and socks in silence. The tide was high, so they needed to walk only a few yards to reach the water.

"Aaaaaeeeeeee!" Ben said when the ice-cold liquid devoured his feet. "Whose stupid idea was this?"

"I can't remember." Evan hissed as he waded deeper, the water lapping just below his kilt. "The past has been obliterated by the pain of the present."

Ben laughed, his lower lip already trembling. "Whoever steps out first loses."

"You're challenging me to a test of physical endurance?"

"That's daft, isn't it? Especially since Orcadians are part selkie."

"Not all of us." Evan rubbed his own arms. "One time when I was four, I was with my mum over at Dingieshowe Beach, mucking about in one of the rock pools looking for fish. She got distracted chatting to one of her friends or something. Anyway, my foot slipped, and I went under."

"Oh my God. What happened?"

"I remember hearing my voice all garbled from the water." He thumped his throat as he cried, "Heeeelp meee" in a cartoonish tone.

"And you got rescued?"

"No. I found my footing again and stood up. Mum never even knew I'd slipped." Evan stood perfectly motionless now, seemingly oblivious to the chill. "It was probably only a few seconds I was under the water thinking I was drowning. But at the time it seemed an eternity."

Ben hugged himself, wishing he could wrap his arms around the four-year-old Evan. "Did you ever go back in the water again?"

"Aye, the next day. That summer I taught myself to swim."

Ben snickered. "Of course you did. A close thing like that teaches you to solve your own problems."

"Among other things." Evan put his hands on his hips and gazed across the harbor at the low hills of the East Mainland.

Ben bobbed in place to battle the deep freeze working its way up his body. "It's not all b-b-bad." He rubbed his shivering lips. "You learned to be self-sufficient. And you don't s-sound like you blame your m-mum."

"I don't. She was never negligent in general. It was just that one moment. Could happen to anyone."

"Okay, you win." Ben dashed out of the water, back to the rough sand, where he hopped up and down to dry his feet in the bitter breeze.

"Your turn." Evan stayed where he was, rocking from foot to foot. "Tell me a scary story from when you were young. Tell me the scariest one of all."

———

"I'VE NEVER HAD a brush with death—so far, at least." Ben hurried to rap his knuckles on a piece of driftwood.

Evan smiled at this superstitious act, though he might've done the same after such a fate-tempting declaration. "It doesn't have to be physical danger. What about frightening news, or an exam where it turned out you studied the wrong material?"

"Let me think." Ben stumbled over the pebbly beach toward the stairs where his shoes and socks lay.

While he waited, Evan did a few calf lifts to keep the blood flowing. The water here was even colder than he'd remembered.

He was suddenly was struck with a memory from last Christmas. He'd been standing on the dock in Stromness gazing out over the wind-ruffled harbor, thinking about how he'd lost Fergus forever, when a sudden obsession had seized him. What would it be like, he'd wondered, to simply walk fully clothed into the water and never come back? To let cold liquid seep into every cell, replacing that eternal pain with an equally eternal numbness?

The impulse had been so fleeting, he'd forgotten it moments later. And of course the pain hadn't been eternal. It had only felt like it at the time.

"This one night when I was eight," Ben said now, brushing the sand from his soles, "I overheard my mum on the phone to my dad. He was overseas at the time, as usual. Oh my God, I cannot even feel my toes. Do you think I've got frostbite?"

Evan stepped out of the water, his feet too numb to mind the rocks and shells beneath them. "It's not cold enough for frostbite, but don't rub your skin. If it warms too fast you could get chilblains."

"Chilblains," Ben said with a titter. "Sounds like something out of a Dickens novel. Anyway, we hadn't seen my dad in ages. It was almost time for him to decide whether to sign up for another overseas tour or come back to the UK."

"Right." Evan bent over to dislodge a piece of seaweed caught between his toes.

"They were arguing." Ben's voice turned soft. "Mum begged Dad to come home. She said if he didn't, she would leave him. That *we* would leave him."

Evan froze. "What did he say?"

"I don't know." He smoothed his sock across his knee. "But he didn't come home."

The wind had died, leaving no sound but the lap of water and the swish of seaweed over rocks. "I'm sorry," Evan said.

Ben sat up straight. "Obviously he came home eventually, on leave. And they're not divorced. That was my fear, that they'd break up."

Evan thought his chest would crack in two at the thought of a young Ben overhearing such a terrifying conversation. Worst, he'd seen that his mum's feelings weren't his dad's highest priority, that asking for what you want gets you nothing.

Perching on the lowest stair, he took Ben's right foot and pressed it against the dry wool of his kilt.

"That feels good." Ben shook out one of his socks and tugged it back onto his left foot, then slipped his shoe on. "Another scary moment was when my boyfriend at school told me he was going to university in America."

"That's awful."

"The worst part was, he told me in August on exam results day. I was so happy to be accepted to Glasgow Uni, and Rhys said he wouldn't be joining me because he was going to University of Miami. When I told him I knew that American universities send acceptances in the spring, he admitted he'd known since April." Ben glared at Evan. "Fucking *April*."

Evan sensed there was a message about secrets he was meant to hear. Perhaps this story was a clue to whatever had made Ben so distant today. "Did you break up?"

"Not officially. We pretended to do the long-distance thing, but I never saw him again." Ben shrugged. "I got over it."

"Was he your last boyfriend before me?"

"Yeah." Ben went still for a moment, then pulled his foot away from Evan. "Talking of which, I've been thinking, since we're kind of in a committed relationship—"

"'Kind of'?"

"—maybe we could stop using condoms? Maybe even tonight?"

Evan felt a mix of relief and apprehension: relief that Ben

wasn't breaking up with him and apprehension because he had to say—

"No."

"I got tested the week we started dating," Ben said, "and you said you'd not been with anyone in ages."

"I could've been lying."

Ben's jaw dropped. "*Were* you lying?"

"No, but I could've been. People lie about loads of things, especially sex."

"So you would cheat on me and then lie about it?"

"I've already *not* cheated and lied about that," Evan said.

"What do you mean, you've—oh." Ben put a hand to his own mouth. "Fergus thought you were unfaithful. You'd been together years, so you weren't using condoms by the time you left him."

Evan could barely look at him for the shame welling up inside. "I had to let him believe I'd endangered his health, maybe his life."

"When in fact you'd done no such thing. Jeezo..." Ben put his head in his hands for a moment, then looked up. "I don't see what that's got to do with me. I know monogamy is hard in the long run, and I hope we have a long run. But we need to trust each other *now*, else why even bother?"

"This is too important to rely on trust." Evan sat on the stair beside him. "If I had to go away again for my job, wouldn't you wonder whether I was putting you at risk?"

"Oh God, it's true." Ben jumped up and began to pace on the sand, one foot still bare. "It's really, really true."

"What, that I sometimes travel for work?"

"That you fuck terrorists out of patriotic duty!"

Evan's gut felt suddenly exposed to the cold night air. "Where did you hear that?"

"From you, last night." Ben's voice was tight and high-pitched. "Saying how you hurt Fergus and then some other lad who was stupid enough to fall into bed with an undercover—"

"Wheesht!" Evan leapt to his feet. "People live near here."

"Is it true, Evan?" Ben's volume hadn't dropped a notch. "Were you some sort of honey bee?"

"You mean 'honey trap'?"

"Whatever! Just tell me the truth. I don't care if it's top secret. I don't care if telling me is against the law. I just need to know."

Evan fought to control his breath. He'd been an absolute dunderhead to get drunk last night. What if he'd said something in the pub? Would his father have stopped him in time?

At least now he understood why Ben had been so distant all day.

What could he even say about Belfast? Legally the answer was *absolutely nothing, have you lost your mind?!?* but Ben already knew enough to imagine the worst. Perhaps if Evan omitted details such as names and places, he could satisfy Ben's curiosity without jeopardizing national security. It was clear that if he refused to reveal anything, Ben would never trust him again.

Evan wouldn't let his secrets break another man's heart. Not this time.

He looked up at the houses on the other side of the road. Their windows were closed, but someone could wander by any moment to walk a dog or smoke a cigarette.

"I'll tell you," Evan said, "but not here."

Chapter 28

DURING THEIR SILENT ten-minute walk back to Stromness, Ben wondered how he could ever handle Evan's secrecy. Such endless trust seemed like a superpower.

Then he thought about what Evan had said last night, that because of his parents' breakup—and his own with Fergus—he'd thought a spook could never find happiness. Ben was determined to disprove that theory. They would find a way.

Right?

On a back street in Stromness, Evan opened the gate of a play park. "Ah good, it's still here." He led Ben toward a six-foot-tall Thomas the Tank Engine and opened its side door. "It'll be a peedie bit cramped, but at least it's out of the wind, and it's as private as this world ever gets."

Ben eyed Thomas's moony face glowing in the nearby street-light and tried to decide whether the cartoon locomotive's smile was creepy or reassuring.

They climbed inside the train, drawing their knees to their chests so they could fit.

Evan took a deep breath, his expanding ribs pressing against Ben's. "How much do you know? What exactly did I tell you last night while I was drunk?"

Ben summed up Evan's confession, how sleeping with an undercover MI5 officer had hurt some guy who'd been dubbed *collateral damage*. "Then something about choosing one's family, and that's when I stopped you talking."

"Thanks. Did I say where this happened?"

"No, but you're MI5, not MI6, so it must have been within the UK."

Evan nodded, then took another long breath. "He wasn't a terrorist, the man I…associated with. His older brother was."

Ben gripped the sill of Thomas's window, bracing himself for a rollercoaster ride of truth—or what he hoped would be the truth.

"About a year and a half ago," Evan said, "MI5 determined that the brother was part of an established terrorist cell that was planning an attack last summer. We knew the region and the month, but nothing more specific. The group was notoriously suspicious of outsiders, so MI5 had failed to infiltrate. The cell members were pure cagey online and on the phone, so surveillance wasn't working either. The Service needed another way in. They hoped that my target would—"

"Does he have a name, this *target*?" Ben's tongue punched the last word.

"I can't tell you names and places."

"Then use filler names so I don't get confused. Mohammed or Reza or Ahmed or—"

"Patrick." Evan swallowed. "We'll call him Patrick, for conversation's sake."

Oh. A generic name like "John" could have been a stand-in for any nationality, but "Patrick" was ethnically specific enough to make it obvious this had to do with Northern Ireland. Ben now felt stupid and a bit racist for assuming the terrorists had been Muslim.

"Anyway," Evan said, "we hoped that even though Patrick wasn't a member of the cell, maybe he'd know his brother's plans. The group had been trying to recruit him, see."

"Did they know he was gay?"

"No. He wanted to come out." Evan sighed. "He wanted so much more from life than guns and bombs." He shook his head. "But his being in the closet made it safer for me to get close to him. His brother wouldn't even know I existed, so I'd never be vetted the way any other new acquaintance would be."

"If Patrick wasn't out, then how did you meet?"

"Our surveillance team knew he frequented a particular gay night club. They also knew that like a lot of Irish Catholics, he loved Celtic Football Club."

The name rang a bell. "You mean Glasgow Celtic? Isn't that—"

"Aye, Fergus's favorite team. So I was well steeped in the fandom." Evan shifted his legs, not that there was a spare inch to do so in their blue plastic confessional. "My supervisors approached me at the start of last year. I'd done some field work but had never gone deep undercover. They explained the attack they were trying to stop and how I could help."

"They gave you a choice?"

"Of course. It was an enormous job for someone so new to the Service. And to be clear, they never told me to sleep with that lad. My instructions were to befriend him. Beyond that I could use my discretion."

Ben was confused. "If you weren't ordered to have sex, then why did you?"

"I thought it would get him to trust me." Evan looked at his hands clenched in his lap. "I was right."

"Did you...like him?" This question felt the most invasive of all.

Evan's face pinched. After a long moment he said, "Going undercover is like becoming a different person. It wasn't me, Evan Hollister, having sex with that man. It was someone else." He paused. "Actually, it was more like being two people at once. The real Evan was always in the background, guiding this other version of me, feeding my other self the right questions, taking every precaution to avoid blowing cover."

"This undercover version of you, is it..." Ben wasn't sure how to phrase this. "Was he the man I met at Dunleven Castle? Was he the man I had Valentine's dinner with?"

"No." Evan seemed offended at the idea. "I've always been myself with you."

Ben recalled how Evan hadn't really changed after the night he'd revealed his job, apart from being a bit more relaxed. "What about Gunnar?"

"Gunnar's a different character," Evan said. "He's nothing like the man I was in-in that other place. When the operation was over, I left that one behind."

Ben hoped that was true. He turned back to the facts of the case. "Did this 'Patrick' tell you what you needed to know?"

"He told me a lot, because he thought I was sympathetic to the cause—and because he wanted to impress me. Some of his information was incorrect, of course, as he wasn't truly part of this group. We were careful which tips we acted on, in case the cell was using him for disinformation. We corroborated every bit of intelligence we got from Patrick—not just for the sake of getting it right, but to avoid exposing him as our unwitting agent. If he ever got caught..." Evan stopped and pressed a fist to his own mouth.

Ben's throat ached. "But he did get caught, didn't he?"

Evan tilted down his chin and began to drag his fingertips over his forehead as he spoke. "One night we were alone together in my flat. In my bed. It was late June, and the investigation was getting urgent. By then MI5 knew the weekend of the planned attack but still no location." He rubbed his arms, though it was far warmer inside the train than it had been on the beach. "By this point Patrick and I had something of a routine. We'd get steaming drunk—well, he'd get drunk and I'd fake it—then...then I'd fuck him senseless, and in the aftermath he'd tell me almost anything I wanted to know."

Ben wanted to stop Evan talking, just as he'd done last night in bed. But his own mouth was frozen open and dry as sandpaper.

"Sometimes he'd repeat himself," Evan said, "so I don't think he remembered later what he'd told me. He was so...naive." He cleared his throat hard. "Anyway, the police would be listening."

Ben shuddered. "This was all being recorded?"

"Firstly, the Service thought as a last resort, they could blackmail Patrick with the recordings. Secondly, this way I wouldn't have to remember everything he told me. But most importantly, the surveillance team were my backup. If I was in danger, they could protect me." His words tumbled out with the force of a waterfall. "I was told that if I went undercover, someone would always have my back. It wasn't a guarantee of safety, but it was pretty fucking close." His jaw clenched. "So they claimed."

Ben wanted to reach out, but feared Evan might snap in half. "What happened that night?"

"It was about three a.m. We were in bed and-and I was...and he was almost...and then suddenly the door opened behind me. Before I could move, someone grabbed me in a choke hold and pulled me off of Patrick. I guess instinct and training kicked in, because my body just went into action." Evan mimicked his own moves as he spoke. "I made my hand into a hook and smashed down on his thumb, enough to loosen his grip on my throat so I could breathe. Like they teach you in Krav Maga?"

Ben gave a wordless nod.

"Then I shoved my shoulder back." Evan's body twitched to the left. "I'd trapped the guy's hand against my chest, so I turned and bashed him in the face again and again until I saw blood, and then I kept punching, sending him down and down, off the bed and onto the floor, with me on top of him."

Ben could barely breathe. "You fought him off?"

"I fought one guy off. But there were four. Two of the others grabbed me and put a..." Evan lifted his hands and dropped them near his neck. "...a black sack over my head. I kept fighting even though I couldn't see, because I knew my life depended on it. But eventually they got me face down and bound my hands and feet. I was still shouting, hoping somebody would hear and call the police. Then one of them kicked me in the stomach so I couldn't shout for a while."

Ben felt his own guts tremble. "Evan…"

"And Patrick, they quieted him right away. I never saw him again after they covered my head."

"How could this happen? What about your backup?"

"The police surveillance van had been hijacked at gunpoint before the other guys broke into my flat. The cops were driven out to the countryside and released alive." He gave a harsh chuckle. "Which shows some things do change, even in places like that. In the past those cops would've been killed—or more likely tortured, then killed."

"What about you?" Ben whispered.

"I wasn't killed." Evan spread his hands to display his presence.

Ben forced out the words, each one splintering his throat. "Were. You. Tortured."

IT WAS EXCRUCIATING TO ADMIT, but Evan knew he'd never truly recover if he couldn't name what had happened to him.

"Yes. I was tortured. Nothing sophisticated or systematic— they weren't CIA-trained or anything—just punching, kicking, pistol-whipping. Quaint, old-school gangster stuff."

Ben gave a little whimper but said nothing, so Evan continued.

"They rolled me and Patrick up in separate rugs and took us to an abandoned warehouse." He glanced at Ben's horrified face. "Apologies for the clichéd setting, but it's true. Anyway, they sat me up in a chair, still naked, and put a gun to my head." Evan ran his hand along the train's window frame to keep himself in the here-and-now. "I knew I should be trying to figure out how to escape, but all I could think about was whether the bag on my head would hold in my brains if they pulled the trigger."

"Fuck's sake, Evan." Ben was leaning forward, head almost between his knees.

"Shall I stop?"

"Only if you want to."

Evan knew he should've taken the out, but he didn't. Didn't want to. Didn't stop.

He'd lost count of how many times he'd told this story. The first was at his debriefing. It had taken hours to blurt all the details amidst his raving agitation and near-catatonic shutdowns. Then he'd told it at the psychiatric hospital the Service shared with its sister agencies and Ministry of Defence—a hospital where every doctor had a top-secret clearance.

Finally, he'd told it over and over to his MI5 therapist. She'd led him through it slowly, using eye movement desensitization and reprocessing therapy to turn the experience into something he could remember without reliving. Thanks to her, the nightmares were now rare; the panic attacks, nonexistent. Thanks to her, he could recall most of the details without falling into the past, without his body feeling every blow.

All of those recounts felt less threatening than tonight's, because this listener mattered more than all the others put together. Would Ben be strong and supportive after hearing this tale, or would he be overwhelmed by the horror and need comfort? They'd not been together long enough for Evan to know how much his partner could take.

"They asked what Patrick had told me. They asked who I worked for, though they already knew. They wanted names of my fellow officers. They'd not had much time to search my flat, see, because one of my neighbors knocked on the door, Mrs…." He stopped himself identifying old Mrs. Barnes, who used to bring him rhubarb-ginger scones when she'd bought more than she could eat fresh.

"What's going on, lad?" she'd called out. *"It's too late for this sort of rumpus."*

"I couldn't answer her," Evan said, "so she announced she was phoning the police. The men had to rush me and Patrick out inside the rugs. Sorry if that part was confusing."

"S'all right," Ben murmured, sounding on the verge of a dry boak.

"They found my weapon—I don't carry one here, but all officers carry one in-in the place I was." It was so hard not saying the word *Belfast*. "They also got my phones, which were fingerprint-protected, but of course they had access to my fingers."

Evan paused, remembering the final text he'd received later that day on his personal phone, before it was smashed to bits:

FERGUS

Go to hell. You'll fit right in there.

"Did you tell them anything?" Ben asked.

"No. I couldn't consider it. If I'd started bargaining with myself, thinking, 'Maybe I could tell them a peedie bit,' then they'd have broken me in minutes." He thought for a long moment before adding, "The Service trains us to resist torture."

"Oh God." Ben leaned over to stick his head out the window. "I need a second."

"Sure." Evan's throat was getting scratchy, reminding him how thirsty he'd felt during his eighteen hours of captivity, how they'd offered him water to drink, then poured it over his head instead, just like in that Clint Eastwood film Ben had shown him.

Ben pulled his head back into the train. "Go on." He took Evan's hand, perhaps as much for his own comfort as anything. "You must have been terrified."

"The worst part wasn't what they did, it was what I feared they would do next. I couldn't see, so for all I knew they had a whole tableful of torture devices: pliers, hammers, hydrochloric acid..."

Ben swallowed so loudly, Evan worried again that he might get sick. "You sure you don't want me to stop?"

"I want to hear how you escaped." Ben squeezed his hand. "But only if you want to tell it."

Evan was relieved to skip ahead. "Patrick's brother—we'll call him Stephen—was the target of our operation. He wasn't at the warehouse when they brought me in, but when he arrived, he asked his men about Patrick."

Another memory washed over him, and this one he didn't share with Ben:

"Hope you boys taught Paddy a lesson about trusting strangers." Stephen grasped Evan's hair through the sack. "They say this face could make a dead man sing. No wonder Patrick fell for it, the eejit."

Evan spat out a gob of blood so he could speak. "Don't call him that. He wasn't—"

The hardest punch yet, Stephen cutting off the truth he most needed to hear. "Don't you dare defend him, spook. You used him." Another punch, this one to the solar plexus. "You fucked the secrets out of him, ya filthy government whore."

Evan fought for his next breath, knowing his last would come soon. Stephen had just admitted that the things Patrick had revealed were true, which meant Evan wasn't getting out alive.

"Wasn't Patrick in the warehouse with you?" Ben asked.

"No. The head thug—we'll call him Des—told Stephen that Patrick had been taken down south to keep him safe until all of this blew over."

"Was that true?"

Evan hesitated, wishing he could let Ben go on believing in happy endings. "They'd been too rough. Patrick died on our way to the warehouse."

"Oh my God." Ben's breath hitched into a sob. "Oh my God."

Tears could be contagious, Evan knew, so he shifted further into debriefing mode. "His death was my only chance. I knew how much his brother loved him. I thought if I could get Stephen alone and tell him his own men had killed Patrick, maybe I could turn him against them. I could win over the most unlikely ally—not only to survive, but to complete the mission."

"The mission?" Ben removed his glasses to wipe his eyes. "How could you still think about that?"

"Focusing on the operation was what kept me alive." He rubbed his palms against the wool of his kilt. "By evening it was obvious I wouldn't tell them anything useful, and they knew MI5 and the police would be looking for me. So Stephen and Des put me in the boot of a car and drove me out into the woods."

Ben yanked a packet of tissues from his inside coat pocket and nodded at him to continue.

"When we stopped, Stephen made me walk into the woods ahead of him, just the two of us so Des could keep a lookout. I was still hooded and gagged." *And naked*, he decided to omit.

"God..." Tears rolled down Ben's cheeks, and though he was clutching a tissue, he wasn't using it.

"After we'd walked a bit, Stephen put me on my knees and took off my hood and gag. For some reason, being able to see again meant everything, even though I knew I was probably going to die."

Ben whimpered again, but he said nothing.

"Des was too far away to hear us, but he had a line of sight through the trees." Evan closed his eyes, seeing the scene on the backs of his lids, the literal moment of truth.

Evan pushed out the words through blood-caked lips. "Patrick's dead."

"I knew it was a gamble," he told Ben. "Stephen could blame me for his brother's death—and in a way, he wouldn't have been wrong—but I figured what could he do, kill me twice?"

"You lie!" Stephen pointed Evan's own pistol at his head.

"Ask Des," Evan croaked. "He's the one who battered him at my flat. Patrick died in the van. I was there. I heard him—" A stream of blood down his throat choked off his words.

"You heard him what?" Stephen loomed over Evan, eyes reflecting the cold light of dusk.

Evan coughed. "I heard him breathing wrong. And then...not at all."

Stephen lowered the Glock for a moment, his hands shaking. Then he raised it again. "I don't believe you."

"It's the truth."

"You're MI5. You don't know the meaning of truth."

"I know Patrick's dead." Evan looked up to meet his captor's eyes. "Because of me, and because of you."

"After what seemed like a year," he told Ben now, "Stephen put my hood back on and said to fall over when I heard the shot."

Ben jerked as though he was bracing for the blast himself.

The gun discharged, and a bullet whistled past Evan's right ear. He collapsed face down onto the damp forest floor, wrists still bound behind his back.

Stephen bent over and put a hand to the side of Evan's throat, as if checking for a pulse. "I'm gonna go sort things with Des. If you're telling the truth, I'll be back to get you. If you're lying, I'll be back to kill you."

"I couldn't hear well after the gunshot," Evan told Ben. "About five minutes later, Stephen was there with my clothes, which they were planning to burn after killing me. I got dressed and followed him to the car. Des was dead." He didn't go into detail—not only to spare Ben but also because his memory of this part was mercifully foggy. "He started driving, and the moment we got a mobile signal, I phoned MI5 to tell them Stephen was ready to cooperate."

"Whoa. Was he a big fish?"

"Not the biggest, but definitely on his way up."

"What did they do with him?"

"I don't know exactly." This was the truth. "All I know is that he told them what the target was. Arrests were made. The public never knew what we'd stopped." Evan paused, wondering what more he should reveal. *In for a penny, in for a pound.* "That attack could've killed dozens of innocent people, including children. Terrorists in that area used to phone in a warning ahead of time, but this cell was different. They didn't just want to scare people or make a statement. They wanted to kill."

Ben finally used the tissue to wipe his eyes and nose. "What happened to you after?"

"First a regular hospital for my wounds, then a psych hospital for my…other wounds. The Service said I could return to work if I continued therapy, which I did. Which I still do."

"Good. Did they give you, like, a medal and all?"

Evan thought of the Certificate of Awesomeness on his fridge. "I got a commendation for bravery. But the best reward was the choice of where to go next."

"You came back to Glasgow on purpose? Why?"

"I wanted to make amends. I knew I'd never win Fergus back." *Not that I was allowed to.* "But I couldn't just walk away from the Warriors." He met Ben's eyes. "I'm glad I took the hard road, else I'd never have met you."

Ben's face softened. "I wish this had never happened." He dropped his gaze. "But we all know what wishes are worth."

Despite the cramped space, Evan managed to pull his arm from between their bodies and loop it over Ben's shoulders. Ben twisted around to hug Evan tightly, his own body shaking with suppressed sobs.

At last he moved back and straightened his glasses. "Can we get out of this train? I can't feel my legs."

With some difficulty, they extricated themselves from Thomas's bairn-size engine cab. Evan marched in place for a few moments to restore his circulation. Then he laid his hand on the engine's roof to remind himself he was in Stromness, not Belfast, and he was with Ben, not Patrick.

As they neared the play park gate, Ben stopped. "I need to know—after surviving something like that, how can you not be…"

"What, crazy?"

"Broken." Ben gazed up at him with eyes still wet. "Others have gone through less and come out shattered."

"Look, I won't lie and say I'm fine, like it never happened. You of all people know I've still got issues." He took Ben's hand, clutching it more tightly than he'd intended. "I wouldn't let those bastards break me, not then and not now. But I know that I could still break one day. You need to know that too."

"I do." Ben squeezed his hand back just as hard. "And you need to know I'm here to help with this burden, even when you think you can carry it yourself." He tugged Evan toward the gate. "Now let's go and get warm."

They left the play park in silence. Evan threw a last glance back at Thomas, where as a child he'd played at being an engine driver, here on an island with no trains.

Chapter 29

BEN LAY awake in the middle of the windy Orkney night, wondering if he'd magically stolen his partner's anxiety. Beside him, Evan slept with an unusual stillness. Gone were the restless limbs and barely audible moans. Now it was Ben whose sleep was haunted by nightmares of black hoods and carnivorous rugs.

But if losing a bit of his own slumber was the price for Evan's peace of mind, Ben was willing to pay it. He couldn't go back in time and take Evan's place, but he could be here for him now, could listen without judgment.

And keep his secret forever.

It wouldn't be easy. It was one thing to know that Evan had left Fergus and the Warriors because of a secret job assignment, and quite another to know that while they'd been badmouthing him, he was being bound, gagged, and tortured.

Ben put his fingertips to his eyelids, trying to blot out the image of Evan fucking "Patrick" from behind, their backs to the bedroom door. Would it have made a difference if they could see the bad guys coming? Did Evan lie awake wondering whether a split-second warning could have saved that poor lad's life?

"All right?" Evan whispered behind him, making Ben jump.

"Sorry. Yes. I'm fine." He swallowed hard. "I can't sleep."

"Because of what I told you in the play park? I shouldn't have shared so many details."

"Thank you for trusting me. Not that I gave you much choice." Ben chose his words carefully, as Evan had warned him they couldn't talk about this in their room, in case it was bugged. "What time is it? Mind, you promised we'd see every single sight on Orkney Mainland tomorrow."

"It's already tomorrow." Evan slid an arm around Ben's waist and snuggled close. "But the time's just gone five, so we can still sleep." He slipped his hand up under Ben's T-shirt to caress his chest, awakening every inch he touched. "Or…"

His mouth found the curve of Ben's neck, the bare skin that met his shirt collar. Ben felt the scrape of teeth, and his cock thickened at this feeling of sure and utter possession—but more than anything, this feeling of normality. Here in the dark they could be two ordinary lovers with no terrible past or terrifying future.

He shifted his arse back a few inches, into Evan's crotch. "Let's do it like this," he whispered. "Lazy Sunday–style."

"That'll be new." Evan lifted up on one elbow to look past him.

"The wardrobe door won't open enough to show us the mirror from here." Ben reached for his tablet on the bedside table. "But we could use this." He brought up the camera app and switched it to front-facing mode.

"We are not recording ourselves having sex."

"We don't have to record." Ben turned on the lamp, then adjusted the tablet's angle so the screen showed both of their faces. Evan's was furrowed with worry.

"Shut off its Wi-Fi."

"Happy to," Ben said. "If you fetch the condom and lube."

After a moment's hesitation, Evan did as he asked, returning quickly under the warm duvet.

Ben watched them on the screen as they made love. He didn't fancy this early-morning closeup of himself, with his hair all mussed and his cheeks crisscrossed with pillowcase creases. But seeing Evan's beautiful face, seeing the rapture he felt at being inside Ben, erased all self-consciousness. It was a captivating sight: those eyes, heavy-lidded with pleasure; those lips, parting with each sigh; that tongue, peeking out whenever Ben—

The tablet's stand suddenly collapsed, sending it tumbling.

"Oops." Ben leaned over to pick it up. "We must have made the floor shake."

A few moments after they began again, Ben realized something wasn't the same. "I can't see your face now." He shifted the tablet. "There you are."

"Here I am." Evan stopped moving and met Ben's eyes on the screen. "As long as you want me." His voice was soft but solemn.

Ben held his gaze. "What are you saying?"

"I'm saying you've no need to worry I'll go away again. For that sort of work." He laid his cheek atop Ben's. "I'll quit first."

Only now did Ben realize he *had* worried about that exact scenario. Beneath his more magnanimous concerns—for Patrick's life, for Evan's sanity—lurked a darker, more piercing dread: that Evan would once again let the government use his body to defend the realm. Now that it had been said aloud, Ben knew how much he'd needed to hear this promise.

"You don't have to commit to that."

"I want to," Evan said. "I love you."

Ben's heart gave a giant thud. He turned his head to look at Evan straight on. "Say that to my face."

Evan smiled. "Say it to *my* face first."

"I love you."

Evan said it again too, then kissed him. Down below, he moved inside Ben with new urgency.

Ben groaned and broke the kiss. "Now I wish we were recording."

"Do you, aye?" Evan reached out to the screen and hit the red dot. The time counter began ticking up.

"Have you lost your mind?" Ben asked, though he didn't stop the video. "What about the cloud?"

"You're offline." Evan ground into him, sending spirals of

pleasure throughout his body. "We'll save it to a folder where it won't upload."

"Okay." Ben clutched his pillow, barely able to speak. He vowed to be worthy of this man's trust, a gift so rarely given.

As their pace increased, their legs grew tangled with the cover. Finally Ben rolled back and said, "Get on top of me."

"What about Lazy Sunday?"

"I don't feel so lazy anymore, do you?"

"Never did." Evan settled between Ben's legs, pulling the duvet up to their waists.

Ben glanced at his tablet screen. "What, no frontal nudity?"

"It's cold in here." He slid his arms beneath Ben's shoulders. "For now."

After a brief adjustment of hips, they found each other again. Ben wrapped his legs around Evan's arse, savoring the rhythmic flex of muscles against his thighs. Knowing he could watch this video over and over, Ben kept his eyes on Evan's, and closed them when they kissed.

Eventually the heat between their bodies overcame the chill of the room. Evan flipped back the covers, removed his shirt, and pushed Ben's up. "Can we take this off? I want to feel you against me."

Ben raised his arms to comply, banishing a brief worry about how his naked body would compare cinematically to Evan's. It didn't matter, because this man was his, and Ben deserved every inch of him.

He cried out now as some of his favorite inches went deeper than ever. Ben reached back to grasp one of the slats of the wooden headboard—partly to keep it from banging against the wall, but mostly to give himself an anchor. He wrapped his other hand around Evan's forearm, feeling the taut muscle propping him up. "Just like that. Don't stop."

"I won't." Evan's body undulated in a steady rhythm. "Want to come soon or make it last?"

Ben almost said, "I don't know, whatever you want" by reflex.

But he knew what he wanted, and he'd learned that with Evan, he could say it. "Make it last. We can edit the video later if I need the hard drive space."

Evan laughed. "Almost forgot about the video." He angled a glance at the tablet. "Fuck, that's hot."

Ben turned his head, pushing aside the bulge of fluffy hotel pillow so he could watch. "It's too close. We need a wider angle to capture your gorgeous legs."

"But if we move the camera back, our faces won't be as clear, plus it'll look porny."

"Heaven forfend."

"More importantly…" Evan spread his knees, then reached both hands beneath Ben's arse. "I don't want to stop."

Ben felt himself lifted and guided toward the ideal angle. Evan's cock pressed against his prostate without moving.

"You'll make me come if you go at me like that."

"No, I won't." Evan smirked. "Not right away."

He began with short, swift strokes, lighting Ben up inside, brighter and brighter, until Ben's cock stiffened and jerked. Then Evan backed off, nearly withdrawing, leaving Ben whimpering with need but also laughing with relief. He wanted more, much more.

"You bastard," Ben panted. "I love you."

Evan just smiled and did it again. And again. And it was glorious.

But the third time Evan tried to slow down, Ben clutched him tighter with his hole.

"Oh." Evan froze as he was squeezed again, harder. "Oh fuck."

"Can we come now?" Ben grasped his own cock. "Please?"

"God, yes." Evan drew back, then rammed into him. "Yes." He went faster now, almost out of control.

"Fuck me." From the first stroke of his hand, Ben could tell he was close, so close. "Fuck me till we come. I need it. Fuck me."

Evan lifted him higher, looping Ben's legs over his shoulders before driving forward again and again. Ben felt the edge of the headboard slat dig into his palm as he clung to it like the safety bar of a rollercoaster.

He tried to bite back the whimpers rising in his throat, not wanting to disturb any neighbors. But in the end nothing could stop his final scream as his orgasm struck, all the more intense for its repeated delay.

Through blurred vision he saw Evan's neck arch, every muscle bulging. He lowered Ben's legs from his shoulders, stretched out upon him, then gave two final thrusts, his whole body shuddering.

Arms aching, Ben pulled Evan close to feel the thump of his heartbeat against his own.

God, how he loved this complicated, contradictory man. Evan had told him the stuff of nightmares, yet Ben had never felt so brave. Evan was clutching him almost too tightly for breath, yet Ben had never felt so free.

"We can be happy. I know it's not easy and it never will be, but we're not fucking doomed."

Like everything else Evan had uttered in his drunken state the night before last, these words were painfully, gloriously true.

Chapter 30

"PLEASE TELL me you ate for the petsitter." Evan set down his bags and picked up Trent, who purred like a chainsaw as she bashed her head against his chin. He carried her into his kitchen, where he found a half-empty bowl of dry food. "Not bad." As usual, the towel beneath the cat's water dish was damp, because she liked to splash when she was bored or happy or awake.

With Trent trotting at his heels like a puppy, Evan went through his flat to confirm that all the items he'd arranged had remained as he'd left them. He'd vetted the petsitter, but one couldn't be too careful.

The stack of mail on the table still showed the corner of a specific envelope poking out at the correct angle. The talcum powder he'd spilled in front of his wardrobe was untouched apart from a single trail of paw prints.

Satisfied at the state of his security, Evan flopped onto his bed for a much-needed nap. He and Ben had taken an extra day off so they could spend most of yesterday in Orkney before boarding the five o'clock ferry. Then they'd stayed the night in Thurso—partly to avoid driving on the peedie Highland roads in the dark, but also to ease the culture shock of returning to real life.

His phone buzzed with a message:

DAD

You still use encrypted texting app?

EVAN

Of course

His father replied with an email address and a long, complex password, followed by the unnecessary instruction to delete this text message.

Evan acknowledged receipt, then fetched his laptop from the safe in his wardrobe. Sitting on the bed, he activated a virtual private network, opened a Tor browser, and logged in to the email address. There he found a drafts folder containing one message.

An email "dead drop" like this was breathtakingly simple and effective. As long as two people both knew the username and password, they could share information without ever technically sending it over the internet. No transmission meant no tracking.

Of course, the drafts could easily be found by MI5's signals-intelligence sister agency, the blandly named Government Communications Headquarters. But first GCHQ would need to know where to look. For a simple file share, this method was a lot safer than handing over a memory stick that could have been lost or stolen on the journey back from Orkney.

Evan clicked on the blank message, then downloaded and opened its PDF attachment:

Russian false-flag operations in Eastern Europe

Evan began to read the summary, his heart beating faster with every line.

The classified Joint Intelligence Committee report described how Russian spies had masqueraded online as Islamic extremists, appearing to associate with well-known non-radical Muslims in two small Eastern European countries. They'd left an electronic trail just clear enough for those countries' domestic intelligence officers to follow—enough to get them chasing their own tails trying to find their targets, to leave them anticipating attacks that never came.

Then the stories would conveniently "leak," framing the Muslims for planned attacks on a beloved landmark. The Russian leaks would be timed with a wave of online trolls boosting phony news reports on social media to whip public anxiety into a froth. By the time the police and security services dispelled the rumors, the damage had been done: rising Islamophobia, social division, and mistrust in authorities to even *tell* the public about a terrorist threat, much less protect them from it. This fear and uncertainty stoked support for extreme-right-wing populist xenophobes, who had already made massive inroads into local and national politics across Europe.

Evan's phone buzzed with another text from his father:

> In Glasgow. Fancy a quick lunch?

"DID YOU READ IT ALL?"

"You didn't give me time." Evan tore off a shred of his falafel wrap and tossed it to a sparrow, provoking a disapproving tongue-click from his father. The peedie bird hopped across the sunlit tile floor of Glasgow Central Station and snatched up the bread. "I read enough to get the general idea."

"Were you surprised?" his dad asked.

"More than I should have been." Evan scanned the train station's wide-open waiting area to see if anyone was close enough to hear. "I get why a fake terrorist plot on same-sex weddings would serve Russia's objectives, but why stage it in Glasgow? Why not in London or Manchester or Birmingham?"

"Russian intelligence likes to test its methods on smaller targets, then optimize those methods before deploying them against their main quarry. It's called capability development. The report I gave you explains this," his dad added with a note of annoyance.

"I told you, I didn't finish it because I had to meet you before your train left."

"Hmph." His father checked the departures board, which showed the train to London's Euston Station running ten minutes late. "Anyway, the report predicts the Russians will eventually execute similar operations in countries like France, Germany, the Netherlands, and of course…"

"The UK. Which Scotland is a part of, so how can it be a small target?"

"It's a less complicated target. There are fewer Muslims here, so it's more likely your office will track the ones the Russians want you to track, even if they're fake Muslims. In London this scheme might never have been noticed."

"But there are same-sex weddings all over Great Britain now, so if this alleged plot gets leaked, it'll scare the entire country." *Including Ben, who could never know the top-secret truth.*

"Exactly." His dad shoved the last two chips from his fish supper into his mouth. "It has all the potential rewards of a London-based operation yet few of the risks. Putin still gets to sow chaos and fear. He gets to remind people of Islam's alleged threat to human rights."

Evan thought about how such a propaganda effort could undermine the open society that most Brits took justifiable pride in, a society that embraced both immigrants and LGBTQ folk. "Can't the government make an announcement before any leaks happen? Like, inoculate the public with a dose of the truth?"

His father gave him a withering look. "Accuse a foreign state of messing with our domestic counterterrorism efforts? They've got nukes, you know."

"So do China, and we wouldn't let them get away with something so brazen."

"The Chinese aren't propping up the British economy." His dad tugged another paper napkin from his takeaway bag and flapped it as he ranted. "Putin's oligarch mates have spent the last decade moving to the UK and buying everything they could get their hands on: Knightsbridge mansions, Premier League football clubs, even fucking castles. No one here batted an eye. After all, the Russians were white, Christian—and most of all, rich. They're part of us now, which means they've got us by the bollocks." He wiped his hands with the napkin, then pitched it into the rubbish bin several feet away.

This was a familiar lament, one Evan had usually dismissed as his dad's Cold-War paranoia. Literally born the day the Berlin Wall fell, Evan had regarded the Soviet Union and its components as matters for the history books.

Evan rubbed the bridge of his nose. After the serenity of Orkney, this bustling train station was giving him a raging headache. "This could be devastating. A manufactured threat against same-sex weddings would poison the way people in this country look at each other."

"And nothing would make Russia happier. They've worked out exactly how to turn us against one another." His father crumpled up his takeaway bag. "It won't happen overnight, but after years of carefully cultivated chaos, the West will eat itself."

Evan wrapped the remains of his falafel, having lost the appetite to finish it. All along, Operation Caps Lock may have been just a peedie piece of someone else's planet-size puzzle. It was too big for MI5—much less a single junior officer—to handle.

"Hang on," Evan said. "Russian intelligence must be doing all this within our country, right? If it were outside our borders, you wouldn't know so much about it, because it wouldn't be MI5's purview. It would be under MI6."

A sneer curled his father's lips, as it always did when their international-facing counterparts were mentioned. "You're right. My branch would be privy to some information, but those stuck-up snakes at Six would probably withhold many of these details out of sheer spite."

Evan doubted that. Then again, he'd entered the Service long after the interagency feuds were at their fiercest. These days the rivalry was friendlier out of necessity, but he'd grown up hearing his father refer to MI6 as "Enemy #2"—after Russia, of course.

"What's your point?" Dad asked.

"Well, if it's happening here, surely someone in the UK is helping them. Maybe several people. Maybe even in Scotland."

"True. They may have agents here, witting or unwitting."

Evan remembered the pure daft articles Jordan had been forwarding to him. Their source could easily be some Russian-operated troll farm like the ones in the Joint Intelligence Committee report.

Then he thought of how David Wallace had called Scotland a "white firewall" at the BVP meeting. And at the rally he'd said, *Mark my words, mate: This is where it starts.* At the time, Evan had thought he meant that the rally itself was the beginning of a movement, but perhaps he'd literally meant *where*. As in Scotland.

"Big people are watching us, Gunnar. And they like what they see."

Evan got to his feet. "I think I know where to look."

Chapter 31

BEN FELT he could burst out of his skin for sheer joy. He was blasting his favorite Persian dance playlist, he was in love with the man of his dreams, and his last university lecture *FOR-FUCK-ING-EVER* had ended two hours ago.

With a fresh travel mug of tea in hand, he shimmied across his flat toward his computer, ignoring the torrential afternoon rain outside and the Krav Maga–induced muscle aches inside, determined to channel this energy into the best wedding he'd ever coordinated. Now that Glasgow Uni's three-week spring vacation had begun, Ben could devote all of his brain to this job—at least for a few days before returning to the realities of exam revision and honors dissertation.

He retrieved the details Michael and Philip had sent him two weeks ago, then opened his wedding spreadsheet template, ready to organize this thing into submission.

In keeping with the football theme, the couple had ordered a sheet cake decorated in black-and-white hexagons, with a double-groomed cake topper upon a scrap of artificial turf. The cheesiness made Ben's eyes cross, but he'd seen worse cakes.

He'd never seen a worse menu, however. Theirs consisted of the classic football-stadium pairing: meat pies and Bovril, a "beef tea" whose smell alone made Ben want to boak. He made a note to suggest alternative beverages. Scottish law prohibited alcohol at football matches, but some sparkling craft cider wouldn't go amiss.

Ben's heart sank when he saw that the "reception tent" was barely big enough for the food and the catering staff. If it rained, there'd be nowhere for the wedding party and guests to retreat.

Michael and Philip were marrying outdoors—in Scotland—with no wet-weather plan.

An hour later Ben's nerves were pure frayed, and his trusty spreadsheets were as messy as a murder scene. With so many variables outside his control, this wedding was chaos-in-waiting.

He needed help, and not just in the form of extra hands. He needed expertise.

At the sound of his mother's voice-mail greeting, Ben felt his courage fade. "Hi, Mum. I just wanted to…to say thanks again for the Naw-Rúz dinner the other night. The *fesenjan* is even yummier as leftovers."

Just ask her. The worst she can say is no.

Ben straightened his posture. "Also, I need your help with a new wedding. I know I told you I was done with them, but this couple were desperate, and you always say we should help those in need. Anyway, the venue…well, they might as well be marrying on an Antarctic ice shelf for all the amenities they'll have. It reminds me of the wedding we did in—"

His phone beeped with an incoming call. Mum.

"Hiya," he said. "Did you hear my message?" He rapped his knuckles against his head at the stupid question. "No, of course not. I was still recording it when—"

"Ben, are you okay?" she asked.

"Ermmmm, yes. No." He explained the situation, even more awkwardly than on the voice mail. Then he held his breath, dreading her answer.

"I'll think about it," she said.

This was the answer he'd dreaded. "In other words, no."

"I'm not saying, 'I'll think about it' to be evasive. I really will consider it."

He wanted to believe her. She seemed to be slowly coming round to the idea of marriage equality, at least for non-Bahá'ís.

"I wouldn't ask if I wasn't at my wit's end," he said. "I don't want to damage your reputation in the Bahá'í community." An idea struck him. "If it feels too public to attend the ceremony, you could simply help me plan beforehand."

After a long exhalation, she said, "I love you, Ben. I promise to pray about this with an open heart and let you know soon."

He echoed her sigh. "I love you too, Mum. That's all I ask."

"No, it's not," she said with a chuckle.

Ben smiled. "No, it's not. But it's a start."

After they hung up, Ben felt bad for offering the compromise of helping with the wedding in secret, thereby implying Mum was some sort of moral coward.

And what was Ben if not a hypocrite himself? Now that he and Evan were in love, there was no swimming back to the safe shores of single life, where he could pretend to the world he was following the rules of his faith.

He went to his bed and studied the painting above it, of an enormous tree bearing fruit of all shapes and colors. UNITY IN DIVERSITY, it read in glittery block letters above the tree, and below its wide roots stretched his favorite quote of the prophet Bahá'u'lláh: YE ARE THE FRUITS OF ONE TREE, AND THE LEAVES OF ONE BRANCH.

He whispered the end of that quote, the part that wouldn't fit on the painting. "So powerful is the light of unity that it can illuminate the whole earth."

To Ben, *this* was the big stuff, *this* was the essence of being Bahá'í. The precept against homosexuality was a small imperfection, a missed stitch in an otherwise glorious tapestry of belief.

He thought about what Andrew had said at the Warriors match, how he and Ben each had to "live in the tension" between their two identities. It was a wise work-around—for now, at least.

But Ben knew that the day was coming when that tension would prove too much to bear. One day soon, he'd have to make a choice that would break his own heart.

———

IN HIS EIGHT years with the Warriors, Evan had kept his cool during hundreds of high-pressure moments: free kicks, corner kicks, penalties. In three years with MI5, while infiltrating two different terrorist organizations and facing death threats from known killers, the ice in his veins had never thawed.

Today, however, his mind was pure panic, and his stomach felt like it had permanently shifted halfway up his throat. For the first time, he was tasked with leading a formal presentation at work.

Detective Sergeant Fowles smiled as she took her seat at the conference table beside Detective Inspector Hayward. "Good luck with the show," she told Evan, "and remember, if you arse it up, probably very few people will die."

"*Brinn in helvete,*" Evan replied, for old time's sake.

"Already in hell, thanks." She gestured to the room, which was growing stuffier by the minute as the rest of the Operation Caps Lock team filed in.

Kay entered last, accompanied by a smartly dressed thirty-something man Evan had never met.

"Good morning," she said as she took her place at the head of the table. "TGIF and all that rubbish. Everyone, this is Grant Kensington from MI6. Please introduce yourselves quickly and efficiently."

The officer from MI5's sister agency nodded to the team. Based on his perma-sneer, Kensington seemed dischuffed at having to slum it with Six's domestic partner—in Glasgow, no less. *The sacrifices one makes for one's country,* said his cooler-than-thou face. The studied carelessness of his golden-brown hair reminded Evan of Lord Andrew, and he briefly wondered whether they shared the same high-priced London stylist.

After the introductions, Kay asked Evan to proceed. Despite the fact his joints had turned to water, he managed to walk to the front of the room and get through the introduction without dropping the remote control.

Evan outlined their hypothesis that the "ISIL-planned attack" had been a deliberate misdirection. "Our main evidence, if you want to call it that, is the eleven-minute evacuation video, which you've all seen." He directed them to his report, which showed a screen grab of the ISIS flag on the filmmaker's laptop, then reviewed how Ned had restored the missing forty-three seconds. "Why make it easy for intelligence officers to discover?" Evan asked. "Did they underestimate our skills, or did they want us to find it?

"This bothered me so much, I looked for other frame-ups of ISIL." Evan clicked to the next section. "Last year there was an attempted bombing of a German football club's bus, resulting in a few minor injuries. A man purporting to be with ISIL claimed responsibility, but within a day forensic evidence linked the explosives to a far-right-wing activist."

His tongue turning to cotton, Evan reached for his glass of water, only to realize he'd left it at his seat. Deirdre picked up the glass and gave it to DI Hayward to pass to Evan. Hayward took a sadistically long pause before handing it over.

Evan took a sip, but even the water seemed dry. "A few months ago, this next video appeared on US Central Command's YouTube account, which had been hacked by a group calling itself the CyberCaliphate."

He hit play, relieved to stop talking.

The video showed militant figures in a training camp, the voiceover speaking in Arabic with English subtitles reading, *American soldiers, we know where you are. We are coming for you.*

When the video ended, Adira chimed in. "There are several issues here, as outlined on page ten of Evan's report. Firstly, while the man's Arabic is more or less correct, his accent is off. I think he's aiming for a Yemeni dialect but not quite getting there."

"This fits a pattern," Evan said. "Another CyberCaliphate video has a man pretending to be American but who sounds almost Australian."

Deirdre looked up from the report. "So if this wasn't ISIS— erm, ISIL—do we know who it was?"

"We have an idea." Ned indicated the screen. "The 'Cyber-Caliphate website'—where they'd posted materials they'd allegedly stolen from CENTCOM—was hosted on an IP block which we know has been used by the APT28 group."

DI Hayward did a double take. "You've lost me. IP block?"

"An IP block is a sort of an internet neighborhood." Evan glanced at Ned to confirm his layperson's definition. "If you don't know a criminal's exact location, but you know they're some-where between two street addresses, it's better than nothing, right?

Hayward nodded. "And this APT…?"

"Advanced Persistent Threat," Ned said. "Basically a long-term cyberattack campaign. APT28 is a notorious Russian one. And by 'Russian' we don't mean people of that nationality. We mean the GRU, Russian military intelligence."

"Whoa." Hayward took off his reading glasses and sat back, scratching the side of his head. "So all this time CyberCaliphate is actually Russia?"

"It's not that simple." Adira said. "We believe there is a real CyberCaliphate connected to ISIL. But some of its products, such as the alleged hacking of CENTCOM, are highly likely to be Russians *posing* as ISIL."

"Let me guess," Deidre said, paging ahead in the report. "Our wedding-evacuation video is also hosted at CyberCaliphate."

Evan tried not to glare at her. *Thanks for ruining my grand reveal.* "Yes. And the site used the same server and registrar as APT28." He spoke faster, sensing the sanctuary of the finish line. "There-fore we can assess with high confidence that Russian intelligence wants us to believe that same-sex weddings are under deadly threat from ISIL."

I did it. I did it, and I survived. Evan set down the remote control, hoping no one else would pick it up before its coating of sweat had dried.

"Thank you, Evan." Kay motioned for him to sit. "Questions?"

Deirdre voiced Evan's own lingering fear. "Couldn't the Russians stage an actual attack and try to frame ISIL?"

"They wouldn't get away with it," Kay said. "A terrorist attack leaves forensic evidence. The story hangs together only as long as it's just a story."

"Also, that's not how they work," Kensington said sharply. "The Russian government prefers covert destabilization. They want us to crumble from the inside out." The MI6 officer rapped his meticulously buffed fingernails against the table top. "An overt attack on our homeland would be an act of war, which means they'd have NATO to deal with. Putin may be audacious, but he's not stupid."

"Unless he knows we won't acknowledge his role," Adira said.

"Aye," Lewis said. "The Kremlin's been murdering their enemies on British soil for years, and we've done next to nothing."

"The public don't care about a few dead oligarchs and their rich pals," Kay said, "but if civilians were harmed, the pressure would be too much for the government to ignore."

It had once puzzled Evan how people in MI5 spoke of *government* as if it was outside the agency, rather than something the agency was part of. Then he'd realized that *government* merely referred to the fragile body constructed by the current ruling party.

Governments came and went. The Service was forever.

"Talking of the public," Evan said, "can they be informed about this?" He knew the answer would be no, but he had to speak up. "Otherwise if the Russians 'leak' this fake threat, it'll cause more Islamophobia—directly before a general election, I might add—all based on a lie."

"Sorry," Kay said. "I know you've worked hard on this investigation, but like most intelligence work, the Caps Lock findings will almost certainly never see the light of day. The Foreign Office will say it's not worth damaging international relations."

"Not to mention," Kensington said, "we've got too many agents in the field who could be in danger if things turn toxic." The MI6 officer spoke to Evan as though he was a child. "It's a very delicate balance, see, and the picture is much bigger than any of you can understand."

Evan simmered in silence as the rest of his team presented their findings. It wasn't just the pushback from the higher-ups that frustrated him; he'd yet to find a direct link between these Russian actors and British XRW groups like the BVP. They seemed to share many of the same values and goals, but their operations could simply be parallel coincidences rather than an organized conspiracy.

He knew he should be relieved there was no threat to same-sex weddings—and by extension, no threat to Ben. He should be satisfied all his hard work had led to a concrete conclusion, a rare thing in the intelligence field.

Yet his father's cynical dread infused him now. Stopping terrorism and saving innocent lives still meant something to Evan. But he could never save his country from a stealthy, hostile takeover by a foreign adversary.

We can't stop them because they own us.

As always, Evan and his colleagues had to bear this burden of knowledge alone. But he wasn't helpless. He would do everything in his power to make Ben safer.

"VOILÀ! A signature Persian New Year dish, duck *fesenjan*." Ben set the stew atop the breakfast bar, trying not to spill any on the narrow ledge. "Except I used meatballs, because I don't trust myself to know when a duck leg is fully cooked and I didn't want to poison you."

"It smells amazing," Evan said, "and I appreciate the lack of salmonella."

"Anything for you, *kjæreste*. Did I pronounce that right?"

"Perfectly, but as a term of endearment it'd just be *min kjære*," he said, pronouncing it *min SHA-rah*.

"Good to know. And that's our *polo*." Ben set the bowl of saffron-infused Persian rice beside the stew, then sat beside Evan in the breakfast bar's cramped space.

They began eating, and Ben was relieved to hear Evan's noises of appreciation. Years of wedding experience had taught Ben to detect when people pretended to enjoy food out of politeness.

As Evan took a second serving of rice and stew, he asked, "Would you consider yourself fluent in Persian?"

Ben appreciated the fact Evan hadn't called it *Farsi*, the equivalent of calling German *Deutsch*, which would be odd in an English conversation. "I can read and write it fairly well, but not speak it. Is this too tart, do you think? The pomegranate paste can be overwhelming, so I added a wee bit of sugar. Don't tell my mum, though—'Acid is our sweet,' she likes to say."

"It's perfect as far as I can taste," Evan said. "Which other languages do you know?"

"I learned French at school. Then I learned Spanish because I love Tejano music. Then I learned Italian because, let's face it, it's sexy as fuck."

"Not as sexy as Norwegian."

Ben laughed, assuming this was Evan's usual dry humor. "I can also read a little Arabic, as it uses the same alphabet as Persian. But they sound nothing alike because they're different language families."

"Your knowledge is impressive."

"Bahá'ís consider ourselves world citizens, so we like to be multilingual. Are you learning Persian for your job? I don't charge much for tutoring," he added with a wink.

Evan looked like he wanted to say something important, but then shrugged. "Maybe."

As they continued eating, Ben sensed a bit of tension. Looking back, he realized Evan had been unusually pensive this weekend. Last night, Ben had written it off as typical Saturday evening post-match fatigue.

"What's on your mind?" he asked. "You getting on all right at work?"

"Aye. There's just been some red tape lately." Evan cleared his throat. "Talking of work…" He slowly set down his fork, then folded his hands over his plate.

The serious pose made Ben nervous. "Go on."

"I love my job," Evan said, "even though the pay is shit and it's wreaked havoc on my life. I love it because it's meaningful and because I'm good at it." He raised his gaze to meet Ben's. "I think you'd be good at it too."

Ben stared at him a moment before a laugh exploded from his lungs. "Oh my God, I thought you were serious." He patted his chest, willing his heart to slow down.

"I am serious."

"Aye, right, because I'm soooo good at keeping secrets."

"You can learn to do that," Evan said. "You're studying GIS, a field the Service desperately needs just now. You've got a natural talent for observation and detail. You read people so well it's almost scary. Add in your background and language skills, and you'd be an ideal asset."

Ben's flesh turned cold at the word *asset*. His eyes fixed on a pomegranate seed that had fallen from the serving dish onto the white ledge.

"I understand if you'd rather work in the private sector," Evan said. "You'd make a far better salary, and you'd be able to tell all your friends what you do for a living." His voice softened. "You know this life is not easy. But if you want to make a difference in this world, this is one way."

Ben blinked as fast as he could, battling back hot tears. How could he have been so naive to think a man like Evan would want him for himself?

"Obviously there's no urgency to decide now," Evan said. "The process usually takes six to twelve months, so even if you applied—"

"Is that what this is all about?" Ben waved his hand between them without looking up. "Us?"

"In a way. There's talk of reassigning me to London. So yes, this is partly my own selfish plan to take you with me."

"I don't mean that," Ben said, so loudly he even startled himself. "I mean, is our whole relationship about you...recruiting me?" He finally met Evan's widening eyes. "I'm ideal because of my background, right? You met me, found out I was part Iranian, and they told you to get me as an *asset*."

"Oh God." Evan raised his hands. "No. Ben, no. I love you."

"Convenient, isn't it?" Ben got up and moved away. "Of all the men you could've had—and let's be frank, you could've had any —you chose me. I've seen the way people look at us, you know."

"Ben—"

"Especially the Rainbow Regiment. But also strangers, when they see a 10 like you with a 6-maybe-7-on-a-good-day."

"Ben—"

"It makes so much more sense now."

"Ben!" Evan stood up. "Would you fucking wheesht for a second and listen to me?"

Ben clamped his mouth shut, then pressed a fist against it for extra security.

"I'm sorry I hurt you by suggesting you apply at MI5," Evan said. "You deserve a life that's free and open and happy. No one in this world deserves more happiness than you."

Ben looked away, emitting a soft snort.

"It's true." Evan twisted the cloth napkin in his hands. "I know I'm a hard person to trust. Most people would say that my words mean nothing. But words are all I've got." He sat down on the breakfast bar stool again. "So I'm going to tell you why I love you. I'm going to list reasons until you get so embarrassed you start throwing *feshatoon* at me to make me stop."

"*Fesenjan.*" Ben flicked a hand at Evan. "List away. This better be good."

"Okay." Evan took a deep breath. "I love when you clap your knees together when something delights you, like you're applauding with your legs. I love how you're learning to ask for what you want in bed, and I love the fact you still struggle with it. I love how you suck on your upper lip when you're thinking really hard."

"Do I?"

"I love that you always see the best in me—until just now, anyway—even though I don't deserve it. I love the way your facial hair grows faster on the left side than the right."

Ben put a hand to his own jaw. "How did you even—"

"I love how you made me a fancy Persian dinner but also gobbled up my mundane macaroni cheese. I love your glasses, but I also love how big your eyes are without them and how surprised I am every time I see them. I love every delicious inch of your—"

"Okay, stop." Ben's cheeks were flaming hot.

"I was going to say body."

"Still, stop." He put his face in his hands. "I'm sorry. I basically accused you of honeytrapping me."

"I don't blame you after what you've learned about what I did last year. You just have to have faith in my feelings for you."

"I do."

"Usually. But there'll be times, like just now, where something I say or do makes you doubt me."

"We'll get through those times. I promise." Ben went to him and planted himself in Evan's lap. "I'll consider your suggestion. I do want to make a difference, and I don't care about salary as long as I make enough to not live with my mother and to afford the occasional pinch of saffron."

"In London?" Evan lifted his gaze to the ceiling, as if calculating. "If you shared a flat with three or four coworkers you might manage a monthly saffron pinch."

"Good enough." Mentioning his mother gave Ben an idea. "If I joined MI5, could I find out where my father's stationed?" When Evan looked away, Ben asked, "Do *you* know where he's stationed? Is it somewhere bad?"

Evan sighed. "Everywhere is bad."

"Right." Ben took off his glasses and rubbed his eyes. "He wouldn't be there if it was a peaceful paradise. He wouldn't be needed."

"If it helps, he's there to make it better."

Ben put his glasses back on. "It does help. I'm proud of him. And I'm proud of you."

"Thanks."

"That doesn't mean I want to become one of you, but I'll consider it. Anyway, like you said, it's not a decision for today." He hopped off Evan's lap and went to the fridge. "What is a decision for today, however, is…" He pulled out a large cling-wrapped plate. "Pistachio biscuits or the world's sloppiest baklava?"

Hours later, after Evan had left, Bed slid out of bed, unable to sleep. He switched on his computer, hoping some uni work would make him as drowsy in the middle of the night as it did during the day.

An alert appeared on his screen, signaling an updated beta version of the profile-tracking software, WhoWhatWhere. He downloaded, installed, and opened it, keen to see the improvements.

Scanning the new beta features, he noticed his previous searches were still saved, as was a search he thought he'd deleted.

As was the search Evan had created a few weeks ago.

Whoa. Evan had rerun this search every time he'd come to Ben's flat and had always seemed frustrated at the results. Either he'd neglected to delete his search last time—unlikely, considering his attention to operational security—or there was a bug in the software, unleashed by this new beta version.

Ben had no clue what to do. If he deleted Evan's search to maintain absolute secrecy, information could be lost. He didn't want to disturb Evan in the middle of the night to ask, especially since he had an early meeting, which was why he'd left in the first place rather than stay the night.

Deep down, Ben knew it was really his curiosity stopping him from deleting the search. Who was Evan so intent on tracking, and why couldn't he do it from work? Was this the "red tape" he'd complained about tonight?

Considering the timing of Evan's WhoWhatWhere query, it could be linked to the bomb threat at St. Andrew's. Evan hadn't seemed happy about Ben's decision to handle Michael and Philip's wedding. Maybe the "hoax" was no hoax at all.

Ben had meant what he'd said earlier: He was proud of his father and of Evan. They risked their lives and made untold sacrifices to keep people safe—as safe anyone could be in this world.

But they'd *chosen* to walk these paths, dragging Ben along with them and forcing him to make his own sacrifices. They may have done it for a good cause, but that didn't mean it was fair to leave him in the dark.

He sat on the edge of his computer chair, fingertips twitching on the mouse, heel jittering against the floor, fear and trust beginning another round of their endless cage match.

Finally, he clicked.

Chapter 32

"I WOULD EAT clear Marmite in a heartbeat."

Evan's declaration was met with a chorus of disgust from his mates gathered around the pub table.

"What?" he asked, trying to keep a straight face. "No matter the color, it still tastes the same and it's still chockablock with B vitamins."

"And it's still bowfin," Robert declared, his face crinkled. "If it was clear-colored, you'd have no idea how much you'd put on your toast."

"Thank God it's just an April Fools' joke," Ben said. "Not that I ever eat Marmite to begin with." He gave Evan a cheeky look and lowered his voice, "There's much better condiments, right?"

Evan felt his face warm at the memory of their adventures with whipped cream and strawberry sauce from the previous night's sundaes.

"The least funny joke today," Andrew said, "was the rumor that the ball from the 1966 World Cup final had been given to the German National Football Museum after proof that it didn't cross the line."

"That was my favorite," Robert said. "England never deserved that trophy. It was never a goal."

Ben sat back in his chair and looked around at the pub. "It's nice being here when it's not pure crammed out with students." He blanched. "Did I sound old just now?"

"A wee bit," Robert said. "You and me, we need to enjoy our last spring vacation." He clinked his pint of lager against Ben's glass of diet Coke.

"Easy for you," Ben said. "You've already got your own company, so your exams are irrelevant. And you've not got an honors dissertation to finish."

"Naw, just crowdfunders breathing down my neck looking for results on the game I'm developing. I've got real-world problems now."

"Gentlemen, please spare us the Stress Olympics." Andrew waved his hand in a shooing motion. "We've all got difficulties. Right, Evan?"

"Right." Evan looked past his companions at the television above the bar, where a news program was discussing the recent rise in acid attacks. He'd just reviewed the trend yesterday morning in a daily threat assessment.

"That's so brutal," Ben said, following Evan's gaze to the TV. "How could anyone walk up to another human and just burn their face off like that?"

"In Scotland it's mostly gang-related," Robert said. "Liam got first-aid training on it last week at the pub, in case any Rangers wanks come busting in looking to burn Celtic fans."

Ben gave a nervous laugh. "They wouldn't really...over football?"

"Football and religion," Evan corrected.

"Either side might try it, honestly," Robert said.

"So what did they tell Liam to do if it happens at Hannigan's?" Andrew asked.

"You gotta get the victim's clothes off, pronto, he said. Then keep pouring cold water on them until the ambulance comes." Robert grimaced. "The scars are nasty. People lose their noses, lips, eyelids. Imagine never being able to blink again."

"Christ..." Ben adjusted his glasses, perhaps wondering if they'd protect him from acid. Evan squeezed his hand, then turned back to the television.

As the familiar red BBC breaking news graphic swirled across the screen, Evan felt his personal phone vibrate. He reached for it, noticing the others fetching theirs as well.

"What earth-shattering event are they pestering us with now?" Andrew said, pulling out his mobile. "Another celebrity breakup, or perhaps Poundland has once again reached record profits."

Evan unlocked his screen to read a news notification:

Police Scotland thwart planned ISIS attack on gay weddings.

"What?!" Ben yelped, gripping his phone with a trembling hand. "Tell me this is an April Fools' joke."

"If it is," Robert said, "it's the sickest one ever."

Evan looked up at the television, trying to keep his breathing steady. On the screen was a video of St. Andrew's in the Square—the very wedding-evacuation video Evan had found on Imageo. The clip zoomed in on the reflection of the ISIS logo.

Oh God.

"That was mine!" Ben stood up and pointed to the TV. "That was my wedding. The evacuation, the false alarm, the—" He turned to Evan, eyes hardening with fury. "I need to go."

"I'll come with you." Evan stood and reached for his wallet to pay for their drinks. As he did, his service-issue mobile rang in his other pocket. Hoping his friends wouldn't notice, he switched his personal phone with his work phone and pulled out the latter. "Yeah?"

"Did you see the news?" Lewis asked.

"Aye. Just a second." Opening his wallet, he saw Robert and Andrew waving him on. "Thanks," he mouthed to them as he grabbed his coat and followed Ben toward the pub's front door. Though it was only a fleeting glimpse, he was sure Robert was eyeing his service-issue phone with suspicion.

"Kay wants the whole team in the office now," Lewis said. "Gonnae be a long night."

"On my way." He hung up, dreading the fallout at work but also anxious to start analyzing all the chatter that must be exploding across the internet. Luckily it was but a two-minute walk to the nearest subway station.

He hoped it would be enough time to make Ben understand.

———

"You lied to me." Ben fought to keep his voice down as he and Evan hurried over the Ashton Lane cobblestones. "That bomb threat wasn't targeting St. Andrew's the venue. It was targeting my wedding."

"I told you the truth." Evan wiped his mouth. "At least, I told you the truth as I knew it that night. That was the provisional conclusion."

"What about since then?" Ben hissed. "Did you find out I was nearly attacked by ISIS?"

"You know I can't say."

Ben's phone rang, but not with the call he was expecting, from his mother. The number was unidentified, so he swiped to ignore it. "Probably a reporter, wanting to know what happened at that wedding."

Evan stopped short. "You can't speak to any media about it."

"Why not, if the danger is out in the open now?"

"Because it's—" Evan gave a frustrated growl and moved close enough to whisper. "It's not what it seems. You have to believe me. But don't tell anyone."

"Tell them what? I don't understand."

"I know you don't. You can't."

"I can't even know whether I'm safe? What about my wedding in two weeks?" His throat tightened, making his voice pitch up in panic. "It's in a public place. Anyone could—"

"Did you not see the headline? It said police have thwarted the planned attack." Evan stepped back and held out his hands palms down. "Everything's fine."

"If it's fine, why do you look so freaked out?"

"I can't—"

"You can't tell me. Right." Suppressing a howl of frustration, Ben walked with Evan to the subway. They were silent as they went through the turnstiles and boarded the crowded escalator side by side.

"It's always going to be like this, isn't it?" Ben asked softly as they descended into the earth. "You'll always say, 'Believe me,' and 'Trust me.'"

"Sometimes, aye." Evan took his hand. "I did warn you."

Ben wanted to let go but didn't. "When I told you I was doing the Rainbow Regiment wedding, were you afraid for my safety?"

"A bit. But I knew I'd be there to protect you if anything went wrong."

Ben rubbed his face, trying to clear his thoughts. He knew he should tell Evan he'd seen his WhoWhatWhere searches about those British Values Party guys, David Wallace and Jordan Lithgow. Then again, Evan would need plausible deniability if MI5 asked him whether anyone on the outside knew about this investigation.

Besides, a crammed-out subway station was no place to discuss this matter.

They stopped at the bottom of the escalator, where Evan pointed behind him, toward the subway's Inner Circle line. "I have to go…"

"Me too." Ben took a step in the opposite direction.

"I'll phone you when I can. Probably not tonight. Just remember—"

"I know." Ben mimed zipping his lips.

The three-minute subway ride felt like an eternity, as Ben turned over this new revelation in his mind. As far as he knew, Evan's operation didn't concern ISIS but rather some far-right extremists. Then again, Evan probably worked on more than one operation. Ben was more confused than ever.

When he got off at Kelvinbridge and neared the station exit, his phone buzzed several times. With dread he pulled it from his pocket to see several missed texts and two more phone calls, including one from the number he'd expected. He dialed voice mail to listen to his mum's message, bracing himself for a plea to quit the Rainbow Regiment wedding.

"I saw the news," she said in a surprisingly steady voice. "I'm calling about the wedding on the eighteenth." She took a deep breath. "Tell me how I can help."

Ben stopped in his tracks. Someone bumped into him from behind.

"Out my road, man!" muttered an annoyed young woman as she continued around him.

Ben stepped aside from the flow of pedestrian traffic, then replayed his mother's message from the beginning. He hadn't heard wrong: She wanted to help with Michael and Philip's wedding. She wasn't planning to attend the actual event, but she would give Ben the preparation assistance he needed.

What had changed her mind? And what did it have to do with the news about—

Oh.

His brief elation faded into a blunt cynicism. Now that marriage equality might be under attack by the same people who'd oppressed her family, she was suddenly all in. No doubt her position was, *If the Muslims want to destroy it, I need to protect it.*

He sighed and continued on toward his flat. If this was what it took to get Mum onside, then so be it. Once she saw that same-sex couples celebrated their devotion as fervently as anyone else, she'd support it for the right reasons.

Assuming they all survived.

EVAN HAD BARELY STEPPED out of the security capsule when he was greeted by Kay.

"You're on troll patrol," she told him as she swept past, heading toward the kitchen with an empty mug. "Enjoy."

Evan sat at his computer and logged onto Twitter, pulling up D Branch's list of 500 known Russian troll and "bot" accounts. Despite their avatars' apparent diversity in age, gender, and nationality, the accounts had three things in common: a creation date from the previous summer, an obsessive support for the Syrian president (friend of Russia), and an equally obsessive opposition to the Ukrainian president (foe of Russia).

The Twitter feed created by this list came up on his screen. Though he'd been expecting it, the sight still took his breath away.

It was wall-to-wall #ISISGayWeddings. Tweet after identically worded tweet proclaimed "sovereignty with LGBT community"— Evan assumed they meant *solidarity*—against the "vial Islamic animals."

Evan clicked on the hashtag, which was already trending #1 in the UK and #9 worldwide. The top-ranked posts were by celebrities who seemed genuinely concerned about the issue, and whose rhetoric was much more subdued—refraining from calling Muslims *animals*, for one thing—and whose spelling was for the most part correct.

He scrolled down the top tweets list until he came to one similar to those of the Russian bots and trolls, from the handle @Pr0udGayScot. The avatar was a model-perfect pic of a handsome young man, but a quick image search showed it to be a stock photo.

Interspersed with stereotypical tweets about men's fashion and Merchant City nightlife were diatribes about not only Syria and Ukraine but also conspiracy theories about the legitimacy of last year's Scottish independence referendum results.

Though @Pr0udGayScot had nearly two thousand followers, his interactions seemed to be nothing but @s to other gay men, asking them to follow him back so he could direct-message "something important": classic honeytrap behavior that could result in the victim's Twitter account being hacked.

"I found more than a dozen of these accounts in the last half hour," Evan told his team in the meeting room. The group, which consisted of Operation Caps Lock plus Adira, had gathered for the first of what would no doubt be many conferences throughout the night. "They were all created mid-February, which suggests this operation, even if part of a bigger disinformation campaign, has been planned for only a short time."

"I looked up the people who'd been asked to follow @Pr0ud-GayScot back," Lewis said. "They were among those showing the copycat Islamophobic tweets. Which means their accounts got hacked."

"Won't they just tell their followers what happened?" asked Detective Inspector Hayward.

"Sure," Evan said, "but you know the saying about how a lie travels around the world before the truth can get its boots on? That's doubly true on social media."

"Remember," Kay said, "disinformation campaigns are about creating fear and uncertainty. They want our citizens to not know whom to trust, to eventually throw up their hands and think they can't believe anything they see or hear."

"Ooft." Detective Sergeant Fowles sank back into her chair. "That's depressingly postmodern."

"What else have you all found?" Kay asked.

Evan held up the report he'd written, which he hoped wasn't riddled with typos. "A lot of the accounts tweeted a link to the Imageo video of the St. Andrew's evacuation I found a few weeks ago. But even more were linking to a new video in Arabic, claiming it showed a direct threat by ISIL. I sent that video to Ned and Adira to analyze."

"Aye, here it is." Ned hit a key on his laptop, and the video appeared on the conference-room screen. On it, a man wearing a black balaclava and brandishing a machine gun stood at a firing range ranting in what sounded like Arabic. Then he turned to face the human-shaped paper target: a rainbow-hued silhouette rather than the usual black.

The man opened fire, demolishing the target's torso and head, all while shouting "Allahu Akbar!"

The video ended.

"Unsurprisingly," Adira said, "this video has the same issues as the one from the CENTCOM social-media hack. The accent is off, the understanding of Islam is cartoonish at best, and, as Ned can attest, it was posted to the same CyberCaliphate website used by the Russian hackers."

"The real ISIL may yet take credit for these threats against same-sex weddings, even if they're not responsible." Kay turned to Evan. "And those threats may *become* real, now that the idea of such attacks is floating about."

He nodded. Just because this episode was a likely Russian false-flag operation didn't mean the danger to the LGBTQ community hadn't just risen—especially as the online troll army had found a brand-new regiment:

"I checked my XRW Twitter list," Evan said, "to see if any extreme-right-wingers were taking part. Piling on Muslims seemed like something they'd enjoy. And sure enough, they were retweeting and sharing along with the bots and trolls. Which in itself doesn't prove anything other than their prejudice, until you look at the timing." He turned to the penultimate page of his team's report. "Normally the Twitter population jumps on a hashtag over the course of hours—or maybe as little as half an hour in the case of breaking news like this. But tonight, these XRW accounts started promoting the hashtag mere moments after the Russian bots and trolls introduced it."

"So they were waiting on Twitter for the signal to spread the word?" Deirdre asked.

"Maybe," Evan said. "Like an army being sent into battle."

"This XRW list you have," Kay asked, "are they real people or just bots?"

Ned cleared his throat. "That's the most unsettling part. A tweet's source field shows which program was used to send it. The bots we track usually use a Russian mass-posting tool, and that was the case here—but only for the bots. Those accounts on Evan's XRW list used everything from desktop browsers to Android and iPhone apps. Just like normal people."

"Let me get this straight," Lewis said. "We got an army of flesh-and-blood white supremacists mobilizing online on behalf of the Russian government?"

"I doubt they know who's pulling the strings," Evan said. "They may just think they're turning public opinion against Muslims. And maybe some of them are getting paid for it." He turned to Kay. "Surely this'll help our case in getting a warrant to surveil David Wallace, Codename Alt-Tab?"

"Not unless you can find intelligence connecting him as an individual to these activities."

"Someone's got to be taking orders from Moscow on how to orchestrate all these trolls. Who better than the BVP chairman? He's got influence, access, and motive."

"So do many others," Kay said. "Let's all keep digging."

The team discussed next steps, then everyone returned to their desks.

After stewing for a few moments, Evan got up and went to Ned. "Is there anything in your toy box that can access a phone's settings remotely?"

Ned gave him a wary look. "You mean hack into a person's mobile?"

"No, of course not," Evan said, as that would be illegal without a warrant. "I'm not looking for the information inside the phone. I just want to switch on the device's GPS and change some of the apps' permission settings."

"Why?"

"So that when they, for instance, post on social media, it leaves a geo-tag." *And I can see it on Ben's WhoWhatWhere program.*

"Ah." Ned thought for a moment. "It depends on the phone's make and model. Also, it's not truly remote. You'd have to be within a few feet—and by *you*, I mean someone else. A specialist."

Evan felt a pang of dismay, but he knew his own strengths as an intel officer, and technological sleight-of-hand wasn't one of them. "How soon?"

Ned lowered his voice. "This is for Alt-Tab?"

"Yes." Evan crouched down, crossing his arms upon Ned's desk. "I can tell you Wallace's phone model, his number, and which crowded Birmingham pub you're likely to find him in when Aston Villa are playing."

Ned ran his hand over what was left of his sandy hair, no doubt contemplating the legality. The action he'd described, though close to hacking, hadn't yet been strictly proscribed by law. It often took years for legislation to catch up to technology, and intelligence agencies happily took advantage of that time lag.

Finally Ned said, "It'll be a delicate operation, so it might take a few attempts, but we'll do our best."

"Thank you!" Evan jumped up, barely resisting the urge to hug him. "You're a god on earth."

The Caps Lock team worked through the night, taking turns napping on the saggy couch in the break room. Every two hours they held a conference call with Thames House to update headquarters on the latest findings.

Heading back to his desk after a twenty-minute nap at ten a.m., Evan spared a brief worry for how his fatigue would affect his performance in Saturday's quarterfinal. Forthside United would be their toughest opponent yet. He couldn't let the Warriors down again like he'd done last year.

Kay met him at his desk. "My office, please."

Evan followed her, wishing for an antacid tablet or six.

"Thames House just phoned," his supervisor said as she sat behind her desk. "Apparently our conference calls provided more questions than answers. They want you in London tomorrow morning for an in-person debriefing. Your train ticket and tonight's hotel room are being booked as we speak."

"The whole team?"

"Just you."

Evan thought of the quarterfinal. "When will I be back?"

"Hard to say. We're making your hotel booking open-ended, just in case." She lifted her chin to meet his eyes. "You've told me everything there is to know about this operation, right?"

"Of course. All of my reports are—"

"What do you know about Ben Reid's work?"

"Erm, his dissertation's got something to do with GIS systems and social media." He decided not to mention he'd used Ben's software to try and track the BVP duo.

"You never told me he'd committed to another same-sex wedding." She glanced down at her jotter, though it was empty. "On the eighteenth, I believe?"

Evan knew his face said it all. He slowly sank into the chair across from her. "No, I never did tell you."

"I don't need to ask why. You probably thought you could protect him."

"I'm sorry," he said.

"I know. I trust you, Evan." She leaned forward and pinned him with her gaze. "Now you must convince our bosses to trust you too."

Chapter 33

As the taxi pulled up in front of his building, Evan saw Ben already pacing outside, beckoned by a cryptic text.

They didn't speak until they were inside his flat with the door securely shut.

"You look shattered," Ben said. "What's going on?"

"I'm away for work."

"Where?"

"I can't say."

"When are you back?"

"I don't know." At Ben's stricken look, Evan added, "Soon, I hope. Maybe even in a couple of days." *Unless I'm in more trouble than I ever imagined.*

"Are you in danger?"

"No." He risked a tiny clue. "This trip, it's administrative, not operational. Can you look after Trent for me?"

"Of course." Ben picked up the meowing cat and kissed the top of her head.

Evan went to the kitchen and fished the spare keys from a container stuck to the underside of a drawer, then slipped a note into the dry-cat-food bin. "She's got enough tins until Saturday. Hopefully I'll be back before—"

"Oh my God, Saturday." Ben set Trent on the couch. "The quarterfinal match."

"The same one I missed last year. I've just spoken to Charlotte, and I'll send my teammates an email today, but I don't know if I can say enough for them to understand." He took Ben's hand and placed the keys on his palm, keeping his gaze upon them. "What I need to know is, is it enough for you?"

"Hey." Ben touched Evan's cheek, forcing him to meet those deep, dark eyes. "I believe you. I trust you. I love you." He kissed him softly. "Those aren't just words to me."

Evan felt his throat tighten. "I wish I could give you some certainty."

"So do I." He kissed Evan again, more deeply. "If you've told me everything you can, maybe we should stop talking."

Evan glanced at the clock. "I need to be at the train station in thirty-three minutes, and I've not even packed."

"Then we'd best hurry." Ben grabbed him by the waistband of his trousers.

They dashed into the bedroom, shutting the door firmly behind them, then threw off their clothes.

As they wrestled atop the covers, hands everywhere, Evan tried to memorize the feel of Ben's skin against his, tried to smother the dread inside that told him this could be their last time.

Ben reached between them to stroke Evan's cock, his fingers and thumb forming a masterful circle. Evan stiffened so fast it made him groan.

Ben bit Evan's bottom lip. "I want you inside me."

"Are you sure?" he gasped, though his body was eager to comply. "There's not much time."

"I don't need much time." Ben rolled away and got onto his hands and knees at the foot of the bed. "Do you?"

"Not when you look at me like that."

Evan readied himself with condom and lube, then did his best to make Ben as supple as he could.

"I'm ready," Ben soon said, his toes curling back around Evan's thighs. "And before you ask, yes, I'm sure."

Still Evan entered him carefully, letting Ben's body guide him into the right angle. Ben pushed back to take him deeper, then deeper still as he emitted a softly moaned "Yes" with each long, shaky breath.

Then he arched his arse against Evan. "Fuck me now. Fuck me hard, and don't stop till you come."

Evan obeyed. He drew back, then slammed forward, again and again, faster and faster. Soon Ben's moans turned to long, ragged howls. His fists bunched the covers, and his arms trembled with the effort to hold himself up.

Evan wanted nothing more than to hold him close and kiss him until the end of the world, the way they had at the inn in Stromness. But right now, Orkney felt as far away as the sun from the earth. So this was all they had, and he would make it as good as he could.

Just as Evan neared orgasm, he felt Ben's limbs begin to give out. He leaned forward, looped an arm around him and pulled him back against his chest. "I'm gonnae come," he gasped into Ben's ear. "Come with me."

"Yes…" Ben stroked himself with one hand and cupped his balls with the other as Evan ground into him.

Evan's body convulsed as he came, the sensations rocketing out from his core to his limbs. Ben buckled in his arms, jerking with his own orgasm.

They parted all too soon. Ben turned to sit on the bed, his cheeks reddened and eyes glazed. "I miss you already."

"Me too." Evan took his face in his hands and kissed him thoroughly, to make up for the lost time ahead of them.

Ben trailed a finger down Evan's bare chest. "Can I stay here while you're gone?"

"Trent would like that." He squeezed one of Ben's knees. "Now I really need to pack."

"On you go." Ben got up and moved toward the door. "I'll fetch your shaving kit and toothbrush from the bathroom."

Evan opened his wardrobe, wondering what one wore to an MI5 inquisition. He instinctively reached for a royal blue shirt and a crimson tie, figuring it wouldn't hurt to don patriotic colors. He probably didn't even need the tie—no one at MI5 apart from directors bothered with suits—and wearing an unaccustomed one might make him seem nervous. He packed it anyway, deciding to decide tomorrow.

When he turned back to the wardrobe, he caught sight of himself in the looking glass. But it wasn't his own image that made him stop short.

They'd not used the mirror just now. He'd fucked Ben without seeing his face—with his own back to the bedroom door, no less. And not for one moment had he thought about being ambushed, bound, gagged, and hooded.

Today, when everything else was falling apart, one piece of Evan had finally mended.

———

AFTER SEEING Evan to the train station, Ben went home for a few hours to finish the dissertation tasks he needed to do on his desktop. Then he packed up his laptop and holdall before returning to Evan's place for the night.

Trent greeted him as though he'd been gone a week.

"You hungry, puppy cat?" he asked over her insistent meows. Their voices echoed against the foyer walls, accentuating Evan's absence. Ben set his laptop bag on the table, then froze.

The lamp beside the couch had definitely been *off* when he and Evan had left.

As he approached it, he spied its cord plugged into a timer device. He remembered with a pang in his heart how the lamp was timed so Evan would never have to walk into a dark flat.

Still, Ben moved through each of the rooms to search for

intruders, his hands raised in the fighting stance he'd learned in Krav Maga class. It was weird to feel…not exactly *confident* in his ability to handle himself against an attacker, but at least *determined*.

"Yes, yes, I'll give you an early snack," he told Trent as he entered the kitchen. "We won't tell your daddy, okay?"

Trent yawped her approval, circling the metal bin that contained her bag of dry food. Ben found a clean bowl, then pried open the bin.

Inside, taped to the bag of kibble, was a note scrawled in Evan's loopy handwriting:

> *Ben,*
> *If the worst happens, please know that I will try till the end of my days to return to you. It's not fair to ask this, but please don't give up on me. I love you.*
> *Evan*
> *PS: Trent gets 1 scoop per day MAX. Don't let her con you into more.*

Ben felt a chill move up his spine. By the time it reached his head, it had warmed into hot tears he couldn't hold back.

What did Evan mean by "if the worst happens"? Had he committed a crime? Had he made a dangerous enemy? Unlike with Ben's father, if the worst happened to Evan—prison or even death—Ben might never know.

He tried to mentally talk himself out of these fears. Evan probably just had to answer questions or maybe even help with the investigation into these alleged attacks.

Ben was more relieved than ever that he'd never told Evan about his own investigation into David Wallace and Jordan Lithgow. He'd copied the BVP men's information into a private query in his own WhoWhatWhere account, then deleted the original search, and finally set an alert to notify him with results on those two phones. If Evan knew about Ben's "helpfulness," he could be in serious trouble.

Trent head-butted Ben's shin. With a murmured apology, he scooped kibble into her dish and set it on the placemat beside her water bowl.

Then he caught sight of the Certificate of Awesomeness on the refrigerator. Evan had told him it was a fake stand-in for an award he'd received at work. Did this wrinkled piece of A4 stationary represent his commendation for bravery, the one he'd mentioned as they'd sat in that play park in Stromness?

The IN RECOGNITION FOR _____ line in the center was still blank. On impulse, Ben found a thin blue marker and filled it in.

AS EVAN ENTERED the polygraph room after his debriefing, he was glad he'd opted not to wear a tie. It would be hard enough to breathe properly without an extra restriction around his neck.

Inside the room, he met a middle-age woman who bore a surface resemblance to Evan's mum, which he assumed was no accident. She gave him a warm smile as she shook his hand.

"Thank you so much for meeting with me," she said, as if he had a choice. "I'm Mariah Hansen, your forensic psychophysiologist. I hope you had time for a sandwich or something after your debriefing?"

"No," Evan said, practicing his minimalist responses. He knew she was trying to establish a rapport and disarm him with her warm demeanor. He'd been trained to do the same himself with interrogation subjects. Next she would be talking about the weather.

"Gorgeous day out there," she said as she led him to the table in the center of the barren beige room. "It's a tragedy we're to be trapped inside all afternoon."

He didn't reply, just sank into the chair and sat forward so she could loop the pneumograph tubes around his chest and abdomen. Then he rolled up his right sleeve for the blood-pressure cuff. Hansen blethered on as she hooked him up to the transducers that would conduct his body's electrical signals to the computer on the table.

Did the Service think Evan was the source of the leak? If anything, he'd wanted to tell the public about the *lack* of threat.

This morning's debriefing had given him no clue as to their suspicions, but it had put all his theories about Operation Caps Lock through the proverbial wringer. The branch director himself had questioned Evan, jabbing holes in his conclusions with the ease of an ice pick through a wet paper towel. He'd never felt so out of his league.

"First we'll just have a little chat, shall we?" Hansen sat across the table without connecting the diagnostic equipment to the transducers.

None of this initial interview would be recorded by the polygraph machine (though it was most certainly being recorded on CCTV). The purpose of this first phase was twofold: to set Evan at ease and to help Hansen choose which questions to include in the actual exam. So far the process was the same as the polygraph he'd taken when he'd first applied to MI5.

Hansen began with the old standards such as Evan's name and place of birth, then asked about Operation Caps Lock: when it had started, what role he'd played in it, and his basic findings—questions he'd already answered at this morning's debriefings. Following each response, Hansen typed in a few notes.

"Your partner's name is Behnam Reid?" she asked. "Am I pronouncing that correctly?"

"Yes," he said. "Reid, as in, 'read a book.'"

Hansen chuckled, and Evan thought, *Two can play this rapport game.*

"Did Mr. Reid know about Operation Caps Lock?"

Evan spoke carefully. "The evening after the evacuation at St. Andrew's, I gave him the information I was cleared to share."

"And what was that?"

He held back a sigh. The answer had been contemporaneously documented by both Kay and Evan. "That there'd been a bomb threat which seemed connected to St. Andrew's—as the events manager there had already told Ben—but that nothing was found and no motives were known. I told him the rest was classified."

"Do you believe that he believed you about there being no threat?"

Evan certainly *hoped* so, but he wasn't inside Ben's head. "I've seen no evidence to indicate otherwise."

Hansen smirked. "Spoken like a true intelligence officer." She continued typing. "When did you tell your supervisor, Kay Northam, that Mr. Reid had ceased to coordinate same-sex weddings?"

Here we go. Evan had dreaded this part—it was his one real misstep, and the truth would probably get him removed from Operation Caps Lock, if not suspended altogether. "February. I don't remember the exact date."

Hansen pushed a calendar across the desk. "Will this help?"

Evan flipped back to the month in question, his chest going heavy with dread. "Monday the sixteenth."

"When did you learn that Mr. Reid had agreed to coordinate a same-sex wedding on the eighteenth of April?"

Evan didn't need the calendar to remember the date of the Warriors' seventh-round cup tie. "March seventh."

"When did you inform Ms. Northam of this new information?"

He pushed the calendar away. "April second."

"As in, yesterday." She made another note, then paused, fingers over the keyboard. "Did you tell Mr. Reid about any threat to same-sex weddings, even in a hint?"

"No." He decided to be extra forthcoming. "I wanted to, but I knew it could jeopardize the operation, maybe even put more lives at risk down the line."

"Hmm." Hansen began to type again, faster than ever. The silence gave Evan time to worry:

Do they think Ben could be the source of the leak? With all the cyber-security forensic evidence pointing toward the Russians, how could they suspect anyone on our side?

Then again, the "bot" army could have been on standby in case the investigation was leaked by someone else. Russian intelligence was clever enough to cover all eventualities. But Ben couldn't have leaked it—like most normal people, he couldn't fake the sort of shock and anger he'd expressed when the news had broken.

A sudden thought occurred to Evan: What if they asked whether he'd told Ben about *any* of his operations, past or present? Ben knew much more than he should about Belfast. They could both be in trouble if Evan offered *that* confession.

So he spit out what he hoped was a less damaging truth:

"I told my father."

Hansen looked up from her laptop, a flicker of excitement twitching the corner of one eye. "You told your father, Hugh Hollister, about Operation Caps Lock?"

"None of the specifics. I only said I was on an op in which there seemed to be intentionally misleading intelligence."

"Why did you share this with him?"

"I needed advice." Evan paused, knowing if the polygraph had been running right now, it might show lingering tension, as though he was leaving something out. "Also, he was having a rough night. Family issues. I thought a bit of work talk might distract him."

"I see." Hansen stood, her chair scraping the bare linoleum floor. "I'll be right back."

For the next half hour, time seemed to pass more slowly than on almost any other day of Evan's life, second only to the one spent in that Belfast warehouse. He knew he was being watched, his every movement or lack thereof scrutinized by people who held his fate in their hands.

Finally Hansen returned—alone, to Evan's surprise. She slid into her seat and picked up her pen as if she'd been gone but a minute. "Evan, where does your father work?"

"Here, right? That is, he's employed by MI5's D Branch, in counterespionage. I don't know if he works at headquarters." Evan's heart started to pound in a way that would drive the polygraph mad. Had his father left the Service? Did he now work for a private intelligence firm? Why wouldn't he have told Evan, of all people?

Hansen gave a slight cough. "Were you aware that your father, Hugh Hollister, is now employed by MI6?"

Evan blinked at her. "He…what? Why?"

"Answer the question, please."

"No."

"You refuse to answer?"

"No! I mean, my answer is no, I wasn't aware. Since when does he work for Six?" he asked, though he knew Hansen wouldn't tell him.

"Did Hugh Hollister give you the idea that Russian intelligence had fabricated a planned terrorist attack on same-sex weddings?"

"Yes, but—"

"Did you conceal the source of this idea when you presented it to the members of Operation Caps Lock?"

"I didn't tell them my father provided the original spark. But I was able to find solid supporting intelligence. And the chatter we tracked after Wednesday night's leak supports that conclusion. We filed reports with headquart—what are you doing?"

Hansen was unclipping the galvanometers from his fingertips. "There's no point keeping you here while the Powers That Be confer with MI6. You go down to the cafeteria and have something to eat, and we'll complete this examination later."

He thought of tomorrow's quarterfinal match and the long train ride from London to Glasgow. "When is later?"

"Maybe today, maybe tomorrow. Maybe Monday." Hansen

unwrapped the blood-pressure cuff and gave his shoulder a brief squeeze. "Sorry, lad. You know how they are."

He did know how they were. The question was, which *they* did she mean?

As he walked out of the examination room, Evan's head spun from the revelation his father now worked for MI6. *Enemy #2,* Dad had always called it, often with a smirk.

But he'd lied. It's what spies did, even to the people they loved.

Chapter 34

"I WANT to call the whole thing off. I don't care how much we've already paid, it's not worth getting blown up."

Ben listened patiently to Philip as they stood to the side of the home stand waiting for the Scottish Amateur Cup quarterfinal to begin. It was hard to focus on his client rather than scan the park for Evan, who was running late thanks to a train delay.

"I tried reminding him that the news report said the police had *thwarted* a planned terrorist attack," Michael said, standing with his arms crossed. "Which means we're safe now."

"From *those* terrorists," Philip snapped. "But what about the copycats?"

Ben could tell that the couple had been having this argument all week, probably since the news had broken on Wednesday. In an intriguing swap of personalities, the usually fretful Michael was now the calmer one. But he seemed to be trying to soothe Philip's emotions with logic and facts, a tactic doomed to failure. Ben knew he had to address the issue straight on.

"What's your worst fear?" he asked Philip. "And Michael, don't interrupt or comment, please."

Philip clutched the shaft of his rainbow flag with both hands.

"My worst fear? That we'll be gunned down in the middle of the ceremony."

"Okay." Ben leaned forward so he could soften his voice while still being heard above the crowd. "And how does that happen? Walk me through the nightmare film in your mind."

Philip sniffled. "Well…we're on the pitch saying our vows, and a sniper bullet goes right through Michael's head while I'm looking down at him."

Ben tried not to blanch at this grim scenario. "So it's being out in the open that scares you?"

"Aye."

"We can work with that," Ben said. "What if instead of holding the ceremony on the pitch after the match, we do it at halftime under the reception tent? It's got sides that hang down in case of rain or wind. That'll make it more private."

Philip shook his head. "Then there won't be room for the caterers."

"We'll hire a couple of box vans for the caterers to store their stuff in, then move it under the tent during the second half. This is basically our wet-weather plan anyway, so I know it'll work. The important thing is for you to feel safe." Ben glanced at Michael to get a nod of agreement. "Philip, if you need to reschedule the wedding or hold it at home, I'll work with you to make that happen, okay?"

Philip's shoulders dropped a fraction at this tiny abatement of pressure. "Okay."

"But as I recall," Ben continued, "it was your idea to marry Michael at a Warriors match, because that's where you met three years ago this month. This is your dream, and I want you to have that." He took Philip's hand in both his own. "But because it's your dream, that means you can let it go if you need."

"Right." Philip's breathing was approaching a near-normal rate. "Can I think about it and let you know after the match?"

"Absolutely. And since I've no interest in football if Evan's not playing, I can spend that time researching security options." He attempted a joke. "Maybe a metal detector that could double as a floral arch."

Philip laughed. "That'd make a cool photo op." He wiped his face with his sleeve. "Thank you. Sorry I'm so fragile just now."

"You're getting married in two weeks. If you weren't fragile, I'd be worried." He patted Philip's arm and handed him back to a grateful-looking Michael, then looked up into the stands to locate his friends.

A deep voice called his name. He turned toward the pitch to see Liam beckoning him, his face red with what Ben hoped was exertion.

Ben stepped onto the turf near the edge of the pitch, trying to maintain the calm confidence he'd gained from interacting with his clients. "Liam, hiya."

"Where is he?" the defender boomed.

"Who?"

"Pope Francis. Your worthless boyfriend, Evan Hollister, who else?"

"Like he told you all, he's away for work."

"Where?"

"It doesn't matter." Ben wished he could say he didn't know, but Evan had told him this morning he was in London. "He feels pure miserable about missing this match. He wouldn't have left if he didn't have to."

"I'm sure you believe that." Liam rubbed his forehead. "You're such a good guy, Ben. It kills me to see him make a fool of you, too."

"I'm not Fergus."

"You will be." Liam leaned in close. "You weren't here this time last year. You never saw my best mate greetin' his eyes out for weeks. You never saw this team so demoralized we couldnae find our own arses with a pair of mirrors." He paused for a second, perhaps reviewing his odd metaphor. "Anyway, Evan Fucking Hollister is a bastard and a coward. Chuck him while you've still got a wee bit of self-respect."

He gave Ben a patronizing shoulder pat as he turned away.

Ben felt the week's pressures rise up inside him: the ISIS threats, Evan's emergency departure, and finally Philip's meltdown. Liam's ignorant tirade was the last straw.

Ben marched forward, fists clenched. With a roar of rage, he shoved the defender in the back.

Liam turned with the bewildered look of a lion bitten by a mouse. "What the—"

"Shut your fucking mouth about Evan." Ben pointed his finger in Liam's face. "If you think he's a bastard and a coward, then you don't know him at all."

"All right, lads?" Robert was approaching, palms out in pacifying position. "What's the problem?" he asked Liam.

"I think your mate here knows where Evan is but won't tell us."

"Why not?" Robert asked Ben.

"Cos Evan's fooled him, too," Liam said.

"Let him talk," Robert growled, then turned back to Ben. "If there's something about Evan we should know, something to help us understand why he fucks off out of town on a moment's notice, then please tell us."

"I can't. Just trust me: If you knew why he left this week—and last year, too—you'd understand."

"Hold on," Robert said. "What's this week got to do with last year? Last year he said he'd run off with another man."

"And why would he say he cheated on Fergus if he didnae?" Liam asked. "Why would he let everybody hate him?"

"It doesn't matter." Ben started to back away, feeling like he was driving on the edge of a cliff with no guard rails.

"Oh, it matters," Liam said, advancing. "I want to know why Evan broke Fergus's heart. What could be worth that?"

Ben wanted to cover his ears and run. "I told you I can't say."

"You always say you cannae say, and then you always *say*. So spill. Tell us why we shouldn't hate that traitor's guts."

"Gonnae leave it." Robert touched Liam's arm. "We've got warmups, and you need—"

"He's not a traitor," Ben said softly.

"Sorry?" Liam shook off Robert and loomed closer. "What did you say?"

Ben's teeth ground together, as if his own mouth was trying to hold back the words. But he'd heard enough baseless attacks.

"Evan's not a traitor," he said. "He's a patriot."

In taxi frm train stn be rt there

EVAN HOPED Charlotte had her phone switched on to receive his text. Kickoff was in thirty-five minutes, which probably meant he'd missed his chance to play, as his manager was required to submit the official team lineup an hour before the match began.

Just in case, he was tugging on his football boots in the back of this cab, having changed into the rest of his kit in the lavatory of his infuriatingly delayed train.

He'd tried to reach his father—because no one had specifically told him not to—leaving what must have seemed a cryptic voice mail (*"I guess you're at work, wherever that may be."*). Unsurprisingly, Dad hadn't returned his call.

Evan jammed his shin guards into the front of his socks, still furious that MI5 had kept him in London overnight, only to inform him this morning that they'd "be in touch" regarding his future with the Service.

He looked up to see the taxi had driven past the match venue. Choking back a screech of panic, he said, "Mate, we've gone too far."

"Naw, it's up here in Firhill Road. Been there a hunner times."

"That's Firhill *Stadium*. I want to go to Firhill *Complex*. The sport center with the football pitches next to it?"

"I know what Firhill Complex is. You said, 'Firhill Stadium.'"

Evan pulled in a deep breath through his nose. *Keep the head. Don't waste energy you'll hopefully need for the match.* "Please take me to Firhill Complex."

When the taxi finally dropped him at the right place, Evan dashed through the car park toward the pitch, his kit bag banging against his shoulder and his rolling holdall bouncing behind him. He was no doubt straining a few back muscles as he weaved through the crowd, but all that mattered was not letting down his team again.

His manager was standing near the home bench, handing the referee two sheets of paper: copies of the official team line without Evan's name on it.

"Charlotte, wait!" he tried to shout, but his voice was swallowed by the Rainbow Regiment's rising cheers at the sight of him.

The referee shook Charlotte's hand, then turned and jogged toward the other team to deliver their copy.

"Charlotte!" he called again, and this time she turned and saw him.

"Wait!" Charlotte sprinted toward the referee. Catching him just before he reached the other manager, she yanked the sheets away and handed him an alternate pair, then dashed back to the Warriors' bench before anyone could protest.

Evan met her there. "I'm so sorry I'm late."

"I got your text," she said, panting. "Officials gave me an extra half hour to turn in the team line—which got the other manager raging, of course. Probably have to pay a fine or something."

"I'll pay it," Evan said. "Thanks for waiting."

"I assume everything got sorted at work?"

"I think so."

"Good. Now hand over your things to your man so you can start warmups." She looked past Evan and cocked her head. "What's he doing with those yins?"

Evan turned to see Ben standing near the touchline with Robert and Liam. They were all staring at him.

As he drew closer, he realized their shared expression was one of fear. "What's going on?" He looked at Ben, whose cheeks seemed to pale under his gaze.

"I'm sorry," Ben said, his voice barely topping a whisper. "I just wanted them to understand."

"Understand wh—" Evan's words halted, then froze in his throat as the icy realization took hold.

Slowly he turned his head toward Liam and Robert, who took a synchronized step back.

Robert raised his hands as if in surrender. "We don't want any trouble. And we'll never, ever tell."

Oh God. Evan covered his face to keep from screaming. Everything he'd done these last three years to keep his work secret, all the hard feelings he'd earned, all the hearts he'd broken...were now for nothing.

"Don't blame Ben," Robert added. "He only said you weren't a traitor. We worked out the rest." He started to stammer. "I-I knew there was something odd on-on Wednesday when you had the two phones, and then when you disappeared after the terrorism news—"

"You suspected he was MI5?" Liam hissed. "And you didnae tell me?"

"It's none of our business," Robert whispered back.

"No, but it sure as fuck is Fergus's business." Liam turned to Evan and let out a hoarse laugh. "He never knew, did he?" He put his hands to his head like he would tear out his waves of ginger hair. "You lied to him all those years."

Evan couldn't speak if he'd wanted to. Words of self-defense lodged in his throat, but they were illegal *and* irrelevant. He deserved this moment of reckoning.

"Carroll, get your arse over here to lead warmups!" Charlotte called.

He waved at her, then thumped Robert's arm as he moved toward their manager. "C'mon."

Robert looked at Ben, then at Evan. "I'll try and buy you a

few minutes to…sort things. It's the least I can do." Shaking his head, Robert jogged after Liam, his broad shoulders heavy with dread.

"I'm so sorry," Ben whispered, his eyes already overflowing.

Evan glanced over his shoulder to see the entire Regiment watching them, though they were too far away to hear. "Let's find somewhere to talk alone."

They walked together round the corner of the main building, Evan dragging his holdall over the uneven pavement.

"How much do they know?" Evan fought to keep his voice calm. "It's important you tell me everything."

"Liam asked where you were. I said I didn't know, but then he said horrible things about you, and I couldn't let—" Ben steepled his palms together over his mouth and nose. "No, I could've walked away. I could've let it go. I should have let it go." He dropped his hands. "But I didn't."

Evan listened as Ben recounted the conversation. He wanted to rage at Ben for blowing his cover, but it was clear he'd done it with the best intentions, to defend Evan's honor.

"Once they started guessing," Ben continued, "I totally froze. I couldn't think of what to say or do, and they read it all on my face. My stupid face." Ben took off his glasses and wiped his wet cheeks. "I wish I could take it back, but I know I can't. I can't ever…"

He sobbed again, and Evan did the only thing he could do, which was to take Ben in his arms and hold him close. Ben's body shuddered against his, and before Evan knew it, his own eyes were hot with tears.

Why had he ever thought he could have a real life—playing football and falling in love—without risking his precious secrecy? Most of his colleagues had little social life outside the Service apart from close family. In his arrogance, Evan had believed he was different, and now he was paying the price.

"I can fix this." He rubbed Ben's back, as much to soothe himself as anything. "I'll say I blew my own cover by accident.

Robert suspected me at the pub—that was my own fault for being sloppy with those phones."

Ben shook his head against Evan's neck. "If you say that, then Liam and Robert'll have to lie too."

He was right, Evan realized with a rising panic.

"Okay, listen." He let go and took Ben's shoulders so he could meet his eyes. "This is hardly the end of the world. Believe me, the Service has much more important things on its mind just now." He drew his thumb over Ben's cheek to wipe away a stream of tears. "We'll work this out."

"No. We won't." Ben pulled away and put his glasses back on. "I can't do this, Evan." He waved his hand between them, in a space that suddenly felt as perilous as the Pentland Firth. "I can't do *us*."

Chapter 35

As soon as the words left his mouth, Ben wanted to take them back. But they were the bravest, truest words he'd said today.

"What do you mean?" Evan asked, though his sickened look said he knew exactly what Ben meant.

"You told me once that you would need to hide things from me, that there were parts of you I'd never truly understand. And I said I didn't care. But I *do* care. I can't be with someone so...unknowable."

"You think you don't know me?"

"Not the way I need to." Ben crushed his palms together, wishing he could smother this truth. "I told myself I could handle it. The secrecy, the uncertainty, the doubt. But I can't."

"Yes, you can."

"Obviously not!" He flapped his hand at the football pitch, where he'd just committed a crime against national security. "Not when people are insulting you to my fucking face."

"Are you ashamed to be with me? Is that what makes it so hard, that my actions make you look bad to your mates?"

"No! It's because I love you too much to let people hate you."

"I know it's not easy lying about something this important. It's hard for all of us, but you learn to live with it." Evan stepped closer. "You and I know the truth, and that's all that matters."

"It's not all that matters." Ben's tears started to flow again. "I can't keep a secret. Remember how I blew your cover at the Glasgow Greens match? Remember how I blurted out the truth about your mum and Magnus? I can't promise this won't happen again, and if you or our country ever got hurt because of me, I'd never forgive myself."

Evan started pacing, no doubt reviewing this damning evidence. Then he stopped and took a deep breath. "You're right. Maybe I shouldn't trust you." He looked at Ben. "But I'm going to do it anyway."

Ben flung up his hands. "Then you're an even bigger fool than I am."

Evan gasped as though Ben had punched him in the stomach. "Why are you doing this? I'm the one who should be saying this won't work. I'm the one who just got hurt by your carelessness. Now I'm meant to believe you're leaving me for my own good? How is losing you good for me?"

"It's obviously safer," Ben said. "I'm not worthy of your trust." *I'm not worthy, full stop.* "I'm sorry."

Evan scoffed. "It's easy to say you're sorry on the way out. It's harder to say you're sorry and then stay to make things right."

"We can't ever be right, Evan. Not with—" Ben stopped himself mentioning MI5. He wouldn't in a million years ask Evan to give up his calling. The world needed a clever, courageous man like him, a man who believed in the greater good.

A man who would let the one he loved walk away forever, if that's what it took.

EVAN WATCHED Ben disappear through the park gates. He wanted to run after him, force him to stop and reconsider. But he was shackled by a hard truth: Ben was better off without him.

At least Evan had proven his father wrong about one thing: This time he was the heart*broken* instead of the heartbreaker.

A voice called his name. Evan turned to see Fergus walking his way.

"I heard you need to tell me—" Fergus stopped when he saw Evan's face. "What's wrong?"

He lifted a hand toward the park exit, then let it fall. "Ben's had enough."

"Enough football?"

Evan didn't have the strength to clarify. "Sorry, what did you want?"

"Oh. Erm." Fergus folded his arms and stood with one foot crossed in front of the other, as though his limbs suddenly felt too long. "Liam said you had something important to tell me."

"I have...what?" It felt like his ex was speaking from another universe.

"He said if you didn't tell me, then he would do it after the match." Fergus scratched his nose with his thumb. "Something about your job."

"Hollister, warmups!" their manager called in a don't-fuck-with-me tone. "Now!"

Fergus grimaced. "I guess we'll talk later."

Evan followed him back toward the pitch, his feet so numb he had to focus on not stumbling. On top of losing Ben, now he had to work out what he could legally tell Fergus about why he'd left last year. A new lie, perhaps, or maybe something between the full truth and that audacious "Belgian lover" story.

Lord Andrew met him at the bottom of the stand. "Where's Ben?"

"Gone." Evan's throat tightened. "He's left me."

"Oh dear. Let me watch your things for you." Andrew took the handle of Evan's holdall. "Listen, this is terrible advice for the long-term, but for now, just try and pretend it didn't happen. Pretend you're okay until you believe it."

Evan could do that. For ninety minutes, he could create a false reality, basically go undercover as a footballer in a happy relation-ship—or better yet, a footballer who had no relationship and didn't care.

But as he joined in with warmups, he thought about last year's quarterfinal match, when Fergus had had to take the pitch mere minutes after Evan had dumped him. Somewhere out there, the universe was snickering, its work of justice complete.

Half an hour later, Evan wasn't the only one on the pitch pretending nothing was amiss. Robert and Liam—the latter wearing the captain's armband—acted as though Evan was just another central midfielder, rather than a secret agent who might know every detail of their lives.

Through what seemed like sheer willpower, Warriors managed to hold Forthside goalless through the greater part of the first half. Offensively, Charlotte took advantage of Forthside's defensive back three by rotating the positions of Duncan, Colin, and Shona. Evan himself was kept on high alert, tracking the three Warriors forwards as they moved this way and that, one of them drawing a defender to the side away from the goal so that another could scoot in behind the defense to take one of Evan's passes. By the twenty-minute mark, Warriors had already had three shots on target.

Now, Colin was dodging a massive center back to try again. This shot was the closest yet, the keeper leaping up at the last second and fingertipping the ball behind the goal.

"Arrrrgh!" Colin stomped in frustration and gripped the ends of his spiky black hair. "Almost." His scowl became a smile as the Rainbow Regiment started chanting his name, led of course by Andrew.

"Next time." Evan clapped him on the shoulder as he jogged toward the corner of the pitch, where the referee was setting the ball for a corner kick.

A gust of wind came up, whipping Evan's hair back from his face. He hoped the players would take a few moments to settle down, delaying the official's whistle until the breeze calmed. To buy time, he turned his back and lifted the hem of his shirt to wipe his face, pretending he had something in his eye. When he turned back round, the referee was watching him with hands lifted in inquiry. Evan signaled he was ready.

The whistle blew. Evan sailed the ball up and over, but despite the delay, the wind still caught it, lifting it higher than he'd intended. Duncan was the first to get his head on it, but the ball just soared back up like it had been struck by a lever in a pinball machine. A defender headed the ball, again nearly straight up.

Evan darted forward to the edge of the eighteen-yard box, finding a spot where he had sight of the goal. The ball descended again, about to land a few feet in front of him. He stepped forward with his left foot, planting it firmly, and swung his right foot as high as a cricket bat. If he missed this volley, he'd end up on his arse.

As his foot slammed the ball, Evan immediately wished he'd missed. By the time his shot streaked past the goalkeeper into the net, he knew something had gone terribly wrong.

Then adrenaline took over, and he sprinted for the touchline to celebrate. His teammates soon swarmed him, whooping and hollering.

Colin scooped him up. "Yaaaaaassss, get in, ya dancer!" he shouted, followed by some Glaswegian words Evan couldn't decipher. Over in the stand, the Rainbow Regiment was going bonkers, but Evan couldn't look at them without seeing who was missing.

When his teammates finally released him, he turned to the center of the pitch for the kickoff, instinctively pivoting on his left leg because the right one was begging him not to use it.

I'm fine, Evan tried to convince himself. He would simply play the role of a footballer who didn't have an injured hip. He reached back and pulled his right foot up to stretch his quad.

"All right, mate?" Jamie steadied Evan so he could stand on one foot without wobbling. "That was a bullet of a shot. If I'd done that, my leg bone would've popped straight out the joint."

"Not sure that's possible." Still standing on his left foot, Evan went to pull his knee to his chest and was met with a stabbing pain he couldn't hide.

"That's you gettin' help now." Jamie steered him toward the touchline, where the physiotherapist was already waiting for him.

"I'm fine," he told her as Jamie returned to the pitch and play kicked off again without Evan.

"We'll see." She had him jog up and down the touchline while she watched. He tried to lift both legs evenly, but the stomp-scuff-stomp-scuff of his gait spoke volumes. Then she had him lie on his back while she manipulated his right leg in all directions, watching for the pain on his face.

When Charlotte came over for an update, the physio told her, "Looks like a hip flexor strain from that volley he scored. Maybe not too severe, but it needs rest and ice, pronto."

"I can still walk and run," Evan protested. "It doesn't even hurt."

The physio crossed her arms. "Then get up and make like you're kicking a ball. You know, as you occasionally do in this sport."

Evan rose to his feet and pulled back his leg with ease. But as he drew it forward, he was sliced with the sharpest pain yet.

Speechless with dismay, he simply shook his head.

EVAN'S first ice session ended just as halftime began. He unstrapped the pack and walked in figures-of-eight on the touchline beside the bench, as much to avoid his teammates' tension as to test his injured hip. Forthside had equalized three minutes after his injury, but Warriors had held fast to keep the game even until the break.

Evan considered hopping into a taxi and following Ben home to beg him to change his mind. But even if he thought Ben would speak to him, he couldn't abandon his teammates.

"Hey." Fergus was at his side, looking expectant.

With the weight of an anvil on his head, Evan remembered Liam's threat. "Let's find a place to sit away from the crowd. I need to change out of my boots."

He picked up his kit bag and led Fergus toward the opposite side of the building to where he and Ben had broken up, wondering what he could reveal. Legally, the answer was *nothing*, but operationally? Evan's stint in Northern Ireland was finished and the would-be attackers imprisoned.

And Fergus was neither careless nor vengeful. Despite his hatred for Evan, he'd welcomed him back to the Warriors because it had been best for the team. Of all people, Fergus had the integrity not to jeopardize national security. If only Evan could have convinced his bosses of that fact a year ago, their lives would be a lot different right now.

Evan came to a halt just past the corner of the building and opted for honesty. "I never left the country last year. I wasn't in Belgium, I was in Belfast."

Fergus gave him a long, blank look, then shrugged. "So you left me for a Northern Irishman. Minor detail, really."

"I left you for no man."

Now Fergus seemed confused. "Was it a woman?"

"It was no one. I left you because my job reassigned me."

Fergus offered his signature harrumph. "If that was true, you could've told me. I could've gone with you. And what was so urgent in Belfast? What sort of architectural emergency..." His eyes widened as he lost his feigned indifference. "Tell me everything. Don't make me ask questions. Just tell. Me. Everything."

Without looking back, Fergus headed toward a bench beneath a bare-branched oak on the far side of the car park.

"You may recall," Evan said on their way there, "I wasn't happy in my job at the firm. You may also recall I wasn't a very good architect." When Fergus didn't dissent, Evan continued. "So I applied at MI5."

Fergus stopped in his tracks and stared at him. "Wh-what?"

"Sorry, that part should've waited until you sat down."

"Please tell me you're joking."

Here was Evan's last chance. He could simply laugh and come up with a new lie. But Liam and Robert would hold him to the truth. "I'm not joking."

Fergus put a hand to his chest and sank onto the bench. "My God…"

Evan sat at the other end. "I wanted to tell you, but I knew you hated the Service for what they'd done in Northern Ireland."

Fergus just stared straight ahead for a long moment, then turned to him. "I never really knew you, did I?"

No one knew me, Evan wanted to say. *Not until Ben, and look how that turned out.*

"I was always myself with you," he told Fergus, "and with the team, and with our families. But I lied about where I went every day, and where I went on business travel during my training."

Fergus eyed him fearfully. "What sort of training?"

"You know, spy things." All of this was public knowledge in one article or another, so he began to list. "Hand-to-hand combat, evasive driving, enhanced-interrogation resistance."

"Fuck!" Fergus leapt off the bench. "I thought you were away learning HSE regulations. But no, you were being practice-tortured."

"I know this is a lot to process." Evan got up, his own nerves making him restless. "Take your time. I'll answer any questions I can."

Fergus paced, faster and faster, his gaze darting over the ground before him. Then he suddenly stopped. "So there was never another man? You never cheated on me?"

"I never cheated on you." Evan emphasized each word, feeling the strangest urge to add, *Sorry.*

He saw the punch coming a mile off—Fergus pulled his arm back, telegraphing the blow—but he didn't dodge or duck. It was what Fergus needed, and what Evan deserved.

He did, however, relax his body and pivot his hips to roll with the punch. So he was shocked to hear a crack when Fergus's fist met his face.

"Aaaaaugh!" Fergus spun away, clutching his hand. "Fuck! Fuckfuckfuckfuckfuck fuuuuuuuuuck!"

Eyes watering, Evan touched his nose. It burned fiercely but didn't feel broken. "Tell me you didn't have your thumb inside your fist."

"Fuck off!" Fergus was bent over, practically kneeling on the ground, his face scarlet with agony. "I fucking hate you. I don't care if you never cheated on me. I *believed* you did."

"I know, and I'm—"

"Did Charlotte tell you? Did she tell you how I fell apart when you left, how I literally collapsed in front of that quarterfinal crowd and cried my fucking eyes out?"

Evan swallowed. "Duncan told me."

"Did he tell you how we were all dancing to 'Copa de la Vida' before the match? How we were all so full of hope before you kicked us in the crotch? I still can't hear Ricky Martin without having a flashback."

Evan's eyes welled up. Duncan hadn't told him that.

"You left me with *nothing*, Evan. No answers, no clues. I had to fill in all the blanks, and they got filled in with the worst..." Tears dripped from Fergus's cheeks. "Night after night I imagined you and your Belgian lover naked, your hands and cocks everywhere. I imagined how amazing he must have been to make you give up your life here with me. How hot and sophisticated and hot and probably French-speaking and really fucking hot." His voice cracked as he raged. "But he didn't even exist! You ripped me apart for nothing. Yes, I'm happy now with John, but I was never the same. That hole you left—" He raised his uninjured hand to his chest. "It's still there. It'll always be there, and there's still days when it chews at me and tells me I'm nothing. Four years together and I wasn't worth a proper goodbye."

Evan wanted to claw his own brain out at the memory of writing that letter and having it delivered it to last year's quarterfinal match. The fact he could even concoct such a brutal breakup, no matter how necessary, said something dark and terrible about him. "I wanted to say goodbye, but I couldn't give you a chance to ask questions. I couldn't look you in the eye and convince you I didn't love you."

"Why not? I believed all your other lies."

Evan felt a spark of old anger. "Why was that, Fergus? When I went away to training, why did you never ask me how it went or what I learned? Because you didn't care. My alleged government architectural job was beneath your consideration. Making buildings safer wasn't art. It wasn't genius."

"You're blaming me for not interrogating you? I didn't give you enough attention, so it's okay to have a secret life from the man you claimed to love?"

"I'm not saying that, I just—"

"No!" Fergus tried to point with his right hand, grimacing at the pain. "This is not the time to justify what you did. This is the time for me to say all the things I wanted to say a year ago. So just shut it and listen."

Evan pressed his lips together. He owed Fergus this much.

His ex sat gingerly on the bench, cradling his right hand. "While we're spilling secrets...I never told John this, or even Liam." His voice fell low and raspy. "But there were nights, lying on the floor of my new bedroom—the one meant to be ours—when I nearly ended it."

"No..." Evan's knees gave out, and he sank onto the other end of the bench. "Fergus..."

"Don't 'Fergus' me, and don't you dare fucking pity me. I wouldn't have killed myself to escape the pain. I would've done it to hurt you. I pictured you finding out. I pictured how it would destroy your life and your mind and maybe even your new love."

"It would've killed me."

"Well, it's a good job I didn't know that, because after the one hundredth unanswered phone call—literally, I counted—I realized you didn't care whether I lived or died. So I decided to keep living, because why not?" He sniffled. "Also, the team needed me."

"They still do." He reached out a trembling hand. "Let's have a look at that thumb."

Fergus shuddered, then held it up. "You think it's broken?"

"Maybe." Evan slid closer. "But even if it's just a sprain, you should see a doctor today. And get that thing splinted right now."

Fergus looked toward the pitch. "I don't think the match physios are allowed to treat spectators unless it's life-threatening."

"Hang on, I've probably got something." Evan unzipped his kit bag.

"A magic spy splint from Q?"

"Aye, it's cleverly disguised as a first-aid kit and a pen." He opened the plastic white-and-red container and pulled out the roll of gauze.

"You always were prepared for anything," Fergus said. "Now I know why."

"Not anything," Evan murmured, thinking of the events of the last two hours. He handed Fergus the pen. "Put this lengthwise against your thumb."

Fergus did as he was told, then hissed as Evan began to wrap the bandage. "So you joined MI5 because you were bored? Was I part of that boredom?"

"No. Look, that wasn't the only reason. Do you remember a few years ago when that Norwegian far-right terrorist Anders Breivik went on a killing spree?" Breivik was one of Jordan Lithgow's idols, of course.

"I remember your gran knew the parents of one of the kids he shot at that summer camp."

"In Utøya," Evan said. "It broke her heart, and with her already so sick…anyway, the next morning I applied at MI5."

"You could have told me. I wouldn't have approved, but maybe in time I would've accepted it. You never even gave me the chance. Ow!" Fergus nearly pulled his hand away. "You were a fucking coward."

"At the beginning. But then later, when I was ready to tell you, when we were going to move in together...I wasn't permitted."

"Why not?"

"Fergus." Evan stopped bandaging for a moment and looked him in the eye. "If I tell you why not, you can never tell anyone. Not John, not the team, not your family."

Fergus tensed. "Will it put me in danger?"

"Not if you keep your mouth shut. But I can assure you, the strength it takes to do that...some days it's almost too much to live with."

"If you tell me, I'll understand why you did what you did?" When Evan nodded, Fergus bit his lip. "Go on, then."

Evan returned to bandaging. "When an MI5 officer starts dating someone, the Service vets the potential partner."

"Like a background check?"

"Aye. Just a basic one at first, but as the relationship progresses or if there are issues, the Service vets the partner's close family members. Then, if there's a deeper commitment, as in living together or perhaps marrying one day, they vet their extended family."

Fergus jerked in a breath. "The Derry cousins."

Evan gaped at him. He hadn't planned to mention Fergus's mum's Northern Irish relatives.

Fergus continued. "The three of them are always banging on about the 'Prods.' They've not spoken to me since I got engaged to John. They don't even know he used to be in the Orange Order."

They probably do know. "Hold this bandage for a second." Evan pulled out the scissors and tape from the first-aid kit.

"What are they involved in?" Fergus asked. "One of those IRA splinter groups?"

Evan didn't want to discuss individuals, but if he said nothing, Fergus would assume the worst, that there were terrorists in his own family. "Not directly. They're sympathizers." He cut the bandage, then taped it in place, trying not to jostle Fergus's thumb.

"This was why you were forbidden to tell me you were a spook?"

"Yes."

Fergus thought for a moment. "Still, you could've quit, right? But you chose your job over me."

"I chose my *country* over *us*."

Fergus gave a gruff laugh. "Whatever makes you feel better."

"I assure you, nothing can do that."

Fergus examined his splinted thumb, then looked up. "What about the text you sent last year? You told me you missed me and you were thinking of coming home."

Evan changed out of his football boots as he spoke. "Someone else sent that message. The people I was working against. On my personal mobile they found the texts you'd sent me after I left."

"Och, those were so pathetic."

Evan took his regular trainers out of his bag, remembering how each message had been a tiny stab in the heart. "They sent you that text about missing you, then they showed me your 'go to hell' response."

It had been the worst of all the tortures that day. The cuts and contusions had healed, but knowing he'd hurt Fergus one last time…*that* wound would fester forever.

Fergus suddenly tensed. "Are we in danger by you telling me all this now?"

"The operation's over. I don't work with those people anymore." *Soon I won't be working in Glasgow at all.* "But you still can't tell anyone."

"I'm not an idiot. And I'll see to it Liam and Robert never say a word."

"They seemed pretty scared," Evan said.

"They grew up with the same tales of MI5 jackbooted thugs as I did, but without the filter of middle-class skepticism." Fergus gave a half chuckle, half grunt. "They probably think you can read their minds."

A steady cheer rose from the direction of the pitch. "I guess halftime's over," Evan said. "And I'm probably due for a second dose of ice."

They returned in silence to the stand, where everyone gaped at Evan's aching face and Fergus's bandaged thumb.

Evan went to the bench, took a fresh ice pack for himself, plus an extra for Fergus, then went to join him and John.

"I've been advised not to ask," John said to Evan as they shifted down to make room, "and I'm gonnae take that advice."

Over the next forty-five minutes, the Warriors played their hearts out, but Forthside scored two more goals before the final whistle to win 1-3. Once again, Warriors' run at the Scottish Amateur Cup was ending at the quarterfinal stage.

Evan tried to take comfort in the fact he'd at least shown up and had made a difference. But if not for today's long train ride and a truncated warmup session, maybe he would have lasted the whole game. Maybe his difference would have counted.

Despite the double heartbreak of losing Ben and the match, Evan felt somehow…lighter now. By telling Fergus the truth—more or less—he'd shed the heaviest burden of all. It wasn't everything, but it was something.

Chapter 36

BEN HAD SLEPT FITFULLY last night, when he slept at all. Mostly he did what he was doing now: staring at the ceiling illuminated by the cold blue light of his mini-humidifier. Allergy season would be over soon, and then he could put that thing away until October. One fewer reminder of his time with Evan.

Robert had texted him after the match yesterday, sharing the news of the Warriors' loss after Evan injured himself scoring a "right screamer." Ben wondered whether it was his own fault. Surely the stress of a blown cover and a sudden breakup would weaken any human body.

Though he knew he shouldn't, Ben rolled over and picked up his tablet. After switching off the Wi-Fi just to be safe, he brought up the video they'd made two weeks ago in Stromness, declaring their love and waking their neighbors with Sunday morning sex noises. He'd already watched it twice with Evan and twice more by himself. This would be the last time. Or perhaps the first of the next hundred times, he wasn't sure.

On this morning's viewing, he didn't focus on Evan's face and body as he'd done before. And of course he wasn't about to watch his own awkward self. Instead he stared at the space between them, at the intersection of skin and skin.

Ben studied the places where hands met chests and shoulders, where lips met lips and tongues met tongues. He searched for distance, for traces of distrust. Surely a warning sign lay here somewhere. Surely the merging of their souls had been a passion-induced illusion. Hormones did funny things to one's mind.

But on this video, not one inch of them seemed a stranger. Every finger was certain in its placement. Their shared, synchronized breath gave and took strength in an endless circle.

In those moments—and in so many others, in and out of bed—he and Evan had been truly united, in that almost mystical way he'd read about in Bahá'í writings or heard about in wedding vows, a way he'd never dared to believe was real. And now that they were over, Ben felt like he was missing part of himself—not just a limb, but something at his very core. How could his heart still manage to beat after he'd given Evan a piece of it, then walked away without getting it back?

When the video ended, Ben dropped the tablet onto the bed beside him. He'd found no hidden clues justifying their breakup, nothing that had to do with them. Circumstances beyond their control had pulled them apart. Ben couldn't help that Evan was an MI5 officer, and he couldn't help that his own curiosity and lack of guile made him constitutionally incapable of secrecy.

Perhaps if they'd met earlier in life, or later, they could have worked. But not as the men they were now.

A buzz came from the wall, signaling a visitor at the building's front entrance.

Evan?!

Ben rolled out of bed and stumbled over to smack the intercom button. "Hello?"

"It's me," his mum said.

Ben stared at the speaker for a moment. "Oh. Right." They were meant to go over plans for the Rainbow Regiment couple's wedding. "Sorry, I just…come on up."

After releasing the lock on the front entrance, Ben put on his glasses, but he could barely see through them. He took them off to see the lenses splashed with small white spots—dried salt from his tears.

He cleaned them with the end of his T-shirt as he went to his desk to get his wedding files. Every muscle in his body ached.

When a knock came at the door, he opened it to his mum. "Hey."

She stared at his face in shock. "Ben, what happened?"

He tried to say, "Nothing, why do you ask?" but when he opened his mouth, the tears choked off his words.

She stepped across the threshold and pulled him into an embrace so strong it seemed it could hold up the world. As he wept against her soft dark hair, she rubbed his back and whispered, "It's all right, *nouré cheshm-am*," which only made him cry harder.

When he could finally talk, he said, "It's over with me and Evan. Like, really over."

"I'm so sorry." Then she asked the question he'd dreaded. "Why?"

The truth was classified, obviously, so he offered the reason that should have been true, if he'd not been such a hypocrite.

"You were right when you said I'd have to choose between him and my faith." He crossed his arms over his chest. "I chose God."

His mother's eyes softened in sorrow at first, but then they narrowed as she tilted her head. "I don't believe you."

EVAN'S shite Saturday had rolled straight into a shite Sunday.

As if losing the man he loved, injuring a hip, and watching Warriors lose another quarterfinal weren't enough, this morning he'd been greeted with the news he was suspended from work. He'd been let off two weeks for the twin sins of 1) failing to disclose that Ben was still involved with same-sex weddings and 2) sharing information about an investigation with his father, who'd not been cleared to know it.

So he was in the worst ever mood, and he was well primed to take it out on his dad. If he could find him.

The Necropolis graveyard behind Glasgow Cathedral was nearly the size of downtown Stromness. When his father would come to visit for Evan's or Justine's birthdays, he would hide somewhere in the town and send his kids a series of clues they'd have to follow to find him.

"This was great fun when I was ten," Evan muttered as he trudged up the sloping pavement in the rain. "Not so much now."

Enter Sandman read the clue on his phone screen. Since as far as Evan knew, no members of Metallica were buried in the Necropolis, he reckoned this was a reference to William Miller, author of the nursery rhyme "Wee Willie Winkie," a shadowy figure who went door to door to make sure all the bairns were asleep. At least Miller's memorial was in the lower part of the Necropolis—if his dad had wanted to meet at the top of the steep hill, Evan would've told him where he could stick his clues.

He found his father smoking a pipe beside the poet's granite obelisk, wearing a black trench coat and holding a black umbrella.

"So you've gone full cloak-and-dagger now you work with James Bond?" Evan asked.

"I thought a wee puzzle would bring back fond childhood memories." He puffed his pipe. "Also, I've been suspended a week, so I've plenty of spare time."

"Just one week? I got two." Then again, he had broken two separate rules, so it was probably fair. "Why did you leave MI5— you of all people, who referred to Six as the enemy?"

"That was a joke, and probably misdirection."

"So it wasn't enough to hide the truth." Evan's fists clenched around the rain-slick cuffs of his jacket sleeves. "You had to deliberately mislead me. I want to know why."

"Then shut your gob for a second so I can explain."

Evan obeyed, hoping to get a straightforward answer for once.

"After 9/11," his dad said, "counterespionage became an afterthought. There was no room in the Service for a Cold Warrior like myself. MI5's D Branch carried on, but budgets are limited, and Russia seemed a shrinking threat in the eyes of the geniuses running our government. I could read the writing on the wall." He looked off into the distance, toward the green roof of the Glasgow Cathedral. "G Branch made me a half-hearted job offer, but counterterrorism is a whole different game, and while you can teach an old dog new tricks, it's a waste of a bloody useful old dog. So I went where my knowledge and talents were better appreciated."

Evan hated the decision, but he understood wanting to be needed. "Why didn't you tell me?"

"You didn't need to know."

"I should have known where my information was coming from."

"It came from British intelligence, and that's enough. Evan, you're not angry for professional reasons, you're angry for personal reasons. You think I lied to you."

"Because you *did* lie to me."

"Yes, it's what we do."

"Not to each other," Evan said. "Isn't that the point of being part of this same strange community? That we can talk about these things, be real together?"

Dad let out a heavy sigh. "You know what I'm going to say."

"That you warned me not to follow in your footsteps."

His father saluted him with his pipe. "Got it in one."

"I tried. I never would have joined MI5 if I'd been a decent architect," Evan said, knowing it was utter pish.

"You were a decent architect. But it wasn't enough for you to be decent. You needed to excel, and I respect you for that. I just wish you'd found another use for your talents."

"Aye, like con artistry or professional gambling. That would've made you proud." Evan tugged his hood as the rain pelted harder. "I don't regret it, you know, not even after all this. Not even after losing Ben."

"Losing—" Dad looked at him in alarm. "What's happened?"

Evan hesitated. He wasn't ready to tell his father the whole truth, about Ben blowing Evan's cover to two of his teammates. He'd had Fergus, Liam, and Robert sign copies of the Official Secrets Act, but due to his suspension, Evan hadn't been able to submit the forms yet (they weren't the sort of thing one casually dropped in the post).

Still, he could share the essential truth of the breakup. "Ben couldn't take the secrecy anymore."

"I'm sorry to hear that. When did this happen?"

"Yesterday."

"And you've phoned him since?"

Evan squinted at his father. "Whatever for?"

"To try and change his mind." Dad shifted his umbrella and pipe to the opposite hands. "Unless you don't want him to change it. Perhaps you'd rather wallow in solitude and feel noble for the sacrifices you've endured on behalf of your country."

"Is that what you did when Mum left?"

His father opened his mouth, then shut it.

Evan softened his tone. "Or maybe it's not so simple."

"Once your mother was gone, I stopped trying to keep her. But before that…" Dad shifted a rock back and forth with his toe, following its movement with his eyes. "The version I've always told you isn't exactly accurate."

Here we are at last. "In what way?"

"I didn't let her go so she could escape the nightmare of marriage to an intelligence officer. I let her go because I had no choice." His shoulders sagged, and in that moment Hugh Hollister looked every one of his fifty-eight years. "She didn't want me anymore. Not because I was a spy, but because I was"— he bit out the words—"someone other than Magnus Muir."

"I'm sorry, Dad," was all Evan could think to say.

His father flicked his hand in a dismissive motion that contradicted the pain on his face. "My point is, unless Ben has some secret Orcadian old flame on the side, there's no reason you can't work this out."

"He seemed dead certain he didn't want this life."

Dad barked out a laugh. "God's sake, Evan, *no one* wants this life. The pay is shit, the recognition is nil, and the damage to our souls is irreparable. But we do it anyway, because it's necessary and challenging and sometimes pretty fucking fun. If Ben really knows you, he'll get that this is who you are. And if he really loves you, he'll realize you're worth the high price of admission."

A sudden gust came up then, catching his umbrella. Evan's father hung on and tried to aim its peak toward the wind, but it flipped inside out with a *thwup*.

"Bloody cheap piece of crap," Dad growled. He dropped it on the ground and stomped on its soggy carcass. For a moment he just stood there, soaked and bedraggled, his pipe smoldering in the falling rain.

Then he pulled a spare travel umbrella from the pocket of his trench coat and deployed it with a deft gesture. "Sorry, where were we?"

"You were telling me to get Ben back."

"Yes. Do that." He stepped onto the paved walkway. "But first, let's go and have a pint of whatever the unemployed drink."

BEN'S MUM had insisted on making him scrambled eggs and a strong cup of tea before they'd continued their conversation, hoping he would talk more sense with an infusion of protein and caffeine.

After the first bite of unwanted food, Ben set down his fork. "I can't tell you the real reason Evan and I broke up. But you're right, it wasn't because of my religion."

"Okay." Standing on the other side of the breakfast bar, she sipped her tea and frowned at his full plate.

"Still, it's true, isn't it? I can't have a boyfriend and still be Bahá'í. And you were right—there's no loophole. I've reread all the writings about it and found nothing to give me hope."

So there was an upside to leaving Evan: At least now there'd be no conflict with his faith. Ben would never have to make that soul-wrenching choice.

"Do you love him?" his mother asked.

"It doesn't matter." He thumbed the edge of his blue dinner plate, remembering how Evan had liked its design. "They say, 'No matter how devoted and fine the love may be between people of the same sex, to let it find expression in sexual acts is wrong.' I burned that quote into my brain. 'No matter how devoted and fine the love.'"

His voice broke then, so he stopped and picked up his fork, though he'd no intention of using it.

Finally his mum said, "It hurts my heart to see you suffer like this again."

"'Again'?" He couldn't remember ever feeling this ravaged.

"When that boy you loved at school went to America."

Ben froze. He'd always thought he'd hidden the true nature of their relationship. "You mean Rhys? We were just mates." He looked up at his mum and knew he couldn't maintain the lie, and anyway, what was the point? "Okay, more than mates eventually. I didn't know you knew."

"I wasn't certain at the time, but the fact you officially committed to the Bahá'í Faith a week after he left rather confirmed it for me."

"I wasn't using religion some sort of rebound relationship, if that's what you're thinking. I really did intend to be true to our laws. I tried to be celibate—and I succeeded, for almost three years."

She looked impressed, as though hearing this for the first time. "What changed?"

"Obviously my 'lower nature' took over," he said bitterly. "That's what our teachings would say."

She leaned forward, crossing her arms upon the breakfast bar. "But what really changed?"

He took a long sip of tea, then another, trying to clear his brain enough to remember what he'd been thinking when he'd started hooking up with men again. "It wasn't all at once. There was this thought that kept coming up more and more often: Why would God make me like this—why would he make so many people like this—just to watch us suffer? It didn't seem like the God I knew."

Now his mum was the speechless one, simply nodding as her eyes began to glisten.

"I tried to remind myself," he continued, "that many people suffered from many things, that being born gay was a 'handicap' my soul would have to overcome through prayer and determination. That's what we teach, right?" Hearing no response, he kept going, staring at the fluffy eggs on his plate as their steam faded. "But Bahá'u'lláh also wrote that the union of two souls is a 'fortress for well-being and salvation.' So being gay can't be the same as being blind or quadriplegic. Vision and walking don't make us better people, but finding that one person…" He looked up at her. "But rules are rules. I either remain a Bahá'í with no partner, or I leave the faith to find happiness with a man."

"Listen." She reached over the breakfast bar and took his hand. "No matter which path you choose, God will still love you. That's not just feel-good wishful thinking on my part. That's from all the writings of our faith. I could recite a dozen passages—"

"No bother. I know you're right." He did know it. He felt it in his bones. "Losing my Bahá'í membership wouldn't mean I'd lose God. But it's still a loss."

"I know." She came to hug him again. This time he didn't cry.

"Promise me one thing?" he asked. "You won't sacrifice your own standing for my sake. Like, if I ever leave, you won't follow me, okay?"

"I can't promise that, Ben." She pulled back and tugged down her black jumper with an air of finality. "Especially not after the decision I just made."

Chapter 37

"Blaaaaa!"

Evan looked down at the pile of sleeping lambs beside him in the orphan pen. One of them was waking up hungry, bleating and blinking into the light of the heat lamp above it.

"You're next, laddie," Evan whispered. "I think." He would check the feeding list in his pocket, because his usually sharp memory could no longer be trusted.

First, he'd finish feeding the newborn in his lap. The peedie beast was snuggled up against his chest, sucking on the bottle's teat, its tiny legs splayed and its eyes set in happy squints. Evan's arms were starting to freeze into this position, holding the bottle in one hand and cupping the lamb's jaw in the other to maintain the proper angle.

After five days and nights in his family's lambing shed, the rest of the universe had ceased to exist. There was no Loch of Stenness, no town of Stromness, no Scotland, no United Kingdom. No world. There were just lambs, lambs, lambs. Lambs and ewes and the damp night air.

Growing up, he'd helped during lambing season for a few hours a day, but like his brothers now, his availability had been limited by school and football. So Mum and Magnus had done most of the work and hired a night lamber for the wee hours.

Evan had volunteered to be this season's night lamber for the cost of a plane ticket and a cat sitter, saving the farm nearly two thousand pounds. He wasn't needed in Glasgow just now anyway, as his hip flexor strain would keep him off the football pitch for two weeks—coincidentally the same amount of time he'd been suspended from his job.

As the lamb in his lap continued feeding, Evan let the back of his head rest on the stone wall. The warmth of the heat lamp was tempting him to collapse on the fresh straw for a nap. But that could mean disaster in the form of stillbirths he wasn't there to prevent.

Evan chomped down on the last unbitten section of his cheek to wake himself. *After this, coffee*, he promised.

So far none of the "orphaned" lambs in this pen were literal orphans. Two were triplets who couldn't be fully fed by their birth ewes, as sheep had only two teats. The one in his lap and its twin had been rejected by their mum, who didn't seem keen on the whole being-responsible-for-another-living-creature thing.

"Don't worry," he said to the lamb as she finished the bottle. "I've got big plans for you."

Evan's hip creaked with stiffness—along with the rest of his body—as he got to his feet and shuffled into the main part of the shed containing the enormous antepartum pen. It currently housed 108 pregnant ewes, which meant nearly half had already lambed. Most of the ewes were sleeping serenely near the center of the pen, making it easy to see the ones with more urgent tasks on their minds.

Over in the corner, one of the older ewes was lying propped against the wall, tail wagging and lip curling—a sign she was close. Her wool bore a red painted dot, indicating she was having a single, according to her ultrasound. A perfect candidate for adoption.

Still, her water bag hadn't come out yet, so he had time for a restorative cup of coffee.

Just as he poured a fresh mug, he heard a deep, roaring bleat. He hurried back to the antepartum pen to see the ewe lift her chin and press her cheek against the wall. Her water bag was now out, which meant the birth would hopefully soon follow.

Evan retrieved the lamb he'd just nursed and brought her back as the ewe was having contractions. He approached slowly and asked, "Whit's on, lass?" in a low, soothing voice.

The ewe's expression said, "What do you *think* is happening, you eejit?"

Soon her baby was entering the world in proper diving configuration, nose between its outstretched forelegs. Evan set the orphaned lamb behind the ewe, then gently but firmly tugged the newborn out. The ensuing placenta drenched the orphaned lamb, who widened her eyes in surprise. Evan draped the steaming newborn over its adopted sibling and started rubbing its "baby goo," as Justine used to call it, onto the orphan to make them smell the same.

Then he paused. The new lamb wasn't breathing. He patted and massaged the newborn's side, and when that didn't work, he picked it up by its hind legs and swung it back and forth. Finally he laid it down and tickled its nostril with a bit of straw.

The lamb gave a hard sneeze, then shook its head and coughed.

"There you are," he said as he wiped the lamb's mouth. "I was getting worried." This was a lie. He was too tired to feel worry or any other emotion.

The ewe got to her feet, snapping the umbilical cord, then turned to nuzzle her offspring. Apparently having lost count on the way to two, she licked both lambs with equal fervor, nickering softly.

Evan cleaned his hands on the straw—more or less—then prepared a small postpartum pen where the new mother could bond in peace with her two bairns.

By the time he'd introduced the family to their temporary home, two more ewes were lambing. One birth was uneventful, the first of twins, but the other needed assistance. Like many singles, this lamb was oversize and thus took forever to get its giant head through the birth canal, even with Evan's help. After massaging, pounding, swinging, and poking it into taking its first breath, he could barely feel his arms.

Then there was a lull. The greatest rush of lambs would come at daybreak—an evolutionary prescription allowing maximum bonding time before predators arrived after dark. But here in fox- and badger-free Orkney, the lambs' only predators came by day: stray dogs, mostly, along with so-called scavenging birds like great black-backed gulls.

He checked the lambs in the postpartum pens for full bellies, then spray-painted matching blue numbers on the sides of each family member as well as a spot of green paint on the hips of the males. Then he updated the tally on the white board and finally headed to the shed kitchen to make more formula.

When he arrived, his coffee was cold. He gulped it anyway, fearing if he took the time to reheat it, a new crisis would pull him away.

As he mixed the reeking imitation colostrum, he took a moment to be grateful that this mind-numbing routine gave him no time or energy to think about Ben or the Warriors or his job. They all seemed like features of a film he'd once seen.

His recurring nightmare was sheep-focused, too: There was always one postpartum pen he'd forgotten to clean and bring food to. When he remembered it existed, he would embark on a fruitless search, knowing it would contain a dead ewe and dying lambs.

He stopped stirring. No, last night the dream had ended with him finding the elusive neglected pen. There was no ewe inside, just one lamb rolled up in a rug, two tiny cloven hooves sticking out of each end.

Evan usually avoided thinking about Patrick outside the safety of a therapy session. But now his mind was too tired to stop the memories flooding in: Patrick's glee at meeting another gay supporter of Glasgow Celtic, his gratitude as the shy nineteen-year-old learned one erotic pleasure after another.

Evan had never been adventurous in bed during his four years with Fergus, but with Patrick he'd abandoned most inhibitions, broadening his own horizons to impress a man he hadn't cared about.

A man he hadn't cared about *at first*. It was impossible, he'd learned, to be detached from a person who knew every inch of his body, who made him laugh and even once cry, who loved pug puppies and Aero chocolate bars and his ma.

Evan closed his eyes and focused on his breath, using a technique his therapist had taught him to let go of these spiraling thoughts. Then he went back to mixing the stinky, life-supporting lamb formula. Patrick was gone, but Evan could still save these sheep and this farm.

The cycle began again: feeding orphans, birthing newborns, attempting an adoption—this one failing—checking bellies, painting numbers, rubber-banding tails, dabbing umbilical cords with iodine, drinking coffee.

As dawn approached, the cycle became all lambing, all the time. His family joined him at five, with Mum and Magnus taking over the births, Sigur feeding the orphans, and Thorfinn helping Evan sort the day-old lambs in the nursery pen, seeing which were strong enough to go out to the hills with their mums.

When daylight broke, the two of them loaded the first set into the trailer, then Evan settled into the driver's seat of the farm's four-wheel-drive vehicle.

Thorfinn handed him a shepherd's crook. "You want the shotgun, too? You never ken what might be oot there."

"Honestly, I'm so knackered, I'd probably blow my own head off."

"Should you be driving, then?"

"If it involves sitting on my arse for even one minute," Evan said, "then aye, I should be doing it." He turned to the two lambs behind his seat. "Buckle up, bairns. It's your first road trip."

He drove out of the shed into the mist-soaked morning. Climbing the hill behind the byre, he steered around the bigger bumps to avoid jostling the lambs.

Once in the field, Evan let the ewe trot down from the back of the transport, then placed her babies beside her. At a day and a half old, they were already a hundred times more hearty than the ones born last night. They nuzzled the damp grass, one of them sneezing as he inhaled the dew.

Thus began the best part of their lives: running and playing on the West Mainland's lush spring pastures—lush by Scottish standards, anyway—and enjoying the occasional sunshine. Next to that first meeting of ewe and lamb, this was Evan's favorite moment.

He pulled out his phone to capture it. As he hit record, one of the lambs kicked up its heels and started bouncing around. Its twin joined the cavorting, jumping up to butt its head against its mum, then falling on its face in the grass. Then, as if remembering what the ewe was there for, both lambs began suckling.

Evan stopped recording and just watched for a moment. Suddenly he was seized by an irresistible impulse.

He attached the video to a text message:

> Thought you might like to see this

As soon as he hit send, he knew it was a mistake. Ben had definitively rejected him. Deep down inside, Evan had always known it would happen. For a brief time after learning the truth about his parents' divorce, he'd let himself hope that he could share this spy's life with a person as real as Ben.

Ben, who somehow still saw the best in him, even after knowing how Evan had betrayed Patrick. Ben, who had filled in the Certificate of Awesomeness on Evan's refrigerator with the words *Being a Hero*.

Despite all that, it had ended as Evan had feared: with tears in the eyes of the man he loved.

He scrolled up through the texts they'd sent each other the last two months. It reminded him of a similar masochistic exercise he'd undertaken in Belfast, rereading texts from Fergus he could never answer. He would have given anything to send one word of reassurance, to tell Fergus things weren't as they seemed.

But no words could make it right, not then and not now.

Evan slowly became aware of a commotion on the other side of the hill. It sounded like a bunch of bronchitis sufferers holding the World Cup of Coughing.

He looked up to see two ravens circling over the area the noise was coming from.

No.

He grabbed the shepherd's crook and sprinted toward the sound. As he crested the hill, he saw his worst fear realized: a quartet of great black-backed gulls surrounding a small white mass. A ewe stood twenty or so feet away, shielding her surviving lamb while its twin was ravaged by thick, sharp beaks.

With a roar, Evan ran down the hill, brandishing the crook. The gulls took off at his approach, thumping the air with five-foot wingspans, their calls pitching up with indignation. From what he could see through his red mist of rage, they were a breeding pair and two juveniles—a mean and hungry family.

"I'm sorry." He knelt beside what was left of the lamb. "I'm so sorry."

Grief washed over him with the force of a gale-ripped wave. This was why he'd left Orkney in the first place: He couldn't accept these routine, unlamented deaths, how animals and crops sometimes perished no matter how hard you fought to save them. *That's just the way the world is, laddie,* Magnus would remind him.

His stepdad had been right, of course. Life outside these islands had shown no mercy either.

Something gray moved in the corner of his eye: a gull feather, its quill caught in the grass, its vane waving in the relentless wind. A murderer's calling card.

He got to his feet, picked up the shepherd's crook, and slammed it down upon the feather. Then he kept going, long after every barb was ripped from the feather's shaft.

With a resounding snap, the crook shattered, and still Evan beat the ground in his endless, pointless fury. When there was nothing left but splinters, he dropped to his knees and stabbed at the cold, hard ground that swam before his eyes.

How many more months would he see Patrick's terrified face smashed by a boot? How many more years would he hear Fergus's plaintive voice mails, begging Evan for a reason to live?

A deep croak came from above. He looked up to see the pair of ravens, circling lower now, no doubt hoping to make a meal of the lamb—and maybe Evan himself, the way things were going.

They called again, together this time, dredging up one pure thought and memory, of Ben's face as he opened a peedie white gift box on his 5.75th birthday.

Wiping his eyes with a dusty sleeve, Evan turned back to the lamb. He took off his jacket, laid it on the ground, then carefully moved the body onto the makeshift stretcher.

When he reached the four-wheel-drive vehicle, the notification light was blinking on his phone. He set down the lamb, wiped the blood from his hands, and swept his finger across the screen to reveal a message from Ben:

I'd like to see that in person

Chapter 38

As HIS PLANE broke through the clouds, revealing the green fields and silver lochs of Orkney Mainland, Ben felt the same lurch in his chest he used to feel when he'd fly into Glasgow after a trip abroad. It felt like coming home.

In the eight hours between decision and takeoff, Ben had prepared for this trip as much as possible: packing his roughest clothes so he could pitch in with the lambing, baking a second batch of pistachio biscuits to bestow upon the Muirs, rehearsing what he'd say to Evan.

But nothing could have prepared him for the sight of the man he loved standing alone upon the rainy tarmac at Kirkwall Airport.

Why had he waited so long to reach out to Evan? he wondered, wishing the airport people would hurry up and stick the stairs on the side of the plane so he could disembark. The last week seemed like a bad dream from which he couldn't wake himself.

It had taken Evan's video to yank him out of that self-induced nightmare. And why that? Ben had no explanation apart from pure and simple *instinct*, the same unstoppable force that led those lambs to rise on their wobbly legs and latch onto a ewe teat.

It wasn't the lambs in that video that had drawn him here, but rather Evan's reaction to them: his soft laughter, the gentleness and joy in his voice. Ben had needed to hear it up close in person, needed to be with the man who, despite all he'd suffered, could still make such happy noises.

He was first out the door, hurrying down the metal stairs, not caring they were already slick with the driving rain, not caring how un-Orcadian he looked sprinting across the tarmac in his black skinny jeans and bright-yellow high-tops.

A few feet from Evan he stopped short. "Oh."

Evan's bloodshot blue eyes widened. "'Oh' what?"

"Nothing. You look…"

"Complete shite?"

Ben nodded slowly. "It's kind of a miracle."

"I've not slept much. I've had a shower, but some of the lambing smells don't really…leave." He opened his arms. "Just as a peedie warning."

Ben stepped forward into the warmest—and yes, stinkiest—embrace of his life. "I'm sorry." Och, he'd wanted to wait until they were in the car before crying. "I'm so sorry."

"No. You're here."

"You don't hate me?"

"I could never hate you." Evan's arms tightened around his back. "Can we make this work? Please?"

"Yes." Ben prayed it was true. "Somehow."

OTHER THINGS BEN had been unprepared for: the real-life cuteness of newborn lambs and the equally real-life stench of all things farming. He'd tried rubbing menthol cream beneath his nose to mask the odors, but it burned like mad on his chapped skin and lips. And anyway, he got used to the smell after the first day.

There was little time for him and Evan to talk, but that was fine. They didn't need words when they could communicate with soft eyes and warm smiles. And though their bodies were too tired and achy for sex—and the farmhouse too small for privacy—they had the strength to hold each other as they plummeted into deep and dreamless sleep.

Wednesday evening, Ben and Evan were laying down new hay in the antepartum pen, which now held but a dozen ewes. Evan would heave a bale from the pile in the corner, unbind it, then pitch the hay onto the floor in big chunks, which Ben would trample into bedding. It was dusty, scratchy work, and after three days he'd barely enough energy to drag his feet, much less lift his knees, but he didn't complain.

"I'm away tomorrow," he reminded Evan. "Need to prepare for Saturday's wedding." His mother had taken over some of the planning work for the event—which she *would* be attending, much to his surprise. "Will you come with me?"

Evan grunted as he clipped the wire surrounding a new bale. "I'll be back in Glasgow Sunday for work Monday."

"What about the friendly match Saturday?"

"I'll not be fit to play. Besides, the flock needs me."

"Lambing's almost done. Your mum said you could leave." When Evan didn't answer, Ben added, "*I* need you."

Evan straightened up, then stabbed his pitchfork down into the bale to secure it. "I need you too." He removed his cap and swiped the dust from his sweaty forehead. "So what do we do about that?"

Ben stopped stomping the hay. Here it was. The Conversation.

"Coffee first?" Evan asked.

"Yes, please." Ben had always been more of a tea person, but farm work required stronger stuff.

They took their mugs and sat on a hay bale near the edge of the shed.

"I'm not sure where to start," Ben said, "other than I'm sorry. I never wanted to hurt you. Quite the opposite."

"I know. You thought you were a danger to my cover."

"Which means a danger to your life. The thought of you

kidnapped by terrorists and paraded in front of a camera to be—"
He shut his eyes hard, but couldn't blot out the image of a
machete to Evan's neck. "And I can't ask you to quit MI5. It's your
calling. You'd hate me for making you give it up."

"Ben, I told you I could never hate you."

"It's more than that. I can't rob this country and this world of
your service. You're too valuable to lose. And to what? What
would you be if not a spy?"

"A farmer."

Ben started to laugh, but then he saw Evan's somber face.
"Really?"

"Listen." Evan set his coffee mug on the floor. "I've decided to
leave the Service and move home." He spread his hands. "This is
where I belong."

Ben's jaw dropped. "You want this to be your life?"

"I want *this* to be my life." He took Ben in his arms and kissed
him softly. "I want you."

"That's what I'm trying to say. You don't need to leave MI5
for me."

"But you said you couldn't handle the secrecy."

"I'll learn to handle it. I'll learn to cope with the unknowable."
He kissed Evan. "You're worth it."

"It's not fair for you to make all the concessions." He let go of
Ben but kept hold of his hand. "We could be happy here. We
could have a flat in Stromness or Kirkwall, and you could get a
job with one of the marine-energy firms. You could even do
weddings on the side."

Ben's head spun—with excitement that Evan was willing to
take this step, and with a bit of annoyance that he'd sorted Ben's
future without consulting him. "And you would work here?"

"Aye, maybe take over the place with my brothers when my
parents retire. It seems boring, but it's not. On a farm, every day is
different. And my family need me. This island needs loads more
young people to keep it—"

"The world needs you more. I'm sorry, but it's the truth." He clutched Evan's hands between his own. "You're right, we could be happy here. But neither of us thinks being happy is enough. You know how dangerous this world is. You can never *un*know that. And to know that but do nothing, to retreat into a world of animals when there are so many humans who need you? That wouldn't make you happy for long."

"It would. And you could be helping the world—actually doing something about climate change—at one of these companies."

"If I got hired. There are hundreds of candidates for each job, and most of the positions I'd want require a Master's degree. So I've put in my application at—" The name stuck in his throat, so he had to literally cough it up. "At GCHQ."

Evan stared at him. "What? Why?"

"Because there are people who'd like to kill me for the sin of planning gay weddings, and I'd rather that not happen. Also, my advisor said I'd be good at signals intelligence. I asked her about MI5, and she said GCHQ would be a better fit. So I'd be safely ensconced behind a computer at Cheltenham, using my GIS ninja skills to thwart bad guys."

"Would you enjoy that, though?"

"I'd be a professional eavesdropper," Ben said. "What's not to love?"

"The fact that GCHQ collect mass surveillance data on British citizens."

"MI5 are the ones who use that data."

"Believe me, I know," Evan said. "I make that moral compromise every day. But you're better than that. You told me once that work which serves others is a form of worship. How could you reconcile a job like that with your faith?"

"I don't know." Ben fought back tears of frustration. *Why is this so hard?* "I thought…since GCHQ are sort of near London, if MI5 transferred you to Thames House, we could live somewhere in between."

"I canna live in London. After this last week I know that more than ever." Evan looked about to shed his own tears. "Glasgow is far enough from this."

"I understand." Ben moved closer and leaned against him. "It's beautiful here."

"It's more than beautiful." Evan slipped an arm around his shoulders and kissed his hair. "This place…it's where I feel most real."

Ben's heart felt like it would rip in two. "You can be real anywhere, because you *are* real."

"It doesn't always feel like it." He tightened his embrace. "I love you, Ben. Please come stay with me here."

Ben buried his face against Evan's neck. "I'll think about it. You know I love Orkney. And I love you."

He was more tempted by Evan's offer of escape than he was letting on. Orkney and its people were lovely. Above all, it was safe. Here they could forget the world and avoid the worst of its evils.

"Not to continue the sales pitch," Evan said, "but mind on, there's the Bahá'í Centre in Kirkwall, the only one in Scotland apart from Edinburgh."

Ben's burning eyes finally overflowed. He pulled away and put his face in his hands.

"What's wrong?" Evan asked. "What did I say?"

Ben forced out the words, though he could barely speak. "This Bahá'í Centre won't accept me while I'm with you. None of them will."

"What? Since when?"

"Since always."

"I don't understand. I know your faith forbids us having sex, but so does every faith." Evan touched Ben's shoulder. "You said it was like Catholics using birth control. You said Bahá'í was an undemanding religion."

"I said all that because I wanted to believe it. But it's more than just not following the letter of the law. I could be basically excommunicated for having a boyfriend."

"Oh." Evan's hand slid off his shoulder. The loss of his touch sent an ache rippling through Ben's body. "But that couple you met here last month—the Milfords, aye?—they didn't seem prejudiced."

"It's not about prejudice, it's about going against the teachings of our faith. Other LGBTQ Bahá'ís have been asked to resign their membership when they entered a serious same-sex relationship. We're accepted and embraced as long as we're single."

Evan let out a soft curse. "If I'd known that us being together could destroy something so important to you…"

"That's the other reason why I never said anything. I didn't want to scare you away." Ben wiped his face with the end of his sleeve—a mistake, as it smelled like newborn lamb. "I truly believe that the leaders of my faith will come around in my life-time. But I can't control that, and I refuse to be without you while I wait for a change of heart that might never happen."

"If it hurts you to make that choice—"

"Then it hurts. That's life, right? Sometimes there's loss no matter what we choose. Perfection's not an option, and neither is giving up." Ben folded his hands, pressing his palms hard together. "I want to be with you, Evan. Somehow."

Behind them, a ewe gave what Ben had come to recognize as an *"It's time!"* bleat.

"Sorry," Evan said. "I should go see she's okay."

An unfamiliar alert pinged on Ben's phone. Curious, he pulled it out and looked at the screen.

Oh my God.

Ben tapped the WhoWhatWhere notification. After a moment, a map came up. "Whoa."

"What is it?" Evan asked.

Ben hesitated only a moment. "I know where David Wallace is."

EVAN STARED DOWN AT BEN, whose excited expression bore barely a tinge of shame. "What? How do you—" He gritted his teeth, wanting to fling his empty coffee mug against the wall. "How could I forget to delete my search?" He'd practiced the utmost operational security at every step.

"There was a bug," Ben said. "You probably told the software to delete the search and it somehow got saved, then belched it back up when I installed the new version. It happened to one of my searches too."

"Then I never should have used it at all. I should never have trusted a beta version."

"You mean you never should have trusted *me*."

Exactly. Evan put his palms to his face and dragged his fingertips over the sides of his forehead, then his jaws, up and down. "I want to."

"But I don't deserve it. I've proved it again and again." Ben's voice was steady instead of pleading. "And this time I'm not even sorry, because if I'd just deleted your search, you'd never have got this new lead." Ben cut off Evan's protest. "And if I'd told you straight away what I was doing, you would've had to report it to your bosses or lie to them. Either way we'd both end up in serious trouble."

"We could *still* be in serious trouble. Ben, you've no idea what you've done."

"I've got some idea." He held out his phone. "Don't you want to see?"

Evan paused only a moment before snatching the device and looking at the screen. "Lerwick? Why is David Wallace in Shetland, of all places?" The BVP leader had never mentioned having friends or relatives there when Gunnar had told him how much he loved visiting Orkney (a drop of truth never hurt in undercover work). As the two groups of Northern Isles, Shetland and Orkney were linked in the minds of most Brits, so mentioning one would naturally bring up the other.

"I'm guessing it's not exactly high tourist season up there?"

Ben took his phone back and tapped the screen. "It was a Twitter post that gave me the notification. Let me see what he said."

Evan realized that this meant Ned's crew had finally switched Wallace's phone settings. If so, there could be more geo-tagged posts to come.

"Wallace didn't tweet about Lerwick," Ben said. "It was just a standard white-supremacist hate tweet."

The lambing ewe bleated again, more insistently.

"I need to see to her," Evan said.

Ben didn't look up from his phone screen. "Give a shout if you need help."

The ewe in question was having triplets, judging by the purple paint mark on her side. Evan was glad this was the first birth of the night, while he still had strength in his arms. Like many triplets, these lambs were wedged together in the confines of their mother's womb. Evan quickly sorted out which leg belonged to whom and got the peedie sheep into position for easier arrivals. Then it was more or less one-two-three happy birthday.

He took the last and largest of the triplets to the orphan pen to hand-feed. "We'll find you a new mum," he told it, "but for now you'll have to settle for me."

Settling into the straw with lamb and bottle, Evan finally had a moment to think about what Ben had just revealed. He felt betrayed—again—but at least Ben had been honest. And if Wallace's trip to Lerwick was significant, perhaps it could be the break in the case Evan had been waiting for.

As for Ben's revelation about his faith, Evan's brain couldn't even wrap around the personal and philosophical ramifications. He still desperately needed a week-long nap.

Soft footsteps approached the orphan pen. Ben leaned round the corner, showing only one eye and the top of his head. "How's it going?" he whispered.

"Triplets. Number 202. Don't let me forget."

Ben tucked his phone into his coat pocket. "I'll feed while you put the others in the postpartum pen." He opened the gate. "Wallace is on the move."

"He's posted again already?" In Evan's experience, David Wallace was sparing with his social-media activity. "What about?"

"Actually, he's got himself into a Twitter spat—or a 'Twat,' as I call it." Ben shifted around him and slid down to sit against the wall. "Every reply is marked with a geo-tag."

That was strange for Wallace—like most controversial figures, he'd learned not to get dragged into online word-wars. "Who's he fighting with?"

"Erm...me."

"What?!"

"Not *me*-me. My alter ego, IllusiveMan. Been a while since I've trotted that one out." Ben petted the sleeping lamb next to him. "Anyway, he's headed southbound from Lerwick."

The newborn lamb in Evan's arms was all that kept him from yelling. "I can't believe you involved yourself even deeper," he hissed.

"Well, again..."

"You're not sorry. But you should be. Ben, this has to stop. You've no idea what you're dealing with." As Evan bent to hand over the lamb, he realized what Ben had just told him. "Southbound from Lerwick, you say?"

"Mm-hm." Ben settled the lamb in his lap. "And too slowly for him to be flying."

"He must be on the overnight ferry to Aberdeen." Evan started to straighten up, then froze halfway. "What day of the week is it?"

"Wednesday."

A thrill of anticipation—the thrill of the hunt—coursed through Evan, a feeling that no amount of farming could make him immune to. "That ferry stops in Orkney tonight."

Chapter 39

"Did you take your Dramamine?" Ben asked as they boarded the giant white-and-blue ferry at Kirkwall's Hatston terminal. His own stomach was fluttering with excitement.

"No, it'll put me to sleep," Evan said. "Besides, this route's smoother than the one we had to take to Stromness last month, so it won't make me as sick." He nodded briskly, as though convincing himself.

"What if we can't find him?" Ben avoided speaking David Wallace's name, in case one of their fellow embarking passengers heard. "What if he's holed up in a cabin?"

"The cabins and berths were all booked when I bought our tickets," Evan said, "so unless he planned this trip ahead of time, he'll be in a regular seat like us, out in the open."

Ben found a map of the ferry on the wall. He and Evan studied it in silence while the flood of passengers went by in a hushed rush, toward bed or a late drink in the midship bar.

He noticed Evan examining his own reflection in the map case's glass. The disguise was a variation on "Bruce," the Glasgow Greens fan who had infiltrated the gay football match with Jamie and Ben. "Am I padded enough?" he asked.

Ben poked Evan's ribs to test the layer of stuffing beneath the purple Highlands and Islands University sweatshirt borrowed from his brother Thorfinn. Then he tugged down the visor of Evan's matching cap. "Looking good, Bruce. And by 'good' I mean fashion-tragic."

"Then let's get started. Mind on, this is just simple reconnaissance, and it's all I'm letting you do."

"Got it." Ben had been cautioned a dozen times on the way to the ferry terminal, and he was determined not to act out of order.

"I'll take the first level," Evan said, "and you take the second. First one to find him texts the other, but regardless, we meet in the third-floor gift shop before deciding next moves."

"Roger that." Putting in his earphones, Ben went up the stairs to the second level. Passing through the lounge and seating area, he took cover a few steps behind one of the crew members, a large man who resembled the Viking painted on the ship's exterior. The crewman's leisurely pace allowed Ben to scan each row of seats, looking *through* the passengers instead of *at* them.

You're an overworked student, he told himself, *who just wants a comfy place to finish that blasted paper.* It wasn't a hard role to play, being so near reality.

He soon lost his man-size rampart when the hulking steward went through a door marked CREW ONLY. When he didn't find Wallace on the second floor, Ben went to the third, approaching the gift shop at the top of the stairs.

Just before he passed through the open, frosted-glass doors, Ben saw David Wallace. He forced himself to keep going rather than screech to a cartoonish stop.

"Hiya," he said to the gift-shop lass arranging perfume boxes. She returned his smile, suppressing a yawn.

Ben quickly texted Evan:

> Found DW outside shop

> Buy something and meet me in level 2 bar

Ben purchased an Irn-Bru and a black-and-white stuffed Shetland pony from the sleepy shop assistant. Instead of going back down the way he came, he strolled past David Wallace—*oh my God, it's definitely him*—and used the rear stairs.

He found Evan in the lounge and handed him the orange fizzy drink. "To keep you awake and maybe settle your stomach." Ben slid onto a barstool. "He seems to be sleeping, but instead of reclining his seat like everyone else, he's sitting upright with his feet on a big black kit bag."

"How big?"

"Big enough it's weird he didn't check it as luggage. It's nearly full, based on how much it sags under his legs."

"That's helpful." Evan twisted off the Irn-Bru cap with a hiss. "Good eye."

Ben basked in the warm sun of Evan's approval. "How shall we distract him so one of us can look in the bag?"

Evan's eyes narrowed. "I'm not involving you. It's too dangerous, not to mention illegal."

"Then why are we here?"

"To observe him."

"To stalk him. Which is also illegal."

"Only when you do it." Evan picked up his rucksack. "Back in a minute. Stay here."

Ben obeyed, and Evan returned as promised, looking like himself again but for his slicked-back hair.

"What happened to Bruce?" Ben asked.

"Gunnar ate him."

Ben put the pieces together. "You're going to just walk up to Wallace and talk to him?"

"Aye. Maybe he'll show me what's in the bag."

"What if it doesn't work? What's your Plan B?" He bobbed his eyebrows. "Aka, your Plan Ben?"

"I'm not letting you anywhere near that man."

"It's not him you're afraid of, is it? It's me. You think I'll blow your cover again." When Evan didn't protest, Ben said, "I don't blame you. But instead of shutting me out, why not deploy me in some way where I won't babble?"

"I'll not be deploying you at all. You're a civilian."

"I'm also all you've got." Ben gestured to the wide, dark window beside them. "Soon we'll be in the middle of the North Sea, in the middle of the night. You need a team, and right now that team is me." He pressed his palms together. "I promise I'll do whatever you say."

"But if things go wrong—"

"We'll make a plan for that." Ben made his final pitch. "Remember the day I broke up with you? You said, and I quote: 'Maybe I shouldn't trust you. But I'm going to do it anyway.'"

Evan sighed, then reached into his bag and pulled out a pen and jotter. "I suppose if we're to be together, we can't leave each other behind." He tore off the jotter's top sheet—to avoid leaving an imprint on the pad, Ben assumed. "Let's make a plan."

BEN SETTLED behind the rear table in the third-floor lounge, which was empty apart from what looked like another tired uni student working on her end-of-term paper. Then he got out his laptop, plugged in his earphones, and waited for Evan's call.

He couldn't see David Wallace from here—which meant the BVP leader couldn't see him—but he could see the two empty adjacent seats, where "Gunnar" would soon sit.

After ten minutes, Ben's phone buzzed in his pocket. When he answered, Evan asked, "He still sleeping? Short answers only."

"Not sure."

"The ship is setting sail any minute, so hopefully that'll wake him enough to see me. Put your phone on mute and keep it that way."

Ben pressed the mute button and laid the phone on the table so he wouldn't accidentally un-mute it in his pocket. Then he opened a blank document on his laptop.

The ferry seemed to suddenly wake, its engine's purr becoming a roar as it prepared to leave the terminal. The rumble worked its way up through Ben's body. He'd never felt so alive.

"David?" came a Norwegian voice in his ear. "It *is* you."

Evan appeared about a hundred feet in front of Ben, extending his hand. He saw David's head as the man stood to greet Evan.

"Gunnar..." Wallace's voice was faint, but Ben caught the words *surprise* and *beard*.

"I always shave it in springtime." Evan sat two seats away from David—per straight-guy rules—and took out his left earphone, leaving in the right wire that held the microphone. "Contact lenses are new, though. Still getting used to them."

Wallace said something Ben couldn't hear, and Evan replied, "I was in Kirkwall to visit friends."

They chatted for a while about Shetland versus Orkney, and Ben typed everything he could hear. Then David must have beckoned Gunnar closer, because Evan shifted into the center seat.

Ben shut his eyes to hear better. David was doing most of the talking, with Gunnar offering *Mmmm*s of acknowledgment. Ben typed snippets of what he could make out, bracketing the less audible parts to jog Evan's memory later:

"Social influence campaign..."

"The Russian model of [operation]..."

"Not exactly propaganda..."

"...know real truth [when they see it?]..."

"Are you okay, mate?"

This last part was louder, and the concern sounded genuine. Ben looked up from his laptop to see Evan slouching in his seat, holding his Irn-Bru bottle to his temple.

"Just a bit hot," Evan said. "Sometimes I become...*sjøsyk*. On the sea."

"Oh, seasick?" David asked. "Sorry, mate. Can I do anything?"

"I came to get medicine from the shop. That's why I'm...here." Evan tried to get up from the seat, then slumped back down as if too weak.

Ben held his breath in anticipation of Plan A's execution: Evan searching the bag while David went to the shop to buy him Dramamine.

"I think it's closing soon," David said. "You'd better hurry."

So much for Plan A. All hail Plan Ben.

"It's too late for the medicine now," Evan said. "I'll either be fine or I won't be fine." He took a deep breath. "Sometimes talking helps. Like, telling a story."

Ben listened closely for one of the code words that meant he should or shouldn't act.

"The people I met in Kirkwall," Evan said. "They're from Norway. I told them about you." After David's inaudible response, Evan continued. "People like us. People with pride in Norwegian heritage, who love and respect that heritage enough to protect it. To keep it pure."

Ben kept typing, though he felt a bit sick himself at these words from Evan's mouth, fake as they were.

"There are organizations like BVP in Norway," Evan said, "but most do nothing but talk because they have no money."

David's reply was indistinct.

"There's a donor now," Evan said, "a man in the oil industry who can...ugh, *helvete*." He took a deep breath. "Can we go outside? Cold air is good."

Yes! There was the code word, *helvete*—hell—which meant Evan wanted Ben to search the bag.

Ben couldn't make out David's response, but he seemed to be dithering about taking his bag outside. It definitely didn't look waterproof, and with the way the boat was rocking, it could slide overboard.

"Can you leave it?" Evan asked. "We're out of the port, so no one can steal it without being found."

More quiet protests.

"I understand." Evan stood unsteadily, grabbing the back of his seat to keep from falling. "I will go to my room now. Also, I will move back to Norway soon, so this might be goodbye."

"No!" David stood up. "I mean, it's fine. Let's go outside and keep talking until you feel better."

Evan lunged for the exit. David followed, glancing back at his bag.

The door shut behind them. A few moments later the sound of Evan retching came through Ben's earphones. He was either truly seasick or a fantastic actor.

Ben put his laptop screen into password-protected sleep but left it open. Then he walked through the lounge, past the other uni student, who was now napping with her head down on her crossed arms, her back to David's seat. The handful of passengers in his section all sat several rows behind him.

Just going to the gift shop for a late-night snack. He pulled out a handful of change, gripping it loosely. A pound coin slipped free and bounced over the carpet toward David's row, rolling beneath the seat beside his.

Ben knelt to retrieve the coin. Then, with a last peek round, he unzipped the bag.

"The sea feeds you, and you feed the sea."

As Evan donated the last remnants of dinner overboard, his grandfather's words came back to him, an old fisherman's Zen acceptance that he might one day drown in a storm.

"Feeling better?" David asked, a few feet upwind.

Evan managed to stand up straight. He searched for the horizon to aid his equilibrium, but on this side of the boat there was no land, just the inky North Sea spilling straight into the sky. The ferry dipped and rolled in what lucky people probably found a soothing rhythm.

"A bit. Thanks." Evan wiped his mouth with a tissue, avoiding the earphone mic that was hopefully still transmitting to Ben through their phone call. "Sorry for that."

David gave a dismissive wave. "When I was growing up, my

brother was carsick every time we went on holiday. At least here there's fresh air." He ran his hands along the ferry's sea-slick railing. "So you were saying about a donor?"

"Yes, this oil man is very interested in supporting the cause. But he's a well-known business leader, so…"

"It's tricky. He's got a reputation to protect."

"Exactly. He needs a, how do you say, boundary? No, that's not the word. Someone to be between him and…"

"A buffer?"

"Yes! So I suggest to him that he donate internationally to help the greater cause. We can help each other, see, Norwegians and British. We are not the same, but we have a common enemy. Anyway, I thought of you." The ferry crested a high wave, and Evan's stomach lurched. "Now I will go inside and try medicine."

He went to the door and rattled the handle before turning it—to emphasize his unsteadiness but also to warn Ben.

Inside, the bag was sitting at the same angle as when they'd left, tucked half beneath David's seat with the zips in the same positions. Either Ben couldn't approach the bag or he'd followed Evan's instructions to leave no trace.

Evan headed for the gift shop, where he nearly collided with an exiting Ben.

"Sorry, mate." Ben offered the sort of awkward smile one gives a stranger, then moved on toward his table, swinging a small plastic bag.

Evan purchased some Dramamine, a motion-sickness acupressure bracelet, and a bag of ginger sweets, prompting a sympathetic *hmm* from the shop assistant. Then he returned to David, whose feet were propped on the black kit bag again.

"I'm going to my cabin to lie down," Evan told him. "Phone me soon and we'll discuss more."

"Definitely." David tugged his rented blanket up over his chest. "Feel better, mate."

As Evan descended the stairs, trying not to pass out, he

murmured to Ben, "Stay and wait for my signal so he doesn't associate us. Hanging up now."

He went to the toilets to put his "Bruce" disguise back on and to procure a stack of paper towels, then found a secluded area of seats on the first floor. Evan wet the towels with cold water, plastered them to his forehead, then turned so he could glance up at the handful of receding Orkney lights as he jotted everything he recalled about the conversation with David.

By the time he beckoned Ben, he felt ten percent better.

"That was the longest half hour of my life." Ben sat beside him, then leaned close and whispered, "The bag was mostly cash. Stacks of shrink-wrapped fifty-pound notes. I lifted it briefly, and it weighed maybe two or three kilos. At a gram for each note—assuming they're all fifties—that's more than a hundred thousand pounds. How are you feeling, by the way?"

"Erm...stunned." Evan tried to wrap his head around this revelation. "Ten thousand is the legal limit to carry over the border without declaring it. But within the country—"

"It's still suspicious, yeah? If the cops caught him with that bag, they'd have questions. They'd probably think him a drugs dealer or a gangster." Ben looked at him. "Is that what he's suspected of?"

I wish. "You said the bag was mostly cash. What else was in it?"

"Documents, I think, but they were at the bottom in what looked like sealed envelopes. No way I could look at them without serious risk of being spotted."

"Wise."

"Also, I got photos of the cash and of the bag itself."

"Wow." Evan touched Ben's arm. "You did well. Thank you."

Ben beamed briefly. "But we're not done, right? What happens now?"

Evan wasn't sure, to be honest, and it was only a matter of time before the Dramamine stole his ability to think clearly. "My supervisor would say we should watch and wait. Let Wallace run free so MI5 can see where the money goes and what it's used for."

"You can't tell people at work about the cash," Ben said, "because they'll ask how you know."

Ben was right. They were already out of the box on this spontaneous operation. With Evan's suspension, he should be staying far away.

"Besides," Ben added, "while you lot are watching and waiting, David Wallace uses that money to do bad things."

Evan remembered what David had told him about all the *"exciting new opportunities in online social influence,"* many examples of which Evan had seen himself the night of the "leak." Perhaps the cash in Wallace's bag was to pay and equip that army of trolls. The documents beneath them could hold the key to everything.

He turned to Ben. "What do you think we should do?"

AN HOUR LATER, Ben was all out of ideas. Not coincidentally, he was all out of snacks. Now he felt frustrated and almost sick.

Evan had "red-teamed" every proposal, poking holes in it the way his MI5 colleagues would do. First Ben had suggested phoning in an anonymous tip. But according to Evan, the police couldn't get a warrant based on an anonymous report. While they could stop and search without a warrant, they needed consent from the person searched. Also, Wallace possessed nothing technically illegal, so a random cop would probably let him go after a few questions.

In an admittedly daft moment, Ben had then suggested *planting* something illegal in Wallace's bag—a knife they'd steal from the bar, for instance. The idea seemed to literally make Evan sick. Upon returning from the gents' after another round of boaking, he reminded Ben, *"This isn't TV, for fuck's sake, where clever characters break the law without consequences."*

Not that Evan had any better ideas.

Now it was nearly two a.m., and they'd taken a break from this operation to focus on the picture of their future together, or at least the future of their jobs.

"There's another possibility," Evan said. "Let me think out loud for a minute before you shoot it down."

Ben mimed zipping his lips, then winced at the memory of having done that before, after the news of the thwarted ISIS attacks.

"In my job," Evan said, "I've often worked with Police Scotland's Specialist Crime Division, which handles terrorism and organized crime. Perhaps instead of working *with* them, I could work *for* them."

He paused, as though expecting an interruption. Ben said nothing, as promised.

"Then I could tell everyone who I work for," Evan said. "You wouldn't have to keep that secret. And I wouldn't have to move to London. What do you think?"

"Have Police Scotland offered you a position?"

"Of course not. They'd never try and poach an MI5 officer."

"Then what makes you think you can just waltz in and say, 'Give me this job'? Wouldn't you start at the bottom as a beat cop?"

Evan frowned. "It'll be worth it to come out of hiding and be real, to have you know where I am and what I'm doing."

"Until you get into this special unit and go undercover again, which is what you really want."

"Not if it means hiding things from you."

"I'll learn to live with it," Ben said.

Evan gave him a withering look that said what they both knew: Ben wasn't going to change. Reining in his curiosity was like imposing a hyper-restrictive diet on his brain—it just made him crave secrets more.

"You shouldn't have to live with it," Evan said. "Being with me shouldn't be a constant exercise of willpower."

"It is exhausting." Ben sat back to ponder Evan's new idea. Fighting terrorists and gangsters was obviously cool. But first Evan would spend years walking the streets in one of those neon-yellow body-armor things, chasing pickpockets and football hooligans—important work but quite a letdown after thwarting international bad guys.

Ben sat up suddenly. "I know what to do."

"About our future?"

"No. About right now."

Ben outlined his plan. After refining it, Evan finally signed off with reluctance. He downloaded an obscure burner-phone app, gave Ben a number to dial, and finally put in an earphone to listen.

"Hiya," Ben said into the phone, using a less fey version of his Wullie McTweedy voice from the Glasgow Greens scouting match. "I want to talk to Detective Inspector Hayward or Detective Sergeant Fowles."

"I'm sorry, neither of them are present at the moment," said a female SCD officer. "How did you get this number?"

Ben ignored the question. "There's a suspicious character aboard the MV Hjaltland, arriving in Aberdeen at seven o'clock. I think he's mebbe one of they gangsters an' all, cos he's got a kit bag of fifty-pound notes and he was making some pretty dodgy-sounding phone calls, so he was."

"Can you describe this suspicious character?" asked the officer, sounding either sleepy or skeptical.

"White guy, about five-ten, mebbe thirteen stone. Blue polo shirt and tan chinos like a right walloper. Also, his name's David Wallace." He rubbed his mouth to hold in the nervous laugh bubbling up his throat. This was deadly serious. "He telt it to someone he phoned."

There was a long silence on the other end of the line. "You're sure he said it was David Wallace?"

"Positive, hen. I reckon it could be an alias, though."

Evan shook his head. Ben clamped his lips together to stop further spontaneous speculation.

"Your name and number?" the officer asked.

"You think my head buttons up the back?" Ben replied. "If this guy's a gangster, and he finds out I grassed him up to the polis, then I'm dead."

"We'll keep your information confidential."

Ben looked at Evan, who nodded reluctantly. "I'm not an innocent bystander," Ben told the officer. "I'm with Wallace. I know him fae the BVP, and I'm no' keen on what he's doing with they Russians. It's no' right. This is our country, int'it? What's the point of taking it back if we do it with foreigners' help?"

There was another long pause, then the officer said, "I'll phone DI Hayward now."

Ben repeated the ferry information, then hung up and immediately burned the phone number. "SCD will know what to do with Wallace?" he asked Evan.

"If anyone does."

Ben took a gulp from his water bottle, hoping his heart would stop racing soon. "Was that call okay?"

"It was brilliant. You followed instructions perfectly tonight. It meant a lot having someone I could depend on as a backup."

The word made Ben think of the police team who'd been carjacked the night of Evan's abduction, leaving him to deal with his captors alone. "I know it's not easy for you to ask for help, especially from someone who's been a bit of a diddy in the past."

"I always trusted you, Ben." Evan gave him a hopeful smile. "I just didn't always know why."

Chapter 40

IT FELT strange to Evan to be near the Warriors' home pitch wearing street clothes instead of a football kit. But everything felt strange about being back in Glasgow. Between the exile of wall-to-wall sheep, then the voyage upon the "HMS Takedown," as Ben called it, the previous eleven days had been like an out-of-body experience.

They'd watched the police take David Wallace into a private room at the Aberdeen ferry terminal, but Evan had heard nothing since. No doubt he'd get an update on Monday at work, assuming he'd not been removed from Operation Caps Lock. For now, he could focus on today's events.

Thanks to the rigors of lambing, his right hip still wasn't fit for this friendly match against Glasgow Greens. It was just as well, since Ben and his mum needed help with Michael and Philip's wedding—especially once the heavy rain began.

Halftime soon neared, and with it the start of the ten-minute ceremony. In the tent beside the fitness complex, everyone seemed ready: the grooms, the celebrant, the bagpiper. The caterers waited nearby in a box van, poised to set up the reception beneath the tent once the ceremony was over.

Evan was distributing miniature bottles of blowing bubbles—

rainbow-striped with the Warriors sword-and-ball logo—to the gathering guests when Fergus approached him, wearing a rain jacket over his mud-stained football kit.

"Can I talk to you a minute?" he asked Evan. "Alone?"

"I have literally a minute." He handed the basket of bubble bottles to Colin, who wasn't playing today out of courtesy to his former team. "How's the hamstring?" he asked as they walked alongside the building behind the tent, out of the others' earshot.

"Good," Fergus said, "but Charlotte subbed me out early to be safe." Fergus stopped and looked back over his shoulder. "I've been thinking…you said you were in Belfast last year. But you came home before the twelfth of July, when the Orange Order has their marches there—or parades, or whatever they call them. So you weren't there to guard the events."

Evan said nothing, since there was nothing he could legally say.

"And my ma's cousins from Derry"—Fergus tugged the front of his rain jacket to shed some of the water—"I saw them at the end of June at her birthday party. They were staying with her in Perthshire for a few weeks. Until after the twelfth."

Interesting. Perhaps Fergus's cousins were more involved with Stephen's cell than MI5 had realized.

"So I put these pieces together." Fergus held his palms facing up, as if holding the pieces, and looked at them in turn. "If you weren't in Belfast to guard the marches, why was it so urgent for you to go there at that time?" He dropped his hands. "My guess is you were trying to stop a planned attack, maybe on an Orange Order parade."

"You know I can't—"

"You can't say, I know." Fergus's lips formed a tight line. "And I can't stop thinking about John's nephew, Harry. Last summer his family took him to an Orange March in Ibrox. He's five years old. Five. Years. Old."

Evan nodded. "Sometimes there's young bairns at those things. Sometimes they're even in the parades."

Fergus wiped his mouth. "Look, I'll never forgive you for leaving, and for lying to me. But working all this out in my head..." He sniffed hard. "It helps somehow."

Evan wished he could confirm Fergus's theory. Letting him find meaning in all his pain would never make up for causing it in the first place. But it might ease it, just a bit.

"I'm glad," Evan said. "You deserve some peace."

"Yeah," Fergus said with a bitter laugh. "I really do."

Just then the wind gusted. One of the tent flaps came loose, followed by a cry of dismay from Ben.

"I'd better go and help," Evan said, relieved to end the conversation.

"Things are good with you two now?" Fergus asked as they headed back toward the tent.

"Things are things."

"Good luck," Fergus said, "and I mean that."

"I know." Evan gave his ex a tentative smile. "Thanks."

He secured the flap and double-checked the other tie-downs as the ceremony began within. Then he began his final assigned task: getting the crowd outside to clear the makeshift "aisle" he'd marked earlier with tape upon the tarmac. As he urged folk to step back on either side, he imagined doing a similar duty while wearing a black uniform and yellow high-visibility body armor.

Evan's research yesterday had revealed that Ben was right: despite his MI5 experience, there was no way Evan could join Police Scotland at the position he wanted. A hierarchy like that required the sort of by-the-book approach that would soon chafe him into rebellion.

But yesterday he'd also explored other options, one of which he couldn't wait to share with Ben.

When the aisle was cleared, Evan climbed atop a chair to the side so he could scan the crowd. He noted which people he'd seen before, which were new, and whether any looked suspicious. At least two dozen more fans had made their way over from the pitch since the start of the ceremony, no doubt beckoned by the bagpipes.

If he someday left MI5, Evan wondered, would this instinct for vigilance fade? Would he ever be able to look at a crowd without searching for a threat? Maybe in Orkney. But maybe not.

Soon applause and cheering came from inside the tent, followed by a single bagpipe note. The recession would begin any moment (due to time constraints, there'd been no *pro*cession).

Ben and his mum came out, each opening a giant rainbow umbrella on either side of the aisle. Then Michael and Philip appeared, beaming in their black tuxedos—worn over Woodstoun Warriors football shirts—and violet-and-green Thistle of Scotland tartan kilts. As the couple paused outside the tent to wave to the crowd, Evan watched each onlooker.

At the end of the aisle on the other side, a young man in an orange hoodie stood with his shoulders hunched, not cheering. Evan couldn't see his face, shadowed by the hood, but his form was chillingly familiar.

It can't be. Not here.

Shifting to the edge of the chair, Evan spied the man's hands. He clutched a bottle of blowing bubbles, but this one was full-size and bright blue, unlike the mini rainbow bottles Evan and Colin had distributed.

The couple began to process, shielded from the rain by Ben and Giti's umbrellas. The bagpiper followed, blasting a strangled-stoat version of the Warriors' unofficial theme song, "Football Crazy."

Evan leapt off the chair and hurried behind the tent, peeling off his rain jacket so he could move silently. Then he ran, hunched over, behind the other side of the crowd.

He wanted to be sure, but if he couldn't be sure, he would act anyway.

At the end of the aisle, Evan came up behind the orange-hooded lad and peered over his shoulder. Sure enough, the right hand fidgeting with the lid of the bubble bottle bore a tattoo across the knuckles: a calligraphied *88*.

The newlyweds were a few meters away now, striding quickly through the deluge of rain and bubbles. Ben was on this side, next to Philip, soon to enter the line of fire.

Evan clamped his right hand over Jordan's wrist and looped his left arm around his other side, pinning his arm.

"Oi!" Jordan's voice was drowned out by the bagpipes.

Evan backed up, spun round, and slammed Jordan face first against the building.

"Drop it!" He pressed Jordan's wrist to the concrete wall.

Jordan twisted his head to see his captor. "Gunnar? What the fuck?"

Evan squeezed his wrist harder. "Drop the acid!"

Jordan let go. Evan stepped to the right, dragging Jordan with him to avoid the splash as the bottle popped open on the ground, spilling its contents.

Behind him, the bagpipes faded out mid-tune, replaced by cries of the crowd.

"Evan, what's happening?" Ben called, his voice getting closer.

"'Evan'?" Jordan's face crumpled in rage. "David said you was a spook! I telt him, 'Nah, man, Gunnar's my mate.'" Still pinned to the wall, Jordan shouted to the crowd, "This guy's a fuckin' spook!"

Evan pulled Jordan's wrists behind his back with one hand and pressed between his shoulders with the other. "Everyone, move away calmly," he said, "and someone phone the police. This man tried to acid-attack the—"

"I never did!" Jordan kicked back, smashing his boot heel against Evan's knee. Evan held on, groaning in pain, but his grip loosened enough for Jordan to twist free and shove him away.

"That was never acid," Jordan said. "That was bubbles, so it was." He reached into his hoodie pocket. "But this is acid."

He pulled out a half-size Lucozade squeeze bottle and popped the top.

"No!" Ben shouted as he flashed past Evan.

Evan leapt forward. Jordan lifted the bottle at him point blank. Liquid surged straight for Evan's face.

The last thing he saw was Ben's arm slamming down upon the bottle.

Then Evan fell back, blinded and burned. He dropped to the ground as the acid melted his skin...his eyes...every inch of muscle and bone.

His face had turned to fire.

CAN'T STOP HITTING. I stop, we die. Can't stop hitting. Can't stop. Can't. Can't. Can't. Can't.

Ben's vision sharpened, despite his glasses slipping down his nose. There was nothing in the world but his own fists meeting the attacker's face, faster and faster. He was vaguely aware of Evan screaming in the background below his own incoherent shouts of rage.

"Hunh! Hah! Fuh! Hunh! Hah! Fuh! HunhHahFuh! HunhHah-Fuh! Haaaaaaaruughhhhh!"

Arms grabbed him from behind, but he tore them off with hands like claws, then began again, smashing, smashing, smashing, smashing.

Down. Down. Stay. Down.

Finally the man's shouts turned to whimpers. He stopped trying to fend off Ben and simply curled into the fetal position, arms shielding his bloodied face.

Ben straightened up and pulled back his foot to kick.

"Son, please stop."

His mum's low voice yanked him back to reality. A reality he didn't want to face.

A few feet away, Evan lay on the ground, restrained by Liam and Robert.

Liam's voice boomed above the shouts of confusion. "Phone

999! Get the match physios! Get me clean water! I need all the water NOW!" The defender held Evan's flailing hands by the wrists. "It's okay, mate," he said calmly. "Let's get you up on your knees so we can rinse this off without spreading it."

Ben stepped closer. Yellow liquid dripped from the left side of Evan's face, neck, and shirt. Was this the acid or was it—*oh God*—his actual skin? Evan was thrashing too hard for Ben to see for sure.

Jamie set an armful of water bottles beside Evan. "Be right back with more."

"Thanks, mate." Liam picked up one of the bottles and twisted off the top with his teeth. "Evan, I'm gonnae start rinsing you now, so hold still."

But Evan only fought harder as the water was poured over him.

"Stop holding him down," Ben said. "Trust me." He tapped Robert's shoulder. "Let me try."

Robert stood and stepped aside. Ben knelt beside Evan, careful to avoid the splatter as Liam kept pouring.

"It's me," Ben murmured as he rubbed Evan's back. "It's your *kjæreste*. Please let them help you."

Evan's flailing eased, but he kept moaning like a trapped animal. Eyes closed, he seemed in another world. The pain in his voice shredded Ben's heart.

The physio arrived, her bag rattling as she set it on the pavement. "We need to cut off his shirt. If it's stuck to the skin, we can't remove that part. And for God's sake, Liam, put on these gloves so you don't get hurt."

Ben held Evan's shirt taut so she could cut it. As the fabric began to part, he dreaded what lay beneath.

But then he steeled himself. He had to look, because he would see it again tomorrow, and tomorrow, and every day. These scars would become part of their life together, and Ben would see and feel and love every inch. Evan wouldn't go through this alone.

With one final snip of scissors, the shirt fell away. Perhaps it was the dim sunlight through the thick clouds, but Evan's skin looked…the same as ever.

"What the—" The physio pulled back. "Hang on." She rummaged in her kit bag and pulled out a torch, which she clicked on to shine over Evan's chest, then his neck and face. "We should see acid damage already." She gently took hold of Evan's chin and tilted it up. "Let's keep rinsing just in case, but I think he's okay. Maybe the solution was very diluted."

Evan gave one last moan, almost in protest. Then he opened his eyes, blinking away the water. "But it's—that's not…" He looked down at his own chest.

"Does it still hurt?" the physio asked. "Does it burn?"

Evan shook his head slowly. "What happened?"

"That's odd." Robert held up the squeeze bottle in one gloved hand, its cap in the other. "I'm no chemist, but I think this is just Lucozade."

Evan touched his neck and face, mouthing the name of the sport drink.

Ben looked over at the half-conscious Jordan, who was being seen to by the other physio. "Why would he fake it?" He looked back at Evan. "And if it wasn't acid, why would you—"

"I don't know!" Evan's breath was still coming fast. "I thought it *was* acid. I thought he was going to hurt you."

"He didn't. Well, except my hands." Ben looked at his own knuckles, raw and bleeding. "Guess I should've been practicing Krav Maga without gloves all this time. Build up a few calluses, heh?"

But Evan wasn't laughing.

EVAN SAT beside Ben in the tent, staring into his own memories.

They'd all come back at once: the punches in Belfast, the PAVA spray at the BVP rally—every moment he'd wondered whether he'd ever see again.

"It felt so real," he whispered.

"I know." Ben reached out to take his hand, then stopped. Evan had already pulled away once, unable to tolerate being touched. "The mind is a powerful thing."

Especially when you're losing it. "A normal person would have been frightened for two seconds before realizing it wasn't acid." He tugged the blanket the physio had given him tighter around his bare shoulders. "I had a full-blown hallucination. I could have hurt someone."

"But you didn't."

"I could hurt *you* one day if I have another…" *Psychotic episode?*

Ben was silent for a moment. "If you feel it's an emergency, I'll drive you to a hospital. But if you're basically stable, let's phone your psychiatrist later and see what they think. Either way, you're not alone."

Evan's voice rasped in his throat. "I warned you I might break someday."

"You're not broken, you're just a wee bit cracked." Ben shrugged. "And if you do need hospitalized, I'll visit you every day. I'll bring you baklava."

This mundane promise made the world feel real again. "Thank you."

"So that guy you grabbed?" Ben lowered his voice to a whisper. "Jordan Lithgow, right? I remember his picture when I looked him up on WhoWhatWhere."

Before answering, Evan checked to see the caterers were keeping their distance. "Aye, that was him."

"Wow." Ben rubbed his bandaged knuckles. "I always wanted to punch a Nazi."

The edges of Evan's face tightened, and next thing he knew, he was laughing. He bent over, pressing his hands to his cheeks to hide his reaction.

"What's wrong?" Ben asked. "Is it happening again?"

"No, no, no." Evan coughed and straightened up. "I just…" He looked into Ben's worried brown eyes. "I just love you."

"Oh, good." Ben went to reach for his hand, then stopped again.

Evan's hand met his halfway in a gentle grip. He examined Ben's bruised fingertips. "You punched him a lot."

"Well, I had to, cos each of my punches is like one of your gentle taps."

Evan felt like laughing again. Instead he put his other hand to Ben's cheek, then leaned in and kissed him. Ben responded with as much fervor as ever, as though Evan wasn't broken or even cracked.

"Oh."

Evan looked up to see Ben's mum standing there holding his discarded rain jacket. He became hyperaware of being shirtless.

"I believe this is yours?" She held it out without coming closer.

"Thanks." He shrugged off the blanket and put on his jacket. "Can I help with anything?"

"Not me," Giti said, "but probably the police. They've just arrived."

Evan stood and zipped his jacket, ready to return to Official Mode.

Outside the tent, the reception and match were in limbo as police cordoned off the area and began interviewing witnesses. One officer was escorting Jordan to a squad car.

Evan introduced himself to the officer-in-charge, showing his MI5 badge for the first time ever—and probably the last. "The man you apprehended is the subject of a joint Police Scotland/MI5 operation. We need Specialist Crime Division, pronto."

The officer did a double take at Evan's identification. "This was a terrorist attack?"

"We'll see." Evan pulled out his phone and rang Detective Inspector Hayward.

Fifteen minutes later, Hayward arrived with Detective

Sergeant Fowles and a dozen crime-scene officers, who fanned out to collect evidence and take over witness interviews.

As Evan was recounting his story to Fowles, one of the officers came over with the bubble bottle in a plastic evidence bag. "Detective Sergeant, we'll send the containers to forensics to confirm, but I'll say right now, this smells like toilet cleaner. Hydrochloric acid."

Deirdre looked up at Evan. "Looks like your instincts were right."

Evan walked over to the blue-and-white police tape and examined the place where the acid had spilled. "I must have smelled it." He pointed to the spot where Jordan had squirted him with his sport drink, a few feet from the spill. "I was there. That's close enough to smell toilet cleaner, right?"

"It's nae wonder you thought you were burnt." Fowles looked at her notes. "Lithgow said, 'This is acid,' then he sprayed you, and you closed your eyes. All you had to go on was scent."

Deirdre's words heartened Evan. Maybe he'd been only half-deluded.

"That's Alt-Tab and Backspace both in custody," Fowles said. "Not a bad week's work."

So David Wallace had been arrested too. "I had nothing to do with Alt-Tab."

"Of course not." Deirdre blinked at him with exaggerated innocence. "I was talking about myself."

"Right. Good work, Detective Sergeant."

"Considering what happened today with Lithgow, I doubt you'll be at our Caps Lock meeting Monday morning."

Dismay washed over Evan as the truth sank in. Everyone here —the Warriors, the Greens, the Rainbow Regiment, and all the wedding guests—must have heard Jordan calling him a spook.

"I'm not saying that to make you feel bad." Deirdre looked round and stepped closer. "I'm saying that cos this is my last chance to tell you what Wallace was up to before someone orders me not to."

Evan's heart beat faster. "Go on."

"Those documents in the bag—and don't pretend you don't know what bag I'm talking about—were instructions on a massive anti-immigrant disinformation campaign. High-level stuff you'd only get from a state actor."

"You mean a foreign government? So the Russians came up with this?"

Fowles shook her head. "I wish we could blame them, but it looks like the idea began with the BVP. Russian intelligence just provided funding and technical assistance."

Evan remembered David Wallace saying how Jordan's "cocka-mamie scheme" had given him an idea for something "visionary." It made him shudder how the bigoted whims of a pathetic man like Lithgow could be the genesis of an international conspiracy.

If the Russians weren't *creating* divisions in British society but merely driving a wedge into the divisions that were already there...that meant that if the BVP were dissolved, another group would rise in its place.

Wherever he worked, Evan would find a way to keep fighting.

Detective Inspector Hayward called to Fowles, ending her illicit debriefing. "Good luck," she told Evan as she moved toward her boss. "Let's do drinks some time."

"Definitely." Evan turned away, noticing that his initial pain at the thought of leaving MI5 was already morphing into something like relief. Maybe he could pursue his big idea a lot sooner than he'd expected.

He found Ben and his mum chatting to the caterers and beck-oned Ben over to the pitch where they could talk alone. "Did they interview you yet?"

"Briefly," Ben said. "Mum wants me to have a lawyer present for the follow-up interview, on account of my beating seven shades out of Jordan."

Evan hoped a lawyer would keep Ben from describing it that way. "Talking of police, I need to go to the station to file an inci-dent report."

"I'll go with you."

"It's top-secret stuff," Evan said.

"Police station's got a public waiting area, right?"

"Aren't you needed here?"

"Mum's got this. She already told me to go if you had to leave." Ben took his hand. "Evan, I'm with you, and not just today. Whatever your job, whatever your state of mind, I'm here for it."

"Are you sure? What about, you know..."

"My faith?" Ben paused a moment and looked past him, toward the place of Jordan's attack. "When I first thought you'd lost your face, I was freaking out. But a moment later, all I could think about was being by your side through every skin graft, every cornea transplant, through all the pain and sorrow and rage." He looked up to meet Evan's eyes. "I would have stayed with you when your body was demolished. So why would I leave you because your mind has taken a beating?"

Once again overwhelmed, Evan could barely speak. "That doesn't answer my question."

"Yes, it does." Ben's grip tightened on Evan's hand. "I know now that it's not you versus God. It's you *and* God, because I can't live without either, no matter how hard it gets sometimes." His lower lip trembled a bit. "If the leaders of my faith ask me to leave, I'll do it, but they'll never stop me being Bahá'í in my heart."

"I can't ask you to give that up for me."

"You're not asking. You wouldn't. That's one of a hundred reasons why I love you, and why you're worth it—why *we're* worth it."

We're worth it. Deep down, Evan had known this all along. He'd risked so much, turning away from the security of solitude because he'd sensed that only Ben could lift his mask, truly see him as he needed to be seen, and still love him.

Only Ben could bring him into the light.

Chapter 41

A few months later

"YOU NAUGHTY, NAUGHTY MAN," Ben murmured, clenching his fist in victory. According to the results on his screen, the target had indeed traveled to the port in question, contrary to what he'd told police. The client would be pleased.

The client in this case was the RSPCA, who'd hired Paladin Private Investigations to track a purveyor of exotic animals and stolen pedigree dogs.

In conjunction with several law firms, Paladin specialized in righting the sort of wrongs the police hadn't much time for: missing persons, animal trafficking, sexual harassment, and work-place and housing discrimination. The company regularly turned away clients who wanted to catch cheating spouses or stalk old flames. *"There's enough shite in the world without us adding another shovelful,"* their president, Hamid, liked to say.

Next month, Ben would start training in both the classroom and the field to become one of Paladin's investigators. For now, he was providing support to the firm's six PIs—and most impor-tantly, upgrading Paladin's GIS capabilities.

The door to their Sauchiehall Street office creaked open. In walked the most handsome man Ben had ever seen.

He wiped his expensive brogues on the mat, then took off his rain-spattered, tortoiseshell-framed glasses and peered through them at the office's geometric steel chandelier. "How do you keep these things dry?" Evan asked Ben.

"I make an awning out of my own hair." Ben tugged forward his quiff, which sprang back into place when he let go. "Next time, wear a fedora for the complete posh prat picture."

Hamid came out of his office to greet Evan. "How'd it go?"

"As expected." Evan slipped out of his raincoat and hung it on the rack. "The flat became magically available once this white guy wanted it." He pointed to himself.

"I knew it!" Hamid smacked his hands together. "Give Ben the recording, and you two can draft the report together. Meanwhile I'll phone the clients." He chuckled gleefully as he returned to his office. "Their lawyer will be thrilled."

Evan undid the top buttons of his shirt and pulled out the wire he'd been wearing. He handed the equipment to Ben. "Won't be long before you're out there with me." He looked at Ben's desk, his eyes widening. "You got your name plaque!"

"I did." Ben beamed as Evan picked up the engraved brass and wooden sign and turned it to face him. Behnam Reid, it said. He'd already sent a pic of it to his mum.

Evan went to change back into his own clothes, then returned to review their findings. Ben was already updating the report on the block of flats in Glasgow's City Centre. When Hamid, a Pakistani man, had attempted to let a flat, he'd been turned away, even though his cover's income and credit history had been far superior to those of Evan's cover.

By the time they'd drafted the report and sent it to Hamid, it was nearly six o'clock. Time to go home.

Evan's flat was *their* home now—for two weeks, anyway, until the lease began on the place Ben would share with their friend Robert, who'd also recently graduated. It was an arrangement that would've seemed impossible a few months ago when Robert's partner, Liam, had hated Evan's guts. But all the Warriors had a different view of Evan now that they had an inkling why he'd left last year.

The day's rain had done little to dispel the summer heat, so they walked slowly down the pavement through the heavy air.

It was rare for them to leave the office together. While Ben worked regular hours, Evan often did nighttime and weekend surveillance or undercover work. But Ben didn't mind, as it gave him time to plan the autumn crop of same-sex weddings—with his mum's assistance whenever possible.

The jobs with Paladin had been Evan's idea, and Ben had been shocked he'd not thought of it himself. He couldn't believe how lucky he was to use his skills to uncover secrets and help people, all without signing over his life and soul to the government.

It seemed a natural turn for Evan, too, after Jordan had blown his cover in public at the Rainbow Regiment wedding. Since MI5 couldn't Official-Secrets-Act the entire football park, that day had been the end of the road for Evan and Her Majesty's Security Service. It was just as well, since after Jordan's attack, Evan was more ready than ever to turn his talents toward an equally meaningful but less traumatic job.

"How was therapy this morning?" Ben asked him now.

"Good. I like going more frequently. We can spend less time dealing with symptoms and more time helping me make sense of myself and what I had to do."

"What do you mean?" Ben knew Evan might not be able to talk about it—emotionally or legally—but he always asked.

Evan looked round before replying. "Leaving the Service. Sometimes I still feel a failure. But my therapist is pure clever. She kens I'm an athlete, so she's always using sport metaphors. She says what happened in Belfast was like having a Grade 3 ACL tear."

"A what, now?"

"It's a knee injury which almost always ends a pro footballer's career. Anyway, she pointed out that after your ACL tear heals, your pain may be gone and you can walk and run, but that doesn't mean the injury hasn't changed what you're capable of. A striker may never again be able to take on massive center-backs week after week. He has to retire."

"How sad."

"It doesn't have to be. That's the point: Pro football isn't life, and neither is MI5. They're jobs." Evan gestured back in the direction of the Paladin office. "I can still make a difference without putting myself in danger—and better yet, without being alone."

Without being alone. After years of thinking he was destined for singlehood, Ben was still learning to accept that he deserved to be in love. Just last week he and Evan had dinner with two of his Glasgow Bahá'í friends, a gathering initiated by Ben even though he was scared they might show the same sadness his mum had felt after meeting Evan.

He needn't have worried. His friends had treated Evan the way they would have treated a girlfriend—with warmth, respect, and good-natured banter. They didn't pull Ben aside and warn him of his sins or say something like, "He's great, but…"

It wasn't an exoneration, as these two Bahá'ís didn't represent the wider community. But it was enough to give Ben hope.

When they arrived at Evan's flat, Trent greeted them as if they were astronauts returning to earth after a five-year voyage. They gave her dinner and playtime, until she finally curled up on her heated window perch, dismissing them with a flick of her tail.

As they moved to the kitchen to make dinner, their phones simultaneously emitted the signature BBC news-alert sound.

Ben pulled his out to read, *'ISIS' threat to gay weddings found to be a hoax.*

"Oh my God." He tapped on the notification to read the article. It briefly outlined how the alleged "leak" of the planned ISIS attacks on same-sex weddings had originated with an unnamed extreme-right-wing group, which had gone on to propagate the rumors on social media. "That's pure twisted."

Evan set his phone on the table. "Must be a relief to know your weddings are safe—as safe as anything can be in this world."

The news didn't totally surprise Ben, not after what had happened with Jordan at the last wedding. Still, something felt off. "It's hard to believe those Nazi dunderheads could manage an elaborate scheme like this all by themselves."

"Mmmm," Evan said. "So how hungry are you? I was thinking of making a curry, but—"

"You know something about this." Ben held up his phone. "You worked on the investigation, didn't you?"

"That was in another life." Evan opened the fridge. "The important thing is that now people know they can't believe everything they read online."

Ben doubted that was the only important thing—and he wondered how long the public would even remember this scam—but for once he didn't feel the urge to press further. At Paladin, he and Evan shared secrets *with* each other instead of keeping them *from* each other. Now their trust had room to grow.

He went to Evan and slipped an arm round his waist. "Have I ever told you how much your detective disguises turn me on?"

Evan pulled him close. "Including today's posh prat?"

"Including that. Though last week's turn as a meter reader was particularly…electric."

Evan groaned at Ben's pun. "It's brilliant being someone else for a peedie while. I canna wait for you to try it."

"Me neither." Ben held him tighter. "And I promise all my selves will love all your selves."

"They all love you too." He bent his head to nuzzle Ben's neck. "Now let them prove it." Ben laughed, and after a moment, Evan added, "Aye, that was an odd thing to say. Let *me* prove it."

"Fire in," Ben said, though the last thing he needed was proof of Evan's love. His uncertainty had faded ages ago, replaced by an ever-deepening faith—in Evan, in himself, and in everything that connected them to each other and to this impossibly imperfect world.

A world worth fighting for.

Thanks for reading!

I hope you enjoyed this latest Glasgow Lads novel. Evan has been part of the series (as a bit of a villain) from the beginning, while Ben was introduced in *Playing With Fire*. Read about how they met at Fergus and John's wedding in a free bonus short story, "Auld Lang Syne," at averycockburn.com/auld-lang-syne.

If you enjoyed this book, please consider introducing the Lads to others—online, offline, or anywhere in between. Thanks.

Want more Warriors all to yourself? How about exclusive bonus material like deleted scenes, commentaries, and photos of characters and settings? Then sign up for my mailing list at averycockburn.com/signup and join the fun!

Author's Note

On capturing shadows

As you might imagine, this book involved a massive amount of research. The magic part about depicting an agency as shrouded in mystery as MI5 means I got to fill in factual gaps using imagination and best guesses.

A few notes on the relationship between fact and fiction in this novel:

- About a decade ago, there were news reports stating MI5 was considering a regional office in Scotland, but I can neither confirm nor deny that it exists now.
- In October 2018, MI5 confirmed it will now take charge of intelligence related to extreme-right-wing (XRW) groups. Evan would be happy to hear this.
- Another fun aspect of writing "contemporary historical" novels is the ability to weave in real-life events on the dates they occurred, including the solar eclipse and Boris Nemtsov's murder.
- Though extensive use of jargon and close adherence to actual MI5 intelligence procedure would have made the

book more realistic, in the interests of storytelling I opted for more straightforward language and processes. If you're curious about MI5's actual procedures, check out "Attacks in London and Manchester Between March and June 2017," an independent report by David Anderson, QC.

Other highly recommended works that helped me a lot:

Spy Nonfiction:

- *Defend the Realm: The Authorized History of MI5*, by Christopher Andrew (OK, I confess I didn't read all 1,056 pages.)
- *Breaking Cover: My Secret Life in the CIA and What it Taught Me about What's Worth Fighting For*, by Michelle Rigby Assad
- Buzzfeed UK's series on Russian activities on British soil, by Heidi Blake et al
- *American Radical: Inside the World of an Undercover Muslim FBI Agent*, by Tamer Elnoury with Kevin Maurer
- *Soldier, Spy: The True Story of an MI5 Officer Risking His Life to Save Yours* by Tom Marcus
- *Open Secret: The Autobiography of the Former Director-General of MI5*, by Stella Rimington
- *Messing With the Enemy: Surviving in a Social Media World of Hackers, Terrorists, Russians, and Fake News*, by Clint Watts

Spy Fiction:

- Slough House series by Mick Herron
- Liz Carlyle series by Stella Rimington (yes, the former head of MI5!)

Other shoutouts:

- Wedding Planner Masterclass podcast series by Amanda Vodic
- BBC Radio's *Around Orkney* program. It's the third thing I hear every weekday morning (the first is my alarm, and the second, my cats' demanding meows).

Acronyms & Agencies

As promised, here is list of acronyms and agencies either directly mentioned in *Playing in the Dark* or which I thought would be useful to know, such as the US equivalents to UK agencies:

- APT: Advanced Persistent Threat
- CIA: US Central Intelligence Agency (human intelligence, aka spies). Equivalent to MI6.
- GCHQ: UK Government Communications Headquarters (signals intelligence). Equivalent to NSA.
- GRU: Commonly known name of *Glavnoye Razvedyvatel'noye Upravleniye* ("Main Intelligence Directorate"). Officially now just GU, it is the Russian Federation's main military foreign-intelligence service.
- HSE: UK Health and Safety Executive
- ISIS: Islamic State of Iraq and Syria
- ISIL: Islamic State of Iraq and the Levant
- MI5: UK domestic counterintelligence/counterterrorism agency. No direct US equivalent. MI5 originally stood for Military Intelligence, Section 5, but since 1931 it has been officially called "The Security Service."

- MI6: UK international intelligence agency. Equivalent to CIA. Officially known as SIS (Secret Intelligence Service).
- NSA: US National Security Agency (signals intelligence). Equivalent to GCHQ.
- SCD: Police Scotland's Specialist Crime Division, dealing with terrorism and organized crime
- XRW: eXtreme Right Wing

About the Author

Avery Cockburn (rhymes with Savory Slow Churn—mmmm, ice cream...) lives in the US with one infinitely patient man and two infinitely impatient cats.

Reach out and say "Hiya!" to Avery at:

- www.averycockburn.com
- avery@averycockburn.com
- Twitter: averycockburn
- Facebook: avery.cockburn.5

Made in United States
North Haven, CT
16 February 2023

32672807R00271